PERFECT STRANGER

Slade broke off the kiss and stepped away from her, knowing that if he didn't leave her immediately, he might never be able to go. "Good-bye, lovely lady."

"Good-bye? But you can't just go," she blurted out, frowning as she tried to understand why he was leaving this way. They had the whole night ahead of them. "Will I see you again?"

"No."

His answer was gently spoken, but there was a flash of some emotion in his eyes—sorrow? pain?—that Alyssa couldn't quite identify. Before she could say more, he turned and walked away, leaving her standing alone. She started after him, wanting to stop his from going, but he had disappeared into the crowd. There was no sign that he'd ever been there.

It shocked Alyssa to realize how powerfully she'd just reacted to a perfect stranger . . . and he had been perfect. She'd never been attracted to anyone like this before. She remained where she was, staring off into the crowd, haunted by the image of her mystery man and the wonder of his kiss.

Outlaw's Lady

Bobbi Smith

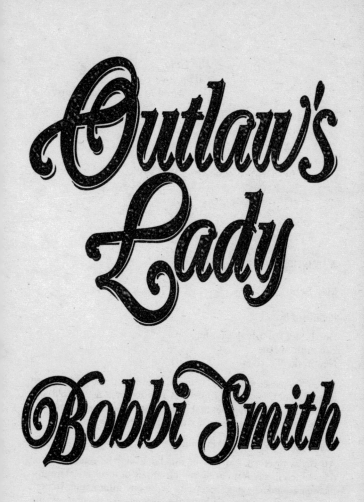

LEISURE BOOKS NEW YORK CITY

For Gina,
With love,
Mom to the Second Power

A LEISURE BOOK®

May 1998

Published by

Dorchester Publishing Co., Inc.
276 Fifth Avenue
New York, NY 10001

ISBN 0-8439-4383-1

The name "Leisure Books" and the stylized "L" with design are trademarks of Dorchester Publishing Co., Inc.

Printed in the United States of America.

ACKNOWLEDGMENTS

I'd like to thank my three favorite attorneys in the whole wide world—Dan Lesseg, Harry Monck and Pam Monck—for their advice. Ann Nelson and Cindy Brown of the Wyoming State Archives were invaluable in their help with research, as well as Lucy Lockley of St. Charles County Library, St. Charles, Missouri. Sandy Freise, Jane Troup, and Mike Weigle helped me put things in perspective. Andy Riccuta of New Castle, PA, was an inspiration, too.

"Hi!" to my friends at Anderson/Austin News in Nashville—the real Vernon Clemans and Nick Ursino, Randy Yarbrough, Patty Warren, Mary, Anna, Lana, Marlene, Delphia, Rochél and Joshua! And June Toon of Anderson/Austin News in Paducah!

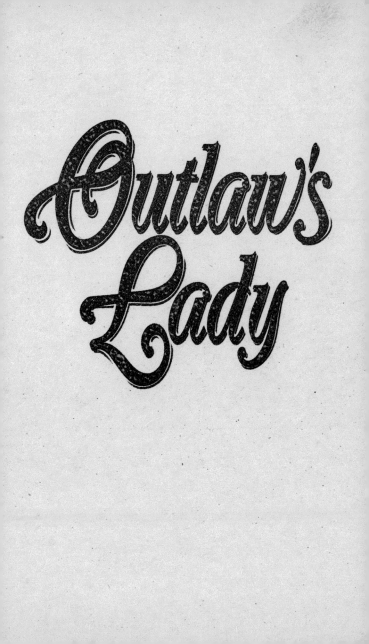

Chapter One

Slade Braxton was hot, thirsty and tired as he strode up to the bar in the Hell on Wheels Saloon.

"Whiskey," he ordered.

"That'll be two bits," Charlie the bartender said as he set a glass in front of him. "You're new in town, aren't you? You just hire on at one of the spreads?"

Charlie eyed the stranger with interest as he poured a healthy portion of potent liquor. There was a menacing, almost dangerous air about the newcomer. He was dressed all in black and wore his gun low on his hip. He looked like the kind of man who could handle trouble that came his way, but Charlie didn't want trouble. He was just making conversation.

"No, I'm just passing through," Slade answered as he pushed money across the bar to him.

"Oh, I thought you mighta come into town for the big doings tonight."

"What big doings?"

"They're having a dance down the street. Everyone in town's pretty excited about it."

"So that's why your business is so slow," Slade remarked, looking around the half-empty bar.

"It was pretty wild in here earlier, but the boys all went down to the dance when the music started about an hour ago." Two other men came in then, and Charlie moved off to wait on them. "When you need a refill, just yell."

Slade nodded, but said nothing more as he took a deep drink of the whiskey. It burned all the way down, and he was glad for its searing intensity. He'd needed a drink right then—badly. He needed to ease the tension within him. He was tired of the massive deception he was caught up in and tired of the life he was being forced to lead because of it.

Slade drank more of his whiskey as he thought back over the last few months. When two gold shipments had been stolen from the railroad by the notorious Dakota Kid's gang, the railroad officials had hired the Pinkertons to bring down the gang and learn the identity of the railroad employee who'd helped them.

Using his own name and a fake background the agency had created for him, Slade had infiltrated the gang. The lies about his past had been so carefully constructed and documented by the Pinkerton office that Slade doubted anyone could disprove them. It had been done to convince the Dakota Kid that Slade

Braxton was a fast gun with a price on his head, dangerous and deadly enough to ride with him. The Kid and his gang were bloodthirsty killers who'd been terrorizing the West for several years, and he had to fit in.

As an undercover operative, it was Slade's job to work within the gang to get the information his agency needed. So far, though, he'd learned little about the train robberies. The gang had been very close-mouthed about them, even when they were drinking. Not that they had stopped their murderous ways. They'd staged many a robbery since he'd joined up with them, and no lawman had ever come close to catching them.

Slade downed the rest of his whiskey in a single swallow, disgusted by some of the things he'd seen over the last weeks. In his mind, he could justify riding along on the robberies. He was getting firsthand information that would ultimately help put all the outlaws in jail. What tormented him, though, was the fact that the gang thought nothing of killing innocent people.

Slade had killed men in his lifetime, but it had always been in self-defense. The men who rode with the Dakota Kid murdered for the pleasure of it.

Slade prayed he'd get the information he needed soon, so he could stop the gang before any more people died. He'd had enough of their deadly ways. In one robbery, he'd managed to bump horses with Zeke, the most murderous of the outlaws, just as he was taking aim at an unarmed shopkeeper who'd come running out of his store to see what was going on. The shot had gone wide, and Slade had been relieved. More than once, he'd been tempted to turn his own gun on the other members of the gang, but he'd held himself back to maintain his cover. Still, it was tearing him apart.

Now, here they were in Black Springs, checking out the town and the bank they planned to rob the following morning. He hoped there was no one on the streets when they pulled off the job. He'd seen enough killing to last him a lifetime.

"You ready for another?" Charlie asked when he saw Slade's empty glass.

Slade nodded and Charlie refilled his tumbler.

"You gonna be in town long?"

"No. I'll be gone by tomorrow, but I'm thinking I'll wander over to the dance tonight. There any good-looking women in this town?"

"A few," the barkeep said with a smile. "All the good girls will be at the dance, but if you're looking for a fast romp, we got some working girls here who could show you a good time."

"I may take them up on that later, but right now, I think I'll go see about doing a little dancing."

Slade paid for his liquor, threw back the drink and quit the saloon. For just a few minutes that night, he wanted to remember what it felt like to be an upstanding citizen. He wanted to smile at someone and get a smile back. He wanted some kindness—and peace.

As he walked through the saloon's swinging doors back out into the street, Slade caught sight of the Kid and Johnson, the Kid's right-hand man, moving slowly past the bank. They looked casual enough, yet he knew that by the time they'd reached the corner of the building, they would know the layout of the bank's interior and just what it would take to pull off the robbery. He wished there was some way for him to stop it. Right now, he knew, there wasn't.

The Kid had asked him to check out the side streets and the sheriff's office before meeting them outside town in two hours. Slade walked in the direction of the dance, making sure his path led right by the jail. A quick look inside told him it was locked up for the night. He figured the lawman was at the dance, too. Slade headed on toward the music, interested in seeing what kind of adversary they'd be facing the following day.

Alyssa Mason laughed in delight as she watched her younger sister, Emily, being squired around the dance floor by an overeager cowboy.

"What he lacks in talent, he certainly makes up for in enthusiasm," John Mason said, looking from his elder daughter to his wife, as they observed the dancing from the side of the outdoor platform that had been constructed just for the party tonight.

"Emily certainly looks like she's having fun," Loretta told her husband.

"Of course she is. She's the center of attention, and she's loving every minute of it," Alyssa said with a warm smile. She loved her little sister dearly and felt no envy toward her for her popularity.

The family knew how much being popular meant to Emily. She was very much aware of her beauty and used it to attract all the handsome men she could.

Women were a rarity in the territory, and Emily loved every minute of being sought after.

"You should be out there dancing, too," Loretta encouraged Alyssa.

"Maybe later," she demurred, not really interested in socializing.

Loretta stifled a sigh at her answer, still not understanding her oldest child even after all these years. She supposed she should just give up trying to convince her to think in terms of marriage. Alyssa had never been one to flirt or try to entice men into matrimony, and now here she was well into her twenties with no marriage prospects in sight. What was the most puzzling to Loretta was that Alyssa was not even concerned about her unattached state.

Not that Alyssa couldn't have attracted men if she'd wanted to, but she truly didn't seem to think it was important. She'd always been a studious child who'd paid far more attention to her books than she'd ever paid to her appearance or more feminine things like the latest styles from back East. When John became the justice of the peace in Black Springs, Alyssa had just naturally fallen into studying the law under his tutelage. She'd loved it so much and had learned so much that she helped him now with his cases, when she wasn't working in the general store the family owned.

Loretta spied Rob Emerson, the town's sheriff, coming toward them and smiled. She'd long suspected that the lawman had feelings for Alyssa, but he hadn't made any real overtures to her. She supposed she could have been imagining things, but she hoped not. She and John thought the world of Rob. He was a nice-looking young man, probably around thirty years old, with brown hair and blue eyes. He was kind and smart, and, in Loretta's opinion, he would make a perfect son-in-law.

"Evenin', folks," Rob said as he came to join them. "You having a good time?"

"It's just delightful," Loretta answered. "How about you?"

"Absolutely. If we keep the young bucks dancing all night, they won't have any time to stir up trouble." He grinned.

"Maybe we should have a dance every Friday night," John suggested.

"That'd be fine with me."

Rob turned to Alyssa. He'd been waiting all night to get up the nerve to ask her to dance. She'd never shown any interest in him other than friendship, but nonetheless, he was attracted to her. Tonight, in her dark green dress with her pale hair worn down around her shoulders, she was the prettiest woman there.

"Would you like to dance?" he invited her.

She was surprised by his request, but quickly accepted with a warm smile. "I'd love to."

Loretta was thrilled as Rob escorted Alyssa out onto the dance floor. She took her husband's arm and hugged it tightly. "They do make a good-looking couple, don't they, dear?"

John smiled indulgently at her. "You've got to stop matchmaking. You know how Alyssa feels about you always worrying that she hasn't married yet."

"I know, but Rob is a wonderful young man."

"Yes, he is. I think highly of him, but the choice of whether to marry or not is up to Alyssa, not us."

"Wouldn't it be nice, though, if—" In her mind's eye, she already had Alyssa in a wedding gown walking down the aisle with Rob.

"Loretta—" There was a hint of a warning in his tone.

She dropped the subject, but was still smiling as she let her gaze follow the couple.

"Are you having fun tonight?" Rob asked Alyssa as they moved in easy rhythm around the dance floor.

"Yes. It's always nice to get out and see everyone," she answered, easily following his lead. "You're a good dancer, Rob."

"Thanks. My mother and sisters insisted I learn back when I was a kid. I guess they didn't want the female population to be seriously injured while dancing with me." He was smiling as he related the story.

"Surely they didn't really say that?"

"Not in so many words."

"Well, when you talk to them again, be sure to let them know I appreciate their efforts."

"I will."

They shared a laugh.

Alyssa knew her parents liked and respected Rob. She often saw him when he came by the office to discuss legal problems with her father. He was a fair and honest lawman, and he was well respected and liked around town.

When the music ended, he escorted her back to

where her mother and father were standing.

"Thank you, Alyssa, and I'll pass your message along to my mother and sisters next time I write to them." He turned to John. "I'd better get back to work."

"Don't work too hard," John told him. "You might miss out on all the fun."

"I'll remember that, but somehow I don't think trouble will let me off that easy."

He said good night and moved away to make sure things were quiet in town.

"Rob is a nice young man. You could do far worse, you know," Loretta said to Alyssa as she came to stand beside her.

"He's very nice, Mother, but we're just friends."

Loretta was tempted to say more. She wanted to tell Alyssa that Rob was a quiet man who needed to be encouraged, but quick intercession by John stopped her.

"Darling, let's dance," he said, distracting her from her concern over Alyssa's unwed state.

"Yes, dear."

Temporarily saved from hearing her mother sing Rob's praises, Alyssa looked around for Emily. She caught sight of her sister standing by the refreshment table surrounded by a group of smitten young cowboys. She smiled, knowing Emily was having a great time. She just wished that she was. Dancing and flirting had never held much appeal for her, but she did like talking with everyone from town. Alyssa looked around, wondering whom she could approach next.

* * *

Slade had been standing in the shadows just beyond the ring of torches that provided the light for the evening's festivities, feeling like the outsider he was. He'd been looking over the crowd, trying to catch sight of the town's sheriff, when he saw the woman for the first time as she stood with an older couple across the dance floor. Once he'd seen her, he hadn't been able to look away.

It wasn't that the woman was the prettiest one there. Certainly, the petite, flirtatious blond who was surrounded by men at the refreshment table earned that honor, but the woman he was drawn to had a classic, almost timeless beauty about her. Her hair was blond, and she had styled it back away from her face and then allowed the thick, heavy mass to tumble over her shoulders in a cascade of curls. The gown she wore was dark green and emphasized her slender figure and her coloring.

As Slade looked on, another man took her out onto the dance floor. When they turned his way while they were dancing, he saw the badge on the man's chest and knew that he'd found the lawman he'd been seeking.

Slade stepped even farther back into the shadows as he observed them together. The woman was gazing up at the sheriff, laughing at something he'd said. Slade found himself wishing that he was the one out there, holding her in his arms, delighting her with his conversation. His frustration over his situation grew even more, and he knew a driving need to be someone other than Slade Braxton, the outlaw and fast gun, for just one brief moment that night.

Slade moved to the refreshment table and helped himself to a cup of punch. He kept careful watch around him. He had to constantly be on guard and aware of his surroundings. When a man had a bounty on his head, there was no telling who might be able to identify him from his wanted poster and think they could face him down and bring him in.

When several people smiled and said hello to him, Slade politely returned the greeting. It felt good—real good. He looked up again after the music had stopped, and he saw the sheriff walking back toward his office and the woman standing alone on the dance floor.

Common sense told him to trail the lawman, to familiarize himself with his routine. Logic told him he had to meet the Kid in less than an hour, but somehow, none of that mattered right then. He put his cup aside and started through the crowd toward the woman who'd caught his eye. He was going to dance with her just one time tonight before he had to leave.

"Miss?" Slade said as he reached her side.

Alyssa looked up, startled. She'd been watching Emily working her wiles on her legion of ardent admirers and hadn't even noticed this stranger's approach—though how she'd missed him before now, she had no idea. He was different from any man there, and she was certain that she'd never seen him before. If she had, she surely would have remembered. He was by far the best-looking man she'd ever seen— tall, dark and somehow dangerous.

"Hello," she said slowly, giving him a tentative smile. "Have we met?"

"No. Would you care to dance?"

A new tune had just begun to play.

Alyssa was mesmerized as she gazed up at the mysterious man who'd appeared out of nowhere. His dark-eyed regard was warm upon her, yet she felt no nervousness at his nearness, only intrigue and—as much as it startled her—desire. She wanted—no, needed—to know more about him.

"I'd love to dance with you."

The words were out before she realized what she was saying, but there was no time to turn back. She followed her instincts. A smile played around the handsome stranger's lips, but he didn't say another word. When he opened his arms, she moved into them. He swept her out onto the dance floor.

The melody was one of the few slow ones the small band had played all night, and Alyssa couldn't have been more pleased at the timeliness of it. She felt as if she were floating on air as they moved together. Looking up at him, she studied the hard, lean line of his jaw. She saw strength and power there. She wondered what his name was and where he'd come from. To her surprise, she had a great desire to know when she could see him again.

Slade glanced down to find her staring up at him. Their gazes met and locked. It was a spellbinding moment for him. All around them the townspeople seemed to fade away until it was just the two of them, moving gracefully to the rhythm of the sensuous music. He did not look away, but held her gaze as they continued to dance.

The whole dance seemed otherworldly to Alyssa, too, as she allowed herself to be mesmerized by this haunting stranger. She was logical and self-possessed by nature, and she found it hard to believe that this was happening to her. Even so, she didn't fight it. The moment was too special, too important. She was here, in this man's arms, and they were moving together as if they were meant to be one.

Alyssa was enthralled. Nothing like this had ever happened to her before. The heat of his hand at her waist as he guided her and the strength of his fingers holding hers set her heart to pounding. She could feel the power of him where her palm rested on his shoulder. He was everything she'd ever dreamed of in a man. This dance with him was heavenly.

And then the music stopped.

They stood, just gazing at each other, for a moment. It seemed to last an eternity, but she knew it was really only a matter of seconds. And then he spoke.

"Thank you for the dance," he said in a low voice.

"You're welcome," she answered, still caught up in the enchantment of the moment.

It wasn't easy for Slade, but he turned and walked away from her, across the dance floor, out of the lighted area and into the shadows. He knew he'd been crazy to dance with her so publicly, but he'd had to do it. Now, it was over. He had to get out of there, and fast. He'd taken too big a chance already.

Alyssa couldn't just let him leave like that. She found herself following him. She wanted to know

21

more about him—who he was, where he'd come from, when she would see him again.

"Wait—" she said, and she was startled to find that her voice sounded breathless and almost sultry.

Slade turned back to her as the music started up again. He wanted to stay. He ached to take her in his arms again and dance with her all night. But he couldn't. He'd forsaken that life when he'd become an operative.

"I have to go," he said simply. "Good-bye, lovely lady."

She was a vision as she stood before him, and the confused, questioning look in her eyes touched something deep within him. Slade could no more have stopped himself from what he did next than he could have stopped breathing. He reached out to her and drew her to him.

Alyssa thought they were going to dance again, and she went willingly into his arms. Instead of dancing, though, her mystery man took a step back even deeper into the shadows of the warm, dark night. And then, as the sounds of the music and revelry swirled around them, he kissed her. It was a quick and passionate exchange that stunned them both with its power and left them breathless and enthralled.

Slade broke off the kiss and stepped away from her, knowing that if he didn't leave her immediately, he might never be able to go. "Good-bye again, lovely lady."

"Good-bye? But you can't just go—" she blurted out, frowning as she tried to understand why he was leaving when they had the whole night ahead of them. "Will I see you again?"

"No."

His answer was gently spoken, but there was a flash of some emotion in his eyes—sorrow? pain?—that Alyssa couldn't quite identify. Before she could say more, he turned and walked away, leaving her standing alone. She started after him, wanting to stop him from going, but he had disappeared into the crowd. There was no sign that he'd ever been there.

It shocked Alyssa to realize how powerfully she'd just reacted to a perfect stranger . . . and he had been perfect. She'd never been attracted to anyone like this before. She remained where she was, staring off into the crowd, haunted by the image of her mystery man and the wonder of his kiss.

"Who was that?" Emily asked as she escaped her suitors long enough to speak with her sister for a moment.

"I don't know," Alyssa answered distractedly. "He appeared out of nowhere and asked me to dance. He seemed nice enough, but I never did learn his name." "Nice enough" didn't come close to describing what she was really feeling for him.

"Pity. He was good-looking. I'll ask around. Maybe somebody knows who he was."

"I'd like to know," she said softly.

"You would?" Emily looked at her in surprise. Her sister had never shown such interest in a man before.

Alyssa realized what she'd revealed, but didn't care. "Yes, I would."

A woman on a mission, Emily returned to her suitors, hoping to learn the identity of the handsome stranger who'd danced with her sister.

Slade shouldered his way through the crowd, heading back to where he'd left his horse. It was time to go. He'd delayed too long already.

"That was one fine-lookin' woman you were dancin' with. I'd like a piece of that."

Zeke Malone's voice came to him out of the darkness. Slade couldn't believe the other man had been there watching him, and he didn't like it.

"Forget it," Slade told him. "There's no time."

"We can make time. Go back and get her to dance with you again. She'd do it. She looked like she liked you a lot. Hell, she even kissed you . . . a good little girl like that." There was a suggestive, lewd quality to his words. "Then when you're done dancin', just lure her over here, so I can get a taste of that sweet meat."

"Let's go, Zeke." Slade kept walking.

Zeke stayed where he was. He was hot for the blond woman—real hot. "I'd let you have her first, if that's what's bothering you. It wouldn't take much to shut her up, and as noisy as it is, nobody'd know what we'd done 'til we were long gone."

Slade had been on edge all night, and Zeke's animal ways sickened him. "No. She's not for the likes of us."

"The hell she ain't! Just look at her! I'd love to see her naked! I just bet she's got some pretty—"

He didn't get any further before Slade's temper

erupted. Slade turned and hit the other outlaw to shut him up. The force of the blow sent Zeke sprawling to the ground. Slade was glad they were in a darkened alley, a short distance away from the crowd, so no one saw them.

"I said no, Zeke." His tone was deadly.

Slade walked off, leaving the man lying in the dirt swearing under his breath.

Zeke's rage was so great that his hand went to his side arm. There had been something about Braxton that he'd despised from the first time they'd met, and he was tempted to shoot him in the back right now for what he'd done. Only the thought of facing the Kid's fury if he caused any trouble in town tonight stopped him from killing the other gunfighter.

Swearing under his breath, Zeke got up slowly and dusted himself off before following him. One day, he vowed to himself, he was going to get even with Slade Braxton.

Slade and Zeke met up with the Kid on schedule and told him what they'd learned. Neither spoke of the incident over the woman. That was private, just between the two of them. The Kid had found a safe place to camp for the night, so they bedded down some time after midnight to try to get some rest.

Slade didn't sleep, though. He expected trouble from Zeke at any time. He lay awake, staring up at the starry sky. Thoughts of his lovely lady stayed with him through the long, dark hours. He would never see her again. He knew that. His dance with her and their forbidden kiss had been a momentary lapse of his usually rigid self-control. She was innocence and all that was good and sweet in life. She had no place in his godless existence.

"I couldn't find out anything about your mysterious, handsome stranger," Emily told Alyssa later that night as they got ready for bed.

"No one knew who he was?" She was surprised; she'd thought surely someone in town would at least know his name.

She shook her head. "And I asked all of them. Nobody had ever seen him before."

Alyssa sighed. "Thanks."

"You really liked him, didn't you?"

She thought for a moment before answering. "Yes . . . yes I did. There was something about him . . ."

Emily grinned impishly and her eyes were twinkling.

"What are you so happy about?" Alyssa demanded, trying to hide her disappointment at the news.

"It's good to know that under your studious, serious exterior beats the heart of a flesh-and-blood woman!"

"Oh, you!"

"Now you know why I like to flirt so much. Men can be such fun! Why, just trying to figure them out could take a lifetime!"

"I wasn't trying to figure him out—"

"All the better. That means you really were attracted to him."

"He was handsome, wasn't he?"

"Very, in a rugged sort of way," Emily agreed. "Maybe he'll be back."

"He said he wouldn't. He said I'd never see him again."

"Maybe he intended to leave, but having danced with you, he'll be so intrigued now that he won't be able to stay away."

"You've been reading too many Sheridan St. John dime novels!" Alyssa teased, knowing how her sister loved that author's Wild West romances.

"I could never read too many! In fact, she just started a whole new series ! Her new hero is Brand, the Half-Breed Scout, and is he ever wonderful! You really ought to read one, Alyssa. You just might like them."

"Maybe I will—one day."

"You've been saying that forever. You don't know what you're missing—handsome heroes, beautiful heroines, good guys and bad guys, and the good guys always win. Romances are wonderful."

"Good night, Emily," Alyssa said, laughing at her hopelessly romantic sister as she headed for her own bedroom.

"Good night." Just as she was about to close her own bedroom door, Emily called out softly, "And Alyssa?"

"What?"

"I hope he comes back. I hope you get to see him again."

"I do, too."

As Alyssa went to bed, she wondered if her sister's

beloved "happily ever after" endings ever happened in real life.

Morning came far too quickly for Slade's peace of mind, but he was ready. If nothing else, he was a professional. He would do whatever his job demanded of him, and he would do it to the best of his ability. They expected no less of him back at the agency. He was considered their top operative. Though he was proud of the distinction, right now it was an honor that weighed heavily upon him.

"This should be an easy one," the Kid said as they got ready to ride for Black Springs. "Some of the boys will be keeping a lookout around the outskirts of town. Johnson and Nash will be holding the horses and keeping an eye on things outside the bank. Slade, Zeke and me will do the actual robbing."

Zeke smiled. He wondered if anyone would suspect anything if a stray bullet took Slade in the back while they were making their escape from town. He'd been thinking about it all night. Surely no one would suspect him with all the bullets that would be flying.

"Let's ride," Johnson said eagerly. He was the Kid's closest friend in the gang and would have followed the outlaw leader into hell and back, if he'd asked him to.

They mounted up and made their way toward town. They dismounted in the alley close to the bank. Leaving the horses with Johnson and Nash as planned, the Kid, Zeke and Slade covered half their faces with their bandannas and moved swiftly inside the building.

"This is a holdup!" the Kid announced, his guns drawn and ready.

Slade and Zeke had their guns out, too. Zeke quickly collected a bag of money from the teller.

"Don't anybody make a move! If you do, I'll shoot you where you stand," Zeke threatened.

A female customer who'd been cashing a bank draft cried out in terror and fainted dead away. Les Anderson, another customer, started to go to her aid, but the Kid turned his gun on him and he stopped. With no one to catch her, the woman fell heavily to the floor and lay still. Tom York, the bank president, had stood up behind his desk at the first sign of trouble, but he was helpless to stop the robbery.

"You'll never get away with this!" he told them, outraged.

"But we already have." The Kid laughed. "Let's go, boys. We don't want to waste too much time here."

They backed from the room, keeping their guns out. They were in the street and running for their horses when Tom York came charging outside after them.

"Help! Help! The bank's been robbed!" he shouted.

John Mason had been about to enter his office a short distance down the street when he heard Tom call for help. Not caring that he wasn't armed, John ran to his friend's aid.

Johnson had brought the horses around, and they had all just mounted up when they saw John running toward them. Slade could see that the man was unarmed, and he feared that one of the others might shoot him down anyway. He rode toward him, trying to block any shots at him, but giving the impression that he was going to take the man out himself.

Shots erupted from the far end of the street, and the gang realized word had gotten out and the sheriff was coming after them. They started to gallop down the street, firing back wildly. Townspeople came running out of their shops and homes to see what was going on.

Zeke had been waiting for just this chance to pay Slade back. He fired in Slade's direction as he spurred his horse to follow the Kid's. He did not look back, thinking he'd hit him. He wasn't worried whether the other gunman was dead or not. If he'd just wounded Slade, it would slow him down enough for the law to capture him. The thought of Slade in jail made Zeke smile.

Slade watched in horror as the man he'd been trying to protect was hit by a shot that had come from somewhere behind him. He whirled his horse around to see Zeke riding away at full speed. With the sheriff closing in on him, Slade leaned low over his horse's neck and raced after the rest of the gang. The memory of the man he'd been trying to shield lying wounded in the street haunted him.

Rob was cursing as he kept shooting at the fleeing bank robbers. When he realized that they were out of range and it was pointless, he stopped and slid his gun back into his holster in disgust. Deputy Clemans ran up just then, gun in hand.

"Go get our horses and gather a posse. We're going after them!'' Rob ordered. Then he glanced toward where John lay unmoving and realized his friend's wound was serious. "But first, send for the doc! And someone go get Loretta!''

Rob went to where Tom was kneeling beside John. "How is he?''

Tom looked up, his face showing all the pain and fury he was feeling over what had happened. "He's dead.''

Rob knelt down beside John, too. He'd been taught from the time he was little not to show any emotion, but there could be no denying the tears that burned in his eyes. John Mason had been a good friend to him. Men didn't come any finer than John.

"I swear to God, Tom,'' he said in a choked voice as he looked over at the bank manager, "no matter how long it takes me, I'm going to find those bastards and see them hang!''

The townspeople began to gather around. The doctor reached them just as they heard Loretta's voice coming from down the street near the general store as Deputy Clemans brought her to them.

"What's wrong? Where's John? Why won't you tell me where he is?''

The crowd parted for her, and then she saw her husband.

Chapter Two

Three Weeks Later

Slade Braxton's well-honed instinct for survival was screaming a warning as he followed the other members of the Dakota Kid's gang down the narrow trail through the rocky gorge. An uneasiness settled over him. He grew more watchful, slowing his pace and lagging behind. He let his gaze sweep the steep, craggy walls of the canyon area ahead. Something wasn't right. . . . He wondered if anyone else had noticed, but they were riding on, seemingly unaware of any danger. Slowly, almost imperceptibly, Slade drew his sidearm and rested it against his thigh. If there was trouble, he would be ready.

And then Slade saw it—the glint of sunlight off a

rifle barrel in the rocks high above them. He wasn't sure who was watching them—he could only hope.

As if realizing they'd been seen, the hidden gunmen unleashed a barrage upon the outlaws below them.

Any hope Slade had had that those watching were with the agency died as the shots struck close around him. These attackers were shooting to kill—and they were aiming at him.

"Let's get out of here!" he shouted, knowing escape back the way they'd just come was their only salvation.

Slade pivoted his mount and raised his gun, ready to take out any of the ambushers he could. He sighted one and took aim. As he did, though, he caught sight of the star on the man's chest. Slade cursed under his breath and deliberately shot wide. He wanted to send the man back into hiding—not kill him. The sheriff dove for cover, giving Slade the chance he needed to head back up the trail.

Nash and Johnson, the two members of the gang who'd been riding closest to Slade, followed his lead. They'd seen several of their comrades fall ahead of them and knew they'd be trapped if they tried to keep following the Kid through the gorge. Spurring their mounts, they raced after Slade.

But there would be no escape for them. Rob Emerson had planned his ambush perfectly. As the outlaws made a break for open ground, the sheriff of Black Springs sent a huge boulder rolling down to block their path. He watched as they reacted like cornered animals, and he smiled with feral intensity. It was just what the damned killers deserved. They were lucky he didn't shoot them down right now like the murdering dogs they were.

"We've got you surrounded. Throw down your guns and give up now!" Rob shouted.

Johnson and Nash whirled their mounts toward the sound of the voice and fired in his direction. Return fire came from both sides of the canyon. A round took Nash squarely in the shoulder. He lost his seat and fell. Writhing on the ground in misery, he called out to Johnson and Slade for help.

Slade silently cursed. He'd almost been ready to bring the Kid and his gang in, and now—

"There ain't no place to run!" the lawman repeated. "Throw your guns down and put your hands up, and we'll let you live!"

Trapped and facing certain death if they tried to fight their way out, Slade and Johnson knew they had no choice.

"Who the hell are they?" Johnson snarled in angry frustration as he tossed his rifle and handgun out where the posse could see them.

"I think we're about to find out," Slade answered as he, too, did as he'd been told.

Slade looked up, waiting for the attackers to show themselves. He held on to the one thread of hope that his supervisor from Denver was among them as he searched the faces of the men who slowly emerged from their hiding places. But Ken Richards wasn't there. All the men were strangers to him. They all wore badges, and they all looked grimly determined. And then the leader stood up.

"It's the sheriff from Black Springs," Slade said, recognizing him from the night of the dance.

Johnson swore out loud at the news.

The shooting continued up ahead of them on the trail, but the sound was growing fainter, as if a running battle continued.

"Sounds like the Kid might be getting away," Johnson told Slade under his breath. "Ain't nobody gonna ever bring the Kid in! He's too damned good."

Slade only nodded in return. He kept careful watch on the deputies climbing down toward them, for the lawmen's rifles were trained on their chests.

"Dismount and step away from your horses," Rob ordered, standing guard, his rifle ready just in case they tried anything. "Hawkins, you cuff them."

Two deputies went to catch their mounts as another came down to handcuff them.

"What are your names?" the deputy named Hawkins demanded as he restrained them.

When Slade and Johnson remained stonily silent, he clubbed them both with his rifle.

"That's Braxton!" one of the men holding the horses called out excitedly. "I recognize him from his wanted poster! And the other one's Johnson!"

"So, you're Braxton, are you?" Hawkins eyed Slade with open hatred. He was glad the outlaw was bleeding from a cut on his forehead where he'd just hit him. He would have liked to shoot him outright, but Sheriff Emerson was watching. "We know all about you."

Everyone knew about Braxton—about the robbing

and killing he'd done. There were wanted posters for him out almost everywhere west of the Mississippi.

"You're under arrest for robbery and murder," Hawkins announced as he searched first Slade, then Johnson for other weapons. He found their knives and took those before going to see to Nash. Once Nash was unarmed, the deputy put a makeshift bandage on his shoulder and handcuffed him, too. They would take no chances with any of these deadly gang members.

Up ahead of them the shooting stopped. Slade wondered if the Kid had managed to get away or if he'd been killed.

"We'll wait here for the others," Rob ordered from his vantage point.

"Do you think they got the Kid?" Hawkins asked.

"I hope so. I want to see him hang."

They settled in, ready to wait it out. Nearly an hour passed before four more deputies rode up. They were leading two horses with bodies tied to their backs.

"Well?" Rob demanded. He'd grown tense waiting for their return. He was pleased that his plan had succeeded this far, but his satisfaction wouldn't be complete until he'd brought in the Dakota Kid, too. He was the leader.

"The Kid got away, but we managed to kill two more of them!"

Rob cursed long and loudly as he stared off in the direction the Dakota Kid had run with the other surviving members of his gang. He was tempted to go after them, but he'd been gone from Black Springs for over two weeks now. They had three of the gang in custody, plus two dead. He would have to be satisfied—for now.

"Don't worry, Sheriff. We'll get him eventually."

"I wanted the Dakota Kid today." His tone was grave.

The others fell silent, knowing there was nothing more they could do right then.

"Well, at least we got Braxton," Hawkins said, and the deputies who'd just joined them were pleased.

They mounted up and made their way carefully around the boulder that had blocked the trail. The posse rode out of the canyon, still frustrated, but knowing they had accomplished some good that day.

Slade swore silently to himself as he rode toward Black Springs surrounded by armed guards. He was a prisoner everyone would just as soon hang as lock up in jail. Nothing was working out as he'd planned. He'd been in some difficult situations in his life, but this was turning out to be the worst. He hoped the truth would be enough to set him free, but considering the circumstances, he doubted it. His expression was grim as they continued on their way to town.

"Sheriff Emerson's riding in!" The shout went up through Black Springs as someone caught sight of the lawmen returning in the distance. "It looks like they caught 'em!"

The townspeople quit what they were doing and hurried outside to see what was happening. They all knew how badly the sheriff had wanted to catch the Dakota Kid ever since the robbery and John's murder. They'd heard talk that he'd set a trap for the deadly gang, and they'd been waiting anxiously for news of its outcome.

The Dakota Kid and his gang had been terrorizing the territory for years now—murdering, robbing trains and banks and generally making life miserable for decent folks. If Sheriff Emerson had caught them, there would be a big celebration tonight.

All eyes followed the progress of their sheriff and his deputies as they rode slowly down the main street of town. They had three handcuffed men in tow and two dead bodies thrown over the backs of horses.

"Did you get them all, Rob?" Tom York called out, eager to see the outlaws get their due.

"We got some of them," he answered tightly.

Cheers went up at his words, but the lawman didn't smile. The Dakota Kid was still on the loose and that left him on edge. During the four-day ride back to town, he'd stayed constantly on guard. There was no telling when the savage bandit might show up or what he might do next. The Kid was amoral, vicious and smart, and that was a dangerous combination to guard against—especially since he would be holding some of his most deadly gang members in the Black Springs jail.

Reining in before his office, Rob dismounted and looped his reins over the hitching rail. He ordered several of the deputies to take the bodies to the undertaker's; then he turned back to Slade and the others and drew his gun.

"Get down, but move slow," he ordered.

"Yeah, we'd hate for you to have an accident now,

after bringing you all the way in,'' Deputy Hawkins said with a scornful laugh.

Slade looked around Black Springs. He'd thought he would never see it again, and now he was back. He eyed the jail and knew it wouldn't be simple to break out of there. He'd had no chance to try to run since they'd been taken into custody, and now things looked even worse. If it hadn't been for bad luck lately, he wouldn't have had any luck at all. Slade knew he'd think of something, though. He had to. Too much depended on his staying close to the Kid.

"Move it nice and easy, Braxton. Don't try anything." Hawkins jabbed Slade in the back with his six-gun. "I'd hate to have to shoot you 'cause I thought you were trying to make a run for it."

Slade didn't respond to his taunting. He just moved steadily toward the sheriff's office as Nash and Johnson followed.

"Did you have much trouble, Sheriff?" asked Al Carson, the editor of the town's only newspaper, *The Gazette*. He wanted to write the story up for the next edition.

"It's never easy dealing with the Dakota Kid." Rob's answer was terse. It had been sheer luck that no one in the posse had been killed or injured in the shoot-out. "We brought in Nash, Johnson and Braxton."

"You got Braxton? Which one is he?" Carson's eyes widened in surprise as he turned to stare at the captives.

Braxton had the reputation of being one of the most dangerous gunmen alive. When the townsfolk heard the rumor that he'd joined up with the Dakota Kid, they'd feared trouble would follow, and they'd been right. In the last few months, the Kid's gang had robbed a number of trains, several banks and two stages out of Laramie. The sooner they were stopped, the better life would be for everyone.

"He's the tall one." Rob gestured toward the man Deputy Hawkins was taking inside.

The newspaperman looked at Slade. The lean, dark-haired gunslinger was dressed all in black and appeared deadly. When the outlaw glanced his way, Al met his regard straight on. He shuddered at the coldness he saw mirrored in the outlaw's eyes. "Is he as mean as he looks?"

"Meaner," Hawkins called over to him. "I'm gonna enjoy seeing him swing."

"So will a lot of other people," Al agreed.

The town wouldn't get back the money they'd lost in the bank robbery. No doubt that was long gone. And hanging the outlaws wouldn't bring back John Mason, but once the gang members were dead, they would never be able to hurt anyone again.

Johnson glared at the townspeople who were gathering round. As he was herded inside, he called out, "The Kid ain't gonna let you hang us. He'll break us out. Ain't none of you gonna be safe until we're free again! You just wait and see."

A murmur of fear went through the crowd.

"You ain't going anywhere but to jail, Johnson!" Rob ground out, barely controlling his fierce desire to pistol-whip the loud-mouthed gunslinger.

"We'll just have to see about that, won't we, Sheriff?'' Nash sneered as he walked past the man who'd managed to outsmart them and bring them in.

"There's going to be round-the-clock armed guards at the jail,'' Rob announced, wanting to ease everyone's fears.

"A few guards won't stop the Kid,'' Nash countered, confident that he would be saved by his friend.

Rob waited until all three outlaws were inside the jail; then he turned back to the townspeople. "You folks can go on home now. There won't be any more excitement today.''

"What about his threat that the Kid's going to break them out?'' someone called out. "I know you said there were going to be guards, but—''

"It's talk, that's all. Just talk. If the Kid does try anything, we'll arrest him and lock him up, too.''

"How come you missed him when you got the others?'' Al asked.

The sheriff scowled at his question. "The Kid got lucky, but his luck's bound to change one of these days.''

With that, Rob went inside and shut the door behind him. He was in no mood to field any more questions. There would be plenty of time for that later, once things had settled down.

The crowd slowly moved away, but the townspeople's mood was still uneasy. Not that they didn't trust Sheriff Emerson. They did. Though he was a rather young man, he'd proven himself to be a good lawman. The only real trouble they'd had in town since he'd been elected sheriff had been with the gang, and now he'd gone out and brought some of them in on his own. That was more than any other lawman had done in the territory.

Al hurried off to the newspaper office. He had work to do.

Inside the jail, the three prisoners were herded into one cell in the back room. Only after Hawkins had locked the cell door, did he tell them to stick their hands through the bars so he could unfasten the handcuffs.

"Make yourselves comfortable," Rob said as he came to stand in the hall outside their cell. "You're gonna be looking at the inside of a jail for quite some time, boys."

Nash glared at him and gave a harsh laugh. "Think what you want, lawman. The Kid ain't gonna leave us to hang."

"If the Kid comes for you, he's a dead man." Rob turned away from them. Ignoring their shouts and taunts, he returned to the front office and closed the door that separated the two areas. He needed some peace and quiet for a minute while he figured out what to do next.

With the door shut, Nash and Johnson grew weary of the game. They flopped down on two of the cots provided in the cell.

"How soon do you think the Kid will show up?" Nash looked over at Johnson. Johnson had ridden with the Kid the longest and knew him better than anyone else.

"It all depends. He'll plan it before he comes into town," Johnson told him. "What do you think, Slade?"

"He's going to have one helluva time getting us out of here if they put armed guards on us around the clock like they said. There's only him, Red and Zeke left."

"The Kid can do it. He can do anything." Nash believed the outlaw leader to be invincible.

"I hope you're right," Johnson said. "Hanging ain't no way for a man to die."

"We ain't gonna die," Nash insisted. "The Kid will save us. You'll see."

Slade made himself as comfortable as he could on a top bunk. He folded his hands beneath his head and closed his eyes as he tried to figure out what his own next move was going to be. He would have to sit tight and wait, and that was going to be the hard part. He had been close . . . so close . . . But that chance was gone. He was going to have to start all over again—providing he got out of this alive, and things weren't looking too good right now.

"How can you even think about sleeping, Braxton?" Johnson demanded, as he got up and paced around the small cell.

He knew the Kid respected Braxton, but something about the man bothered him. Maybe it was the way Braxton was so quiet most of the time, or the way he never tried to make friends with any of the others in the gang. Johnson always kept an eye on him, not trusting him completely. And he wasn't the only one who felt that way. He knew Zeke did, too.

"I can't sleep if you keep talking to me," Slade drawled, not bothering to open his eyes. Johnson was one of the coldest men in the gang. Slade knew he

43

would just as soon kill a man as talk to him.

"We need to be planning something. We need to—"

"There isn't anything we can do right now but wait it out. You may as well follow the lawman's suggestion and make yourself comfortable. We're going to be stuck here for a while, even if the Kid does come after us."

"Don't tell me what to do, Braxton" Johnson said angrily. The Kid was the only one he listened to. He'd been riding and killing with him since he was thirteen. He was twenty-five now, and he knew no other life than running with the gang. The thought of spending his days locked up in this small cell was enough to make him crazy.

Slade heard the edge in his voice and looked over at him. "I don't care what you do, Johnson. Suit yourself. I'm just saying, the Kid would be a fool to ride straight in here and try to break us out now. And one thing the three of us all know for sure is that the Dakota Kid is no fool."

"He's right, Johnson," Nash added, his voice strained from the pain of his wound. "Take it easy. We're stuck for now, but it won't last long."

Johnson looked over at Nash and managed to bring his temper under control. This was no time to fight among themselves, though it irked him to admit Braxton was right. He'd just have to wait and hope the Kid would come for them soon.

Johnson was sure the wait wouldn't be a long one. The Kid would never desert him. Never.

* * *

Rob sent one of the deputies to fetch the doctor so he could examine Nash's wound. That done, he settled in behind his desk, glad for a moment of peace.

"What are you going to do with them?" Hawkins asked.

"I'm going to see that they have a fair trial."

"I don't know why you're so determined to waste time," Hawkins scoffed.

"Because it's the law, Hawkins, and I'm sworn to uphold it."

"It would have been so easy to rid the territory of them while we were still on the range. It would only have taken three shots."

"That's the difference between us," Rob said, his gaze narrowing as he studied his hot-headed deputy. He liked Hawkins, but he knew he couldn't trust him completely. He had to keep an eye on him. "I like to do things by the law. You like to dispense your own brand of justice."

"Is that so bad? We know who these men are, and we know what they've done." Hawkins didn't understand how the sheriff could be so fair. The outlaws hadn't been fair when they'd killed John Mason.

"We have to let justice take its course."

"But we know Braxton was in on it! And Nash and Johnson, too! There were witnesses who saw them do it!"

"And they'll get their say at the preliminary hearing and at the trial. Until then, it's our sworn duty to keep those men safe."

"I'd feel a lot better if they were in pine boxes, six feet under somewhere."

"Everybody in the territory would, but we're going to do it legal-like. I don't want to hear any more talk about vigilantes and lynchings."

The deputy was silent, but sullen. "What are we going to do about the Kid? You know he's going to try to break his men out."

"If he shows his face in Black Springs, I'll arrest him. But I don't intend to give him any extra time to cause trouble. I'm going to see Alyssa Mason right now and arrange for the hearing to be held first thing tomorrow morning."

Hawkins shook his head. "Ain't that something . . . Our biggest case in years, and it goes before a woman justice."

"Who better?" the sheriff countered. "It was her father who was killed."

"I know, but still—" The thought of a woman justice of the peace left him uneasy, even though there had been several others in the history of the territory who'd done fine jobs.

"Don't be a damned fool, Hawkins. You know how smart Alyssa is about the law," Rob said, scornful of his narrow-mindedness.

Rob was glad to see capable women in positions of authority. The territory had given women the right to vote years before, and to his way of thinking, only good had come of it. And Alyssa was one special woman. She was smart and kind. She was pretty, too, in a quiet sort of way.

"I know," Hawkins groused, "but she's still a woman. It just don't seem right to me."

"If we had lady lawyers out here in the territory,

I bet she'd be qualified to be one. We were just fortunate to have her to fill in for her father after the bastards shot him.''

The deputy gave a grunt. ''So, once we hold the hearing and they're bound over for trial, how fast are we going to head for Green River for the criminal trial?''

''The sooner we're out of here, the better. I don't want to give the Kid any time to plan a jailbreak.''

They shared a grave look, knowing how dangerous the trek across country with the prisoners would be.

''I'll start making the arrangements.''

''And I'll go talk to our judge.''

Rob put on his hat, checked to make sure his side arm was loaded, just in case there was trouble, and left the office. He was pleased that he was going to see Alyssa and that he had some good news for her. He might not have the Kid yet, but at least he'd brought in part of his gang.

''They just brought in some of the Dakota Kid's gang! I can't believe they actually caught them!'' Emily Mason hugged her mother as tears of joy filled her eyes.

''Thank God,'' Loretta Mason breathed.

They had been working in the small general store they owned when a customer had come running in to tell them the good news.

''I just wish they'd caught the Dakota Kid, too,'' Emily said as she and her mother moved apart.

''Rob's a good man. If there's any possible way to do it, he will. You'll see. He's already accomplished

47

more than any other lawman in the territory.''

"I hope nothing goes wrong now that they've got some of the gang in custody.''

"I wonder what Rob's going to do about the hearing? I wonder if Alyssa will preside?''

"I know judges are supposed to excuse themselves if they're personally involved in a case, but if she doesn't handle it, who will? Besides, she'll only preside over the preliminary hearing and bind them over for trial. It's not like she's going to be sentencing them or anything.''

"I wish she could try them," Loretta said fiercely. "*And* sentence them.''

When John was murdered, Alyssa had been chosen by the townspeople to finish out his term as justice of the peace. There had been no one better qualified in the law to take over. Though she'd only held the office for a few weeks, so far Alyssa had upheld their belief in her completely. Many who had doubted a woman's ability to administer justice had changed their minds after watching her conduct the business of her office. Her father would have been proud.

"Don't worry. They're going to hang whether she's in charge of the sentencing or not. There are witnesses who saw everything that day. There's no way the gang can get away with this.''

"I hope you're right, but you know how vicious the Dakota Kid is. Anything might happen before they go to trial.''

"Rob will make sure everything goes smoothly. He worked too hard to catch them to let them get away.''

Even as she tried to sound positive, though, both

Emily and her mother knew the dangers involved. They offered up silent prayers that justice would be done.

Rob knocked at the door to Alyssa's small office.

"Come in," she called out from her desk, where she sat poring over a thick law book.

"I need to talk to you right away," he told her, taking off his hat as he entered the room. His gaze was upon her as he went to stand before her desk. Her blond hair was pulled back in a tight bun; she was wearing glasses for reading; and she was dressed in a mourning gown, as she had been since her father's death. Even so, he thought she looked lovely.

"You're back!" Alyssa was excited at seeing him. She'd heard of his plan to trap the Dakota Kid's gang and hoped it had gone well. "Did you get them?"

"I got some of them," he told her, and he felt ten feet tall at the look in her eyes as she gazed at him.

"Thank you, Rob," she said with heartfelt sincerity.

"Don't thank me too much. I only brought in three of them, and we managed to kill two. The Kid got away, though."

"Who'd you catch?"

"Nash, Johnson—and Braxton."

"You got Braxton," she repeated, stunned.

"Yes."

She felt a great weight lift from her soul. The eyewitness to the shooting claimed that Slade Braxton was the one who'd gunned down her father. Now, thanks to Rob, justice would be served.

"Thank you," she whispered, fighting back the tears as she looked up at him. He was a fine man, and she was proud to call him her friend.

Alyssa looked so feminine and helpless and beautiful to Rob right then that he felt an overwhelming need to go to her and hold her, but he didn't. She'd never given him any indication that such a forward, personal gesture on his part would be welcomed, so he held himself back.

"It was my pleasure, believe me."

"What can I do to help you?"

"That's why I'm here. I want them arraigned as quickly as possible. Can you do it tomorrow? In the morning?"

"How's nine A.M. tomorrow? Is that soon enough?"

"Yesterday wouldn't have been soon enough for me," Rob said gruffly, giving her a half smile.

"Me, either." Alyssa managed a grim smile of her own. "I should disqualify myself, you know."

"Don't even think about it." He admired her for taking her job so seriously.

"But I am personally involved in this."

"Aren't we all? Everybody in town could say the same thing. But this case is too important to us. We can't take any chances with delays."

"All right. What about the Kid? Do you have any idea where he's holed up?"

"No, not yet, and that's the reason I don't want to waste any time if I can help it." His expression grew even more determined. "When I get back to the office, I'm going to interrogate each of the prisoners individually. Maybe I can persuade one of them to tell me where the Kid is right now.''

''Good luck.'' She saw the steely glint in his eyes and knew that if anyone could get information out of the prisoners, Rob could.

''It's going to take more than luck. I doubt any of them will talk, but I have to try. I'll be posting armed guards around town and in the jail tonight. We're going to keep watch every minute.''

She nodded, respecting his precautions. ''I'll see you first thing in the morning, then.''

''I'm looking forward to it.''

Alyssa's relief that the outlaws had been brought in was tinged with fear as she watched Rob head back to the jail. Everyone knew how deadly the Dakota Kid was. No one involved would rest easy until the trial was over, so she would do everything within her power to help.

Alyssa stayed late at her office, going over more of her father's law books. She didn't want to make any mistakes during the hearing the next day. She would do things by the letter of the law.

Chapter Three

"All right, Braxton. It's your turn. The sheriff wants to talk to you next," Hawkins said as he shoved Johnson back into the cell later that night.

Slade got down off his bunk as Hawkins took the handcuffs off Johnson. He offered no protest as the deputy fastened them around his wrists. Since they'd taken Johnson out to be questioned, he'd been trying to decide the best way to handle his situation. There were risks involved in telling the truth, but there was a bigger risk of dying by staying silent. Slade knew what he had to do. It angered him, but he had little choice. He followed the deputy from the cell and waited while the man relocked the cell door behind them.

"The sheriff's really looking forward to talking to you," Hawkins told him in an almost gloating tone as they made their way to the outer office. "Go on through that door over there." He pointed toward a door off to the side.

Slade did as he was told. He was pleased that he and the sheriff were going to have some time alone. What he had to say needed to be said in private. It was important that no one else knew of their conversation.

The windowless room was starkly furnished with only one table and chair. A single lamp burned on the table top. The sheriff stood across the room, his expression unreadable.

"Sit down." Rob's order was terse as he fought to control his anger. His interrogation of Johnson had been infuriating. The outlaw had been arrogant and had refused to cooperate with him in any way. And now he had to face Braxton—the worst of the three in his opinion. He'd read the wanted posters. He knew what this man was capable of, and he hated him with a passion. "I've got some questions I want answered, Braxton."

Slade sat down at the table and waited. He was trying to judge Emerson's mood so he could figure out the best way to handle things.

"Where's the Dakota Kid?" Rob demanded abruptly.

"I don't know. He could be anywhere right now." Slade was serious in his answer.

In the time Slade had been riding with the gang, he'd learned that they had any number of places to hide out—friends with ranches who'd cover for them, abandoned mining cabins up in the mountains, box canyons that were easy to guard and sometimes even caves in the wilderness. That was what had made this assignment so difficult. He'd needed just another few weeks, and he could have set up the arrests. As it was, he was now trapped in a deadly web of his own making. He only hoped the truth would be enough to save him.

"That's not good enough." Rob moved threateningly toward him. He grabbed Slade by the shirt front and glared down at him with murderous intent. "Deputy Hawkins out there would just love an excuse to put a bullet in you, and I'm beginning to feel the same way about you and your friends. I've taken all I can from the likes of you. I want some answers and I want them now!"

"Sheriff—there's something you need to know," Slade began.

"What's that?" Rob released him and stepped back, eyeing him coldly. Braxton was a deadly gunslinger—a bank-robbing, cold-blooded killer, who deserved to hang.

Just remembering that terrible day of the robbery filled Rob with an even blacker rage. Black Springs was his town. He was the law here. If outlaws decided to cause trouble, they'd soon learn that there was a steep price to pay.

"I've been working with the gang undercover. I'm a Pinkerton agent." Slade had not wanted to reveal his true identity, but he could see no other way out.

"And I'm the President of the United States!"

Outraged by the lies and the arrogance he'd faced first with Johnson and now Braxton, Rob lost control.

He hit Slade, knocking him from the chair.

"You're a lying, no-good bastard is what you are! A Pinkerton agent?" He scoffed. "Witnesses put you at the scene of the crime, Braxton! We all know what a killer you are!"

"My reputation is a cover," he argued. There was blood seeping from his cut lip, and his jaw ached. "The agency created it to convince the Kid to let me ride with the gang."

Slade slowly started to rise, but Rob was lost in a white-hot rage. He kicked him in the side and sent him sprawling back on the floor.

"Stay down in the dirt where you belong!"

Slade bit back a groan as he looked up at the lawman. "I can prove it. If you wire Denver—"

"You're just stalling for time. While I'm waiting for a telegram, the Kid will have the chance to break you out! I'm not going for it. I'm going to see you hang, Braxton, all nice and legal, and as far as I'm concerned, it can't happen a minute too soon!"

"Check my story out."

"*Story* is the right word! It's a big one, and a lie!"

"Wire Denver. They'll tell you the truth about me."

"The truth is you're a wanted man—a killer with a price on his head in more states than I can name! I brought you in. The only thing I want anybody to tell me is the location of the Kid's hideout, and the only wire being sent is already gone. I wired the district judge in Green River a while ago and told him to get ready for a trial—and a hanging."

"You've got to listen to me—"

"All right. I'm listening. Where's the Dakota Kid?" Rob was oblivious to any protest or logical argument. Slade Braxton was going to face justice. He was going to pay the price for his killing ways.

"You're making a big mistake—"

Emerson hit him again. "I'd say you were the one who made a mistake, Braxton. You're the one on the wrong side of the law. The only mistake I made was not following Hawkins's advice and shooting the three of you dead when I had the chance out in the canyon."

Slade was bleeding from a cut over his eye, and his eye was already swelling shut. His side felt as if it were on fire, and his jaw was aching. He wanted to prove his identity to this man, to convince him they were on the same side of the law, but he had kept nothing with him that would show his connection to the Pinkertons. If he had, someone in the gang might have found it. Slade realized his only hope was that his supervisor, Ken Richards, was keeping track of the gang and would learn through newspaper accounts what had happened. He hoped Ken would get there in time to save him from hanging—unless the Kid managed to break them out first.

"Now, get the hell out of here before I do something I might really regret." Rob's regard was condemning as he watched Slade struggle to his feet and start from the room. He smiled thinly at seeing him in pain. "If you think you're hurting now, wait until that noose tightens around your neck."

Johnson and Nash both looked up as Slade was returned to the cell and unhandcuffed. They'd always known he was a tough man, and from the looks of him, he'd just received a beating that reaffirmed it. Johnson had suffered some of the sheriff's wrath, but nothing like what had happened to Slade.

"I take it you didn't tell him anything," Nash drawled, managing to smile in spite of his own pain.

"They're not going to find out where the Kid is from me," Slade answered, climbing slowly back into his bunk.

"He didn't get anything out of me either," Johnson said with pride.

"I guess it must be my turn," Nash remarked as Hawkins glared at him from where he was standing by the open cell door.

"You think you're pretty smart, Nash, but let's just see how smart the sheriff thinks you are." Hawkins was waiting to put the cuffs on him.

Nash got up. The deputy quickly restrained him and led him away after securing the cell door once again.

"Let's make a break for it when he brings Nash back in!" Johnson told Slade when he was sure they were alone.

"I'm all for getting out of here, but we're not going anywhere without guns. The sheriff's got armed guards posted all around the building and the town."

"But there's just the two of them here in the jail. We'll kill them and take their weapons." He was excited about his plan. He was sure they could pull it off. "It's late, nearly midnight. Once we get away from here, we can sneak out of town without anybody seeing us. No one will even realize we're gone until tomorrow morning.''

''Your plan's all well and good, but you're talking suicide if anything goes wrong. If either Emerson or Hawkins managed to get just one shot off while we were trying to break out, we'd be dead men before we got out the front door.''

Johnson shot him an ugly look, knowing he was right, but not wanting to die without a fight. ''We're as good as dead anyway. We gotta find a way out of here.''

''Do what you want. You're going to anyway. But I'm telling you, we stand a better chance of escaping while they're transporting us for trial. They'll need to take us to Green River, and there's bound to be an opportunity somewhere on the trek.''

Patience wasn't one of Johnson's stronger traits, but this time he accepted the truth of Slade's words. Breaking out of the jail wouldn't mean much if they never made it to their horses. He would wait for his chance, but the waiting wouldn't be easy.

Alyssa rose early the following morning. She'd stayed up long past midnight, thinking of the day to come, and now it was here. In less than two hours, she would be presiding over the preliminary hearing of the men responsible for her father's death.

So much had changed in her life since that terrible day. It was hard for her to believe that just a few weeks before, she'd allowed herself to be carefree. The light-hearted memory of her dance with the mysterious stranger had faded now, replaced by the responsibility that had fallen heavily on her shoulders. Her mother and her sister looked to her for strength and guidance. She could not let them down.

Alyssa dressed with care, though she had little choice in gowns. Because of her state of mourning, she donned a black, long-sleeved, high-necked day gown. She pinned her hair back in a tight bun at the nape of her neck. She didn't want anyone in the courtroom to have any reason to criticize her or be distracted by the fact that she was a woman. This hearing was serious business.

A quick glance in the mirror told her she was ready. She looked exactly as she'd wanted to look—staid and serious. For the first time in her life, she was glad she had to wear glasses to read. It added to the studiousness of the image she wanted to project.

"Are you ready?"

The sound of her mother's voice startled Alyssa, and she jumped nervously as she turned toward the open bedroom door to find her mother standing there, watching her.

"I'm as ready as I'll ever be." She drew a steadying breath. "You're coming to the hearing, aren't you?"

"Yes, Emily and I both are. We decided not to open the store until it's over. Nobody will care anyway. The entire town is eager to see what's going to happen today."

Alyssa nodded. "I hope it all goes well."

The constant, nagging fear that the Dakota Kid might somehow find a way to disrupt the proceedings stayed with her, but she knew Rob would have planned for possible trouble and be prepared for it.

"You know it will," her mother said with confidence. "Your father trained you. You know the law. You'll do fine."

"I have to," she declared fiercely. "The Dakota Kid's gang is one of the meanest in the West. I want to make sure they never have the chance to hurt anyone else again."

Loretta gave a small sob as she went to embrace her daughter. "I'm so proud of you, and I'm sure your father is, too."

"I want him to be proud of me."

"I miss him so." Loretta choked, struggling not to give in to the tears that threatened. "I never really thought his killers would be caught. But Rob never gave up. He's a wonderful man and a true friend to have tracked them down the way he did."

"If only he'd caught the Dakota Kid, too, then we could put this all behind us after the trial."

"The law will catch up with that man some day. I know it!" Loretta refused to believe anyone as evil as the Kid could remain untouched by justice.

"I hope you're right," Alyssa agreed.

Classes were canceled at the one-room schoolhouse that morning so the building could be converted into a courtroom. As soon as they were allowed, the townspeople packed into the building. Nearly everyone in Black Springs had been affected in one way or another by the robbery and killing, and they were eager to see justice finally done. Though this was just the first step, they were glad some progress was being made. They waited, talking quietly among themselves, for the hearing to begin.

Al Carson was in the front row, taking notes for *The Gazette*. Tom York was there, too. He was to be called as a witness today. He had seen everything. There were several others who'd been notified by Alyssa that they would be called upon as well. All were eager to do their civic duty in helping see these men convicted.

"They're coming!" someone sitting near the back of the room shouted.

A hush fell over the crowd, and everyone looked toward the doorway as the sheriff and his deputies entered the room with the prisoners. The townspeople's mood grew tense, and they glared with open hostility at the gunmen.

Slade was led shackled into the courtroom. His mood was as dark as the townspeople's was angry. He looked around at the sea of condemning faces and recognized no one. He kept telling himself there was still time for Ken Richards to save him, but he knew there wasn't a lot.

The only thing that kept Slade from complete despair was the knowledge that the sheriff hadn't told anyone of his claim that he was a Pinkerton. The night before, he'd waited tensely for Nash's return to the cell, fearing that the lawman would use what he'd told him on Nash to try to get more information out of him. Luckily, it hadn't happened. For whatever reason, Emerson hadn't said anything. His cover was still in place.

"Sit down here," Hawkins said, shoving him

slightly toward one of the chairs at a table in the front
of the courtroom.

Slade sat down and kept his eyes directed straight
ahead. He wondered how long the hearing would last.
Judging from the eagerness of the crowd to have their
revenge, he doubted it would take long. The comments he'd heard coming up the aisle convinced him
the crowd was already certain of their guilt and was
ready to hang them even now—without the benefit of
a criminal trial. Vigilantes were everywhere these
days, and he knew the threat they posed.

Nash and Johnson were seated next to him. The
sheriff sat down at the end of the table while his deputies took seats directly behind them.

"All rise," Rob announced when he saw Alyssa
coming up the steps into the courtroom.

Everyone stood as she entered and walked briskly
toward the desk at the front of the room. Slade rose,
but didn't bother to look over at the judge. He'd be
seeing enough of him as it was.

"What the hell?" Nash swore in outrage.

"I don't want no damned woman judge!" Johnson
was furious.

A woman? Slade glanced toward the female walking up the aisle, and he went still. It was *her*—the
siren who'd haunted his dreams every night since
he'd taken her in his arms and held her close.

He scowled as he watched her walk by, her head
held high, dignity in her every move. She looked different . . . pale and strained. The glory of her hair had
been ruthlessly tamed and was secured back at the
nape of her neck in an unbecoming bun. She was

wearing a black dress that gave no hint of the sweet curves beneath it. The beauty who'd enchanted him the other night had vanished, replaced by this woman who looked cold and unfeeling.

"What kind of justice is this?" Johnson insisted.

"Shut up," Rob threatened under his breath.

The deputies sitting right behind them tensed, expecting more trouble. They were glad that they'd decided to keep the prisoners handcuffed for the duration of the hearing. There was no telling what these three might try.

"Judge Mason knows more about the law than everybody in this room put together," Rob said.

"Her name's Mason?" Slade looked over at him.

Rob glared at the three of them. "That's right. She's Alyssa Mason, the daughter of the man you killed in the shoot-out after the robbery. He was the justice of the peace here in town, and she was chosen to take his place. It seems fitting that she's going to be in charge of ruling on your future, doesn't it?"

Slade wondered if things could get any more complicated in his life, and he wondered, in even greater irritation, just how much life he had left.

"Sit down." At the command, everyone was seated.

Alyssa was as ready as she would ever be. She'd heard the outlaws' comments about her as she'd passed them, and they only hardened her resolve to do a fair and just job in presiding over the hearing. She suppressed a shudder at the knowledge that these miserable excuses for men were responsible for her father's death.

She lifted her gaze to the three outlaws and silently studied each one of them in turn. The dark-haired, mustachioed prisoner who was wounded, she knew to be Rick Nash. He was looking straight at her, his expression filled with loathing and hatred. The fairer man next to him must be Carl Johnson. He was glaring at her with the same sneering disgust as Nash, and there was more than a hint of arrogance in his manner.

And then she looked over at the man named Slade Braxton.

Alyssa's gaze collided with the outlaw's, and her breath caught in her throat. She couldn't believe it! It was him! Her mysterious, enchanting stranger was a killer. Her mysterious stranger was Slade Braxton!

Her hands began to tremble as she stared at him in disbelief. Even as bruised and battered as he was, there was no denying that he was handsome, and he exuded an aura of power and danger. Her regard hardened as she continued to look at him, and so did her heart. The man who had so mesmerized her that night hadn't been a prince out of a fairy tale coming sweetly into her life. His courtly manner and gentlemanly ways that evening had all been an act. He was an outlaw—a thief. A murderer.

Alyssa realized that he'd probably been in town that night to check out the bank before robbing it the following morning. She cursed her own gullibility in having been so swept away by his charm and warmth. It was obvious he was a conniving liar, and she'd allowed herself to be hoodwinked by a ridiculous romantic fantasy that had never even existed.

She would never allow anything like this to happen to her again.

Tearing her gaze away from Slade's, Alyssa used the gavel to bring the court to order.

"We're here today to determine if these three men—Slade Braxton, Carl Johnson and Rick Nash—are to be bound over for trial. Could we hear a reading of the charges against them?"

Rob stood to address the court. "The charges against Braxton, Johnson and Nash are bank robbery and murder. As part of the Dakota Kid gang, they robbed the Black Springs Bank. As they were fleeing town, they shot and killed Judge John Mason."

"Thank you." Her voice was tight and her expression was harsh and unforgiving as she looked back at the three defendants. "Gentlemen, were your names correct as read?"

Each answered "yes" individually.

"And how do you plead to these charges? Mr. Nash?"

He gave her a sneering look as he answered, "Not guilty."

"So noted. Mr. Johnson?"

Johnson was openly hostile, muttering under his breath about women judges and what he thought of Wyoming's brand of justice. Finally he replied, "Not guilty."

"So noted. And Mr. Braxton?" Alyssa said his name as impassively as she could when she looked his way.

"Not guilty." His voice was deep and steady in response.

"So noted."

She tried to ignore the effect the deep, resonant sound of his voice had on her. She'd thought she would never see him again. She'd thought he was gone from her life forever . . . and now he was back. But in all her wildest imaginings, she had never thought she would be facing him this way—in a court of law with him accused of murdering her father. She gave herself a fierce mental shake and got back to business.

"I call our first witness, Mr. Tom York, to the stand."

Tom hastened forward. He took the oath as administered by Rob and sat down in a chair by Alyssa's desk.

"Mr. York, tell us of your involvement in this robbery."

"I'm president of the Black Springs Bank. I was in the bank on the morning of the robbery, and I saw everything," he said with force, glaring at the three gunmen.

"Can you identify the men here before you?"

"Yes, all three of them took part in the robbery."

"You're certain?"

"Positive."

"Even though they were wearing masks at the time of said robbery?"

"I followed them outside. The shooting started as they were getting away, and I got a real good look at them."

"Did you see who was doing the shooting?"

"They all had their guns out."

"Do you know which man is responsible for the murder of John Mason?"

"I can't say for sure, but it was probably Braxton who did it! Everybody knows what a killer he is," he said angrily, looking at Slade with open hatred.

A rumble went through the crowd, but Slade didn't react to it.

"Thank you, Mr. York. You may step down," Alyssa said, dismissing him. "Our next witness is Guy Shoaf."

A tall, distinguished, white-haired man came forward and took the oath.

"Mr. Shoaf, can you tell the court what you witnessed that fateful day?"

"Yes, ma'am. I sure can. I was walking down the street, not far from the bank, when the Dakota Kid came running out. It was then that I noticed two men holding a bunch of horses off to the side of the building. I shouted for someone to get the sheriff. The Kid must have heard me, because he turned and shot me."

"Where were you wounded?"

"I was lucky. His bullet just grazed my head, and I've recovered." He showed everyone in the court the mark on his temple.

"We're happy about that."

"So am I," he said with a grin that brought chuckles from his friends in the crowd. "I guess the Dakota Kid's not as good with a gun as everybody says."

"Give him another chance, old man," Johnson snarled, drawing startled looks from everyone.

"Silence in the courtroom!" Alyssa directed sternly, turning a cold-eyed look on Johnson.

Hawkins jabbed Johnson in the back with his gun. "Go ahead, just make a move," he told him in a low voice for his ears only.

"Did you see anything else, Mr. Shoaf?" Alyssa continued. "Can you identify any of these men?"

"Yes, I saw all three of them there by the bank right before the Kid shot me."

"Did you see who shot and killed John Mason?"

"No. I had already been wounded by then."

"Thank you. You may step down."

Guy made his way back to his seat. Alyssa called Les Anderson to the stand.

"Mr. Anderson, you were also in the bank at the time of the robbery, weren't you?"

"Yes, I was."

"Tell us what you remember about that day."

"I had just made a deposit and was starting to leave the bank when the Dakota Kid came charging in with his men. They all had their guns drawn and looked deadly. He ordered the teller to give him all the money, and then they backed out of the bank with Mr. York, there, following them."

"Can you say positively that these three men took part in the robbery?"

"Yes, ma'am."

"Even though they wore masks?"

"Yes, ma'am. I watched from the window as they were getting away. Their masks were down, and I could see their faces real plain-like."

"Did you see who shot John Mason?"

"I can't be sure, but I think it was Braxton," he

said. He knew of the outlaw's deadly reputation and wanted to see him hang.

Slade tensed, but otherwise showed no outward display of emotion. He had fired his gun during their getaway, but he had deliberately made sure that he'd missed everyone. He'd been trying to protect Mason, not kill him. Damn the cover the agency had created for him! The public had believed every word of it!

"You said you 'think' it was Braxton. Would you be willing to testify under oath that he shot John Mason?"

Les paused, thinking. "Well, I—"

"Mr. Anderson, are you positive that Braxton was the one who killed John Mason? Yes or no?"

"Yes!" In truth, he couldn't really be sure who'd shot whom in all the wild gunplay that had gone on that day. But he reasoned that these men were murdering thieves who deserved to die. If swearing Braxton had done it helped put away the gang and make the territory safe, then he'd do it.

"Thank you. You may step down."

"I call the final witness. Chris Turner."

When the man had been sworn in, Alyssa went on with her questioning.

"Mr. Turner, tell us your experiences that day."

"I was walking up the street when someone shot Guy. I went running toward him to see if I could help, and the bastards shot me, too!"

"How badly were you injured?"

"I was wounded in the side."

"But you're recovering?"

"Yes."

"Did you witness John Mason's murder?"

"I saw him fall."

"Did you see who fired the shot? Is that man in this courtroom?"

"I couldn't say who shot him. Everything was so crazy. Everybody was screaming and shots were being fired wildly. It was pandemonium."

"Thank you. Is there anything else you'd care to add to your testimony?"

"Yes! I hope they all hang." He turned a vindictive gaze on the three prisoners. "It's just what they deserve! John Mason didn't deserve to die! But these men do!"

"You're dismissed."

Alyssa had grown pale as she'd listened to the witnesses' testimony. This was the second hardest thing she'd ever done in her life. The first had been burying her father.

"That concludes the list of witnesses for our hearing." She was quiet for a moment; then she looked up at the three men whose fate rested in her hands. "Gentlemen, judging from the eyewitness testimonies we've heard today, I find I have no choice but to bind you over for trial for bank robbery and murder."

A wild cheer went up from the crowd. Alyssa was forced to use the gavel to bring order to the courtroom.

"Said trial to take place as soon as possible in the county seat. Sheriff Emerson, these men are remanded into your custody and are to be escorted under full armed guard to Green River. Witnesses will be expected to appear at said trial. This hearing is adjourned."

At the back of the room, Loretta and Emily were sitting quietly while all the others around them were celebrating. They looked at each other, knowing how terrible the proceeding had been for them and for Alyssa—especially Alyssa.

"I can't believe it was him!" Emily said to her mother in a low voice as they made their way from the courtroom. She'd managed to stay silent during the proceedings, but could no longer hold back her astonishment.

"Who? What are you talking about?" Loretta asked, confused.

Emily drew her mother aside to a quiet place where no one could hear them. "Slade Braxton. He's the stranger who danced with Alyssa the night before the robbery."

Loretta's eyes widened. "Dear God . . . Alyssa danced with that man?"

"She didn't know who he was, and he disappeared right after the dance. We thought he was just a cowboy passing through town, because none of my friends had ever seen him before. Alyssa thought she'd finally found her dream man, and she feared she would never see him again. Now—"

"Now we know he's no dream man. He's the man who killed your father!"

They shared a tormented look, understanding how devastated Alyssa must be. The discovery must have been crushing for her.

"I wonder how she managed to stay in control." Emily couldn't believe how calm and deliberate her sister had remained after discovering her mystery man's true identity.

"She's your father's daughter. He couldn't have done a better job. She was magnificent."

"I wish this had never happened! I wish Papa was here!" Emily said in a tear-choked voice, missing him desperately.

"I know." Loretta slipped her arm supportively around her daughter's waist. The pain of her own loss was nearly unbearable as she sought to offer Emily comfort.

Though these men would stand trial and justice would be served when they paid for their crimes, their hangings wouldn't bring back her beloved husband. He had been lost to her forever, and all because of the man named Slade Braxton.

Loretta and Emily returned to the store, speaking of the hearing no more. The pain of their loss would never go away, but maybe, in time, it would dull a bit.

They could only hope.

Chapter Four

"My husband says the hearing this morning was enough justice for the likes of them. It's just a shame we can't lynch them here and now, and be done with it!" Darlene Hayes told Emily as she paid for her purchases at the general store that afternoon. "What with your father being killed and all, I'd think you, your mother and your sister would be leading the call for a hanging."

"As difficult as it is for us, we have to let the law handle it. That's what my father would have wanted. That's what my father stood for," Emily said quietly, though she, too, found the biblical "eye for an eye" brand of justice tempting.

"That he did. Your father was a fine man. Your sister did him proud up there today. She handled things real good—for a woman."

Emily managed a smile at Darlene's disparaging addition. "She did, didn't she?"

"I'll see you later. Tell Alyssa what I said."

"You can tell her yourself," Emily said, spying her sister coming through the door even as they spoke.

"Why, Alyssa, I was just telling your sister what a fine job you did with the hearing."

"Thank you, Mrs. Hayes."

"Now, if Sheriff Emerson can just keep them alive long enough so they can go to trial—"

"What are you talking about?" Alyssa grew alarmed at the unspoken threat in the other woman's words.

"Oh, some of the men were talking wild and crazy about saving the territory the cost of a trial and a hanging. But don't you worry none. It was just talk, that's all." She tried to sound casual when she saw how Alyssa had reacted to her statement.

"Sometimes talk can lead to other things," Alyssa said. "I hope they understand that taking any such action would have serious legal repercussions."

"I'm sure they do, dear, but seeing as how your father was the one killed, I would have thought that you'd be the most eager to see some frontier justice done. Sometimes a noose or a bullet makes sense, don't you think?"

"No, I don't. We may still be a territory, but that doesn't mean we're uncivilized."

Mrs. Hayes smiled patronizingly at her. "Of course not, dear, and congratulations, again, on a job well done."

With that, she left the store.

"My job's not over yet, not by a long shot," Alyssa muttered, staring after the departing woman.

"What do you mean?" Emily asked.

"I'm not going to rest easy about any of this until the three prisoners are gone from here and locked up good and tight in Green River."

"I don't blame you. That must have been so terrible for you—coming face-to-face with Slade Braxton today."

Alyssa glanced sharply at her sister. "So, you recognized him. I was afraid of that."

"You have to admit he's not an easy man to forget," Emily said, thinking of her first impression of the darkly handsome gunslinger. She shuddered visibly, though, as her initial admiration of him was replaced by loathing.

"That's a good way of putting it, Emily, because I'm never going to forget Mr. Slade Braxton . . . never."

They shared a look that spoke volumes, remembering the eyewitness testimony against him.

"What are you going to do now that the hearing's over?" Emily asked.

"After listening to Mrs. Hayes, I think I'd better go have a talk with Rob. It was bad enough just worrying about the Dakota Kid showing up to break them out, but now we've got possible vigilantes to contend with as well."

" 'We'? Isn't that the sheriff's worry?"

"I guess, but I feel that it's mine, too. After all, I am the judge who bound them over for trial."

"What's Rob going to do next?"

"He's already wired Judge Banks in Green River to let him know what's happened here. I was just on my way over to the jail to find out the rest of his plans for transporting them."

"From the sound of things, he'd better get them out of here as quickly as he can."

"I know. In fact, I was just thinking that I'd ask him if I could ride with him when he goes."

"What?" Emily was shocked that she'd even consider such a thing.

Alyssa had expected just such a reaction from her sister, and she deliberately ignored it. "I want to make sure the outlaws are delivered safely into the hands of the proper authorities."

"That's why Rob has deputies," Emily argued. "Alyssa, you're a—"

She stopped before the statement she was about to make initiated a fight she knew she wouldn't win. Telling Alyssa she was a female and shouldn't be doing these things would only encourage her to prove that she could.

"I'm a justice of the peace," Alyssa said, finishing the sentence for her. "I'm the one who ordered them held for trial. I'm the one responsible for their being in our jail, and I'm going to make sure that the criminal trial takes place."

"I wish it was already over."

"So do I. Have you and Mother talked about going to the trial?" Alyssa asked. "Do you want to attend?"

"We discussed it earlier for a few minutes. I want to go, but Mother said she didn't. You and I both know I can't go off and leave her here to run the store alone, so I'll stay here.''

Alyssa nodded. ''I'll plan on staying in Green River then, until the trial's over.''

''It would be good for you to be there, but do you really think you should travel with the sheriff and those . . . killers? Aside from the fact that you are a single female and you'd be traveling with men who are unrelated to you, the trip might prove dangerous.''

''Papa taught us both how to use a gun,'' she said, trying to calm her sister's fears. ''I'll carry my side-arm, and then I'll be ready just in case there is any trouble. I doubt there will be. I'm sure there will be a number of deputies riding with us.''

''Is it proper, though?'' Emily was one who always worried about convention.

''Rob is a good man. I trust him implicitly.'' Alyssa didn't care about propriety. She was only interested in seeing justice done. ''Besides, I'll be traveling as Judge Mason, not Alyssa Mason. I have a legal, not to mention moral, obligation to do this.''

''Do you think he'll agree to your riding along?''

''I hope so. Rob knows I can handle myself if there's trouble. He also knows that I won't cause him any unnecessary delays. I want to help him, not hinder him.''

''I can't believe you're so daring.''

''It's what Father would have done.''

''But Father was a man.''

''No, Father was a judge, and so am I. I'll go talk to Rob now.''

When Alyssa had gone, Emily returned to business,

but her thoughts were still on her older sister. Emily was constantly amazed at how different they'd turned out. Alyssa was always so serious about life, while she preferred more frivolous pursuits like flirting and dancing. She adored men and was actively looking for Mister Right, while Alyssa paid little attention to her single state. That was why Emily had been so delighted by her reaction to the stranger at the dance. It had proved that her sister was a flesh-and-blood woman after all, and not a prig destined to be an old maid. But now that Alyssa had learned the truth about her mystery man, Emily doubted she would ever allow herself such a flight of fancy again. And that was a pity, for Emily believed a woman's main goal in life was to attract and marry the richest, handsomest man she could find.

Alyssa rarely thought of matrimony, though. Emily could only remember one man her sister had ever seemed to care deeply about, and that had been back when she was eighteen. It hadn't worked out between them, so Emily supposed Alyssa hadn't really loved him. Still, her sister's lack of interest in catching a husband puzzled her. Emily sighed. The law had now become her sister's whole life, and if she wasn't careful she was going to end up an old maid.

Emily glanced at her own reflection in the small mirror behind the counter. She thought she looked dreadful in the black gown she was wearing, but she knew there was no escaping her period of mourning. She'd loved her father dearly and would not sully his memory in any way. As much as she enjoyed a busy social life, she would curtail her activities as was proper.

Smoothing her pale curls back from her face, Emily managed to smile at her own reflection as she envisioned herself in a beautiful, brightly colored gown, dancing with a handsome suitor. Though she was in mourning for her father's passing now, it wouldn't last forever. When her mourning was over, she had every intention of catching herself a good-looking husband.

"Alyssa, is something wrong?" Rob asked as he looked up to find her entering his office, her expression very serious.

"I'm not really sure, but I'm glad you've got the guards posted outside."

"Why?"

"Darlene Hayes was at the store when I stopped by just now to see Emily. She said there's been talk about a lynching."

The lawman tensed. "I thought the hearing would help calm things down around here. It looks like I was wrong."

"How soon are you planning on leaving with them?"

"Dawn, tomorrow. I have a few things I have to put in order here before I can go."

"How many men are you taking with you?"

"Four deputies."

"How would you like a fifth?"

"Who?"

"Me."

"You're a woman. . . . I can't deputize you," he sputtered, surprised by her offer.

"You don't have to, but I would be another gun if you needed it. I want to ride along. I'm not going to be able to rest easy until this trial's over."

Rob was quiet for a moment, considering her suggestion. Alyssa was good with a gun. John had trained both his daughters to shoot straight, as well as to ride astride. Any other female he would have forbidden outright to come along, but Alyssa—

He didn't have to think long to make his decision. Making the trip together would allow him to spend time with her, and that would be a rare treat, indeed. He'd been wanting to court her for some time now, so it looked like something good might come of the arrests after all.

"All right, you can go. Be ready to ride at first light."

"I'll see you then."

When Alyssa returned home, she found her mother at the house waiting for her.

"How are you doing, dear?"

"I'm fine. Have you had a chance to talk to Emily?"

"No, why?"

She knew her mother wouldn't be pleased with her decision to accompany Rob and his deputies to Green River, but she also knew she would eventually come to understand. She quickly explained her reasoning and how Rob had agreed to let her make the trip with them.

"Do you think it's a wise thing to do?"

"Father would have ridden with them. I can do no less. Once we're there, I plan to stay on in Green River through the trial."

Loretta nodded. She wanted to argue with Alyssa, but knew it was pointless. Once again she thought of how her oldest child was so like her father—smart, brave and stubborn. It was a pity she hadn't been born a boy, for those traits were very admirable in men. In a female, however, society considered them less attractive qualities.

"When will you be leaving?"

"Rob said they'd be riding out at first light."

"I'll pack a few things for you to take along with you."

"Thanks." She kissed her cheek. "I think I'll go take Spartan out for a quick run. I need to get away for a little while."

"Just be careful. You know the Dakota Kid's still out there somewhere."

"I will."

Alyssa disappeared into her room just long enough to change into clothes suitable for riding—her split skirt, blouse, vest and boots. She'd fallen in love with horses as a young girl and gloried in the feel of the wind in her face as she rode across country. As she got ready to leave the house, she picked up her leather riding gloves, donned her western hat and buckled on her gun and holster. She couldn't be too careful when she was riding alone.

Within minutes, she'd saddled her horse and ridden off to enjoy a moment of freedom. It wasn't often that she got to run wild this way, and she treasured every minute.

When they left for Green River the following day, she was going to have to be Judge Mason all the time. No trace of Alyssa could be revealed. She would be staid, serious and competent. She would have to be on watch and ready for any trouble that might come their way.

Alyssa rode steadily. Spartan enjoyed the workout and settled into an easy pace as they headed back toward town. She rode down the main street on her way home. It was near dusk, and she knew she should hurry, for dinner would be almost ready.

"To hell with a trial! Let's hang the bastards ourselves!"

The drunk's shout made her saw back on her reins as she was passing the Royal Straight Saloon. She paused to listen to the men inside. Though she couldn't make out clearly everything that was being said, she could pick out the general drift of things, and it didn't sound good.

"It's what the bastards deserve! Let's do it! Right now!"

"Yeah! Sheriff Emerson wouldn't stop us if we went down there. He don't want no trouble with us."

"He'd probably hand 'em over on a silver platter!" another man insisted.

"What are we waiting for?"

"Wait a minute . . . wait a minute. You men are talkin' crazy. You don't want to go bustin' them men outta jail just to hang 'em. You'd end up having the law comin' after you!"

"Naw . . . Ol' Hawkins wants 'em dead, too. I heard him say so earlier tonight. He was saying how it wouldn't have bothered him at all to shoot 'em down just like they shot John."

The reference to her father hurt, but Alyssa ignored the pain as she tried to make out their words.

"I heard tell, some of the other boys over at the High Noon were talking about doing the same thing. It's a good thing the sheriff's getting them killers out of town right away. If he kept them around here too much longer, he wouldn't stand a chance of holding them."

"When are they riding out?"

"I heard tomorrow, but I ain't sure."

"Then what are we waitin' for?"

A sense of dread filled Alyssa, and she urged Spartan forward in the direction of the jail. She had to let Rob know what was going on in the saloon.

"Rob!" she called out as she ran inside his office.

"What is it?" He jumped to his feet at the sound of alarm in her voice.

"I was just riding past the Royal Straight. A lot of the men have been drinking all day. They're pretty riled up and talking about a lynching. From what I heard, there's another bunch over at the High Noon talking the same way."

Rob cursed under his breath as he strode to the gun cabinet and took out a rifle. He checked to make sure it was loaded. "We can hold them off if we have to."

"To what end? Even if you back them down tonight, it'll only make them angrier."

"And if I try to move the prisoners out now, they'll see us and try to stop us."

Alyssa thought quickly. "Not if you stay here and act as if everything's going according to plan. While you're playing decoy, Hawkins and I, along with several of the others, can leave for Green River with the prisoners right away."

Rob frowned. He knew she was talking sense, but he didn't like it. He didn't like it at all. "Wait here."

He strode outside and said a few words to the two guards. They hurried off in the direction of the two saloons.

"I sent Clemans and Ursino to check out what you were saying. They'll report back in a few minutes. Then I'll decide. You may as well sit down while we wait."

"How are the outlaws doing? Have they given you any trouble?" She motioned toward the cell area.

"No. They've been real quiet since we got back here. Almost too quiet, really, but that's all right. I've got a lot on my mind right now, and I don't need to be putting up with anything from them."

"If we're forced to leave tonight, there's almost a full moon out, so riding won't be too difficult. We could travel most of the night and give ourselves a good head start."

He nodded thoughtfully. "I could catch up with you tomorrow."

"That would work. No one will ever be the wiser, unless they actually do try to force you to give them up."

"Let's just hope it doesn't come to that. I'd hate

to fight anybody from town over these three. They aren't worth it.''

''And that's exactly what the drunks are thinking. Upholding the law isn't easy, is it?'' She managed a pained smile.

''No, it isn't.''

They fell silent as they awaited the return of Clemans and Ursino. They didn't have long to wait.

''She's right, Sheriff,'' Clemans told him. ''They're drunker than skunks at the Royal Straight, and the talk is running hot and heavy toward lynching them tonight.''

''Ursino?''

''They're hot at the High Noon, too. I don't know if they'll really do anything. But do you want to take the chance?''

It would have been easy to let things stand as they were and simply turn the three outlaws over to the crowd of vigilantes if they came for them. But Rob prided himself on being an honest lawman. He was not going to take the easy way out on this one. He'd worked too hard to bring these men in.

''All right. You two go find Hawkins and Brown. I want you on your way to Green River—now. And tell Connors and Drake that I need them back here to stand guard at the jail again. I want things to look the same to anybody who might be watching us.''

''I'll get them and be right back,'' Clemans promised.

''And I'll go get the prisoners' horses and tie them up behind the building.''

''Good. That way we can get them out of here by

85

the rear door, and nobody will see us. I'll just spend the rest of the evening sitting here at my desk, pretending like nothing's going on. If anybody comes down to check on us, everything will look like the prisoners are still locked up nice and tight.''

''Rob? Could you get word to my mother and sister about what's happened? I mentioned to them earlier that I was making the trip with you, but they both expect me to leave tomorrow morning. There's no time for me to go back home now.''

''I'll let them know as soon as I can. Are you going to be all right?''

''I'll be fine,'' she said, giving him a half-smile. ''I have my gun, so I guess I'm ready to ride.''

''Here, take this, too.'' He handed her a rifle he'd taken from the gun case. ''Be careful, I keep it loaded.''

''Thanks.''

''I already stocked up on some supplies for the trip. You can take those with you, too. You'll be needing them. It's a good three days' ride. And here's some money. It's not much, but I'll bring more when I come along after you tomorrow.''

''Looks like you've thought of about everything.''

''Except a lynch mob. I'd worried about the Dakota Kid showing up and causing trouble, but I hadn't expected this,'' he said, thoroughly disgusted.

''It'll be fine. You'll see. We'll be watching for you to catch up with us on the trail.''

''I'll be there. I intend to see this through to the end, just like you do.''

They shared a knowing look, satisfied that their plan would work.

"Now, let's get the three of them ready for their little trip." He got the handcuffs and his own six-gun, then led the way back to the jail cell.

Slade looked up when he heard someone coming. He was surprised to see a woman with the sheriff. It was dark there, so he couldn't quite make out who she was.

Nash stirred, too, and drawled, "You bringing us a little entertainment to help pass the time, lawman?"

"Watch your mouth, Nash," Rob threatened.

"I doubt you'd find me very entertaining, Mr. Nash," Alyssa said in her coldest tone.

Slade recognized her voice immediately—the woman was none other than Judge Mason. He felt a moment of hope that Emerson had investigated what he'd told him about being a Pinkerton and was coming to release him. His hope was instantly erased when he saw the handcuffs.

"All three of you, get over here. You're going for a ride tonight," the sheriff instructed.

"Where to?" Johnson challenged.

"You don't need to worry about that or anything else except getting out of here while you're still alive."

"Why? What's going on?" Nash asked.

"There's talk around town of a lynching, so I want you on your way to Green River before anything happens. Johnson, you first. Come here," he ordered.

Johnson rose slowly and stalked to the bars. The sheriff fastened the cuffs on him, then on Nash. He looked over at Slade. He had never even considered that the outlaw's story about being a Pinkerton could be true. There was so much evidence to the contrary, he hadn't bothered to wire anyone in Denver. Braxton was a killer with a reputation known far and wide. He was guilty. They even had an eyewitness who'd seen him shoot John.

"Let's go, Braxton. We haven't got all night."

Slade climbed slowly down from the top bunk and walked toward the lawman. He said nothing as the irons were clasped about his wrists, but he took the opportunity to let his gaze run over Alyssa where she stood next to Emerson. Gone was the cold, proper lady judge from that morning. She'd forsaken her mourning dress and gavel for riding clothes and a six-gun.

She was carrying a weapon and that surprised him. He wondered how many facets there were to this woman who'd so intrigued him. First, she'd seemed an enchantress, beautiful and elusive. Then he'd discovered she was a prim-and-proper, no-nonsense judge, and now, it seemed she could handle a sidearm as well. He wondered which woman she really was.

Alyssa looked up at Slade just then, and their gazes met. Taking care to stay in character, Slade gave her a slow, seductive smile.

"Pity."

"What is?" Rob asked.

"That she's not the entertainment for the night."

Alyssa bit back a gasp, keeping tight control over her reaction to him and to his words. She would not give him that power over her. Standing this close to him, she could see the dark shadow of his beard on his lean jaw, the slight sardonic twist to his lips and the challenging spark in his gaze. His shoulders were broad and powerful. She remembered all too clearly how it had felt to be held in his arms, but that had been when she'd thought him a gentleman. Now she knew better. Now she knew him for what he really was. She was tempted to step back, to distance herself from him, but she stood her ground, refusing to be intimidated.

"I think you're going to be very *entertained* tonight, Mr. Braxton," she ground out, angry with him and herself for the conflicting feelings he aroused in her. "An all-night ride should keep you quite occupied."

"An all-night ride?" Slade repeated in a low, suggestive voice, and his gaze darkened as he considered the double meaning of his words.

Alyssa couldn't stop the slow heat that crept into her face as she realized what he was referring to. She decided to ignore his crudeness. "That's right."

"Too bad you're not going on the *ride* with us," Johnson leered.

"Oh, but I am," she declared. "I intend to see you three all the way to Green River."

Slade frowned at the news. The sheriff had to be out of his mind to let her ride along. It was pure stupidity. No one knew what the Kid might try while they were on the trail, and she'd be caught right in the middle of it. Determined to convince her to stay behind, he gave her another meaningful look, "We're going to have a lot of nights out on the trail then. You sure you're up to it?''

Alyssa stiffened this time at his insinuation and tightened her grip on the rifle she was holding. ''I'm up to anything the three of you might try.''

''Anything?'' Johnson taunted.

''Anything,'' she answered.

''Let's get out of here,'' Rob said, wanting to end the exchange right then and there, before the outlaws grew too crude in their remarks. ''The horses should be out back by now. Let's go.''

He unlocked the cell door and kept his gun ready as he directed them out the back door and into the alley behind the jail. As he'd promised, Ursino was there with their horses, as were the other deputies. All were heavily armed and ready to ride. Alyssa went around the building to get Spartan and rode back to join the group of riders.

''Be careful,'' Rob told them quietly, hoping all would go well for them.

''We will,'' Hawkins promised.

''Alyssa, you take care.'' He went to stand beside her.

''You, too. Catch up with us as soon as you can. We'll be watching for you.''

''I will.''

With that, they rode quietly from the alley and disappeared into the night.

Rob went back inside and locked up again. He settled in at his desk, acting as if nothing had changed. He hoped there would be no trouble.

* * *

Nash and Johnson shared a knowing look as Black Springs disappeared from view. Soon the Kid would come and rescue them. The thought buoyed their otherwise grim spirits. They glanced over at Slade, wondering what he was thinking, wondering if he was as glad as they were to be out of that cell and on the move, but as usual, the other gunman's expression was inscrutable. He betrayed none of his inner feelings.

They'd been riding for over an hour when Johnson finally spoke up. "When are we stopping for the night?" He wanted to move as slowly as possible to give the Kid time to locate them and work out a plan to free them.

"We're not stopping at all, unless you've got a real hankering to be the main attraction at a necktie party," Hawkins told him sarcastically.

"You think they'd chase us this far out of town?" Nash asked. His injured shoulder was paining him, and he would have liked to make camp for the night.

"The ones who might cause the trouble were a bunch of drunks. They didn't want to wait for you to have a jury trial. They wanted you to hang. Who knows what lengths they might go to if they got in the mood to see someone swing tonight?"

Nash grunted in acknowledgment and tried to ignore the pain from his wound. At least, as long as he was in pain, he knew he was alive.

Alyssa rode in silence, her rifle safely in its scabbard, her handgun ready should she need it. The moonlight provided enough light for them to make good time, and she was glad for that.

Slade Braxton was riding directly in front of her. She tried to ignore him and the way he rode easily in the saddle, as if he were born to it. She reminded herself again that the witness in town had claimed he was the one who'd shot her father. It didn't matter that something about Slade attracted her. He was a killer. The man who'd lived briefly in her fantasy didn't exist. She had to remember that.

Alyssa silently prayed for the hours and miles to pass quickly, and she concentrated on staying alert and watchful. The trip was going to be a long, tedious one, but in the end it would be worth it.

It was long after midnight when emotions reached a fever pitch in Black Springs. The men from the High Noon and the Royal Straight were determined to replace the slow court system with justice of their own making. Guns in hand, the drunken vigilantes quit the saloons and banded together in the street to advance on the jail. They knew guards were stationed around town, but they figured no one would think members of the Dakota Kid's gang were worth dying for. They expected little resistance from Sheriff Emerson or his deputies.

Rob heard the warning shouted from one of the building's guards, and he grabbed his loaded shotgun and strode out of the jail. What he saw approaching was worse than he'd expected. The entire street was filled with men, all intent on getting their hands on his prisoners.

''Hold it right there!'' Rob ordered, holding his shotgun up for all to see.

"We ain't here to hurt you, Sheriff. We just want to get Braxton and the others and show 'em what happens to their kind here in our town!" the self-appointed leader of the rowdy crowd shouted.

"You're going to have to go through me to get them, Meyers!" Rob yelled back, recognizing Cam Meyers as the spokesman.

"We don't want trouble with you. We just want to see the killers pay for what they've done."

"You will, just as soon as the trial takes place in Green River. I got a wire from Judge Banks a little over an hour or so ago, telling me he was all set to hold the trial just as soon as all the witnesses were there."

"We don't care about no trial!"

"We want justice!"

"So do I, but there is no justice in mob rule."

"We want an eye for an eye!"

They started forward en masse. This time, Rob lifted his shotgun and fired a round off high over their heads.

The boom of the gunshot shocked many of them. They fell back a few steps, arguing among themselves about what they should do. Once again, they decided to overrun the jail.

"I don't want anyone to die, but if you try to come in here, I will fire into the crowd, and I won't care who I hit!" Rob told them. "And neither will my deputies!"

"Step aside, Emerson!"

"There'll be no lynchings in my town. Go home and sleep it off!"

They surged toward him again, testing him, daring him to use deadly force. Even though some of them might wind up injured or dead, they were too drunk to care. They wanted a hanging.

Rob was trapped as they advanced on him. There was no way for him to win. If he fired on them as he'd threatened to do, someone would surely die. If he stepped aside, they would learn the truth about the prisoners. It would be far too soon to suit him, but at least his men had a few hours' head start.

"Don't shoot!" he called out to his deputies.

They did not fire as the drunks took their weapons. Instead, they stood aside while the mob overran the jail.

"Where are they?" Meyers demanded, when he discovered that the killers were already gone.

"On their way to Green River. They've been gone for hours. You'll never catch up with them."

The mob was angry and frustrated. They were cursing loudly as they abandoned the jail and returned to the saloons to drown their frustration in more liquor.

When they'd gone, Rob and his deputies stood alone in the office.

"Thank God we got the prisoners out of here when we did," he said wearily.

"And nobody got hurt," Connors added, thinking how differently things might have turned out had they not sent the prisoners on ahead.

"What are you going to do about this in the morning when everybody's sobered up?" Drake asked.

Rob shook his head as he all but collapsed back into his desk chair. "Same as I planned all along. I'm going to ride out after Hawkins and catch up with them on the trail.''

''Don't you want us to arrest Meyers and some of the others who were riling them up the most?''

''No. There was no real harm done—just a few tense moments. We outsmarted them, though. That's all that matters. I'm just glad the men decided to keep drinking, instead of going after the outlaws. If they'd decided to do that, I don't think we could have stopped them even if we'd wanted to.''

The deputies were silent in their agreement.

''I think you boys can go on home now. The rest of the night should be real quiet.''

Chapter Five

It was in the early morning hours when Red Parsons reached the hidden campsite where he knew the Kid and Zeke would be waiting for him.

"Where are they?" the Dakota Kid asked, stepping out from behind a boulder, his rifle in hand, as Red rode in alone.

Zeke, too, had been keeping watch, and he appeared nearby.

"They're on their way to Green River," Red answered as he reined in and dismounted. He wasn't the least surprised to find that they'd had their guns on him as he'd approached the camp.

The Kid wasn't a physically powerful man. Thin and wiry, he stood just under six feet tall. But he was smart, and that was why Red rode with him. There wasn't anybody in the territory good enough or fast enough to bring the Kid in, not even Sheriff Emerson—for all that the lawman had been trying real hard.

"What happened? I thought for sure they'd hold them over in Black Springs for at least a week." The Kid was disgusted at this news, for he'd already been formulating a plan to break them out of the jail there.

"Emerson must have figured trouble was brewing in town, so he got them out of there real fast," Red explained as they moved to sit by the small campfire. He noticed that the Kid was still limping heavily. "How's your leg doing?"

"It's sore as hell, but I'll live," he growled. During the ambush in the canyon, he'd taken a bullet in the thigh. They'd managed to dig it out before Red had ridden into Black Springs, but the Kid was still favoring the limb and cursing the deputy who'd gotten lucky with his shot. "What did you hear while you were in town?"

"I was drinking in the saloon, trying to find out what was going on. There was a bunch of drunks wanting to string them up right then and there. They finally got their guns and went to the jail to face down the sheriff. I went with them as part of the crowd. I thought if they did break them out, I could figure out a way to rescue them and get them out of town before they got hanged."

"You mean some drunks tried to overrun the jail?"

"Tried to? Hell, they did it."

"What did that Emerson do?" He hated the sheriff of Black Springs with a growing passion.

"He tried to back them down, but when they came

97

at him, he didn't shoot or anything. He just stepped aside. He told his deputies not to shoot and to turn over their weapons.''

"Are you serious?''

"Yeah. The drunks nearly tore the place apart looking for our boys. They weren't too pleased when they found out that they were already gone, but I was glad. The thought of trying to get Nash, Johnson and Slade away from fifty or sixty drunks who wanted to see them hanged real fast—'' Red shook his head, glad that he'd been spared the necessity of trying to break them free of the mob all by himself.

"So, how many guards went with them on the trip to Green River?''

"I don't know. They were long gone by the time we showed up.''

The Kid was thoughtful. "We'll ride after them at dawn. Maybe we'll have better luck finding them on the trail than your friends in Black Springs did finding them in jail.''

"They weren't no friends of mine. That was an ugly crowd. I was glad to get out of there in one piece.''

The Kid smiled thinly, wishing ill will on Emerson. "I bet that sheriff was, too. Too bad they didn't take some of their anger out on him.''

"I know,'' Red agreed, thinking how clever the lawman had been to accurately judge the mood of the town. "You sure you're feeling good enough to ride out so soon?''

"I can live with it. We gotta find them before they

reach Green River. It'll be our best chance of freeing them.''

They settled in for what was left of the night.

The Kid did not sleep, though. He was too busy trying to think of ways to outwit the deputies who were guarding his men. There were only the three of them to pull it off, but he'd always considered himself smarter than any ten lawmen around. He just had to find the right place and the right time, and he would save the boys.

The Kid knew how being locked up must be affecting Johnson. He'd known Johnson since he was just a boy. He was as close to family as he had. He would not stand by and let anything happen to him.

He respected Nash, too. He was loyal and fast with a gun. Though Nash was hot-tempered, the Kid had always known he could trust him.

He was proud to have Slade Braxton in his gang. Slade was the only man he knew who was colder than himself. The other gunfighter had nerves of steel and the guts to match. He would find a way to save all three of them from hanging.

Thoughts of the men who'd been killed in the ambush troubled the Kid. He was going to miss them. He didn't like the fact that Emerson had come that close to trapping him. Somehow, he was going to find a way to pay the lawman back.

As the eastern sky lightened, the Kid was already up and saddling his horse. They rode for Green River before full daylight had claimed the land.

*   *   *

Hawkins was still leading the way as the new day dawned. They had stopped only a few times during the night, for he had been intent on putting as many miles between themselves and Black Springs as he could. Now, with the advent of daylight, he picked up their pace. He was tense and on edge. The Dakota Kid could be anywhere around, watching them, waiting for the right time to attack. The darkness had been their friend, but daylight was their enemy. At midmorning one of the other deputies finally convinced him to stop.

Alyssa had kept up with their grueling pace without complaint. If the men could do it, so could she. She understood their concerns about reaching Green River as quickly as possible, and she would not cause them any trouble. Though Spartan was weary and she was exhausted, she said nothing. She would match them mile for mile.

"We'll stop here for a while. Let's rest the horses and eat," Hawkins called out as they reached an open area where they could keep an easy watch on their surroundings.

Clemans and Ursino took first guard over the prisoners, while Alyssa joined Hawkins and Brown, eating a light, cold meal. It wasn't much, but it helped revive her.

"You doing all right?" Hawkins asked, eyeing her skeptically. He had been less than enthusiastic about her riding with them, but he'd had no authority to override the sheriff. It didn't matter to him that she was the one who'd alerted them to the possible lynching. She was just a woman and shouldn't be involved in these things.

"I'm fine," she told him, sensing how he felt about her and refusing to give him any reason to criticize her. "I wonder how things went in town last night."

"It'll be interesting to see what Sheriff Emerson has to say when he catches up with us," Brown remarked.

"I hope he didn't have any trouble, but the talk I heard was pretty ugly," she said.

"Yeah, me, too. If we'd waited much longer, we might not have had any prisoners left alive to take to trial," Hawkins said.

"So you're all heroes?" Johnson taunted. "You saved our lives, so we should be grateful to you?"

Hawkins turned a deadly glare on him. "Damned straight, Johnson. You'd probably be a dead man right now if we hadn't got you out of town."

"I'll remember to have the Kid thank you when he comes for us," Nash said with a sneering smile.

"I wouldn't put too much hope in being rescued," Hawkins told him. "I'd just as soon shoot you as let the Kid free you."

Johnson and Nash glared at the deputy. "You'd have shot us the other day if the sheriff had given you the chance."

"That's right," he said coldly. "And you'd do well to remember that."

Slade looked on without making any comment. He'd been watching the guards, keeping track of who seemed the sharpest. He was trying to judge their chances of escaping the deputies without the Kid's help. It didn't look good. The handcuffs were trouble enough, but just trying to get a gun away from one of the deputies was going to be next to impossible. He ate the cold, tasteless food they gave him and wondered where Ken Richards was.

As Slade sat lost deep in thought, his gaze drifted to Alyssa. She was standing and stretching, and he knew she had to be feeling the effects of long hours in the saddle. She'd wanted an all-night ride, and she'd gotten it.

"You think she's good-lookin', Slade?" Nash asked, following the direction he was looking.

"Not particularly. I was just thinking how she'd gotten her all-night ride," he said, watching her as she walked away out of earshot.

"Don't think she enjoyed it."

"Damn right. We sure could have shown her a better time," Johnson added with a leering smile.

"Ain't that the truth," Nash complained. "But then again, if we'd stayed in Black Springs, we might be stretching some ropes right now."

"Yeah, but if we'd had some of her first, it might have made it worthwhile," Johnson went on, watching her every move. "Wonder what the Kid will do with her once he gets us out of this?"

"It'll be interesting to find out. Maybe we'll get *our* all-night ride after all."

"She's mine, if it comes to that," Slade declared tensely, fearful that just might happen.

The other two men laughed loudly, drawing the attention of their guards.

"What's so funny?" Ursino asked, looking at them suspiciously.

"Not a thing, deputy," Slade answered.

Alyssa heard their derisive laughter and glanced their way. She found Slade's gaze upon her across the distance, and once again she was struck by the intensity of his regard. She told herself that she hated him. This was the man who'd killed her father. Yet, even from their first encounter at the dance, she hadn't sensed any evil in him. For some reason, she didn't get the same feeling of decadence from him that she got from the other two. There was something different about him, and that troubled her. Her judgment and intuition about people were usually right on target, and she had always trusted her instincts—until now. Until Slade Braxton.

She gave herself a mental shake and turned her back on the gunman. In a few days, they would be safely in Green River. She would be done with him then, except for sitting through the trial and watching him hang for what he'd done. She was looking forward to the end of this ordeal.

"Miss Mason? You all right?" Hawkins noticed that she'd moved off away from them.

"I'm fine."

"Well, don't wander too far off."

"Don't worry, Deputy. I'm armed." She rested her hand on her sidearm as if to demonstrate that she was not a woman to be dismissed lightly. She was a woman to be reckoned with.

Nash glanced over at Johnson, wondering if his friend was thinking what he was thinking. The lady judge might believe she was good with a gun, but up against the three of them, she didn't stand a chance. She was their biggest and best hope for making a break for it. If one of them could get hold of her, they could get her gun away from her and then use her as a hostage.

Johnson met Nash's regard and gave a slight nod in her direction. He wondered when he'd get the chance to talk to Nash and Slade without being overheard. Whatever they tried, they would have to try soon, before Emerson caught up with them. It was going to be hard enough as it was, without worrying about the sheriff being there, too.

There was no time then to plan anything, though, as Hawkins and Brown replaced Clemans and Ursino guarding them. The other men went to eat, and then it was time for them to mount up and ride again.

Slade's mood was black as they continued on, late into the afternoon. He'd seen the looks Johnson and Nash had exchanged earlier and knew they were planning something. He'd kept a careful lookout for some sign that the Kid was closing in, but had seen nothing out of the ordinary. There'd been no sign of Ken Richards, either, and that troubled him even more. Things were complicated and getting worse—especially with the lady judge along. It was one thing to deal with Nash, Johnson and the deputies. It was another to have involved her.

Slade looked up at Alyssa. She was riding alongside Deputy Brown, just up ahead of him. He watched her, studying her. She was different from any woman he'd ever known, and he wondered how she'd come to be so involved with the law.

It had been his experience that females were interested in one thing and one thing only—well, maybe two things—marriage and money, and not necessarily in that order. It just depended on the particular female.

But Alyssa obviously had no interest in finding a husband. If she did, she certainly wouldn't be involved in such an unladylike pursuit as the law. And he knew what money was involved in her kind of work, and it wasn't much.

She was riding astride, and that was unusual for a woman, even in these parts. She also handled her horse with a practiced hand and could use a gun. Whether she was a good shot or not, he had no idea. She moved easily with the gun on her hip, though, so he figured she had some working knowledge of which end of the weapon the bullet came out.

Alyssa Mason intrigued Slade, but she irritated him even more. She had distracted him that night in town, and now she was complicating an already treacherous situation just by her mere presence. He scowled, wishing the trek to Green River was over, and at the same time dreading reaching the town, for it would mean their trial was imminent.

"Thinking about your future, Braxton?" Hawkins taunted, grinning as he saw Slade's expression.

"No, I was thinking about yours," he countered.

Hawkins's hatred for him grew even more intense at his quick comeback, but it didn't deter him from continuing to belittle him. "I know. Your kind should be worried. One day soon, I'll be a sheriff in these parts and scum like you won't be allowed within a hundred miles of my town.''

"That's if you live long enough, Hawkins," Johnson mocked.

"Oh, I'm not the one who should be worried about living long enough. You three should start measuring your lives in days now, and not years.'' He was laughing as he spoke.

Slade turned a steely look on the deputy, finding no humor in his words. "We're innocent until proven guilty, lawman. Remember that.''

"You suddenly a lawyer, Braxton?''

"I know the law," Slade answered firmly.

"That's because you're always so busy breaking it,'' Hawkins told him. "All the knowledge in the world ain't gonna save your asses. You're dead men. We're just going through the motions here.''

"We'll see what the Kid has to say about that when he shows up,'' Nash put in.

"Since you ain't seen or heard from him since the shoot-out in the gorge, maybe he ain't coming for you like you think.''

"The Kid would never desert us. He'll be here," Johnson insisted, trusting in his one and only friend.

The other deputies heard the fierceness in his tone and doubled their alertness. They would be stopping to make camp for the night soon, and it would be then that they would be most vulnerable. They would have to keep a close watch all night to make sure they weren't ambushed.

Some time later, they found a suitable place to stop. It was secluded, shielded from open view by boulders and some trees. Hawkins knew two well-placed guards could easily keep a careful lookout. They made camp and built a small fire. The meal that night wouldn't be much, but at least it would be hot.

"What d'ya think?" Johnson asked Nash when they were sitting close together, a short distance from their ever-watchful guards.

"The woman?"

"Yeah. All we'd have to do is get her gun. Are you up to it? What about your shoulder?"

"I'll be just fine once we're away from here," Nash said, grimacing a little in acknowledgment of the throbbing pain he was enduring. "We gotta tell Slade what we're thinking so he'll be ready when the time comes. We're gonna need his help. It'll take all three of us to pull this off."

Johnson nodded slightly as he glanced over at their companion. "Slade—"

Slade moved to join them. He'd been standing a short distance away, studying the lay of the land. He knew there was no chance of making a break for it, but he always took a look around just in case of trouble. Hawkins had chosen the campsite well. It was easily defendable and would be difficult to run from. He sat down by the two other gunmen.

"There's no easy way out of here. Hawkins knew what he was doing when he picked this spot," he told them.

"We're not worried about that right now," Nash began in a low tone. "We got an idea about what we can do."

A guard moved nearer, trying to hear what they were saying.

"Yeah, once the Kid gets us out of this, we can head for Kansas or Texas and have us some real fun," Nash went on, speaking loudly.

"You should have gone there in the first place," Ursino said, keeping an eye on them. He didn't mind them talking among themselves, but when they got to talking so low that he couldn't understand them, he worried. He didn't trust them for a minute. He knew their kind. They were deadly and without conscience—a very dangerous combination.

They ignored him and spoke of ordinary things until Ursino moved away from them again.

"I'll take her. They won't be expecting me to make any kind of move," Nash said.

"Her?" Slade glanced at him sharply.

"We'll grab the lady judge. It'll be the easiest way to get a gun—and a shield," Johnson explained.

"We'll only get one shot at it," Slade cautioned. He betrayed nothing of what he was feeling, but he was swearing silently again over Emerson's stupidity in letting the woman ride with them. He could only hope that the moment never came when Nash had the opportunity to lay a hand on the lady judge. If it did, though, he hoped he was close enough to keep her from harm without giving himself away to the others.

"I know. That's why it's gotta go right the first time." Johnson saw Ursino looking their way. "When are we eating?" he demanded, wanting to allay any suspicions the deputy might have that they were planning something. "We ain't had nothing to eat in hours, and we're hungry."

"Quit your complaining, or you won't get anything when we do eat," Brown called over to him from where he was stirring a pot over the campfire.

It took a little while longer, but eventually Brown was dishing up hot beans on tin plates.

"Why don't you serve our *guests?*" Brown said as he handed two plates to Ursino.

The deputy headed their way as Alyssa went to Brown.

"Can I help?"

"Sure. Give this one to Nash." He handed her a plate, and she followed Ursino to where the outlaws were sitting, waiting for their meal.

Slade took the plate Ursino offered him with a grunt of thanks. Ursino moved on to Johnson then, just as Alyssa approached Nash.

It happened quickly, as Slade had known it would. Nash appeared to be taking the plate, but instead he snared Alyssa by the wrist and shoved her roughly sideways and off-balance, toward Slade. Nash grabbed her gun from her as she fell, screaming in surprise. He then dove for cover behind a nearby boulder.

Johnson was ready, too. The instant Nash made his move, he tossed his plate of hot food directly in Ursino's face. Throwing his shoulder against the deputy's legs, he brought the big man down. He scrambled to grab his gun before he could recover from the attack. Johnson shot wildly at the deputy, wounding him, and then scurried to Nash's side.

Slade realized that all hell was breaking loose. He pushed Alyssa to the ground, near some rocks, shielding her body with his own.

Alyssa thought Slade was attacking her, and she fought like a wildcat to escape him. Her efforts proved futile against his overpowering strength. He pinned her down easily. They lay pressed intimately together, his hard-muscled chest against her back, her hips nestled tightly against his groin.

"Lie still! You're not going anywhere," Slade ordered.

But she continued to struggle against him. Her attempts to hit out at him were weak, but the feel of her wriggling hips beneath him stirred fires deep within him that he didn't want stoked. At least, not right now. He tightened his hold on her even more, wanting to still her completely.

"Let me go!"

"No! Now, quit fighting me!"

"The deputies are going to shoot you!" she snarled, expecting any moment to be freed by avenging lawmen.

"Getting shot is no different from hanging—it's just faster," he said, pressing her down even harder. He wanted her safe. If any shots came their way, he'd take them, not her. But it seemed Nash had other plans, and he silently cursed the outlaw's viciousness.

"Hawkins! Brown! Clemans! Don't any of you fire unless you want to see your pretty little lady judge here be the first one killed!" Nash shouted as the other three guards dove for cover and prepared to return fire.

"Let her go, and nobody gets hurt!" Hawkins ordered, watching as Ursino managed to crawl away from the outlaws. He was glad his friend wasn't dead, but he was furious that they'd been outwitted. He'd show these bastards, if it was the last thing he did.

"We're dead men either way, you fool!" Johnson called out to him. "What happens next is up to you!"

"Let her go now!" Hawkins yelled, ready to fire as soon as he could get a clear shot. He was sorely tempted to shoot Slade. The gunfighter had tried to seek cover, but was still partially in his line of fire. The only thing that held him back was the fear that he might miss and accidentally wound Alyssa.

"Why? So you can take us into Green River and hang us? We ain't that stupid that we're gonna sit around and wait to get hanged, Hawkins. We got nothing to lose. Now, be good boys and put your guns down before you force us to do something you'll regret."

"Go to hell!"

"We're already there!" Johnson shouted back.

Nash slanted a quick look at Slade and Alyssa. "Get her standing up. I want them to know that I'll kill her if I have to."

Slade muttered a vile oath under his breath, then ordered her in a low voice, "If you want to stay alive, don't fight me. Just do exactly what I tell you to do."

Alyssa's mind was racing as she tried to think of a way to escape the outlaw's hold, but Slade's grip on her was unyielding as they slowly started to rise.

"Stay close to me," Slade told her.

"I'd rather die!" she said in disgust.

"That could happen if you don't do exactly what I say! Don't try anything stupid—it might get you killed!"

He was rough as he lifted his arms and looped them over her, drawing her back against his chest. He wanted to be able to get her out of Nash's line of fire as fast as possible if it came to that, and this was the surest way.

"Throw down your guns!" Nash called out to the deputies again.

Hawkins was furious. The way Slade was holding Alyssa in front of him made it impossible for him to draw a bead on him.

"You listen to me! Anything happens to her, you're gonna die! All of you!" Hawkins yelled.

He silently signaled for Clemans and Brown to try to maneuver into a better position in hopes of getting a clearer shot at them.

"We may end up dead, but the lady judge will die first!" Nash returned coldly.

"Then I'll personally make sure you're second, Nash!" Hawkins countered.

It was then that a shot rang out from behind the outlaws and ricocheted off the rocks nearby.

"What the hell?" Slade dove for cover with Alyssa held firmly in his grip.

Both the deputies and the outlaws went still as they tried to see who was there.

Nash and Johnson prayed it was the Kid, along with Red and Zeke, coming to save them.

The three deputies hoped that it was Sheriff Emerson catching up with them at last.

Silence hung heavily over the campsite as they waited in tense expectation for the other gunman to show himself.

"Let her go, or so help me God, I'll plug all three of you right now!" Rob's voice boomed with righteous, outraged authority from his place of hiding somewhere behind them.

Nash and Johnson cursed their bad luck and spun around, trying to locate the sheriff so they could get a shot off at him. But he was too well hidden. They could see no hint of his hiding place.

Alyssa tried to get up, but Slade held her down.

"It's Rob! Let me up! Now!" She'd never been so glad to hear Rob's voice in her life. How like him to show up just in time to save her! Her father had always said he was an outstanding lawman, and he'd been right.

"No—not yet!" He didn't trust either Nash or Johnson not to shoot her anyway, just to get even. "Wait . . ."

She struggled against his hold, kicking and hitting out at him where she could, but it was useless. Her blows didn't faze him.

"Alyssa! Can you hear me?" Rob called down, fearing she'd already been killed.

"Yes!"

Rob breathed a sigh of relief. "Braxton! Let her go. I want her to stand up real slow so nothing happens to her."

Nash and Johnson were furious. They knew that Slade still had the woman and that she was their only hope of escaping.

113

"Slade, don't do it! Don't let her go! She's our ticket outta here! She's our shield!" Johnson shouted.

"Listen to him, and you'll all end up dead!" Rob dictated.

Slade was trapped. If he let her go too easily, he'd be branded a coward by Nash and Johnson. If he didn't let her go, she might get killed in the crossfire he was sure would come. He had no choice. He would not be able to live with himself, knowing he'd been responsible for her being harmed in any way. He could live with being called a coward.

"Go on! Get out of here! But be quiet and stay down low as you go," he ordered as he freed her.

Alyssa tore herself from him, as if she'd been burned by his touch. She scrambled quickly away from their hiding place.

"What the hell did you do, Slade!" Nash shouted, angry beyond reason when he caught a glimpse of her getting away. "Why did you let her go?"

"She's free, Emerson!" Slade called out. "I'm standing up now."

Nash and Johnson both aimed at Slade, ready to shoot him. He was nothing but a damned, miserable coward. They could have shot their way out of there! They could have freed themselves! And now he'd gone and let their one and only bargaining chip go!

"Don't try anything, fellas," Clemans said with glee as he crept up behind the two of them. "Me and Brown got you covered. Any sudden moves, and you're both dead."

They had been concentrating so hard on Slade and the woman that they'd forgotten about the other deputies. They cursed their luck and threw down their guns in disgust.

"We got 'em!" Brown shouted as he quickly grabbed up the guns.

Hawkins ran to Ursino's side as Clemans and Brown herded Johnson and Nash out of their hiding place. The two gunmen glared at Slade as they were forced to stand with him. He returned their regard without emotion.

"You're a damned fool! We coulda ridden outta here!" Johnson snarled.

"You're the fools. We aren't dead yet, but we would have been if you'd tried to shoot your way out just now. There's still two more days' ride to Green River. The Kid's not going to let us hang."

They were too angry right then to realize the truth of his words. They thought only of his betrayal.

"The Kid'll want to know why you gave up the woman so easy."

Slade turned a deadly look on them. "The Kid'll thank me for saving your worthless, stupid necks!"

They fell silent.

Once things were under control, Rob came riding down from where he'd been keeping a gun on them. Alyssa ran out to meet him.

"Thank you! You saved my life!" she told him tearfully.

"I'm just glad I got here in time. Are you all right?" he asked worriedly as he dismounted before her.

"Yes . . . I'm fine." She tried to sound convincing, refusing to show how scared she'd really been. It had unnerved her to discover that no matter how hard she'd fought, she'd been unable to free herself from Slade's commanding hold.

"Good." He was thrilled to see that except for being a little bruised and dirty, she was unharmed. He wanted to hold her and reassure her, but he held himself back, unsure how she would react to him if he did. He glanced over to where Clemans and Brown were holding the three prisoners at gunpoint.

"What do you want me to do with them, Sheriff?"

Rob smiled. It was a cold, conqueror's smile. "I want them to be real comfortable the rest of the night. Handcuff all three of them together, back-to-back. Even if they try to run, they won't get far that way. Then sit 'em down over there by the fire, so we got a good view of them."

"Yes, sir!" Clemans hurried to do as he'd been ordered while Brown covered him.

When that was done, Brown came to where Alyssa was sitting with Rob.

"Here's your gun, ma'am." He held out her firearm to her.

She took it. "I'm sorry for the trouble I caused you."

"No need to apologize. Look what they did to Ursino." Brown nodded to where the other deputy was lying, his shoulder swathed in bandages.

"How's he doing?" Rob asked.

"He's hurtin' pretty bad and needs to see a doc. We can't get the bullet out."

"There's a bottle of whiskey in my saddlebags," Rob said. "Let him have all he wants. In the morning,

116

Clemans can take him back into Black Springs.''

"Are you sure? That'll only leave three of us to guard them."

"We'll be fine," the sheriff told him. He would make sure there were no more escape attempts.

Alyssa didn't bother to remind them that she would be a fourth gun. After today, she had a long way to go to prove her worth to them in that way.

As she settled in for the night, she relived the terrifying events of the day and began to tremble. It was late before she finally fell into an exhausted slumber.

Chapter Six

Alyssa woke before dawn. She was unable to get back to sleep, though, for in her mind, she kept reliving the horrifying moments when she'd been helpless in the outlaws' hands. It had been a terrible feeling to be totally defenseless. She'd thought that by carrying her gun, she'd be safe and able to protect herself, but yesterday she'd found out just how wrong she'd been.

As terrifying as the experience had been, though, her thoughts kept returning to Slade Braxton. He could have used her for a hostage or a shield or let one of his friends shoot her; instead, he'd released her. She found his action puzzling. Slade Braxton was a murderer without a conscience. She knew that. Yet he had let her go.

Alyssa knew they were expecting the Kid to rescue them, so she supposed that could have been part of the reason he'd ignored Nash's and Johnson's shouts to let them shoot her. Slade must have realized their escape would have turned into a slaughter if he'd kept her, and obviously he hadn't been quite prepared to die. Thinking of it that way, it only made sense that he'd give her up.

As logical as it seemed, though, Alyssa still found herself wondering about a man who could face his companions' hatred and ridicule without the slightest show of emotion. They were a frightening, unnerving lot, and she would be glad when the trial was over.

When the deputies started to stir, she decided to get up, too. There was no point in lying there, sleepless and tense. They might as well get on the trail again.

Rob and Clemans had taken turns tending to Ursino through the night. They planned to ride for home as soon as they could.

Alyssa went to see if she could help them in any way. Her nursing skills were limited—Emily was far more gifted in that area than she was, but she wanted to help if she could.

"How's Deputy Ursino doing?" she asked Rob.

"He'll make it, but the ride home is going to be tough on him—even after all that whiskey."

She looked over to where Clemans was helping the wounded deputy to stand. She flinched when she saw the pain reflected in the man's ashen features.

"Truth is, though," Rob went on. "I'm just glad he's alive . . . and you, too. That confrontation could have turned into a bloodbath yesterday."

"I know. I was thinking about that last night," she

told him. "Braxton seemed to be the only one without a death wish."

"Maybe he knows something we don't," Rob said tersely.

"Like where the Dakota Kid is and when he'll make his move?"

"Exactly. Braxton's the worst of the lot. He was wanted for murder before he ever joined up with the gang, and he's only gotten worse since. It'll feel real good to see them put that noose around his neck."

Alyssa shivered in spite of herself. "It's terrible to be so bloodthirsty, isn't it?"

" 'An eye for an eye,' " he quoted. " 'Course, Braxton would have to hang twenty or thirty times to match his reputation."

"I wonder how a man comes to be like that?" Her gaze followed Slade as Brown freed him from the other two prisoners and shackled his wrists in front of him again.

"Who knows? I figure the man's probably half-crazy. He'd have to be to do the things he's done."

"Crazy?" She looked at him, a bit startled. Of all the things she'd suspected of Slade Braxton, crazy had never been one of them.

"Not crazy like a raving lunatic or anything, but sly and cunning. He's got to be smart to have stayed alive this long with the big bounty that's on his head. No doubt there were bounty hunters gunning for him everywhere. But we're the ones who brought him in, and his days are numbered now. Once that jury hears the evidence against him, we won't have to worry about Slade Braxton killing anybody ever again."

Alyssa knew she should feel good about that, but as Rob was speaking, she glanced toward Slade to find that he was watching her from across the campsite. His dark-eyed gaze was intent upon her, and she felt the power of his regard to the depths of her soul. He looked every inch the dangerous gunfighter this morning. His beard shaded his jaw with dark shadow. He looked disreputable, a pirate of the high plains.

Alyssa found herself mesmerized and had to force herself to look away. As she did, though, she remembered his words to her the day before as he'd released her—*Be quiet and stay down low as you go.* If he was as amoral as Rob believed, why would he have cared if she'd gotten shot or not?

"Rob . . . ?"

He looked at her expectantly.

"What happened yesterday was my fault, and I was thinking maybe I shouldn't be wearing a gun," she admitted, regretting having been caught off guard by the prisoners.

"Don't even think about it. I've seen how you handle a gun—you're good. I know it and you know it."

"But they might have escaped yesterday—"

"They tricked Ursino, too, you know, and he's one of my best deputies," he reminded her.

"I know, but—"

"Forget it."

"You're sure?"

"Positive. You handled yourself well yesterday. Any other female probably would have fainted dead away or done something stupid, but you kept your wits about you. That took guts."

121

Alyssa nodded tightly. His praise helped bolster her flagging self-confidence, for she felt she'd failed them by not being more careful.

"Looks like they've just about got Ursino ready to ride. We'd better start packing up."

"Thanks for going to see my mother for me."

"She was worried about you, but once I explained what had happened, she understood. Did she send along what you needed?" he asked, having given her the small bag Loretta had packed for her the night before.

"Yes, thanks. I wasn't looking forward to making the whole trip in one set of clothes. I wouldn't have been a pretty sight by the time we got to Green River."

"Glad to oblige." He grinned at her.

They bade Clemans and Ursino good-bye as the two men started back to Black Springs. It wasn't going to be an easy trip for the injured deputy, and they hoped he made it without too much trouble.

Once Clemans and Ursino had gone, it was time for them to head out. The terrain they were to cover this day would be rougher than it had been the day before. They would be following the river for part of the way, and the opportunities for ambush would be many. They would have to take care and watch for any sign that the Kid might be waiting.

Slade was exhausted as he mounted up. Handcuffed to the others as he'd been all night, he'd gotten no sleep. Now as they headed out, he knew it was going to be a rough ride. He'd traveled this way before and knew the trail was narrow and rocky.

Hawkins and Rob rode up front, with the prisoners following behind. Brown and Alyssa brought up the rear. They kept up a steady pace and stopped only when necessary to rest the horses.

It was late afternoon when dark clouds began to gather. Rain soon followed. They paused long enough to don their slickers, then started up again.

Rob refused to let the wet weather stop them. An occasional shower wasn't unusual at this time of year, but when the rain didn't let up after an hour, he became concerned. The river was running higher and faster than normal. He knew how treacherous the water could become if the storm was as heavy behind them as it seemed to be up ahead.

When the lightning began in earnest, Rob started to look for shelter. The narrow canyon with its steep, rocky walls offered little in the way of cover for them, though, so they kept going. They would have to get to the other end before they could find any real protection from the downpour.

Though Alyssa was wearing her slicker and had her hat pulled low over her eyes, she was still getting drenched. She told herself that if the men could do this, so could she. Sighing, she tightened her grip on the reins and straightened her shoulders. Surely, the storm would end soon.

A bolt of lightning split the sky directly in front of them, cracking loudly and startling the horses.

Spartan shied at the brilliant flash and the crashing boom that followed. Alyssa brought him under control with an effort and tried to calm him.

"You all right?" Rob called back to her, seeing how her horse had tried to bolt.

"I'm fine."

"We'll stop as soon as I can find a safe place on some high ground." He was forced to shout, for the thunder continued at a deafening roar and the sound of the rising, rushing waters threatened to drown him out.

They moved on, battling the elements.

"The good news is, it isn't a freak snowstorm," Brown told her as a particularly strong gust of wind blasted them.

"Don't even talk about it!" Alyssa cautioned. She knew how fierce the winters could be in the territory, and an unexpected snowstorm could prove deadly to the unprepared. "But you're right. Thinking about it that way, the rain doesn't seem quite so bad." She managed to give him a soggy smile.

Up ahead, Johnson kept watching for some sign that the Kid was near.

"I wonder if he's up there somewhere, just waiting for the right time to make his move?" he muttered to Nash.

"I hope so," Nash answered. He looked over at Slade and added, " 'Course, we wouldn't be in this fix right now, if our good ole buddy Slade, here, hadn't gone yellow on us."

Neither one of them had spoken to Slade yet that day. They were still angry about the way he'd turned the girl over to the deputies without a fight. They firmly believed they could have negotiated their way to freedom if he'd just gone along with their threat to kill her.

"Yeah," Johnson agreed. "I wonder if the Kid knows what a coward he is?"

Slade heard them talking and looked over at them. His expression was cold. "I wonder if the Kid knows how stupid some of his men are?"

Both Nash and Johnson tensed at his insult and glared at him, wishing they had their guns.

"It made more sense to me to stay alive and have the chance to escape again later, than to get shot down like a dog by a sheriff who already had the drop on us. Emerson is a smart man. He wasn't about to negotiate with us. He didn't have to."

"We could have shot her!"

"And then Emerson and the others would have shot us," he said, amazed at their complete lack of logic. But then, he'd known when he made his decision about Alyssa that they were going to brand him a coward. Their opinion of him didn't matter, though. What mattered was that she hadn't been hurt.

"Maybe," Nash said sullenly.

"There was no maybe about it. They had us in their sights. It was over. We're just going to have to find another way out," Slade went on.

At that comment, they looked at him with a little less disgust.

"So what's your big plan?" Johnson asked snidely, confident that he didn't have one.

"I haven't thought of one yet."

The other two snorted in ridicule.

"But I will."

"Sure you will," they agreed sarcastically and turned their attention back to the trail as lightning rent the sky again.

"It doesn't seem to be clearing off at all," Rob told Hawkins as they rode on through the drenching rains.

"I thought it would have started to clear by now."

"How are the others doing?"

Hawkins looked back over his shoulder. "It looks like they're keeping up all right."

"Good. With any luck at all, we should be able to find some kind of shelter soon."

The river was flowing fast and swift. Alyssa was holding her own. Though Spartan was still shying at the lightning, she was able to keep him under control. There were occasions when he could be headstrong, so she was glad that he was proving manageable in spite of the miserable weather.

And then it happened.

Lightning cracked frighteningly right in front of them again. Brown's horse reared and threw himself toward Spartan. Spartan panicked as the other horse crashed into him. He bolted forward, blindly charging into Slade's mount, then lost his footing and slipped sideways. He stumbled down the low, sloping bank and into the deadly current.

"Alyssa!" Rob had turned at the first sound of trouble. Seeing her danger, he tried to ride to her.

Alyssa was battling to regain control of her frightened mount as Spartan fought to keep his footing against the power of the rushing waters. She was not one to lose control, but as she felt herself slipping from her seat, she knew she was in trouble. Spartan lurched toward the bank, and as he did, she lost her grip on the reins and made a desperate grab for the saddle horn.

Slade was the closest to her. When he saw what was happening, he didn't hesitate. He urged his mount forward directly into the river.

"Hang on!" he shouted over the roar of the crashing waters and booming thunder.

He reached her before Rob, so the sheriff stayed back at the water's edge, not wanting to make things worse. Maneuvering the horses would be rough enough with just the two of them. Three could be chaotic.

As Slade urged his mount next to Alyssa's, Slade violently cursed the handcuffs that limited his freedom. If his hands had been free, he could have grabbed her around the waist and hauled her to safety before him on his horse. They would have been all right then, but restrained as he was, there was no simple way to get a grip on her.

"Grab onto me and hang on!" he ordered as he kneed his horse in as close to hers as possible.

He leaned toward her as he fought to control his own balking mount. Alyssa kept one hand on her pommel as she reached out to grab Slade's arm. She missed on her first try as Spartan shifted and stumbled, whinnying in terror, and in spite of her fierce self-control, she let out a scream.

"Now!" he ordered, knowing it wasn't going to get any easier.

Lightning cracked nearby again, and Spartan partially reared and shifted backward. His eyes rolled in fright as the thunder boomed around him.

Alyssa cried out again. She could feel herself losing her seat completely, and she clung to the pommel in desperation.

Slade knew he had to do something. He moved in closer once more and tried to reach out to her. He managed to grab her arm, and she reached out toward him just as both horses panicked. Slade kept his hold on her, but then his horse shied and he was forced to release her to keep his own seat. He made a grab for his saddle horn, but missed.

"No!" Alyssa screamed as she realized he was falling into the torrent.

She made a desperate attempt to reach him and managed to grasp his arm for a moment, but the current was too strong. Slade was torn from her grip and swept away by the fierce, battering current.

It was at that moment that Spartan, bumped by Slade's frantic horse, gave a lurching leap toward the bank that completely unseated her. Alyssa managed only one cry for help as she, too, was tossed into the raging torrent.

On the bank, Rob had gotten out his rope, hoping to lasso Alyssa and pull her in to shore. His lasso fell into the water near her, and she tried to make a grab at it, but it was too late. She missed his lifeline by inches and was swept away downstream.

Nash and Johnson saw that the lawmen were distracted with their rescue attempt and decided to make a run for it. Hawkins anticipated their move, though, and turned on them, his gun in hand. He was in no mood to tolerate anything from them today.

"Don't go getting any ideas about taking off, boys," Hawkins ordered.

Rob and Brown rode along the bank, trying to find a way to save Alyssa and Slade, but there was nothing they could do as the rushing river washed them farther and farther away. They could see them, surfacing and going under as they were battered by the massive rocks and boulders. He knew that handcuffed, Slade was helpless to save himself, let alone help Alyssa.

"Let's go!" Rob ordered, grabbing the reins to Alyssa's horse as Brown took charge of Slade's. Both mounts had managed to climb back up the bank to safety, escaping the river's wrath.

Rob and the others raced down the trail, trying to keep Alyssa and Slade in sight. They feared they would disappear beneath the torrent before they could catch up to them, and they did. Torn from their view by the rushing waters, Slade and Alyssa disappeared in the thundering river.

Slade was pummeled by the rocky riverbed as he was washed downstream. Bruised and battered, he clung to the hope that eventually he'd get close enough to shore so he could get his footing and climb out. With his hands bound, though, it was appearing more and more hopeless. There was no way he could swim and save himself. He choked as he was dragged under again, and he struggled with all his might just to keep his head above water.

Alyssa fought the current as she swam toward Slade. She knew he was going to drown unless she could get to him and help him in some way. The current was vicious and unforgiving, slamming her against the submerged rocks, but still she kept on. Never before in her life had she appreciated the fact that she'd learned how to swim, but she did now.

It was growing so dark that she could barely make him out ahead of her in the rapid flow. She struck out toward him, but then he disappeared beneath the water again, and she knew she had to hurry. It was pure luck that brought her nearer to him when he surfaced, fighting for breath and weak from the struggle.

Alyssa wanted to shout to Slade that she was almost there, but she couldn't waste the energy. It would take all her strength just to make her way toward him. With one lunge, she managed to touch his shoulder, but he slipped from her grip before she could get a firm hold on him.

"Don't try!" he managed. "I'll only pull you down—"

She heard him, but ignored his warning as she swam toward him again. This time she grabbed his shirt just as he went under. The current pulled them both down, but she kicked fiercely and fought her way back to the surface. Gasping for breath, she somehow managed to get his head above water. She linked her arm around his neck as she struck out for the shore.

"Kick if you can!" was all she could choke out.

The current had not lessened. Despite their efforts, they were swept along at breakneck speed, down the canyon away from the others and off into the growing darkness of the coming night.

* * *

Rob was devastated. Alyssa and Slade were gone. As night fell, he and Brown ceased their headlong chase and doubled back to where they'd left Hawkins guarding the prisoners. Rob was silently praying that Alyssa and Slade had made it to safety, but he feared the worst.

"Where are they?" Hawkins yelled as he saw them approaching. He'd kept the prisoners moving, following Brown and the sheriff to help if they could.

The rain was still pouring down, the cloud cover making the night even darker than normal.

"We couldn't catch up to them. I'm afraid they're lost!" Rob answered as he reached them.

Hawkins couldn't believe what had happened. Lightning cracked high above them again, reminding them of the severity of the storm.

"Let's get out of here. Maybe Alyssa made it to the riverbank farther downstream, and we'll be able to find her in the morning," Hawkins said, not wanting to consider the possibility that she might have drowned.

Brown gave him a disbelieving look. "In this current? Hell, she's probably dead already . . . Braxton, too."

Nash and Johnson didn't say anything. Though they thought Slade a coward, they hoped he'd survived. If he was smart, he'd let the deputies think he was dead, and then come back and rescue them. As for the lady judge, they hoped she'd met a miserable end. It was what she deserved, and her death would leave them with one less gun to worry about.

Huddling down against the continuing rain, they

traveled on through the night. They hoped Sheriff Emerson found a place to camp soon. They'd had enough riding and excitement for the day.

The rocks scraped at Alyssa's legs as she tried to paddle toward where she thought the bank was. It was next to impossible to see anything in the darkness, and she was growing weary of fighting. Time and again the current threatened to pull her under, yet somehow, she resisted its deadly grip. Clutching Slade, frantic to save him and herself, she continued her struggle to survive. She refused to die this way!

A rock loomed just ahead of her and off to the side. Her anger gave her the strength she needed to make the final, desperate lunge for it. She had to let go of Slade to do it, but as she grabbed the sturdy boulder that could save them, she positioned herself to snare him again as the current swept him past her. It took all her flagging strength to get a grip on his shirt again. With one last herculean effort, she managed to drag him toward her, out of the main force of the water's flow.

Alyssa collapsed back against the rock. She was still half in the river and had to take care to keep Slade's head above water. She knew she should be afraid that he might regain consciousness and overpower her, but right then, she didn't care. She was too exhausted to fight anymore—either the river or him.

The water's chill had numbed her, and in a way she was grateful that she could feel nothing. As soon as dawn came and with it the warmth of a new day, she knew she would be in pain, for she was certain she was bruised and bleeding. Right now, though, that wasn't important. They were out of the current, and she'd saved Slade. That was enough.

Alyssa remained where she was, resting, until a long time later when she started to shiver uncontrollably. She knew she had to get out of the water completely to be safe, so she struggled toward the bank, hauling Slade with her. As the water grew shallower and the tug of the current lessened, she almost collapsed. Slade was a big man, and once they were out of the deeper water, she could barely move him. She didn't give up until she'd dragged him partially up onto the rocky river bank, though. Only then did she allow herself to collapse. Falling to the ground beside his still form, she couldn't summon the strength to move any farther.

Slade regained consciousness slowly. His last coherent memory was of Alyssa crying out as she started to fall from her horse into the river. He vaguely remembered losing his own seat as he tried to reach for her and being washed away toward a looming boulder. He had no real recollection after that, but judging from the way he felt, he was certain he'd lost the battle with the rock.

Slade wondered why he was still alive. The current had been the worst he'd ever fought in his life. Yet he *was* alive. There was no doubt about that. If he'd died, he wouldn't have been in such pain. Every inch of his body felt as if he'd been bludgeoned, and his head was throbbing. He started to lift one hand to his head and was jarred back to reality at the biting tug of the handcuffs. Lifting both hands to his forehead, he flinched in pain. When he drew them away, they were covered with blood—proof that, indeed, the boulder had won.

Slade struggled to sit up, wondering how he'd gotten to the bank and wondering how he'd managed to survive. It was dark and the rain was continuing, but it did seem to be letting up a little. Not that staying dry mattered after his swim. . . . As he pushed himself to a sitting position, his head reeled and pain sliced through him. It was then that he saw her.

Alyssa was lying beside him, and she was so quiet that he feared she was dead.

"Alyssa!" he groaned.

He forced himself to move and painfully crawled the short distance to her side.

In the darkness, it was difficult to discover her condition. Slade leaned over her, wanting to make sure she was breathing. His concern was only for her well-being. He forgot that he was a wanted man. He forgot that his cover was so good that even a fair-minded sheriff had been convinced of his evil ways. He thought only that she was hurt, and he had to help her.

Kneeling beside her, Slade gently brushed a lock of wet hair from her face and tenderly touched a bruise that was already beginning to discolor her pale forehead. He leaned closer, whispering her name.

"Alyssa . . ."

"What . . . ?" She heard his voice as if from a great distance and stirred, opening her eyes to find Slade leaning over her.

A surge of joy welled up inside him as he realized that she was coming around. It ended abruptly, though, when he felt the dig of her gun in his ribs.

"Back off," Alyssa said in a hoarse voice as she pressed the gun even harder against him for emphasis.

And Slade did, sitting back a short distance away from her.

"You're alive—"

"And if I wasn't, you were going to finish off the job, right?" she accused him.

He weakly rested his head in his hands. Dizziness threatened to overwhelm him, and his stomach was churning in rebellion over the river water he'd swallowed.

"Actually, I was worried about you."

Alyssa would have laughed, but she felt too miserable. "Don't concern yourself."

He fell silent. It hurt too much to talk, and he certainly wasn't up to an argument.

Alyssa sat up, gun still in hand, ready for any sudden, threatening moves from him. She didn't know what stroke of fate had brought her to this moment—alone and abandoned, on foot in the wilderness with the man who'd killed her father—but here she was. As she thought about it, she realized it was her own fault. She'd convinced Rob to bring her along, and she'd convinced herself she could handle any situation that might arise. So far, she'd failed miserably. Now was the time for her to prove she could do it. She had to take charge. She had to bring the prisoner back in.

There was no telling what kind of trouble she might

run into trying to locate Rob and the others, but she'd worry about that later. Right now, it was too dark to go anywhere. She needed daylight to traverse this terrain, and it was just past sundown. A long, dark night of keeping Braxton at bay loomed ahead of her.

"We'd better see if there's some place around here to sit out the night."

She forced herself to stand and swayed slightly as she got her balance. As much as she hated to admit it, she was glad Slade was in worse shape than she was. If he'd come out of this unharmed, it would have been easy for him to overpower her and disarm her. Because of his injuries, she still had the drop on him, and she thanked heaven for that. She didn't like wishing pain on anyone, but having him partially incapacitated and handcuffed helped her.

"You wouldn't consider shooting these cuffs off me, would you?" he asked, peering up at her in the darkness. He could just barely make out her grim, determined expression. "I didn't think so."

"You're smarter than I thought you were," she said sarcastically.

"I'll take that as a compliment."

"You can take it any way you like. But let's move. There's no sense sitting here in the pouring rain. Let's go find some shelter."

He considered trying to take the gun away from her, but quickly gave up the notion. They weren't going anywhere, and as jumpy as she was right now— like a half-broken filly—she just might shoot him. He felt bad enough as it was. He didn't need a gunshot wound, too.

Chapter Seven

The going was not easy as Alyssa and Slade made their way along the riverbank in the rain. Slade was leading the way with Alyssa following, her gun in hand. Weak, battered and bloodied though he might be, she didn't trust him, and she had no intention of giving him the chance to escape.

"It looks like there might be something up ahead," Slade called over his shoulder after they'd been walking for some time. There appeared to be the entrance to a cave or at least a protective overhang.

Alyssa offered up a silent hallelujah and trailed him through the rocks and heavy brush to the haven. It wasn't a cave. It was more like a naturally scooped-out den of sorts, but she didn't care. At least they would be out of the storm's wrath for a while.

"Let me go in first and make sure it's safe," he offered.

"Just remember I've got the gun and I'm not afraid to use it," she returned. Rob had told her how cunning Braxton was. She would not allow herself to be fooled by anything he said or did.

Slade understood her caution, so he moved with deliberate care, not wanting to scare her with any sudden, unexpected actions. He had to stoop down to enter the retreat, and he half-crawled inside. The shelter wasn't much, but it was definitely better than spending the night trekking across rough terrain in miserable weather.

"Come on in," he told her when he'd made sure there were no snakes or other creatures that might not welcome their intrusion.

"All right. But you get on the far side, over there, so I don't have to worry."

When he'd done as she'd ordered, Alyssa made her way into the haven. Slade was sitting with his back braced against the opposite wall. She took a seat near the opening, so she could keep some small distance between them. She wanted to have time to fire if he decided to attack her.

"I never thought sitting on rocks could feel as good as an overstuffed sofa, but they do right now," she said with a low groan as she allowed herself to relax a bit.

"At least it's dry in here," he added wryly. He almost smiled, but his head hurt too much. His jaw clenched as he fought to control the throbbing pain.

"Let's hope it stays that way."

"If the rain was going to come in, it would have done it by now. We should be safe for the rest of the night. All that's left to do is get comfortable, get some sleep and wait for daylight."

"You go right ahead." She sat straighter, deliberately not making herself too comfortable. She tightened her grip on her gun.

"I will," he said, shifting positions. "I didn't get any sleep at all last night. Nash and Johnson weren't too happy with the way things turned out, and being handcuffed together like we were, it was impossible to get any rest."

"Sometimes life is rough," she said with little sympathy. If he wasn't a killer, he wouldn't have been there in the first place.

She fell silent as she began to unbraid her hair. It would dry more quickly if the thick, wet tresses were unbound. She combed her fingers through it, wishing she had a brush. But that wish was as far from being fulfilled as her hope for a warm bath.

Slade had meant to close his eyes and try to sleep, but as he watched her free her pale mane from its confinement, he found himself mesmerized. No longer did she appear the gun-toting judge; she'd transformed herself into the intoxicating woman he'd held in his arms that night of the dance.

"You should wear your hair down all the time," Slade said.

She ignored his comment.

"You look very pretty that way."

Alyssa said nothing in response. She would not allow herself to be affected by anything this man said or did.

"Why haven't you married? Were you too busy studying the law to realize you were turning into an old maid?" he asked, being deliberately provocative.

She stifled a gasp at his obnoxious comments. "Perhaps I'm an old maid, as you so candidly put it, because I choose to be."

"Pity."

"I thought you were going to sleep." She was terse, wanting to discourage any further conversation with him.

He managed a half-grin at her display of temper. "I plan on it. But first, there was something I wanted to tell you." He sat up and leaned slightly toward her.

His movement made Alyssa nervous and she pinned him with a challenging glare as she pointed the gun straight at the middle of his chest. "Yes?"

He did not back down from her unspoken threat. Instead, he looked straight into her eyes as he spoke. "I wanted to thank you for saving my life. It would have been very easy for you to have let me drown out there. No one would have been the wiser, and there probably would have been some celebrating at the news."

"I don't doubt it."

"Well, thank you."

She wondered at his ploy, trying to figure out what he was up to. She glared at him, sure that he was planning some kind of deception. "You're alive and well, so don't make me think I made a mistake."

She was one spirited woman. He managed a smile, but she didn't respond.

"What would your father think about your being in this position?"

At the mention of her father, she was immediately furious. "Don't you dare even speak of my father! You're not good enough to say his name!"

He understood her anger, but wanted to know more. "What kind of man was he?"

"Nothing like you!" she said coldly as she aimed the gun at Slade's heart. "Besides, what do you care about my father? You're the one who killed him!"

Slade studied her. "What if I told you that I didn't shoot him, that your eyewitness is lying?"

"I'd say you were every bit as miserable and rotten as the sheriff told me you were."

"If I told you the truth, would you even listen?" he countered sharply.

"I'm as fair as my father was. I go by the letter of the law. Witnesses saw you with the gang, robbing the bank. One man saw you shoot my father down in cold blood. I bound you over for trial on the basis of evidence presented against you at the hearing. Now it's up to a judge and jury in Green River. They can decide who's lying and who's telling the truth."

Slade was quiet for a minute as he debated whether to take the chance and tell her everything. He probably wouldn't get another opportunity. He was certain that the sheriff and his deputies were scouring the countryside looking for them right now. There was no way he could reveal his true identity in front of Nash and Johnson, and he couldn't be sure Ken would show up in time to save him from hanging. He had to find someone who would be willing to wire Denver for him and verify his story. He hoped that person was Alyssa.

"If you're as fair and just as you say you are, then you'll listen to what I have to say."

Alyssa turned an icy regard on him, but she didn't invite any further discussion.

"I tried to tell your precious sheriff the truth when he first brought me in, but he didn't believe me. All it got me was a beating in his back room. There's something you need to know—I am not who and what you think I am."

Alyssa couldn't believe he was going to try to lie his way into her good graces. "Save your breath, Braxton. I know all about you."

"What do you know?" he demanded.

"I know that you're a sly, conniving liar."

"Listen to me," he snarled, interrupting her. "I'm an undercover Pinkerton agent."

"Oh, please . . . " she scoffed, her eyes widening at the magnitude of his lie.

"I work out of the Denver office. Send a wire to them and they'll verify what I'm telling you."

"How dare you continue to lie!" She was furious.

"How dare you and your precious sheriff not listen to the truth?" he snarled back at her. "All I asked Emerson to do was send that wire, and he refused!"

"He didn't believe you, because he knows what kind of man you are!"

Alyssa gave a disbelieving shake of her head as she stared at Slade. Everything Rob had told her about him was true. She was glad now that they'd had the time to talk about Braxton earlier. If she'd been a weaker woman, she might have been swayed by his story. He certainly seemed earnest enough, but that was what Rob had warned her about. Rob had told her how killers like Braxton were vicious, conniving bastards. Braxton had just proven it.

"You're damned right I'm a liar! I have to be to work undercover! How else could I convince someone like the Dakota Kid that I should be riding with his gang?"

She was shocked by his words, but she still refused to believe he was a Pinkerton. "You just admitted you are a liar!"

"Damn it, woman!" Slade swore, furious over all that was happening. No one would listen to him; he had no way to prove his true identity. "I've been working on bringing in the Dakota Kid's gang for months. I was *this* close to making the arrests, and now the whole thing has fallen apart—thanks to your wonderful sheriff!"

"Well, he got you!" she retorted.

"But he didn't get the Kid!"

She fell silent, ignoring his outrage. She was certain it was all part of the act Rob had warned her about.

When she didn't say any more, he went on, "Look, Alyssa, all I'm asking you to do is to send one telegram when we reach Green River. My supervisor's name is Ken Richards."

She gave him an icy smile. "You know, you're almost convincing in your righteous anger. It's a good

143

thing Sheriff Emerson warned me about you and told me what kind of men you murdering gunslingers really are.''

His frustration was growing. ''You have to understand that it took the agency months to create my background and my dangerous reputation. We did it all just so I could infiltrate the gang. We'd been retained by the railroad to find out the name of the Kid's informer at the express office and to bring in the Kid's gang. I was just getting close when Emerson trapped us in the canyon.''

''Sheriff Emerson's a fine lawman. He wasn't about to let my father's killers get away.''

''If he's such a damned fine lawman, why didn't he recognize the truth when he heard it?''

''The truth is what we know happened, not some farfetched fairy tale you'd like us to believe.''

''What will it take to convince you that I'm telling you the truth?'' His rage would have intimidated her had she not been armed.

''A witness saw you shoot my father!''

''Your witness is wrong!'' Slade turned on her, ignoring the gun. ''Don't you realize I could have taken that gun from you any time I wanted to since we climbed out of the river, but I haven't even tried? Do you think for one minute that if Nash or Johnson had been washed down river with you, they would have gone along with any of this, like I have? Listen to me! I'm an undercover Pinkerton agent who wants the Kid brought in just as badly as you and Emerson do.''

Her hand tightened on the gun as she met his challenging gaze. For a moment, she froze, startled by the burning intensity of the emotion she saw mirrored there. "Back off."

"Are you so cold—so full of hate for me that you won't even consider that I might be telling you the truth?" He shifted position, leaning toward her, his eyes boring into hers.

"I don't trust you," she told him tightly, not daring to look away.

"When we get to Green River, send that telegram to Denver, please." He lowered his tone as he spoke. "All I'm asking is for you to take a chance on me."

Conflicting emotions filled Alyssa as Slade leaned ever closer to her. She thought about firing at him. What she'd been told about his involvement in her father's shooting warred with what she'd experienced with Slade herself. . . . He'd released her when he could have held her hostage, and he'd warned her to be careful when he'd let her go. He'd been the first to try to rescue her when she'd been stranded in the river and had almost lost his own life in the process. And now he told her that he could easily disarm her any time he wanted and yet he hadn't even tried. . . . She hesitated, gazing up at him, all her doubts and fears revealed in her eyes.

"Trust me, Alyssa," Slade said in a low, hoarse voice. He saw her confusion and took advantage. Slowly covering the last distance that separated them, he completely ignored the gun she held tightly in her hand, and leaned forward to kiss her.

Alyssa was stunned. She gasped at the intimate contact that she remembered so clearly from the night of the dance. She remained unmoving as his lips plundered hers. This was crazy—she knew it was—but for just this one fleeting moment, she didn't want his kiss to end. For an instant, she was once again the innocent he'd danced with that night in town. She was floating in the arms of her mystery man, thrilling to his embrace.

Slade had wanted to kiss her again ever since he'd left her the night of the dance. He'd been wondering if she was truly as cold and indifferent to him as she seemed. He wondered if she was feeling anything toward him but the need for revenge. His lips moved over hers in a soft yet sensual caress, and her response was his answer. She did feel something for him.

And then he felt the cold metal of the gun suddenly pressing against a very personal, very intimate part of him.

"Get away from me, Braxton, or you'll be singing soprano," Alyssa ground out. Her hand was shaking as she fought to control the urge to follow through on her threat. She was furious with him and furious with herself for giving in to her weakness for him. He had killed her father. How could she have forgotten, even if only for a few moments?

Slade slowly backed off. He studied the look on Alyssa's face, hoping to see a flicker of understanding, but he saw only anger.

"That's not the way to get me to listen to you!" She wiped her mouth with the back of her hand, wanting to erase any evidence of his compelling kiss. "You're a very dangerous man. I'm taking you in for murder."

Slade stared at her and then at the gun she aimed at him with renewed deadly intent. He fell silent and sat back against the far wall.

It was going to be a very long night.

Rob passed the night in the shelter they'd found, haunted by his concern for Alyssa. His imagination gave him no rest. Terrible visions played in his mind—that she was alone, injured and suffering; that Slade had gotten her gun away from her, killed her, and was now hunting them; or that both Alyssa and Slade had drowned in the raging river and he would never find their bodies.

"You all right?" Hawkins asked his boss when he found him staring silently off into the distance.

"I hate these bastards," Rob told him heatedly, tension in every line of his body. "All of them."

"I know," the deputy agreed. "I don't think I've ever heard of a meaner, more vicious gang."

"I've been sitting here worrying about Alyssa. I hope to God she's alive, but—" He shook his head, revealing the hopelessness and the helplessness he was feeling.

"If she's alive, we'll find her." Hawkins tried to sound encouraging.

"And if she's not . . . How will I ever tell Loretta? To first lose John that way, and now her oldest daughter—"

"It's almost light and it looks like the skies have cleared. We can start searching again right away."

"I just hope we find Alyssa—and soon."

"Me, too."

"The longer we delay getting into Green River and locking them up, the better chance we give the Kid to find us and try to free them."

"I'll get everybody moving," Hawkins told him as he went to wake the others.

Breakfast was cold and fast. Though Nash and Johnson complained, the lawmen cared little about what they wanted.

Rob and Hawkins combed the riverbanks for some sign of Alyssa and the lost prisoner, while Brown kept watch over the outlaws. Their search turned up nothing. They had no idea how far downstream the two might have washed. As the morning hours passed, Rob and Hawkins slowly came to fear the worst—that they might never find any trace of the missing pair.

"It's light out, Braxton. Let's start moving," Alyssa said as the sky brightened in the east. She left their haven and surveyed the surroundings as she waited for him to emerge.

Slade had managed to get some sleep. He was still sore from the battering he'd taken over the last few days, though, and his mood was black as he faced her in the morning light.

"Which way?"

"Back toward the river." She waved him on his way with her gun. "We've got to find a place to cross. With any luck, it's gone down since last night."

He nodded and started off. Alyssa followed. She was past exhaustion, but she couldn't give in to her weariness. There was too much at stake. She had to keep going.

As Alyssa watched Slade walking ahead of her, she thought of what had happened the night before, and her anger returned. In the light of day, she found it particularly irksome that he'd taunted her by telling her that he could take the gun away from her any time he wanted to. She wondered if she truly seemed so defenseless. She feared she did.

Her mood soured even more at the realization that he considered her helpless and weak. Why else would he have kissed her? He'd probably thought she was a pitiful, love-starved old maid who'd surrender everything to him after a little male attention. Well, she'd certainly shown him. She'd been more than tempted to geld him.

Looking up at Slade, she had to admit that he was attractive, in a rugged sort of way. She remembered how she'd reacted to him at the dance, but that had been before she knew him for what he really was.

Or did she?

All his rantings about being a Pinkerton had led her to believe everything that Rob had told her. Slade Braxton was a known robber and killer. And the witness at the hearing had testified that he'd seen him shoot her father. As far as she was concerned, the case against him was cut and dried—no matter what outrageous tales he might concoct.

Still, there lingered the smallest of doubts in the back of her mind, and that fact added to her fury with him. Was he such a good liar that he could convince her, a woman who prided herself on her intellect and logic, that the possibility of his innocence was real?

And his kiss . . . What had been the reason for his kiss, and why was she still haunted by it?

Alyssa was angry and glad of it, for that powerful emotion sustained her and kept her moving. She glared at Slade's back and kept trudging after him. They'd found no trace of Rob and the others yet, and if they didn't locate them soon, she wondered how she was going to be able to stay in control. She was going to have to get some sleep sometime, but there was no way she could safely restrain him while she rested.

Her options were limited. She could fire a warning shot, hoping to alert Rob and the others to her location. It might work—if they were close enough to hear it. But if they weren't, she'd have wasted a bullet, and once she was out of ammunition—

Alyssa realized worriedly, too, that Rob might not be the only one out there within hearing range. By signaling her position, she might also be letting the Dakota Kid know exactly where she was, and she definitely couldn't risk that. Her situation was difficult, and she could only hope that they were reunited with Rob—and soon.

"Let's take a break," she called out to Slade, needing to rest for a while.

Slade didn't bother to answer, but merely found a shaded spot and sat down, glad for the reprieve. He was certainly in no hurry to be returned to the sheriff and his deputies. The longer they were separated, the more time Ken had to hear what had happened to him and to get to Green River. He knew, too, that the longer they were out here, the more time the Kid had to try to come up with a plan to free them.

Slade wasn't particularly thrilled with the idea of being rescued by the Kid, but it was far better than going to trial and hanging. And the way things had been going lately, it seemed that was the way it was going to turn out.

He glanced over at Alyssa. He wasn't sure he wanted to broach the subject again, but he had little choice. "Have you given any more thought to what I told you last night?"

She glanced at him coldly.

"Will you send the telegram?"

"If Sheriff Emerson refused, I'm sure he had a very good reason. I'm abiding by his decision."

"I thought you were an independent, logical, intelligent woman? I thought you could think for yourself?" he challenged her.

His comments stung, but she did not lose her temper. "That's quite discerning of you, and you're right, I am. But that changes nothing. It's out of my hands. Like I said before, your fate is up to the judge and jury."

"But they'll never get the chance to hear the truth if you don't get word to the Denver office."

Slade was so frustrated that he was tempted to tackle her and grab the gun. He ran the risk of being shot, but being wounded and free was sounding better and better to him all the time. It was certainly better than being hanged. He was seriously contemplating the move when the decision was taken away from him.

"Alyssa! Is that you?"

Rob's call came from the top of a rise about a quarter of a mile away, and Slade felt his hope of being saved from the hangman sink even lower.

"Rob! Yes! We're here!"

She jumped up and ran toward Rob. She was thrilled to hear the sound of his voice. She'd begun to believe they would never be found. She'd also had the feeling that Braxton was planning something, and she was relieved at Rob's timely arrival.

Rob rode down the slope and was off his horse beside her in an instant. Unable to restrain himself, he snatched her up in a warm embrace.

"Thank God you're all right!" Rob said in an emotional voice as he held her close.

"Thank you for searching for me!" She relaxed in his arms, feeling safe at long last.

"I would never leave you alone out there, Alyssa. How did you survive the river? And Braxton? Where is he? Is he dead?"

"I'm right here, Emerson," Slade said as he came forward. He could have run, but saw no point in it, and he was more than glad to break up this cozy little scene. The sight of Alyssa in the lawman's arms irritated him for some reason.

Rob put Alyssa from him as he looked over at the gunfighter. He saw the cut on his forehead. "You were injured?"

"Our lady judge saved me. She pulled me out of the river. If it hadn't been for her, I would have drowned."

"We'll get you to a doctor once we get into town."

Slade gave a mirthless laugh as he stared at them. "Why? I'm not much worse off than when you got done with me a few days ago."

Rob looked irritated. "All right, then let's go. The others are waiting just over that rise."

Slade started walking. He'd come this far on foot— what was another mile or two?

"I'm so glad I found you," Rob told Alyssa, as he turned back to her. "I was so worried. I was afraid that you'd—"

He lifted one hand to touch her cheek. His gaze went over her, taking in the glory of her hair, unbound and falling about her shoulders.

"I was afraid, too," she admitted, drawing a deep, sustaining breath. "I was awake guarding Braxton all night, and I didn't know how much longer I could have kept going."

"You've been magnificent," he praised her. "I don't know another woman who could have done what you did. Look at what you accomplished—you rescued yourself and Braxton from the river, and you managed to keep him in custody while walking miles through the wilderness."

Alyssa was warmed by his praise. "I couldn't let him escape."

"Alyssa—" Rob said her name softly. His pleasure in finding her was so great that he had to let her know how he felt.

"What?" She looked up at him and saw the tender emotion in his eyes.

"I am so glad you're all right." He bent to her and gently kissed her.

It was a soft, sweet exchange that startled her. She'd always thought of Rob as a good friend, but she'd never thought of him in a romantic way. She accepted his kiss without protest, finding it pleasant and unthreatening—a far cry from Slade Braxton's exciting embrace.

Rob ended the kiss and, smiling, walked her over to his horse. He mounted first and then helped Alyssa climb up behind him.

"Put your arms around me," he told her. He enjoyed every minute of having her pressed tightly against him as they followed slowly after Braxton.

Their reunion with Hawkins and Brown was a happy one. Nash and Johnson merely glowered sullenly as Slade was brought back to join them.

"We were hoping you'd gotten away and had gone for help," Johnson told him.

"I never had the chance," he answered, refusing to say more.

"We're just going to have to sit tight and wait for the Kid to come for us," Nash put in.

"Yep, he'll be here soon," Johnson said. "He won't let them make it to Green River without trying something."

"I hope you're right," Slade replied. "Freedom would feel real good right now." And he meant it.

He stared down at the handcuffs that held him captive, and he wondered how he would have fared in getting the gun away from Alyssa had the sheriff not shown up when he had.

* * *

"We'll ride on another hour or two and then make camp for the night," Rob told her once they were back on the trail again. "That way we'll be assured of still making it into town tomorrow. It'll be late in the day, but we'll be there."

"I'm going to be really glad to see Green River. This three-day trip has turned into a real adventure." She was glad to be back riding Spartan again, and though she was still exhausted, at least now she could relax and let Rob run things.

"Adventure or nightmare? I'm not sure I'd care to live through it again."

"Me, either."

They shared a smile.

It was almost dark when they made camp. Alyssa ate hungrily, glad for some hot food. The memory of Slade's story kept bothering her, and she decided to broach the subject with Rob. She hoped he could give her insight to convince her that Slade was lying.

"Rob? There's something I want to ask you about," she told him when she found him standing a short distance away from the camp.

He looked up expectantly, glad that she'd sought him out. He'd been a bit concerned about being so bold as to kiss her earlier. He feared that he might have been too forward. "What is it?"

She glanced back toward the outlaws to make sure they were far enough away that they wouldn't be able to hear what she was saying. "While I was alone with Braxton—"

"He didn't hurt you, did he?" Rob immediately stiffened, ready to do battle to protect her honor. If

Slade Braxton had laid a hand on her, he'd kill him.

"No—no, nothing like that!" She touched his forearm to put him at ease. "It's just that he told me something about himself, and I wanted your opinion on it."

Rob frowned, worried. "What did he tell you?"

"He said he was a Pinkerton undercover agent and needed me to send a wire to their Denver office to verify his story. He said he told you, but that you didn't believe him. That you beat him up instead."

Rob spoke down to her as though she were a difficult child in need of careful explanations. "Alyssa, I told you what kind of man Braxton is. He's a liar, a thief and a murderer. For God's sake, he's the one who shot your father!"

She paled at his painful reminder. "I know! Don't you think I told myself all those things? I told him I didn't believe him, but—"

"But what?"

"What if he *is* telling the truth? What if he really is an operative? He said the agency had spent months creating his deadly background so the Dakota Kid would believe it was true and let him join up with the gang."

"What would you expect a man to say if he thought he was going to be hanged in another few days? Wouldn't you be trying to come up with the best story you could to save your own neck?"

"Yes, but Rob—"

He looked at her expectantly.

"Braxton is a big, strong man. It was just the two of us out there alone. He could have overpowered me at any time and taken the gun, and he didn't even try.''

''All that means is that he believed you knew how to use your gun and that you just might do it.''

''Do you honestly think so, or do you think there's a possibility that he might really be a Pinkerton?''

Rob couldn't believe that she was buying into Braxton's ridiculous story. ''Alyssa, there's only one truth you need to remember, and that is—Slade Braxton killed your father.''

She nodded grimly, annoyed with herself for having been tempted to believe anything the gunslinger had to say. She should have known better. Rob was right. ''You're right. I'm sorry.''

''There's nothing to be sorry about, Alyssa. I just hate to see you tortured this way.''

''Good night, Rob.''

''Good night, Alyssa.''

Alyssa returned to the campfire and bedded down for the night under the watchful eyes of Brown and Hawkins. They were relieved and happy that she'd returned to them unharmed. They were going to be very glad to reach Green River and turn over their prisoners to the sheriff there.

Sleep came quickly to Alyssa, and with her deep slumber came a dream.

Slade was walking toward her. His expression was serious. His gaze captured and held hers. He stopped before her, and then slowly, deliberately, he bent to kiss her.

Alyssa knew she should fight him. She wanted him

157

to go away. She hated him! He was a terrible, horrible man! But as his mouth sought hers, the gun she'd been holding slipped from her fingers. Instead of struggling to be free of him, she lifted her arms to loop them around his neck, aching to be closer to him. She accepted his embrace. She reveled in his kiss. His name echoed in her mind and her heart. Slade—

Alyssa jerked awake, breathing heavily, trembling from the force of the emotions that her wayward dream—or was it a nightmare?—had conjured up.

Shifting position, she stared across the fire to where Slade was sleeping. The miserable man slumbered on, completely unaware of the havoc he'd just wreaked upon her peace of mind. Furious at her traitorous dream, she tried to get comfortable again and put all thoughts of him from her. But sleep would not come.

Alyssa lay restless and awake, staring up at the stars—remembering. She wondered why Slade's kiss was the one that haunted her and not Rob's.

Chapter Eight

The Kid, Zeke and Red were ready and waiting. It seemed they'd been frustrated at every turn in their attempt to rescue their friends, but things had finally turned around late the day before. Once the rain had stopped, they'd managed to get ahead of the lawmen and were now in position to ambush them before they reached Green River.

"They should be showing up any time now," the Kid told his men, as they crouched low behind rocks above the trail.

Though there were only three of them, they figured they wouldn't have too much trouble getting rid of the lawmen. They would have the element of surprise on their side, not to mention position. The Kid smiled.

"Why are you smiling?" Red asked. He wondered how the Kid could be enjoying this.

"I was just thinking how I'm turning the tables on Emerson. He thought he was so smart surprising us like he did in the canyon, and now we're going to even the score."

"It will feel good, won't it?" Zeke agreed, though he couldn't have cared less about saving Slade's neck. He only cared about rescuing Johnson and Nash. He still regretted that the shot he'd taken at Slade after the bank robbery had missed and hit the old man.

"It's gonna feel real good." The Kid lifted his rifle to sight down the barrel and make sure he had a clear shot in the direction they'd be coming. "All we got to do is wait. Once they ride this way, it's going to be real simple—just make sure all your shots count."

"I wish we knew how many deputies were making the trip."

"I wish Emerson had ridden out with them, instead of staying back at the jail. I'd really enjoy being the one to put a bullet in him."

"You'll get your chance one of these days. Once we get the boys free, maybe we can pay another visit to Black Springs—and Sheriff Emerson," Red said.

"I like the way you think." The Kid's smile broadened at the thought of facing down the lawman who'd caused him such trouble.

They stayed alert and ready as they kept watch.

Over an hour passed before they heard the first sound of horses nearing. They tensed, expecting the riders from Black Springs to appear at any time.

"What the . . . !" the Kid muttered angrily as he discovered the horses they'd heard were coming from the other direction—from Green River.

He counted close to fifteen men and wondered who they were and where they were going. Just as they were almost out of range, he caught sight of the group from Black Springs coming down the trail.

"There they are. . . ." he told the others in a low voice, excitement surging through him. Now was the time. He was going to rescue his men.

"What are we going to do?" Red asked.

"Nothing for now. Just sit tight until we see what's going on."

They remained quiet, waiting for the deputies and their prisoners to draw near. The Kid grew furious, though, when the two groups met, talked for a minute, then joined forces and started back toward them and town.

"What the hell is going on?" he demanded, straining to try to identify the riders from town.

"Who are those men?" Zeke wondered.

As the group rode closer, they were finally able to make out the badges on the chests of the men from Green River.

"Damn! They must have been expecting trouble." The Kid swore violently under his breath as he realized that his chance for a successful ambush had been ruined. "And look! Emerson's with them! The bastard must have hightailed it out of town that same night right after the drunks raided the jail!"

"We can still take them!" Red encouraged him, seeing Nash, Johnson and Slade among the riders.

"Like hell, we can!" the Kid snarled. "There's close to twenty armed guards down there and only three of us. We could have taken just the men from

Black Springs, but there's no way we can shoot it out with this many.''

He stared down at the small army of deputies passing by, and his hatred and anger grew even more. As they drew ever closer, he could see that Nash had been wounded. There was a woman with them, too, and that really surprised him.

''Who's the woman?'' He looked over at Red.

''She must be the lady judge they had in Black Springs.''

''A lady judge?''

''Her name's Alyssa Mason. From the talk I heard in the bar, her daddy, the local justice of the peace, was the man we killed during the robbery. She was the one in town who knew the most about the law, so they picked her to fill in for him. She's the one who held the hearing and everything.''

''Ain't that something.'' He watched her pass by. ''A woman bound my men over for trial. I think I'm going to find a way to pay her back, too.''

Zeke looked back down at the female and suddenly began to swear.

''What is it?'' The Kid looked over at him, puzzled.

''That woman! I recognize her! The night before the robbery, when we were casing out the town, Slade went up to where a dance was going on. I know for a fact that he damn well danced with her that night!'' Zeke remembered that night far too well, and now that he'd found the woman again, he just might finish up what he'd wanted to do to her in the first place.

The Kid smiled at the news. ''I wonder what our

lady judge thought when she found out the man she'd
danced with was Slade Braxton?''

They found the thought most amusing.

"I bet Slade enjoyed it, too," the Kid remarked.

"What are we going to do?" Zeke wondered.

"Right now, there's nothing we can do, damn it!
Whatever we do, it'll have to be in Green River."

"I sure don't like trying a jailbreak in that town,"
Zeke said.

"You think I do? But we can't just stand by and
let them hang the boys!"

The Kid immediately began trying to come up with
a new plan to save his friends. There had to be a way,
and he was going to find it.

"It's good to see you," Rob said, grinning at Steve
Jones, the sheriff from Green River. "How'd you
know to come meet us?"

"Judge Banks told me what was going on. He
thought it would be a good idea to give you an escort
into town." He looked back at the three outlaws.

"I appreciate it."

"You did a good job."

Rob grunted, still a little disgusted with himself.
"If I'd gotten the Dakota Kid, too, I'd be feeling a
lot better right now."

"Yeah, but you got Braxton, not to mention Johnson and Nash, and the others that you shot during the
ambush. A lot of people are sleeping easier in the
territory these days now."

"That's my job."

163

"We'll do some celebrating tonight, what d'ya say?"

"That sounds real good. I could use a little relaxation. With the Kid still out there, I've been worried he might try something on our way in."

"That's what Judge Banks was thinking. We can't be too careful right now, but once we get them locked up nice and tight, it'll be fine."

"I'm looking forward to seeing them behind bars again."

Alyssa was riding farther back with Deputy Brown. She was feeling uneasy, and she wasn't sure why. They had a large force escorting the prisoners now, and only the Dakota Kid and two of his men were still running free. Yet even though everything seemed fine, for some reason she felt as if someone was watching them.

Looking around, Alyssa tried to see if there was anything unusual going on, but all seemed quiet. Finally, she told herself she was just tired and over-reacting. They were safe now that the other lawmen were there. Everything was fine.

Even as she told herself that, though, Alyssa found herself looking over at Slade. She tried to put all thoughts of him out of her mind, but his nearness was a constant reminder of the forbidden kiss he'd given her the night before. Even though she knew Slade was a liar, some of what he'd said to her had been true. She considered what it would cost her to send the telegram to Denver and wondered if she should. She was certain his story would turn out to be a lie.

Surely, there was no one there who could vouch for his being a Pinkerton. She was almost positive he had made the whole thing up. But could she live the rest of her life knowing that she hadn't at least tried to verify his story?

It was that question she had to answer before the trial ended.

The man appeared very much a dandy as he climbed down from the coach in front of the stage office in Black Springs. He was sporting spectacles, a derby hat and a tailored suit, and he looked completely out of place in this dusty Western town.

"Here's your bag!" the driver called as he tossed a small valise down to him.

The man caught it deftly, belying his outward appearance of being uncoordinated and ill at ease. "Which hotel is the best?"

"There's only one, Mr. Wiley, so I guess it's the best," the driver said drolly. "It's Becker's, one street over."

"Thanks."

Bag in hand, Ken Wiley, also known as Ken Richards, started off in that direction, taking careful note of the lay of the town as he went. The hotel was small, but that didn't matter to Ken. He hoped he wouldn't be there long enough to worry about his accommodations.

"You staying long, Mr. Wiley?" the lady at the desk asked after he'd signed the register.

"I don't rightly know, ma'am," he said in his most courtly manner.

"Well, welcome to town. If you need anything, just let me know. My name's Maisie. I'll be glad to help you with whatever you need."

What he needed and what she could give him were two very different things. "Thank you, ma'am. I appreciate it."

Ken went up to his room and stayed there only long enough to leave his bag and check his appearance. After all those hours on the stage, there was no telling how well his fancy-dude clothes had held up. A quick check in the mirror over the washstand told him he was still passable, so he was ready.

Glad that he'd finally reached Black Springs and hoping he wasn't too late, Ken quit the hotel and headed straight for the sheriff's office. In his guise as a reporter for the *Denver Daily News*, he hoped he could contact Slade when he found him. He could imagine the mood his operative was in right now, and Ken was certain that he didn't know the half of all that had happened.

The newspaper report he'd read on the ambush of the gang by the sheriff of Black Springs had been short and scant on details. All it had relayed was that Sheriff Emerson had trapped the Dakota Kid's gang and brought in Braxton, Johnson and Nash for trial. It had reported that some other members of the gang had been killed, but the names of the dead outlaws had not been given in the article.

Ken glanced through the window of the sheriff's office and was surprised to see a pretty young woman dressed in black talking to the man sitting behind the desk. Taking care to stay in character, he entered the jail and looked expectantly at the lawman.

"Are you Sheriff Emerson?" Ken asked eagerly.

Deputy Clemans and Emily both looked up at his interruption.

"No, I'm Deputy Clemans. Can I help you?"

Clemans was irritated by the man's intrusion. He thought Emily the loveliest woman within a hundred miles, and the fact that she'd come to the office to speak with him and to ask him if there'd been any news from her sister had bolstered his self-esteem quite a bit. He'd been enjoying having her all to himself for a little while, and now this man had shown up and ruined everything.

"My name's Ken Wiley. I'm a reporter with the *Denver Daily News*. I need to talk to your sheriff."

"That's not possible, I'm afraid."

"Why not?" he pressed.

"Because Sheriff Emerson is not in town right now."

"But I've come all the way from Denver to cover your big story about the Dakota Kid's gang."

"You're too late, Mr. Wiley," Emily said, insinuating herself into the conversation. She'd been intrigued by this man when he'd walked into the office. He looked very much like an Eastern gentleman, and they were a definite rarity in this town.

At her words, Ken knew a moment of fear. He turned toward her, the distress in his expression real. "I don't understand, ma'am."

"My name's Emily Mason. My sister, Alyssa, was the judge who—"

"You mean they've already been tried and hanged?

But I just heard about the arrests! I hurried straight here and promised my editor I'd wire him a follow-up story as soon as possible."

"No, no," she said. "They haven't been hanged yet."

"It's like Miss Emily was telling you," Clemans put in. "The preliminary hearing was held here. Judge Mason bound them over for trial, so right now Sheriff Emerson and some of the deputies are escorting the gang members to Green River."

Relief washed through Ken at the news. He pulled out a pad of paper from his vest pocket and a pencil, presumably to take notes, and looked at Emily.

"Well, thank heaven. This trial is going to be the story of the year, you know. I'm glad I didn't miss it. Can you give me details about the hearing? You say your sister was the judge? Isn't that highly unusual?"

"Not in Wyoming Territory," Emily told him. "We've had female justices of the peace for years now."

"I see." Ken pretended interest, although he really just wanted to get to the bottom of what had happened with the gang. "How did the hearing go?"

"It was very difficult for us. . . . Tragic really," Emily explained.

"How?" Ken wondered at her involvement.

"You see, my father was the justice of the peace in town and he was killed in the robbery that day. My sister had to preside over the hearing."

"That must have been very difficult for her—and for you."

"It was," Emily agreed.

"My sympathies on your loss."

"Why, thank you, Mr. Wiley."

"How did your sister hold up going through such an ordeal?"

"Alyssa is well versed in the law and she did not let her personal feelings interfere with her job."

"So there were no problems at the hearing?"

"No. None."

"It went fine," Clemans added. "We had eyewitnesses who saw the three of them rob the bank, and one man—Les Anderson—swore under oath that he saw Braxton kill John Mason."

"This Anderson says he saw everything and swears that Braxton was the one who killed them?" Ken repeated, shocked, and knowing immediately that for some reason Anderson had lied under oath.

"That's right."

Ken knew Slade was in big trouble. He was going to have some investigating of his own to do—and fast, from the looks of things. "Were there any other witnesses?"

"Yes." Clemans quickly told him of Tom York, Guy Shoaf and Chris Turner.

"When did Sheriff Emerson leave for Green River?"

"Three days ago. So they should be arriving there some time today."

"Do you know how soon they'll have the trial?"

"Last wire Sheriff Emerson got from Judge Banks, the judge told him they'd start the trial as soon as the witnesses were all in town."

"So they may already have left Black Springs?"

"I'm not sure. You can check around town and find out."

"I'll do that. And what about the Dakota Kid? Do you have any idea where he's hiding out?"

"If we did, I'd be there arresting him right now. Sheriff Emerson was real worried about him. He was afraid the Kid would come after them while they were on their way to Green River. It was rough enough as it was."

"Why? What happened?"

Clemans quickly told him about the escape attempt by the outlaws, and how the sheriff had showed up just in time to save the day and rescue Alyssa.

"Your sheriff sounds like quite a man."

"He is. They don't come much braver than Rob Emerson."

"It's hard to believe that he let a woman ride along on such a dangerous trip, though. What ever possessed him to take her with them?"

"My sister is not just any woman!" Emily found herself speaking up in Alyssa's defense. "She can handle herself and a gun, and as you can see, everything's turned out all right."

Not that Emily and her mother hadn't nearly swooned at the news Deputy Clemans had brought them about the thwarted escape attempt. It had taken Emily the rest of the day to calm her mother's fears about Alyssa's safety.

"Well, Deputy Clemans, I thank you for your time." Ken shook hands with him. "I appreciate all your help. Do you want to give me your full name so I can put you in my story?''

Clemans beamed. ''Vernon Clemans.''

''And you, Miss Mason? May I quote you?''

''Why, of course, Mr. Wiley.'' She smiled at him in her most coquettish fashion. ''In fact, if you'd like to speak more about my sister's involvement, I'd be happy to tell you whatever you'd like to know. Would you like to interview my mother, too?''

''Yes. I would. Perhaps you could direct me to the witnesses, too, so I could interview those who haven't left for the trial yet?''

''I'd be delighted. Deputy Clemans, I'll speak with you later. You'll let us know the minute you hear something?''

''I certainly will, Miss Emily.''

''Thanks.''

''Deputy.'' Ken nodded to Clemans and started from the office, leaving the lawman glowering behind him.

Ken held the door for Emily and waited as she moved past him. He watched her for a moment, enjoying the sweet scent of her perfume and the gentle sway of her hips. Then he followed her outside. He didn't know how much more useful information he could learn from her, but at least interviewing her and her mother would be a start. There wasn't much time. He had to work fast.

''Tell me, Mr. Wiley, how did you come to be a reporter?'' Emily asked as he walked beside her.

''It was a roundabout route,'' he answered quite honestly. There was no need for deception there. ''It

171

all came down to the fact that I like getting straight answers to my questions, and this seemed the best way.''

''I find reporters so . . . interesting,'' she said as she gazed up at him. She wondered how he would look without his glasses, and she decided he would look quite handsome. ''Have you been one for long?''

Ken grinned, not lying again as he answered, ''Not long enough. I enjoy my work. How else would I get to meet an interesting, lovely lady like you?''

Emily glowed at his compliment. ''I do believe I like you already, Mr. Wiley.''

They both laughed.

''We own the general store,'' she told him. ''Mother and I run it by ourselves since Alyssa's taken on being the justice of the peace.''

''It must be difficult for you, having lost your father.''

''It was terrible, and we still haven't recovered. I doubt Mother ever will. I just look forward to the day when that terrible Slade Braxton hangs for what he did.''

He heard the ferocity in her tone. ''Are you really positive that Braxton did it?''

''Les Anderson said so. He was there when it happened.''

''And you trust this Les Anderson?''

She was quiet for a moment, considering his words. ''I think so. Why do you ask?''

''It's my job to ask hard questions.''

''Isn't eyewitness testimony the best?''

''If the eyewitness is reliable and trustworthy, yes.

But if the man's just interested in seeing someone hang, then I question his motive and the truth of his sworn statements.''

''I see. Well, I don't think there's a problem there. Les is a very nice man.''

''Good,'' Ken said, but he didn't mean it. He already knew the man was a perjurer.

''Here we are,'' Emily said as they reached the store. ''Mother, I've brought someone along who wants to talk to you.''

Loretta looked up from where she'd been sorting through some newly received merchandise behind the counter. ''Oh?''

''This is Mr. Ken Wiley. He's a reporter from Denver, and he's here to write a story on how Rob brought in the Dakota Kid's gang.''

''It's nice to meet you, Mr. Wiley.'' She thought him a very nice-looking young man.

''Please, I'd feel much better if you both would call me Ken.''

Emily smiled brightly up at him and hoped he planned on being in town for a while. ''All right, Ken. And I'm Emily.''

He gazed down at her and couldn't help smiling back. She was pretty, just about the prettiest girl he'd seen in months. . . . The direction of his thoughts annoyed him. He had no time for a flirtation—innocent or otherwise. Slade's life was on the line.

''Is something wrong, Ken?'' she asked, seeing how serious his expression had become suddenly.

''No, not at all. I was just thinking of the outlaws and wondering about the trial.''

"We'll be closing the store in another half hour. Would you like to join us for dinner tonight?" Loretta suggested.

"I would like that very much, but, please, allow me to take you out."

"Why, thank you. We'd enjoy that," Emily answered quickly, thrilled that he wanted to spend more time with her. "Would you like me to tell you where you could find the other witnesses, and then you could meet us at our house about seven o'clock?"

"Yes, thank you."

"Actually, Emily, why don't you just go on with Ken, and then you can make all the introductions for him."

"Would you do that?" Ken asked.

"Why, I'd love to. We'll meet you at home in a little while, Mother."

"That'll be fine, dear."

Loretta was smiling as she watched them go. Emily certainly seemed taken with the handsome reporter. She found it interesting that a newspaper from as far away as Denver would be covering Sheriff Emerson's ambush of the Dakota Kid's gang, but she supposed the capture of a notorious gang was big news.

Her heart was heavy as she thought of how much the gang's actions had affected their lives. It was tragic that John had been killed. He'd been a good man, a fair and loving man. Tears threatened as she realized how much she missed him. Thank heaven, she had Alyssa and Emily to sustain her through these hard times.

For not the first time, Loretta thought about her

decision not to attend the trial. She wondered again if she should go to Green River to see justice done. It was good that Alyssa would be there, but somehow she felt the growing need to be there, too. She wanted to watch the men who'd taken so much from her pay for their terrible crimes. It seemed bloodthirsty, wanting revenge so badly, but her soul wouldn't know any peace until the ones responsible had been punished. When she got the opportunity later that day, Loretta decided she would speak to Emily again about attending the trial.

It was several hours later when Ken and Emily arrived at the house to meet Loretta.

"How did your interviews go?" Loretta asked him as he sat in their small parlor with them.

"Tom York, Les Anderson and Guy Shoaf have already left for Green River," he answered. "I did get the chance to speak with Chris Turner, though. He's not leaving until tomorrow."

"Did it go well?"

"Yes. From what I've learned, that must have been a terrible day for just about everyone in town."

"It was," Loretta agreed. "John was killed, and two men were wounded. The bank was robbed. . . . The Dakota Kid will have a lot to answer for when he goes to meet his maker."

"Let's just hope that's real soon," Ken said.

He'd despised the Kid and his men for a long time now, and the fact that they'd proven so hard to bring in had only increased his hatred of the killers. They had wreaked death and destruction wherever they'd

ridden. That had been why he'd sent Slade undercover to bring them down. Slade was his best operative. Now, though, it was beginning to look as if all
their hard work had been for nothing. The Dakota Kid
was still on the loose, and Slade was going to trial
for a murder he hadn't committed.

Ken had to get to Green River right away. He had
to prove to the law there that Slade really was an
agent and completely innocent of the charges against
him. It wouldn't be easy to do with Anderson testifying that he'd seen Slade gun down Emily's father.
It was going to take some good detective work on his
part to free him, but he would do it. His friend's very
life depended on it. He would take the ladies to dinner
as planned, then forget about getting any rest and ride
out tonight.

Emily was in heaven as Ken held her chair for her
at the restaurant.

"Thank you," she murmured politely as she sat
down.

He did the same for Loretta, then joined them at
the table.

"I can't tell you how long it's been since I was
privileged enough to dine with two such lovely ladies."

Loretta found him most charming and laughed at
his blarney. "Are you Irish, Ken?"

"On my mother's side," he returned with a smile.

"Somehow, I knew that, but your compliment is
very much appreciated."

They ordered, and, when the meal was served, they
found it to be delicious.

As they dined, Ken regaled Emily and Loretta with stories about his past experiences as a reporter. He wasn't lying. The stories he told them were true; the only false part was the role he played in them. He'd been doing the investigating he told them about as an agent, not as a reporter.

Emily was finding Ken even more attractive as she got to know him better. There was something about him—his sharp wit and his obvious keen intelligence—that drew her to him. He had been courtly and attentive during the short time they'd spent together, and she was most impressed with him. He seemed a gentleman through and through, a far cry from the usual rough-talking cowboys she put up with. She hoped she could find a way to get to know him better. If he left for Green River right away, she might never see him again, and feeling as she did about him, she just couldn't let that happen.

"So what will you do next?" she asked as they were finishing dessert.

"I need to find the other witnesses and interview them. Then I'll stay on for the trial and report back to Denver about its progress."

"So you'll be leaving Black Springs soon?"

"I have to, but I appreciate all your help and co-operation. This could have been very tedious today, and you were both a great help to me."

"It was our pleasure," Emily told him.

"Indeed, Ken, you are a charming young man," Loretta added. "I wish you luck with your reporting."

"The way things are going, I think I may need all

the luck I can get.'' He meant it, knowing the challenges he was going to face dealing with the law in Green River.

When they'd finished eating, Ken escorted them back home.

"Thank you for a delightful evening," he said as he saw them to the door.

"And thank you for dinner."

"My pleasure, ladies. Good night."

"Good night."

Ken looked at Emily, and in the moonlight, he thought she was even more beautiful than before—if that were possible. If he'd had more time, he would have found an excuse to stay and talk a little longer with her, but he didn't. Slade was counting on him. He turned to walk away once the ladies had started to go inside.

"Ken . . ." Emily softly called his name after her mother had disappeared indoors.

He paused to look back at her. "Is something wrong?"

"I was just wondering . . . Will I ever see you again?"

He stared at her, seeing an innocent beauty who could become important to him if he let her. Unfortunately, he didn't dare let that happen. This job was too dangerous. Just look at what had happened to Slade. He answered her honestly when he told her, "I don't know."

"Oh." Her disappointment sounded in her tone.

"Good night, Emily."

Ken turned and walked away. He did not look back.

Emily stayed where she was, watching him go. He was different from any man she'd ever met before, and she wished they'd had more time. She wished there was some way she could get to know more about him. Filled with disappointment, she went back inside.

"Is Ken gone?" Loretta asked.

"Yes. He just left."

"You liked him, didn't you?"

"Very much. He's so . . . different from the men I usually meet."

"Yes, dear. I think the term is 'civilized.' "

"I doubt I'll ever see him again," she said, sighing as she sat down beside her mother on the sofa.

Seeing how Emily was acting, Loretta knew that she'd decided to do the right thing. It had been a hard decision, but one she knew now she wouldn't regret.

"That may not necessarily be true."

"Why?"

"Because I've just decided that you and I should go to Green River and attend the trial."

"Are you sure, Mother? It won't be easy for you."

"I'm very sure. I want to see the men who killed your father get what's coming to them."

"We'll have to close the store—"

"It doesn't matter. This is more important. I want to be there with Alyssa. I want to know what's going on firsthand."

"Do you want to leave tomorrow?"

"Yes. The stage leaves about noon, I think."

"I'll make a sign for the store telling everybody we're going to be closed for a while, and I'll put it in the window tonight."

"While you take care of that, I'll start packing for both of us."

Ken went to the stable he'd seen earlier and made arrangements to buy a horse and the gear he needed for the trip. Returning to the hotel, he changed out of his city clothes and resumed his normal identity. He had no time to play the gentleman anymore. He had to get moving—fast. After strapping on his gunbelt, he checked out of the hotel and was ready to ride.

Ken put all thoughts of the beautiful Emily out of his mind as he headed out of town. Slade's situation was too serious to allow himself to be distracted. He was first and foremost an operative. His friend's life depended on his doing his job.

Emily had finished the sign and left the house by herself to put it in the window of the store. Ken had been in her thoughts since they'd parted, and she was considering stopping by the hotel on her way home to leave him a note. She wanted to tell him him that they would be making the trip to Green River on the stage the following day, too, and she was looking forward to seeing him again.

She put the sign in the window, relocked the shop and started off toward the hotel. It was then that she saw the lone rider coming down the street toward her. She was in the shadows, so she was pretty sure the man couldn't see her, yet she wondered who would be riding out of town this late at night.

As the rider moved past her, Emily realized with a start that it was Ken . . . but it took a moment for her to be certain for he looked so completely different from when she'd last seen him. The man on horseback bore little resemblance to her sophisticated dinner companion. Gone were his glasses and suit. Ken looked like a gunman now—tough, hard and dangerous.

Emily was tempted to call out to him, but held back. For some reason, he'd deliberately deceived her and everyone else in town. She wondered why he would do such a thing. Suddenly, it occurred to her that Ken might be one of the Kid's gang trying to get information about the witnesses and the prisoners. Unsure of what to do, she hurried home to tell her mother what she'd discovered.

Chapter Nine

Rob breathed a deep sigh of relief at the sound of the jail cell door slamming shut. They'd made it. They were in Green River, and the prisoners were behind bars.

"They're all yours," Rob said as he walked back out into the front office with Steve Jones.

"Good job, Rob," Jones complimented him.

"Now all we have to do is get through the trial."

"We will. Judge Banks should be on his way over to talk with you. I sent one of the deputies to get him."

Rob nodded. "We can't go to trial soon enough for me. The witnesses should all be here in another day or two, so we'll be ready."

"I'm glad things have worked out so smoothly. I

got a wire from Clemans, and he said Ursino is doing fine.''

"Good." Rob was relieved to know that his wounded deputy had made it safely back to town. "Any word on the Kid?"

"Nothing, damn it."

They shared a troubled look, knowing the outlaw was probably somewhere close by, just out of reach.

"I don't think he's going to let this go."

"I don't either, and I'm not sure where to start looking for him. If I send my deputies out on a wild-goose chase, that doesn't leave us with enough men to guard the jail, just in case he should try something here in town."

"Our best bet is to sit tight then."

Judge Banks entered the sheriff's office, and both lawmen were glad to see him. They discussed the plans for the trial and were relieved to learn that he intended to select the jury the next day and start the trial the day after. When he'd gone, Rob finally allowed himself to relax a bit.

"I think I need a drink," he said wearily.

"I'd love to go celebrate with you, but the way things are looking, I think I'd better stay here."

"We'll do our celebrating when the trial's over."

"You're on."

"If you need any extra help, just let me and the boys know."

"I will, don't worry."

They shook hands and Rob headed for the hotel. He wanted a bath and a shave and a drink, and not necessarily in that order. As he reached the small lobby, he saw Alyssa just starting upstairs to her room.

"Need any help with your bag?" he asked, going to join her.

"Oh . . . Rob." She smiled warmly at him as she saw him crossing the lobby toward her. "No, it's not that heavy. I'll be fine. How did it go at the jail?"

"Everything's all right. We can take it easy now. The hard part's over."

"For you maybe," she said softly, knowing how she was going to be affected by hearing the descriptions of her father's murder again during the testimony at the trial.

"Alyssa, if you need anything—anything at all— just let me know."

"Thank you, Rob."

"Have you thought about dinner yet tonight? Would you like to join me?" Rob invited her.

"I'd love to."

They agreed to meet in half an hour and then parted. Rob registered at the hotel and made a quick trip to the bath house to get cleaned up. He was taking Alyssa to dinner. He wanted to look his best, and he knew he certainly needed a shave.

A short time later, Rob was back in his room shaving off several days' growth of whiskers. He was tired, yet the excitement of knowing he was going to be dining with Alyssa renewed him. Since that terrible moment when he thought she'd died, he'd known the truth of his feelings. He loved her and wanted to marry her.

The fact that she hadn't been angry over his kiss that day and had accepted his invitation to dinner tonight all fueled Rob's hope that she might one day return his affection. It was too soon after her father's death to think about courting her right now. She needed more time to come to grips with all that had happened. But once she'd recovered from her terrible loss, he was going to let her know how he felt.

When Rob reached the lobby a short time later, Alyssa was waiting for him, wearing her mourning clothes once again. They decided to dine in the hotel's small dining room and ordered quickly.

"I think I could eat one of everything on the menu," Rob said when the waitress had left them.

"I know. Three days of trail food makes you appreciate a good meal."

"Are you saying you don't like my deputies' cooking?" he asked her with a grin.

She smiled back. "There's a definite reason they're deputies and not chefs."

The meal was delicious, and they both ate heartily. He told her what he'd learned from Judge Banks and the sheriff.

"So the trial is going to begin that soon," she said thoughtfully.

"Yes, and it's going to be wonderful to be done with it."

"I doubt it will ever be completely over for my family," she said solemnly.

"I understand, but there will be some solace in knowing the ones responsible have been punished."

"I just wish there was a way to bring my father

back.'' Though she kept up a good front most of the time, her father had been her best friend. She missed him terribly.

Rob couldn't help himself. He saw the distress in her eyes and reached out to cover her hand with his. ''If I could turn back the clock and make things different that day, I would, Alyssa.''

She lifted her pain-filled gaze to his and gave him a wavering smile. ''You're a good man, Rob. Father was very fond of you. You were the son he never had.''

''I wouldn't want to be his son,'' he remarked with a wry grin.

She frowned, puzzled by his words.

''That would make us brother and sister, and my feelings for you are anything but brotherly,'' he admitted.

''Oh.''

His confession surprised her. She enjoyed his company, and his kiss had been pleasant. He was a nice man, and she liked him. Maybe in the future she could think of him in a romantic way, but for now, her entire being was focused on the trial.

''I know this isn't the time, Alyssa. I just wanted you to know that I do care about you and I want you to be happy. If you need anything, anything at all while we're here, just let me know.''

''I appreciate your thoughtfulness.''

They ended the evening then. He escorted her to her room, but did not try to kiss her. Once he was sure she was safely inside and her door was locked, he decided it was time for the drink he'd promised himself.

Rob made his way to the saloon down the street. He knew Steve was still at the jail, keeping a close watch, so he bought a bottle of whiskey and went off to visit with his friend. They might not be able to celebrate in the saloon, but they could sure share a drink or two at the jail.

Alyssa stood at the window of her room, staring out into the night. The streets were dark and deserted, and the scene below matched her mood. She felt alone, lost and confused. She'd been tempted to speak to Rob about Slade again during dinner, but had decided against it. She trusted Rob's judgment, and he was convinced of the other man's guilt. If she brought the subject up again, he might think she didn't have any faith in him.

Knowing this, Alyssa didn't understand why Slade's request that she wire the Pinkerton office in Denver kept plaguing her. The trial would begin in one more day. There was still time enough for her to send the wire and get a response—if she dared to do it. As she fell asleep that night, her last thoughts were of her father and the troubling gunman who was accused of his murder.

When the sheriff entered the cell area to talk with the prisoners, Slade looked up.

"Well, gentlemen, it looks like things are going smoothly," Steve told them. "This morning, the jury was selected. The trial is scheduled to begin tomorrow.''

''Only if the Kid doesn't get here first,'' Johnson declared.

''We'll be ready for him if he does show up,'' Steve said confidently.

''I don't care how many men you've got, lawman, you still ain't good enough to stop the Kid,'' Nash bragged, still certain that the Kid would save them.

''We ain't worried,'' Johnson added as he lay back on his cot and folded his arms beneath his head.

Steve's expression hardened as he stared at the accused killers. ''I would be if I were you.''

With that, he turned and stalked back to his office.

''Johnson,'' Nash said in a low voice once the lawman had gone.

''Yeah, what?''

''You really think the Kid's gonna get here in time?''

''I know he will.''

Nash nodded. ''What's taking him so long? I figured he'd bust us out before we went on the trail.''

''So did I, but something must have happened. He ain't gonna desert us.''

''What do you think, Slade?'' Nash asked.

''The Kid won't give up,'' he answered.

If there was one thing Slade had come to understand about the outlaw leader during the time he'd ridden with him, it was that the Dakota Kid didn't like to lose. He was sure the gunslinger was just waiting for the right time to make the attempt to free his friends. Whatever he did would be fast and deadly, and Slade hoped the sheriff was ready for it.

"Damn right, he won't," Johnson repeated with emphasis.

"I just hope it's soon," Nash added.

Red sat in the Gold Dust Saloon, nursing a beer and listening to the talk going on around him. It seemed the whole town was excited about the trial that was to start the following morning. From the sound of things, the townsfolk didn't think it would last long. Red knew he should get word back to the Kid right away. He finished his drink and strolled from the bar.

It was early evening, but still light enough outside for him to be able to see the deputies who were stationed around town. There were several patrolling the streets and even more watching over things from rooftops.

Red swore silently to himself as he tried to judge their chances of rescuing their friends. It didn't look good. They would need some kind of big distraction to draw the guards away, if they were going to have any chance at all of saving the others. Mounting up, he rode for the campsite where Zeke and the Kid were waiting for him to give them the bad news.

Alyssa had passed a quiet day in Green River. Rob sought her out around midday to let her know that the jury had been picked and that four women were among those who would serve on it—Mary Ann Bovier, the local schoolteacher; Kaye Friese, the minister's wife; and two other ladies, Clover Noack and

Sandra Stetson. He'd also informed her that all the witnesses but one had arrived in town, and the other was on his way. She'd been pleased with the news and was as anxious as the lawmen for the proceedings to begin.

As the day passed, Alyssa tried to keep herself busy, but thoughts of Slade kept intruding. Once, she even found herself heading for her hotel room door, intent on going to the telegraph office to send his requested wire, but she stopped. She knew what kind of man he was. Why did she still harbor doubts?

Alyssa dined alone that evening and was looking forward to retiring early. She wanted to be well rested for the excitement of the coming day. She was just getting ready to undress when she heard a commotion outside in the street. Looking out her window, she saw people running wildly toward the far end of town.

''What's wrong?'' she called down to them.

''There's a big fire! They need all the help they can get!''

She leaned out a little farther and could see a terrible red glow in the sky. She saw the deputies who'd been posted around the jail running to help, too. It was then that she realized that all might not be exactly what it seemed. She looked back toward the jail and saw that there was only one guard left out front. The men who'd been posted to keep watch on top of the building next door had gone to help fight the fire.

Alyssa frowned as she went to her holster and got her gun. She was glad that her purse was large enough to hold it as she hid it in the handbag. Leaving her hotel room, she hurried downstairs.

The lobby was deserted, and the scene in the street outside was eerie. She could hear the shouts and warnings of the townspeople in the distance by the fire, but down the street near the jail, it was quiet—too quiet for her peace of mind.

She'd learned enough about the Dakota Kid during the last few weeks to put nothing past him. He was smart, devious and patient. It would be just like the outlaw leader to cause some major trouble somewhere else in town in order to create a diversion to give himself the time he needed to pull off a jailbreak.

Her sense of disquiet grew stronger. The guard she'd seen outside the jail just a few minutes before had now disappeared, too. Then she noticed that the jail door was ajar and felt relieved. No doubt the guard had stepped inside to report to the sheriff about what was going on.

Alyssa almost let herself relax, but then she saw that the shades had been drawn in the office, and she wondered . . . Moving quietly, she stayed in the shadows as she made her way along the wooden sidewalk to the front of the jail. As she drew near, she could hear voices coming from inside.

"Shoot the bastard!" a man demanded angrily.

"No. The gunfire will bring everybody back here at a run, and then we won't have time to get out of town. Just leave him locked up in the cell. Think how much explaining he's going to have to do when his deputies come back and find out that the Kid outsmarted them," Slade responded.

"He's a lawman! He deserves to die!" a different outlaw insisted.

"Zeke"—Slade sounded furious—"one gunshot will give the whole jailbreak away."

"Slade's right," Johnson told the other gang members. "Let's just get out of here while we got time. I've had enough of the inside of jail cells to last me a lifetime."

"I could always use my knife on him, just like I did the guards outside," Zeke said. "That won't make no noise."

"Quit wasting time! If he's locked up in the jail cell, he ain't going anywhere. Let's go. I want outta here!" Nash put in.

"Emerson's gonna love this when he finds out." Johnson was chuckling.

Alyssa had been holding her breath as she listened to the exchange. She backed away from the jail, desperately wondering what to do. It was then that she saw him waiting in the alley nearby—the Dakota Kid. She recognized him immediately from his wanted poster and a frisson of fear went down her spine. Knowing there was no time to waste, she pulled her gun out of her purse, ran out into the middle of the street and fired off several rounds.

"Jailbreak!"

Since his wounded leg was still giving him trouble, the Kid had decided to wait outside with the horses. At the sound of her shots and scream, though, he spurred his mount forward, intent on silencing her. There was too much at stake! He had to shut the screaming woman up!

Alyssa saw the Kid coming toward her and almost panicked. There was no time to run, so she did the only thing she could do. She took aim, fired at him and then ran for cover just as townspeople came running to her aid.

The Kid was shocked as his hat was shot from his head. At the sight of help on the way, he wheeled his horse around. Though he wanted to kill the woman who'd caused him so much trouble, he wanted to save his own skin more.

"Red! Zeke! Get the boys outta there now!"

The Kid galloped from the scene, leaving the rest of his gang to follow.

"Alyssa! Are you all right?" Rob called. He'd been helping with the fire when it had occurred to him that there might be trouble down at the jail. His hunch had proven right, and he was glad that he'd reached the sheriff's office when he had.

"Yes!" she called from where she'd taken refuge behind some barrels in front of the general store.

"Stay down!" he ordered, not wanting to worry about her safety while he was storming the jail.

Rob was ready as Red and Zeke came running out. The outlaws had their guns drawn and were firing, but only Zeke made it to his horse. Rob gunned Red down as he tried to make a run for it. Before Nash or Johnson could get outside, Brown and Hawkins showed up, along with several of Sheriff Jones's deputies.

"You in the jail! It's all over! We're coming in!"

They rushed the sheriff's office together, firing steadily, determined that their prisoners would not get away.

"Red's dead. The Kid and Zeke must be, too!"

Johnson shouted to Nash and Slade as he returned the deputies' fire.

Slade cursed the luck that left him trying to break out of jail with an army of deputies waiting outside to kill him. He'd hoped for a minute that they were going to make a clean get away, but now he knew it was over. He was trapped, looking as guilty as hell, and there wasn't a damned thing he could do about it.

Rob dodged bullets as he threw himself at the door, crashing against it with his shoulder. As he did, he lost his balance and fell into the room. His gun went flying from his grip. He looked up and found himself face to face with Braxton, who stood over him, gun in hand. Rob believed he was a dead man.

In that instant, Slade had the perfect opportunity to kill the lawman. Instead, he deliberately fired into the wall over his head just as Hawkins's and Brown's shots shattered the front windows and sent Nash and Johnson diving away from the flying glass.

Rob didn't have any time to waste wondering about Slade's missed shot. He went for his gun just as Hawkins and Brown charged into the room, their own guns ready.

"Throw your weapons down or you're dead men!" Rob ordered.

Nash and Johnson were furious. They had almost been free! But now, they faced certain death if they tried to shoot their way out. In complete disgust, they laid their guns down and raised their hands over their heads. Slade did the same.

It was over.

"Emerson! Is that you?" came Sheriff Jones's shout from the cell area.

"Yeah." Rob hurried to free his friend as the deputies took charge of the outlaws.

Slade said nothing as they were herded back into their cell. He only wondered how many hours he had left until the noose was tightened around his neck. He knew it wouldn't be long.

Once the shooting had stopped, Alyssa came out of hiding. She still had a bullet left in her gun, so she kept the weapon in hand as she slowly approached the jail. She had seen Rob rush into the office first. After all that gunfire, she feared that he might have been hurt in some way.

"Rob?" she called as she neared the doorway.

"It's safe. You can come in." Hawkins stepped into the doorway to speak with her.

"Is Rob all right?" She hurried inside, wanting to make sure he was unharmed.

"I'm fine," Rob told her.

Relieved that he hadn't been shot, she went straight to the cell area, where he stood watching the prisoners being locked up. Almost without thought, Rob's arm went around her shoulders, and he gave her a warm hug.

"Do you realize what you did?" he asked, looking down at her with admiration in his gaze.

"What did she do?" Hawkins asked.

"She was the one who figured out what was happening. If it hadn't been for her shots, I wouldn't have gotten here in time. That was very brave of you."

Alyssa blushed at his praise. "I heard all the shouting about the fire, but it was so big that I just had this feeling that maybe the Kid had had a hand in it.''

"And you were right," Brown agreed. "They would have gotten clean away if it hadn't been for you."

"She even took a shot at the Kid," Rob said.

"But I missed," she emphasized. "I only hit his hat."

"You did?" Brown and Hawkins were shocked.

"If she'd gotten a better a shot at him, she would have put him six feet under. As it was, she sent him hightailing out of town and gave us time to get here to help."

They started back into the office. Alyssa just happened to glance toward the three gunmen as she went. She shivered at the looks of hatred both Nash and Johnson were sending her way. She was very glad that there were jail cell bars between them.

Just before Alyssa disappeared out of the cell area with Rob, his arm still protectively around her shoulders, she glanced at Slade and found him watching her. She saw no hatred in his regard. His expression was inscrutable as he watched her walk out with the other man.

"I can't thank you enough," Sheriff Jones said as they joined him in his office after closing the door to the cell area behind them.

"You're lucky you're still alive," Rob told him. "They're a deadly bunch."

"They could have killed me and been done with it. I don't know why they didn't. God knows, they murdered the two guards I had posted outside." The pain of losing his two friends was evident in his voice.

Alyssa remembered the outlaws' conversation. "I heard Slade Braxton saying they shouldn't kill you because a shot would give the jailbreak away."

"I was just lucky that they didn't have a lot of time. Whoever killed my men used a knife on them, and they could have done the same to me."

"I'm so sorry," Alyssa said.

"So am I," he responded. "They were good men."

"It was probably Zeke Malone. He's a cold one, who's known for being real proficient with a knife," Rob told them. "It's small consolation, but we did get Red Parsons during the shootout."

"Good," Jones said savagely, "that means there's one less murderer on the loose. Who's left of the gang now? Just the Kid and Zeke Parsons?"

"It looks that way."

He nodded, pleased. "Good. We may be taking them down slowly, but ultimately, we're going to win this. They are not going to escape us."

The two lawmen shared a look. They both hated the Kid and wouldn't rest until he'd been brought in to face justice.

"I'm just sorry I missed him tonight. I was so close—" Rob regretted not figuring out what was going on more quickly.

"His day's coming—one way or the other."

"Will you need any more help tonight?"

"I will, Rob. Thanks. We're stretched pretty thin, the way things are."

"Just give me time to escort Alyssa to her room, and then I'll come back and stand guard with you."

"We'll stay and help, too," Hawkins and Brown volunteered.

Jones appreciated the other lawmen's aid. He turned to Alyssa as they prepared to leave.

"Miss Mason, I can't thank you enough," he said. "If it hadn't been for you, things would have turned out quite differently tonight."

"I'm just glad I could help."

"You did. You foiled their whole escape attempt. Without you, they would have been long gone by now."

"Your father would be proud of what you did," Rob complimented her. "Maybe you should forget about being a judge and hire on as a deputy. We're the first territory to have female jurors and justices of the peace—why not deputies?" He found the thought of working more closely with her quite appealing.

"I think I'll stay right where I am. I like using the gavel to bring order much better than I like using my gun."

With that, she said good night to Sheriff Jones and the others, and Rob walked her back to her hotel room.

"Since we've been together on this trip, you've been in one adventure after another," Rob remarked as they reached the door to her room. "I think you're due for some peace and quiet pretty soon."

"I hope so. I think I've had enough excitement to last me quite a while."

There was an awkward pause in their conversation as she turned to unlock her door.

"Well, good night, Rob."

"Good night, Alyssa," he said softly.

She looked so beautiful that he was tempted to kiss her, but he controlled the urge. He waited until she was safely inside; then he returned to the sheriff's office. As he passed the long hours of the night with Jones, though, Alyssa stayed in his thoughts.

Chapter Ten

Alyssa awoke several hours before dawn and was unable to get back to sleep. She rose and, without lighting a lamp, drew a chair to the window to wait and watch for the sunrise.

Today was the day. Today, the trial would begin.

She had expected to be excited that the outlaws were finally being brought to justice, but she only felt numb . . . especially after last night. The memory of how Slade had argued with the other men and saved the sheriff's life stayed with her. And again, she was haunted by the possibility that he was not the killer he seemed to be.

Staring out into the pre-dawn darkness, Alyssa debated with herself about what to do. She knew how Rob felt about Slade's guilt, yet her own doubts could not be erased. They had been troubling before, and now, after listening to his argument with the other killers last night, they were even more so. Alyssa remembered, too, the way Slade had looked at her as she left the cell area with Rob, and she wondered . . .

An hour later, when the eastern sky had brightened, Alyssa dressed and prepared for the eventful day ahead. She would be in court from the opening moment, but first, she had a stop to make—at the telegraph office.

Judge Banks was a strictly by-the-book, nononsense judge. He called the court to order right on schedule and the trial was under way. Guards were posted inside and outside the courtroom. They were taking no chances with security after what the Kid had tried with the fire the night before.

The jury was made up of four women and eight men. They paid close attention to all the evidence presented and seemed, to those watching them, intelligent and rational. Alyssa was pleased with the twelve selected.

The hours passed quickly. The witnesses who'd testified before her court were all present and more than willing to cooperate. One by one, they were called and took the oath to tell nothing but the truth, so help them God.

When court was adjourned for lunch, Alyssa hurried back to the telegraph office.

"Did you get an answer from Denver yet?" she asked Jonas Howard, the telegraph operator.

"No, ma'am. Not a word." At her look of disappointment, he quickly went on, "But if anything comes in this afternoon, I'll bring it to you over at the courthouse.''

''That would be wonderful. Thank you.''

As she returned to the proceedings, she couldn't help wondering what was taking the Pinkerton office so long to respond to her query. If Slade Braxton was an agent, wouldn't they want to save him from hanging? And if he wasn't, wouldn't they want to notify her of that, too?

The thought that Slade was nothing more than a liar and a killer seared her soul as she listened to the rest of the day's testimony. Judging from the remarks she overheard from those attending the trial, there seemed little doubt in anyone's mind that Slade was her father's murderer. The following day, Les Anderson would be testifying. He was the witness who'd sworn under oath that Slade was the man. But if Slade was an amoral killer, why had he been so insistent that the outlaws not gun down the sheriff during the jailbreak?

Alyssa had no answer, and so she waited—for news from Denver and for the final jury verdict.

It was sundown when Ken rode into Green River. He was hot, tired and exhausted, but he didn't care. The good news was he'd made it. He reined in before the hotel and, after checking in and washing up a bit, he went looking for the nearest saloon. He knew it would be the best place to learn the latest information on what was happening with the trial.

''Give me a beer,'' he ordered.

The barkeep quickly set the glass before him. Ken

paid him and took a deep drink of the brew.

"You staying in town long?" the bartender asked, trying to make conversation. It had been a slow night for business, and he was glad to see a new face.

"For a few days," Ken answered.

"Where are you from?"

"Denver, originally, but now I move around a lot. What's going on in Green River? Anything exciting?"

The bartender was wiping down the bar as he replied, "Last couple of days have been the most excitement we've had in years. We're holding a trial for some of the Dakota Kid's gang."

"The Dakota Kid? Is he still alive?"

"Hell, yes, and causing trouble every chance he gets. He set a fire last night, and while we were fighting to put it out, he tried to break his boys out of jail."

"Did he get away with it?" Ken stiffened, fearing Slade was gone.

"No. Someone saw them and yelled a warning. There was a shoot-out. Two guards were killed. The Kid escaped and so did one of his men. But Red Parsons was gunned down and we've still got the three prisoners we had originally. They never made it out of the jail."

Ken nodded. "You were lucky."

"I'll say. The Kid probably would just as soon have shot everybody in town. The sheriff was lucky, too. They just locked him up in a cell while they were trying to make the escape. It's pretty frightening. No one knows when—or if—the Kid will try again, but we don't put anything past him.''

"You've had some excitement, all right, but that kind of excitement you don't need.''

"The deputies who were killed were good men. The town's going to miss them. The trial started up today, so maybe we'll see justice done real soon. It shouldn't take long. There weren't that many witnesses who needed to testify.''

"So, you think there'll be a hanging?''

"Oh, yeah—especially after the fire. People are out for blood now. Not that they weren't before, what with Judge Mason getting shot down in cold blood and all in Black Springs, but now they've killed some of our own.''

Ken downed the rest of his beer. He'd learned all he needed to know. "Thanks for the beer.''

"There's more where that came from. Come on back whenever you're thirsty.''

Ken left the saloon and went back to his room. He had no time to waste. He'd already missed one day of the trial, and he could just imagine Slade's mood. Ken would have smiled at the thought, had the situation not been so serious. He knew what he had to do, and he would do it—now. After getting his saddlebags, he headed for the jail.

Pete Riley was standing guard at the sheriff's office, and he eyed the stranger approaching suspiciously. The man was wearing a side arm, so Riley leveled his rifle at him.

"What are you doing here?''

"My name's Ken Richards, and I've come to speak with Sheriff Jones."

"What about?"

"That's between me and the sheriff," Ken answered tightly. "If you'd like, I'll leave my gun with you."

"All right, and what's in your saddlebags?"

"You can look through them, too, if you'd like. I heard from the barkeep about your trouble last night."

"Maybe the barkeep talks too much," Riley said tersely as he took Ken's weapon and sifted through the papers he was carrying. "Go on in."

He opened the door for him.

"Sheriff, there's someone here who wants to see you," Riley announced.

He went back to standing guard, keeping careful watch. He had no intention of ending up dead like his two friends.

Steve Jones looked up at the tall man who came to stand before his desk. "What can I do for you, stranger?"

Ken glanced toward the cell area and saw that the door was closed. Satisfied that they were talking in private, he explained, "My name is Ken Richards. I'm a Pinkerton supervisor out of the Denver office. Slade Braxton is one of our operatives who's been working undercover with the Dakota Kid's gang for months now."

Jones was stunned. "No."

Ken had expected just such resistance. He produced all the necessary identification papers to convince the shocked lawman of the truth.

Jones studied them, reading each document carefully, recognizing the signature of the territorial governor vouching for Braxton's true identity as an operative. He shook his head in disbelief.

"But there are witnesses who saw him rob the bank and kill John Mason in Black Springs. Les Anderson is due to testify tomorrow that he saw Braxton shoot him down."

"The man is lying . . . or should I say, mistaken. Our agency went to great lengths to create the myth of Slade Braxton's deadly reputation. Slade does know how to handle himself and a gun, but I can tell you right now, there is no way Slade Braxton shot anyone down in cold blood."

"Wait a minute—" Jones was troubled by this newly revealed information. He got up and called for Riley. "I want you to go find Rob Emerson. I need to see him—now."

Riley hurried off.

"Mr. Richards, why don't you have a seat for a moment. I just sent one of my men to find the sheriff from Black Springs. I want him in on this."

Ken did as he'd suggested, and they waited in tense silence. Rob came rushing to the office within ten minutes.

"I appreciate your coming so quickly," Jones told him. "Mr. Richards here has some very interesting information to share with us."

"Richards?" The name sounded vaguely familiar to Rob. Hoping the papers Jones handed him would jog his memory, he began reading. He was in shock when he looked back up at Ken. "It was true."

"You knew?"

"Braxton tried to tell me back in Black Springs, but—"

"But his cover was so good you didn't believe him," Ken finished for him.

"Exactly. All the posters say he's wanted for murder in Colorado and Texas," Rob said, defending his decision to ignore Slade's claims.

Ken smiled tightly. "We do a good job when we send our men undercover. We take no chances with their lives and carefully document everything. Obviously, all of Slade's hard work and ours was convincing. I'm just glad I got here in time. If you still have any doubts, I'm sure a wire to the territorial governor will put your minds at ease."

"It's all right. You won't have to do that," Rob said, turning to Jones. "We can trust him."

"You're sure?"

"There was a time during the break-out attempt when Braxton could have killed me and didn't. I had just crashed through the door, and I'd accidentally dropped my gun. Braxton was standing over me. He could have shot me dead, but instead he fired into the wall above my head. I should have realized the truth then."

"Everything was happening so fast, you couldn't have known," Jones reassured him.

"There was a lot of shooting going on. I thought maybe he'd been distracted by the other deputies rushing in. But now, I know why—he deliberately missed."

"Slade's one of our best agents. He's a good man.

That's why I'm certain he's not the man who killed Judge Mason. Your witness is mistaken on that account.''

"How do you want to handle this?" Jones asked. "Should I talk to Judge Banks and make arrangements to let him go?"

"No. I have an idea I'd like to share with you. Since the Kid is still on the run, our job's not finished.''

"Do you want to fake an escape and let him get away?" Jones suggested.

"No. You're sure they're going to be convicted, aren't you? And the trial's almost over?''

"Yes," both men answered.

"Then I want you to go through with the executions. I want you to hang Slade with the other two outlaws.''

The following morning found guards posted outside the courthouse once again. Judge Banks and Sheriff Jones had no intention of letting anything going wrong.

Slade was tense as he was led into court with Nash and Johnson. He knew the trial would end today, and the verdict was not going to be in his favor. There was a hunger for blood in the people of this town, and the blood they wanted was his.

He remembered how one of the deputies had taunted them to start counting what was left of their lives in days, but now he knew it was down to hours.

Slade had seen no sign of Ken, and it was obvious that no one had wired the Denver office. He was, as

Thrill to the most sensual, adventure-filled Historical Romances on the market today...

FROM ▥ LEISURE BOOKS

As a home subscriber to Leisure Romance Book Club, you'll enjoy the best in today's BRAND-NEW Historical Romance fiction. For over twenty-five years, Leisure Books has brought you the award-winning, high-quality authors you know and love to read. Each Leisure Historical Romance will sweep you away to a world of high adventure...and intimate romance. Discover for yourself all the passion and excitement millions of readers thrill to each and every month.

Save $5.⁰⁰ Each Time You Buy!

Each month, the Leisure Romance Book Club brings you four brand-new titles from Leisure Books, America's foremost publisher of Historical Romances. EACH PACKAGE WILL SAVE YOU $5.00 FROM THE BOOKSTORE PRICE! And you'll never miss a new title with our convenient home delivery service.

Here's how we do it. Each package will carry a FREE 10-DAY EXAMINATION privilege. At the end of that time, if you decide to keep your books, simply pay the low invoice price of $16.96, no shipping or handling charges added. HOME DELIVERY IS ALWAYS FREE. With today's top Historical Romance novels selling for $5.99 and higher, our price SAVES YOU $5.00 with each shipment.

AND YOUR FIRST FOUR-BOOK SHIPMENT IS TOTALLY FREE!

IT'S A BARGAIN YOU CAN'T BEAT! A Super $21.96 Value!

▥ *LEISURE BOOKS* A Division of Dorchester Publishing Co., Inc.

GET YOUR 4 FREE BOOKS
NOW — A $21.96 Value!

*Mail the Free Book
Certificate
Today!*

Get Four Books Totally FREE — A $21.96 Value!

▼ Tear Here and Mail Your FREE Book Card Today! ▼

PLEASE RUSH
MY FOUR FREE
BOOKS TO ME
RIGHT AWAY!

Leisure Romance Book Club
P.O. Box 6613
Edison, NJ 08818-6613

AFFIX
STAMP
HERE

far as anyone in Green River was concerned, a wanted man, and it looked as though he was going to hang for terrible deeds he hadn't done.

The murmur of voices grew louder as they were ushered inside, and Slade let his gaze sweep the room. He saw Alyssa sitting in the same place she had occupied yesterday. The proud way she held herself touched him. He could imagine the turmoil she was feeling, sitting through the trial. It couldn't be easy for her. He wanted the chance to talk to her again, to let her know he was not a killer, but he would never have another opportunity. He was going to hang, and he would go to his death with her believing that he'd murdered her father.

His mood was dark. His hopes destroyed. His life was over.

And then he noticed the man sitting next to Alyssa.

Slade's spirits soared!

Ken was there!

It took all of Slade's considerable willpower not to reveal his relief. Instead, he scowled blackly at the people who were staring at him as he was led to his seat in the front of the courtroom.

Alyssa had taken the same seat as she had the day before, but today a strange man sat down near her. She had never seen him before and wondered who he was. He appeared to be a gentleman, for he was wearing a suit and was well groomed. He seemed very interested in all that was going on.

Alyssa was distracted from her curiosity about the stranger as Slade was brought into court. She battled with herself not to look his way, but once he'd passed by, she let her gaze linger on him as he walked up the aisle under armed guard.

Judge Banks brought the court to order, and the first witness of the day was called. The judge kept things moving along at a deliberate pace. He wanted the trial over as soon as possible.

The court was dismissed at noon for the midday break. Alyssa had intended to speak with the stranger beside her, but he rose and left the building quickly before she had the chance.

She left the courthouse and was making her way to the hotel restaurant when she heard someone call her name. She turned to see her sister and her mother hurrying toward her. Alyssa was overjoyed.

"You came!" she said as she was swept into her mother's warm embrace.

"We couldn't let you go through this all alone," Loretta told her as she hugged her close. "How are you?"

"I'm fine. When did you get here?"

"We came in on the stage about an hour ago. We've already checked into the hotel and just started looking for you. How's the trial going?"

"The judge dismissed everyone for lunch. Testimony should resume at about two o'clock."

"We may as well have something to eat, then," Loretta said. "And you can tell us everything that's happened so far."

They went on to the restaurant and ordered a light meal. As they began to eat, Emily brought up the news they'd heard about her trip to Green River with Rob.

"Deputy Clemans told us about the trouble you had and how Deputy Ursino was wounded."

"I'm so thankful you weren't injured by those terrible men," her mother put in. She had been horrified when the deputy had described the thwarted escape attempt and how Rob's timely arrival had saved the day. "Thank heaven Rob showed up when he did."

"I'll say, and there was even more excitement after Clemans and Ursino left to go back to Black Springs."

"There was?" Loretta looked worried. "What happened?"

She told them about the rainstorm and being swept away with Slade.

"Dear Lord, you could have been killed! And to be alone with that *man* in the wilds . . . How did you ever manage?" Loretta had always known that Alyssa was a strong woman, but she'd never imagined she could handle anything that terrifying.

"It wasn't easy," she answered, and was quiet for a minute as she remembered the danger she'd faced from the water—and from Slade.

"What was it like to be all alone with him?" Emily asked, curious about the outlaw.

"He was handcuffed. Otherwise things might have turned out very differently. But as dangerous as Slade is, I never felt threatened by him." As she spoke, she wondered if that was a lie. The memory of his kiss was very threatening—to her peace of mind.

"And you managed to find your way safely back to Rob?"

"I had my gun, so I was in control. Once daylight came and the rain stopped, we started out on foot and headed toward town. Rob had been looking for us, too. I don't know how much longer I could have kept it up, especially since I hadn't slept for so long."

Her mother patted her hand as she smiled gently at her. "You are so brave, Alyssa."

"I hardly think I'm brave," she denied. "I just seem to be in the wrong place at the wrong time lately. The Kid tried to break his men out of jail the other night, and I was the one who discovered it."

Loretta went pale at this news. "I don't understand."

Alyssa quickly explained to them how the Kid had started the fire and then tried to free his men.

"It's hard to believe all this has happened," her mother said, dazed at the danger Alyssa had faced and survived. "There aren't many women who could handle so much excitement."

"Why, thank you, Mother."

"For what?"

"I thought you were going to lecture me on how I shouldn't have made the trip here." She managed a grin.

"Would there be any point?"

"No. It was important that I be here."

"Then we'll just be glad that everything turned out all right in the end."

Alyssa was relieved that her mother had responded so calmly to her harrowing tales. "It's almost time for the trial to resume. We ought to be getting back.''

They left the restaurant and returned to the courtroom. They took their seats. Alyssa wondered where the stranger who'd sat by her earlier had gone, but she could see no sign of him. She had no time to worry about it, though, as the three outlaws were already being led back into the room. She felt her mother tense beside her and reached over to take her hand in a reassuring grip.

Judge Banks called court back into session, and the trial continued. Les Anderson took the stand to give his damning testimony against Slade Braxton.

Alyssa found her gaze drifting to Slade as Anderson was sworn in. She noticed how Slade held himself rigidly as the witness testified under oath that he'd positively seen Slade kill her father. Other than tensing, Slade betrayed no outward sign of emotion. His expression remained inscrutable. Only once did he glance her way, as if sensing her regard upon him. Their gazes met for an instant, but she could read no emotion there—no regret, no sorrow.

As Anderson's testimony continued, Alyssa forced herself to look away from Slade. She watched the jury instead, trying to read their reactions to Anderson's description of the robbery and shooting. He embroidered his testimony with even more detail than he'd used at her hearing and evoked looks of disgust and loathing from the women on the jury.

Her mother's grip on her hand tightened, and Alyssa knew it was torturing her to hear her husband's murder spoken of with such brutal frankness again. She was sure from the way things were going that all three men would be convicted and sentenced to hang.

It was late afternoon when the last witness finished his testimony and the case went to the jury. Alyssa, Loretta and Emily rose and started from the courthouse. They stopped outside, weary and deeply worried about the outcome.

"Are you all right?" Rob asked as he joined them.

"We're fine," Alyssa answered.

"It's just difficult hearing it all again," Loretta told him, smiling gently at his concern. "There will be no rest for us, though, until they're convicted."

"I hope the jury won't be out too long," he said, trying to reassure her.

"If they do convict them and sentence them to hang, when would the hangings be carried out?" Emily asked.

"As soon as possible, probably," Rob answered. "Most everybody wants the three of them to pay for all the trouble they've caused both here and in Black Springs."

"Will you let us know when they reach a verdict?"

"I'll send word to you the minute I know something. If you need me for anything, I'll be down at the jail. I told Steve Jones I'd help him keep watch again tonight."

As Rob left them, Emily caught sight of Ken Wiley mingling with the crowd. She was stunned. He was once again dressed as a gentleman. Any trace of the dangerous-looking man she'd seen ride out of Black Springs several nights before was gone. She wondered how he could so completely change his identity, but dismissed her concerns about him now as ridiculous. The Ken standing nearby was the same Ken she'd met and been intrigued by. Probably, he had just dressed that other way because he'd been riding across country at night. She rationalized that he could hardly have worn his suit on the trip since he was in a hurry and going by horseback.

"Ken . . . ?"

He looked up at her and smiled as he walked straight to her.

"I didn't know you were coming to Green River for the trial. I thought you'd decided to stay behind in Black Springs."

His straightforward approach put her even more at ease. It was obvious he had nothing to hide. Emily realized how silly her imaginings had been.

"You'd already left town when we decided to go ahead and make the trip. Mother and I just arrived on the stage this morning. Let me introduce you to my sister," Emily said. "Alyssa, this is Ken Wiley. He's a reporter for the *Denver Daily News*."

"It's a pleasure to meet you," Ken said. "Emily and your mother told me all about you when we first met in Black Springs."

"So, you're a reporter," Alyssa said. "You sat next to me this morning, and I noticed you were taking notes."

"Yes, I have to file my stories as quickly as I can. Members of the Dakota Kid's gang being brought in is big news. In fact, I'm on my way to the jail right now. Sheriff Jones has agreed to let me interview them."

"Why would you want to?" Emily asked, surprised.

"I want to understand what motivates these men. What makes them want to kill and rob? They're deadly predators, and I want to reveal that part of the story to my readers."

"It sounds so . . . grisly."

"But it's the truth of who they are. Perhaps I could take you ladies to dinner tonight, and we could speak of other, more pleasant things?" he invited them.

"We'd enjoy that," Emily answered quickly.

They made plans to meet in the hotel dining room at seven P.M. and then parted company.

"He's a nice man," Loretta observed.

"Isn't he? I have to tell you, though, the other night he had me worried."

Alyssa slanted her a curious look. "The other night? What happened the other night?"

"Nothing really," Emily stated with just the right propriety. "It was just that it was late when I went down to put a sign in the store window that we would be closed for a few days, and I saw Ken riding out of town. He looked—different."

"What does 'different' mean?" her sister asked.

"Well, he looked downright dangerous . . . almost like a gunslinger. For a while, I thought he might have been a member of the Kid's gang in town trying to get information to help break the gang members out of jail."

"I think your imagination was running away with you."

"It was. Now that I've seen him here again, I know

he really is who he says he is. I'm sure he only dressed that way to make the ride to town. He could hardly wear his suit and tie across country.''

As they continued on their way back to their hotel, Alyssa fell silent. For all that she was quiet, though, her thoughts were deep and troubled. The trial was essentially over. All that remained was for the jury to bring in a verdict. That could come at any time now— and then Slade Braxton would hang.

Pain tore at Alyssa as she faced reality. She tried to hide from it, but she couldn't. There had been no response to her telegram. She had no real proof that Braxton was the Pinkerton agent he claimed to be. What he had told her had been a lie—just as Rob had insisted it was from the beginning.

Alyssa could deny the truth no longer.

Slade Braxton was a killer.

''Alyssa, what's wrong?'' Emily asked, catching a glimpse of her sister's dark, troubled expression.

''I was just thinking about Braxton and the testimony against him today.''

''No wonder you're looking so angry,'' her sister said, hating the man with all her heart.

''That certainly explains it,'' her mother agreed.

''Yes, it certainly does.''

But no matter what her mother and sister thought, Alyssa's personal torment had nothing to do with hating Slade Braxton.

Chapter Eleven

Slade looked up as the door to the sheriff's office opened. He was hard pressed not to smile at the sight of Ken following the lawman into the cell area. He knew better than to think they were coming to let him out, so he was ready to play along with whatever scheme his friend had devised.

"Gentlemen," Sheriff Jones said as he stopped before them in their cell. "This is Mr. Ken Wiley, a reporter from the *Denver Daily News*. He wants to interview you, and I told him you would be very cooperative."

Nash and Johnson got up from their cots and came to stand closer to the "newspaperman."

"You're here lookin' for a story? Well, we got one for you, don't we, Nash?" Johnson said.

"Did the sheriff tell you how the Kid outsmarted

him the other night? We had your lawman there all locked up in this very jail cell, nice and tight like. He looked real good behind bars, too,'' Nash went on.

"We would have been long gone, too, if it hadn't been for that damned lady justice of the peace showing up when she did," Johnson added.

"It seems to me the Kid can't be very smart, if one woman could ruin his entire plan." Ken taunted them deliberately as he looked around at the small facility. "If he can't bust you out of this jail, how good is he?"

"There ain't nobody as good as the Dakota Kid," Nash said in defense of his leader.

"Well, it is true that he is free—and you're not. So I guess that does make him a lot smarter than you," Ken said with emphasis, wanting to see if he could make them angry enough to reveal information about the Kid that he could use to his advantage.

"We haven't been convicted or hanged yet," Slade countered as he got up from his cot and came to eye Ken up close. "The jury's still deliberating."

"But the talk on the street says you're guilty as sin, Braxton. There were witnesses at the trial who testified that they saw you do it. The townsfolk are convinced—"

Slade shrugged expressively as his gaze locked knowingly with Ken's. "I'm innocent until proven guilty."

Ken said flatly, "You're going to hang—all of you."

"No, we ain't!" Johnson declared. "The Kid's

somewhere close. The minute he gets the chance, we'll be free again.''

"But if you're innocent like Braxton says you are, why would you need the Dakota Kid to set you free? The jury should find that you're not guilty and let you go.''

"You write that in your column, Mr. Newspaper-man. You tell the people that we're innocent and being wrongly tried. And make sure you spell our names right, too,'' Nash sneered.

"Yeah, I'd hate like hell to have my name spelled wrong in a big-city paper like yours,'' Johnson agreed.

Ken turned back to Slade. "How does it feel getting ready to pay with your life for the crimes you've committed?'' He looked straight at his friend again, his pencil poised over his note pad, pretending to want to take notes on his next remarks.

"It's like I said, Mr. Wiley.'' Slade gave him a slow, predatory smile. "I'm an innocent man.''

Ken pressed, "Do you really believe the Dakota Kid can save you, considering how heavily guarded you are?''

Nash made a threatening move toward the reporter. "The Kid can do anything. He could be watching you right now! I'd be real careful if I were you—''

"Yeah,'' Slade said seriously, drawing Ken's full attention. "If you're smart, you'll watch your back. The Kid has ways of finding out things.''

Ken pretended to be intimidated by their unspoken threats and backed nervously away from the jail cell. He understood exactly what Slade was implying.

"I think I've got enough material for now, Sheriff Jones. Thank you."

"All right. You boys settle back in now. We don't need any trouble tonight," Steve ordered as he and Ken left them. "If I hear anything from the jury, you'll be among the first to know."

He closed the door.

"What do you think?" Jones asked him.

"I think the Kid is still somewhere real close by. You're right to keep such a heavy guard around town. After listening to them, I think I'd better keep an eye on Alyssa Mason, too."

"You think he might come after her?"

"Sooner or later. I've already befriended her sister and mother, so it shouldn't be too difficult to insinuate myself even more into their good graces."

"There's not much else we can do right now, except sit and wait. Once the jury comes back in and this is over, I'm looking forward to continuing the hunt for the Kid and what's left of his gang."

"You're not the only one. I'm not going to rest until the Kid's brought in."

"So what they say about you is really true," Jones mused.

"What's that?"

"That the Pinkerton Agency is 'The Eye That Never Sleeps.' "

"Not when we've got work to do," Ken replied. "I have to go wire Denver right now. I'll talk to you again later."

"I'm not going anywhere."

* * *

The first thing the following morning, the jury announced that it had reached a verdict in the case. Word went out, and Judge Banks convened the court at a little after ten A.M.

"I understand you ladies and gentlemen of the jury have reached a verdict in this case," he stated, addressing them in front of the packed courtroom.

"Yes, Your Honor, we have," the jury foreman said as he handed the paper with the verdict written on it to Jones, who carried it to the judge.

Banks read it solemnly, and nodded. "What is said verdict?"

"We, the jury, find Slade Braxton, Rick Nash and Carl Johnson guilty on all counts."

A cheer went up in the room, and the judge had to use his gavel to restore order. He looked down at the three convicted men, his expression cold and unfeeling.

"You have been found guilty. I sentence all three of you to be hanged by the neck until dead. The sentence is to be carried out by sundown today. Court is adjourned." He banged the gavel again.

A roar went through the room as Slade, Nash and Johnson were led away.

Loretta and Emily embraced each other, shedding tears of relief.

Alyssa sat alone, her head slightly bowed, her shoulders slumped. She knew she should be glad that justice had done, yet all she felt was emptiness. Her father was dead, and soon Slade would be, too. He was a liar and a killer, yet she remembered far too clearly for her own peace of mind how he'd saved her from harm when Johnson and Nash had tried to escape on the way to Green Springs and how he could have tried to disarm her during the time they were alone together in the wilderness—but he hadn't.

Memories of Slade's forbidden kisses and dancing with him plagued Alyssa, too, and would not be dismissed. Silently, she cursed him and her own weakness for him. Try though she might, she couldn't forget him. He was an outlaw, a convicted killer, and soon he would be dead. There would be no one to mourn his passing—except her.

As Slade moved up the aisle past her, he glanced her way. Their gazes met and, for just that moment in time, there was nothing else in the world but the two of them. The noise of the courtroom faded away; the knowledge that his life would be over before sundown grew hazy. All that mattered was that they were looking at each other, and remembering what might have been.

And then he was gone.

And she was alone.

"Oh, Alyssa, this is so wonderful! At last, justice has prevailed!" her mother told her, sobbing.

She embraced her mother, knowing she needed comforting. Loretta would never understand the power of her daughter's turbulent feelings—feelings that even Alyssa didn't fully comprehend—so she said nothing. Slade Braxton had come into her heart and her life, and Alyssa knew she would never be the same because of him.

"Shall we go back to the hotel?" Emily suggested.

"I'd like to accompany you, if I may?" Ken said as he came to join them.

"That would be fine," Loretta agreed. "I'm sure you're very excited now that the trial's over and you can file your story."

"I'll wire my paper about the verdict and the sentencing, then follow up with another story this evening after the executions are over."

"You live a very exciting life," Emily told him.

"It can be. There are days when I'm constantly chasing leads, and then there are days like today when I'm just sitting around, waiting for things to happen so I can write about them."

"Well, all of our waiting is over. Justice has been served," Loretta said.

Alyssa was quiet; the burden her heart carried was too devastating for speech.

Slade Braxton was guilty.

By sundown tonight, he would be dead.

The crowd gathered around, watching as the finishing touches were put on the hastily constructed gallows. The sheriff would soon be bringing out the prisoners, and the townspeople didn't want to miss anything. It wasn't often that the law caught up with gunslingers like the Dakota Kid's gang, and they were going to enjoy the gruesome spectacle of the hanging.

In the hotel, Alyssa lingered in her mother and sister's room.

"Do you want to go down and watch?" Emily asked them as the time drew near.

"No," Loretta answered quickly. "I don't need to

see them dead. I just need to know that they've paid for what they did. I hope Braxton suffers the most. God knows, he's the most vicious one.''

''How does a man become that savage?'' Emily wondered aloud.

''What if he really isn't as bad as they say?'' Alyssa asked quietly. Her torment had been unrelenting all afternoon.

Both women looked up at her, stunned. ''What are you talking about?''

''Braxton . . . What if he isn't as terrible as everyone believes he is?''

''Alyssa,'' Emily began, remembering the night at the dance and how her sister, a woman who had never shown any great interest in romance, had fallen so completely under his spell. ''Think about what you're saying. Braxton shot Papa.''

''What if he didn't shoot him? What if Les Anderson was wrong? Remember at the hearing how he first said he wasn't sure who'd killed Papa, but then he changed his testimony?''

''Braxton had just robbed the bank! He was riding out of town and he was firing his gun! Anderson was right there!''

''But did he really see him shoot Papa or does he just want Braxton to hang?''

''Does it matter?'' Emily demanded angrily.

Alyssa stiffened as she lifted her troubled gaze to her sister. ''The truth would matter to Papa. Braxton might not be the one who killed him.''

For the first time, Emily realized the depth of Alyssa's misery. ''How can you still feel this way about him?'' she asked in a low, disbelieving voice.

''I don't know. All I do know is that I believe he's not as cold-blooded as everyone thinks he is.'' She told them how he'd saved her life in the escape attempt and how he could have tried to take her gun when they were out in the wilderness alone, but didn't. ''During the Kid's jailbreak attempt, I heard Slade arguing with Nash and Johnson, trying to convince them not to shoot Sheriff Jones. The others wanted the lawman dead, but Slade convinced them not to kill him. If Slade really was that vicious, do you think he would have cared about saving Jones's life?''

''But Alyssa . . . Braxton's going to die.''

''I know.'' She drew a ragged breath, finally understanding what she had to do. She headed for the door. ''I have to be there . . . I can't let him die alone.''

After she'd gone, Emily and Loretta stared at the closed door in silence. They finally understood the truth—Alyssa had fallen tragically in love with the handsome, deadly stranger, and there was nothing they could do to help her. They could only be there to comfort her when it was over. And it would be over soon. . . .

Alyssa left the hotel and went straight to the telegraph office, only to find what she had feared the most—there had been no response to her wire. With that news, her last, desperate hope of proving Slade innocent died.

Making her way down the street, she neared the site where the executions would take place and stood on the edge of the crowd, watching and listening. The others' comments seemed ghoulish to her as she heard them say how they hoped the gang members would suffer.

Crazy thoughts assailed Alyssa as she kept her silent, hopeless vigil. She imagined a stranger riding into town at top speed at the last minute with proof that Slade was, indeed, an undercover Pinkerton operative. . . . She imagined the Kid attacking with a gang of gunmen, setting Slade free just in time . . . She fantasized what it would have been like if the robbery and murder had never happened—how she would have gone on with her life, enchanted by the memory of the mystery man who'd so charmed her with a dance and a forbidden kiss one sweet summer night.

Alyssa bit her lip as she fought to master her runaway heart. She had to bring her traitorous emotions under control. She could not give in to the hysteria that threatened. She had to be brave.

But logic could not overcome the truth of what she was feeling—she did not want Slade to die.

The thought that she should try to rescue him jolted her. Before she could even react to the electrifying, wild possibility, Ken's voice sounded close beside her. She jumped nervously at his intrusion, fearing the reporter might have been perceptive enough to have read her thoughts somehow.

"Are your sister and mother going to come down to watch?" Ken asked as he stood with her.

"No. They were satisfied enough that things had

turned out as they'd hoped. They had no need to see the hangings."

"And you?" he asked, his regard penetrating.

"I *had* to come," she answered honestly.

Ken sensed the unspoken tension in her. He'd gotten a coded wire from Denver informing him of her inquiry about Slade's status as an operative. To protect Slade, he'd ordered them not to respond to her in any way—to neither confirm nor deny his association with the office. It was important to maintain his cover. They could take no chances with his life—not even by revealing the truth to the justice of the peace from Black Springs.

"I'm glad Sheriff Jones stationed the deputies around town again. I'm worried about the Kid. There's no telling what he might do today to save his men."

"I hope the sheriff's precautions will be enough," she said, remembering the other night. With the hanging just minutes away, she knew it was a very dangerous time.

"Short of asking the governor to bring in troops, there isn't much more he could do."

Alyssa nodded and looked back toward the gallows. They had just finished hanging a heavy drape around the bottom of the platform, to shield the bodies from public view after the executions.

It will be over soon, she realized painfully.

Too soon! her heart cried out.

Before the sun set in the next hour or two, her father's killer would have paid for his crime with his life, and she would be free to go on with hers. Her mother and sister were going to feel some sense of peace, but Alyssa would not. For her, there would only be devastation and heartbreak.

A low murmur ran through the crowd as the door to the jail opened and the sheriff walked out with Johnson. The outlaw's hands were cuffed behind him. The gunman glanced around at those gathered for the hanging and sneered at them with open hatred. The sheriff urged him on, and they moved together to the steps and mounted them slowly.

Johnson looked up at the noose that awaited him, and for an instant, the terror he'd been fighting showed on his face. He was expecting the Kid to save him, and now was the time. *But where was he?*

With each step he took, Johnson knew he was moving closer and closer to his death, and he had no intention of dying that day. He'd told himself over and over again that the Kid would rescue him, but there was no sound of shots, no ambush, no one coming to his aid. He was alone.

Terror and fury tore at him. He refused to believe that this could really be happening. Surely, he wasn't really going to hang! He paused at the top step.

"Move it, Johnson," Jones ordered, digging him in the back with his rifle.

"Go to hell!" he snarled. He would have made a run for it, but there was nowhere to run to, and he refused to be shot down like a mad dog.

"You're going first, my friend," Jones said tersely, pushing him toward the spot where the hangman waited for him. "Do you need a blindfold?"

"No."

The noose was slipped over his head.

"You got any last words?"

"The Kid'll see you pay for this! All of you!" he shouted to the crowd.

Then the time for talk was over.

"I have to do something!" the Kid said fiercely as he watched the noose being placed around Johnson's neck.

He was crouched down, hiding in an alley with Zeke within view of the gallows. He started to draw his gun. He wanted to get up and shoot anyone and everyone who got in his way. He had to stop his friend's hanging! But Zeke grabbed his arm when he would have charged forward.

"Don't!" he told him in a harsh, low voice. "There's no way we can save them!"

"I can't just watch them die!"

The Kid turned on Zeke. There was a fire of madness shining in his eyes. He was usually a cold, calculating man, who carefully thought out his every action, but standing by watching his friends die while he could do nothing to stop it left him enraged.

"Then leave. Now. It's suicide to try to stop the hangings. There are guards everywhere, just watching for us. We're lucky we got this close without getting caught. You try to shoot your way out of here and save them, and we're dead men."

The Kid valued his own skin more than anything else in the world. Zeke knew that by appealing to his innate sense of self-preservation, he'd be able to get the Kid to control his fury.

"I want them all to die for what they've done!"

"Then I know what we should do," Zeke told him with a cold smile.

"What?"

"We can't stop them from hanging the boys, but we can make them suffer just as good. We'll kidnap that lady justice of the peace, the one who ruined the jail break. That shouldn't be too hard. We'll make them sorry they ever messed with the Dakota Kid's gang."

The Kid looked back toward the gallows just as the trap door was sprung. His friend dropped heavily through it. Johnson was dead almost instantly, his neck broken in the fall.

Pain stabbed at the Kid. It was an ugly way to die, and there had been nothing he could do to stop it. He swore to himself then and there that if the time ever came when the law was closing in on him, he would never allow himself to be taken in and hanged. When he looked back at Zeke, there was hatred in his eyes.

"Johnson was right. They are going to pay."

The Kid turned back toward the scene in the street just as Nash was led out, kicking and screaming and fighting all the way. He could hear Nash yelling about how the Kid was going to save him, about how he wouldn't let him die like this. The Kid's cold hatred grew even stronger as he witnessed Nash meet the same fate as Johnson.

"It's your turn, Braxton. Are you ready?" Rob asked as Jones returned to get his last prisoner.

"Is any man ever ready to hang?" Slade asked with a pained half-smile.

"There's been no sighting of the Kid, so it looks like everything's going to go smoothly."

Slade's smile twisted even more. "That's easy for you to say."

"Ready?"

"Yes." He grew solemn as they led him from the cell.

When they left the jail, a wild murmur ran through the crowd. Slade remained stoic. He showed no emotion whatsoever as they made their way to the steps. But just as he started up the steps to where the noose awaited him, he caught sight of Alyssa standing in the back of the crowd with Ken at her side.

Her presence shocked him. He would have thought that she would be celebrating his demise, but instead, he saw no joy in her expression, only dark pain, anguish and torment.

For an instant, Slade relived the moment when he'd first seen her at the dance. He remembered how her innocence and purity had touched him. He wanted to go to her and tell her everything, to let her know that it would be all right.

But there was no time.

Later, once the Kid had been brought in and the express office informant's identity was uncovered, Slade vowed to himself that he would go to Alyssa and try to explain. Until then, he had to continue with the charade of his death. He silently prayed that at some time in the future, she would forgive him for the deception and come to understood their need for secrecy.

"Let's go, Braxton! Move it!" Jones ordered, playing his role to the hilt, forcing Slade to climb the stairs to his "death."

The shouts of the crowd grew even louder as he mounted the steps one by one. He walked straight to the noose and waited. The hangman put the noose around his neck and, with a sleight of hand, did what had to be done with the secret harness Slade was wearing.

"Any last words?" Jones asked.

Slade glanced at him, fighting down the fear that Ken's harness contraption might fail. "No."

He turned back to the crowd, seeking out Alyssa. His gaze found her where she stood with Ken, and it was her tearstained face he held in his thoughts as he felt the trap door give way beneath his feet.

Alyssa cried out when the door was sprung, and she swayed as if she were about to faint.

"Are you all right?" Ken asked, putting a supportive arm around her.

She had tried to stay in control, but the horror of knowing Slade was dead tore at her. She clutched at Ken's arm, fighting the terrifying blackness that spun around her, fighting the tears that came from the depths of her soul.

"Let me get you back to the hotel," he offered, and he led her away.

Around them, the townspeople looked on with sympathy. They thought she was distraught because her memories of her father's death had been too painful.

"Braxton will never hurt anyone again, Miss Mason," one well-intentioned soul said, trying to cheer. Alyssa as she passed by on Ken's arm.

The words only increased her misery.

"Do you want to go to your mother's room, so you'll have someone with you?"

"No! No . . . I need to be alone for a while. I'll go on up to my own room. Thank you," she said, drawing away from him when they reached the hotel.

"If you need anything—anything at all—just let me know."

"What I need, no one can give me."

With that, she left him and disappeared up the stairway to her room.

Ken watched her go and then hurried back outside. He wasted no time in heading for their prearranged meeting place—the undertaker's parlor. They had a lot to do and little time.

Alyssa had been alone in her room for over an hour when her mother and sister came for her.

"You haven't had much to eat all day, young lady, so you're going down to dinner," Loretta insisted.

"I'm not hungry." She resisted, not wanting to talk to anyone tonight.

"I don't care. You're going," Loretta ordered in a strict motherly tone.

"You heard her," Emily said.

Outnumbered, Alyssa gave in, but she had no appetite. She was numb, emotionally and physically.

She left a lamp burning low on the dresser, for she knew it would be dark when she returned.

The dining room was quiet that evening. Alyssa ate sparingly of the hot meal set before her. The food seemed tasteless as her mind kept offering up a torturous vision of Slade standing on the gallows, the noose being put around his neck.

"May I join you?" Rob asked, approaching their table.

"Of course, Rob. How good to see you," Loretta said, smiling at him. "Sit down."

"Thanks."

"Have you eaten yet?"

"No, I haven't. I was helping the sheriff over at the jail," he told them.

When the waitress appeared, he ordered a meal of his own.

They spoke of general things for a while, and then Emily and Loretta excused themselves, having already finished eating. Alyssa remained behind to talk with Rob about the plans to bring in the rest of the Kid's gang.

"Do you have any idea where the Kid's hiding?" she asked.

"No, and we were really lucky he didn't try to stop the hangings today. It could have been deadly and disastrous with all the people there."

"So no one's seen or heard from him since the night of the breakout attempt?"

"That's right. There's been no word at all, and that bothers me. You should have seen how certain Johnson and Nash were that he was going to bust them out. Even up to the last minute, I don't think Johnson really believed he was going to hang—not until the noose was around his neck.''

Alyssa shivered at the gruesome memory.

Rob saw her reaction and reached across the table to take her hand. He said fiercely, ''I promise you, Alyssa, I'm going to bring in the Kid and the rest of his gang, or I'm going to die trying.''

''Don't talk like that! There's been enough death already!''

''It's the way I feel. I want the Kid, and I want Zeke. I want the killing to stop, and I'm going to do everything I can to put an end to it.''

Rob was more than tempted to tell her the truth. She deserved to know that Slade had not been lying, that he really was a Pinkerton, but Ken had sworn him to secrecy. Rob was going to continue the hunt for the Kid, but he was going to be working in co-operation with the Pinkertons this time.

''You're a brave man, Rob.''

''Determined is more like it,'' he said with a wry grin. His thoughts turned to another hunt he was on— the hunt to capture Alyssa's heart. ''When are you returning home?''

''On tomorrow's stage,'' she answered, for she had just discussed the arrangements with her mother before he'd joined them.

''I'll be heading back the day after. Alyssa—'' His tone turned more serious, and he tightened his grip on her hand a bit. ''I know you're still in mourning, but now that the danger is behind us, I'd like to see you more often, if that's all right?'' His expression was earnest as he gazed at her across the table.

His ardency surprised her and she wasn't quite sure what to say. Her emotions were shattered from the shock and sorrow of Slade's death. "Rob . . . I . . . I do care about you, but it's just too soon for me . . ."

He thought she was referring to her father's death, and that it was too soon for her to think about seeing anyone socially. "I understand, Alyssa. Just know that I'm here and I care about you—deeply."

"We can talk about this more later," she responded, caught off guard by his serious declaration. "I'd better go upstairs and start packing for the trip home."

"I'll walk you up to your room."

"No, that's all right. I'll be fine. But thank you for everything, Rob." She stood up, ready to go.

Rob stood, too. "Good night, Alyssa. I'll see you tomorrow."

"Good night, Rob."

He remained standing by the table, watching her until she'd disappeared from sight upstairs. Then he walked back to the sheriff's office. They still had some planning to do.

Alyssa returned to her room and closed and locked the door behind her. Leaning back against it, she sighed and closed her eyes. It took her a moment to regroup. She was exhausted and felt completely drained emotionally.

Rob's declaration had been sweet, and while she did like him a lot, it would be some time before she could deal with any kind of romantic involvement. True, in all the time she'd known Rob, he had been nothing but good to her. She did hold him in the highest regard, and perhaps she could have come to love him—if Slade hadn't come into her life.

The dangerous gunman had devastated her with his lies and deceit. It would be a long time before she could trust her own judgment again—a very long time.

Wearily, Alyssa stirred herself to action. She turned up the lamp on the dresser and started toward the bed, ready to turn back the covers, undress and call it a night. She would get up extra early in the morning and pack then. She was reaching for the bedspread when she saw it—a note propped up right on her nightstand, with her name scrawled brazenly across the front in crude handwriting.

Her hand was trembling as she reached out to pick it up. She carefully unfolded it, and as she read the missive, she began to tremble in terror.

Lady Judge

   Know this—you're next!

   It's your fault that my men were hanged, and I'm gonna see you pay for it! If you hadn't shown up at the jailbreak, Johnson, Nash and Slade would be alive right now.

   I got your daddy, and now I'm gonna get you! You'd better keep watch because you're never gonna be safe from me.

                                            The Dakota Kid

Chapter Twelve

Alyssa's hands were trembling so violently that she could barely finish reading the letter. Icy fingers of fear traced up her spine. The Dakota Kid had been there—in her room! Her terror grew, and her eyes widened in horror at the thought that he might still be there!

She backed toward the dresser where her gun was safely stowed and grabbed it up out of the drawer. If the Kid dared to come after her, he would have a fight on his hands. The note was still clutched in her hand as she ran for the door. She had to find Rob! She had to let him know the Kid was here in town!

She fumbled at the lock in her haste, but finally got the door open and threw it wide. Feeling as if she'd escaped some dreadful fate, she rushed out into the hallway. She stuffed the note in her pocket and hid her gun in the folds of her skirt as she crossed to her mother's and sister's room. She wanted to make sure they were safe before she went in search of Rob.

"Mama? Emily?" she called out as she knocked softly on their door.

"Yes, dear? Has Rob gone already?" her mother asked as she unlocked and opened the door to speak with her.

Alyssa managed to keep her expression calm as she faced her. "Yes, he left a short while ago. He had to go back to the sheriff's office, but I just remembered something else I wanted to ask him about the case. I'm going to walk over there now to speak with him, but I wanted to make sure that you and Emily were all right before I left."

"We're fine, darling. We're just getting ready for bed. You be careful."

"Don't worry," she answered, tightening her grip on her gun. "I will be, and I'll be back as soon as I can."

"Good night, dear."

"See you in the morning."

Loretta went back inside and closed and locked the door.

Satisfied that her family was safe from the Kid's wrath, Alyssa hurried from the hotel. She was watchful as she made her way to the sheriff's office. She cut a wide path around the dark alleys and store entrances. The Kid might be anywhere, just watching and waiting for her. She held the gun down low, but she was ready for trouble if it came. She was glad she'd had the foresight to bring the weapon along.

She would not hesitate to use it if she had to.

As she neared the sheriff's office, Alyssa noticed that the shades were drawn and thought it strange. There were lighted lamps inside, though, and so she did not hesitate when she reached the office, but walked right in. Her only thought was to find Rob as quickly as possible.

Sheriff Jones was sitting at his desk, and he looked up, his expression revealing that he was clearly shocked by her unexpected intrusion.

"Sheriff Jones, I—"

"Miss Mason?" he stuttered in surprise.

"I was hoping to—" She moved farther into the office and was relieved to see Rob sitting at a chair before the sheriff's desk. "Oh, Rob, there you are. Thank heaven. I have something important I have to show you—"

Intent on giving Rob the note, Alyssa closed the door and hurried toward him. Rob, who had nervously risen to his feet, quickly tried to head her off.

"I found this on my nightstand. I thought you might want to see it—"

Rob wanted to avoid trouble. He took her arm, paying no attention to the note, and tried to usher her back outside immediately, but she resisted his effort.

"Alyssa, it would be best if we talked later. We're in the middle of something important here and—"

He got no further. At that moment, Ken and Slade appeared in the doorway from the cell area. They were deep in conversation and had not heard her come in.

"No one knows you're alive except us," Ken was saying, "and we want to keep it that way for now."

"Slade?" Alyssa gasped. She took a step back as if physically struck by his completely unexpected appearance. Her eyes grew wide in disbelief, and she paled. Looking from Slade to Rob and then back again, she managed, "You're alive . . . ?"

"Alyssa, I wanted to explain everything at dinner, but—" Rob began, agonizing over how shocking this must be for her. He wanted to calm her.

"But how?" She ignored Rob and stared straight at Slade. "I saw them hang you—" Her shock was so great that she couldn't say any more.

Slade had remained frozen in place at his first sight of her, but seeing her distress, he moved forward now to talk to her. It was time to tell her the truth. He'd planned to seek her out later, after the Kid had been brought in, but fate had dealt him a new hand, and he would play it.

"They used a specially designed harness that made everything appear like a normal hanging, but—"

"I don't believe this!" Her joy, relief and happiness at finding him alive were completely and utterly overwhelmed by her fury at having been so deceived. She had been mourning him. She had cried for him . . . and he was alive.

"Alyssa . . . I told you the truth that day on the trail. I really am a Pinkerton," he explained gently as he came to stand before her. "I was working undercover in the gang to help bring it down."

"But I wired the Denver office like you asked me to! They never answered! I kept checking at the telegraph office and hoping—I even went there again right before the hanging was scheduled just in case word had come—''

Slade was deeply touched. He wanted to reach out to her and take her in his arms, but he restrained himself.

''I'm sorry,'' Slade offered, and knew his apology sounded lame in the face of her very real distress.

Alyssa stared up at him, torn between the desire to cry hysterically in relief that he was alive and the impulse to slap him with all the force she could muster for having lied to her this way. Watching him ''die'' that very afternoon had nearly destroyed her!

''It's my fault that the Denver office didn't answer your wire,'' Ken put in. ''I've been in touch with them almost daily. When your request came in for information about Slade, I ordered them not to respond.''

''But you're a reporter!'' She stared at him in disbelief.

Ken's expression changed, and she caught a glimpse of the real man she was dealing with. He looked hard-edged, shrewd, cunning and capable of anything. The change in him was chilling.

''I'm Ken Wiley, the reporter, when it suits my needs,'' he explained. ''Otherwise, I'm Ken Richards. Slade and I work together out of the Denver office.''

''But I'm a justice of the peace! And you deliberately kept the truth from me!'' She grew even angrier, if that were possible. ''You let me go on believing that Slade was a killer and a thief—even when I knew in my heart that it couldn't be true! You let me stand there in that crowd today and listen to the others rejoice in the fact that a 'cold-blooded killer' was getting what he deserved! You let me believe that I was really watching him die! How could you?''

''It's my—our job to bring in the Dakota Kid,'' Slade answered simply before Ken could say anything. ''If the Kid believes I'm dead, we'll have a lot more freedom while we're trying to track him down.''

Still reeling from all that had just been revealed to her, she held up the note that had brought her there in the first place.

''Well, you won't have to track him very far!'' she snapped. ''Take a look at this!''

She shoved the note at Slade, glaring up at him as he quickly read it. She saw the change in his expression and smiled in grim satisfaction.

''What is it?'' Rob asked, coming forward to read over his shoulder.

''And you! How dare you!'' She turned her outrage on Rob, her anger with him showing in her every move. ''You knew the truth about Slade when we were having dinner, and yet you said nothing to me! Not one word!''

''I couldn't tell you, Alyssa. I gave Slade and Ken my word that I wouldn't tell anyone of his faked death. They want the Kid to believe he's dead.''

''But I thought he was dead, too,'' she said in a choked voice.

''I'm sorry, but it had to seem real. Slade was convicted of killing your father. If you'd known the truth about him and what was really happening today, you might have acted differently at the execution. Then someone might have become suspicious,'' Rob told her, trying to make it all seem quite logical.

Alyssa looked at Slade, her regard cold. "If you're innocent of shooting my father, then who murdered him? What happened the day of the robbery? I want the truth!"

"Your father came running toward the bank just as we were making our getaway. I tried to block the shot, but Zeke gunned him down," Slade answered, remembering far too clearly that fateful morning.

"And Zeke is the one who is still alive and riding with the Kid," she finished for him.

"Not for long, if I have anything to say about it," Rob declared, his determination to see the gang completely destroyed growing even stronger.

Slade looked down at the note he held, then back up at Alyssa again. His expression was deadly serious as he spoke. "You found this note in your room just now?"

She nodded. "Yes, I found it when I went back upstairs after having dinner with Rob."

Rob was furious as he took the note from Slade to show it to Jones. "The bastard was actually in her room tonight and no one saw him! Her room's the last one down the hall. He had to walk past at least six other rooms to get there, not to mention take the stairs! How could he do that? He was right here in town under our noses, and we couldn't catch him. Thank heaven Alyssa wasn't in the room when he went in. God only knows what the bastard might have done to her."

"He would have killed her," Slade answered tightly, unable to look away from the blond beauty who stood so proudly and defiantly before him.

Alyssa was still furious with him, and he knew she had every right to be. The thought of her in danger, though, sent a shaft of pain through Slade. He led a mostly solitary existence, but since she'd come into his life like a soft breeze on a hot summer night, she'd haunted him.

"We're going to have to put a round-the-clock guard on Alyssa," Slade said. "Her life's in jeopardy as long as the Kid and Zeke are on the loose."

"No problem," Rob agreed. "She's taking the stage home tomorrow. Once we're back in Black Springs, it'll be easier to keep a close watch over her."

"The Kid thinks I'm dead, so I've got the edge of surprise on my side. I'll stay with her. He won't be expecting me."

Rob resented Slade's intrusion in making the arrangements to safeguard Alyssa. "I can stand guard, too."

Slade and Rob regarded each other solemnly, each recognizing the unspoken claim of the other.

Alyssa was standing there beside them, torn between fury at the two men and terror over the Kid's threat. She wanted to slap Rob and Slade for daring to discuss her safety right in front of her, as if she didn't have a brain or a say in the matter.

She turned an icy glare on them both, wondering whom she hated most right then—them or the Dakota Kid. She lifted her gun for emphasis as she said, "Gentlemen, I'll have you know that, right now, I feel perfectly capable of taking care of myself. Thank you very much for your concern!"

Slade gave her a slow, appreciative grin as he remembered the last time she'd held a gun on him—and where she'd held it. "I'm well aware of just how good you are with your gun, ma'am."

Heat flamed in her cheeks as she remembered, too. "Good, and don't you forget it either, Braxton!"

For an instant, she was caught up in the power of his smile. His very presence there—alive and well—tore at her. She'd thought him dead, yet he was alive!

Torn by conflicting emotions, Alyssa turned her back on them all and stormed out of the office.

The small group of men stood dumbfounded, staring after her.

"I'm going after her." Rob spoke up first. He took advantage of the situation, for he knew Slade couldn't walk the streets of Green River openly.

Slade, Ken and Steve remained in the office, stunned by all that had just happened.

"As dangerous as this is for her, it's just the break we needed," Ken said, thinking only in terms of the cold, hard facts.

Slade looked over at his friend, his gaze deadly. "This kind of break I can live without. I don't want her hurt in any way."

"It's perfect. Alyssa's our bait now—our lure. We know the Kid's after her. We know he'll make a move to take her at some point in time. We just have to wait it out and see what he tries. My guess is he's probably on his way to Black Springs right now. He'll be there ready and waiting for her return."

"Sometimes you're a cold bastard," Slade remarked without emotion.

"In this business, you have to be."

*   *   *

"Alyssa! Wait!" Rob called out as he followed her from the sheriff's office.

But Alyssa had had enough. She did not slow her pace, but marched on, heading straight toward the hotel.

Rob lengthened his strides and finally managed to catch up with her.

"I'm sorry," he said immediately, wanting to put things straight between them. He valued her friendship and didn't want anything to ruin it—especially not anything involving Slade Braxton.

She heard him, but did not slow down or even look over at him.

"Alyssa, listen to me. The last thing in the world I'd ever want to do is hurt you. Braxton needed to keep his identity secret. They asked me to give my word that I wouldn't reveal what I knew. I had no choice."

"I know that, Rob. It's all right," she said stiffly, still walking without pause.

Her emotions were in such turmoil that she wasn't sure exactly why she was so angry. She'd been devastated at first, because she'd thought Slade had been executed. But now that she'd discovered he was alive, she was furious! She'd been torn apart because there'd been no answer from the Pinkertons when she'd been trying desperately to prove Slade was innocent and save his life. She'd wanted him to be an operative—and not the cold-blooded killer who'd gunned down her father. And yet, now that she'd learned he *was* on the right side of the law, she was angry about that. Nothing she was thinking made any sense to her.

They had reached the hotel, and she stalked inside, ahead of Rob.

"I'm walking you up to your room, and I'm going to check every square inch of it before I leave you tonight," Rob declared, determined not to take no for an answer.

"Fine." She did not pause in the lobby, but kept on walking straight for the stairs.

"I'll stand watch all night down here, once I know you're safely locked in your room."

"Thank you."

Alyssa still did not look at him, and she did not stop until she reached the door to her room. As she drew her key out of her pocket, Rob took it from her and opened the door.

"Wait here."

She stood in the doorway, watching as he started a thorough search. He checked in the small closet and under the bed for her, and then made sure her window was securely locked.

"All right," Rob announced. "It's safe."

Some of the tension drained from her as she entered the room.

"I'll be close by if you need me," he told her as he went to her. "Alyssa . . . I want you to know that I would never do anything to hurt you . . . Never."

She looked up at him then and saw the true depth of his devotion in his eyes. The intensity of his feelings startled her. She'd known that he wanted to court her for some time, but she'd never guessed he felt this strongly.

"Rob—"

Unable to help himself, he took her in his arms. "Alyssa, I love you."

He hadn't meant to declare himself so openly so soon, but the thought of the Kid trying to harm her terrified him. He could only imagine what might have happened if she'd walked in on the outlaw in her room earlier that night.

His lips sought hers in a devoted kiss. He would protect her with his life. He would keep her safe. The Kid would not harm her as long as he had a breath in his body.

Alyssa accepted his kiss quietly. It was pleasant and he was kind, but his embrace stirred no deeper emotion in her. She would have liked to love him. Rob was a good, strong man who took care of his own, but she knew that there could never be more than friendship between them. When Rob released her and stepped back, she could see the fierceness of his desire for her in his expression.

"Keep this door locked, Alyssa. If you need anything—anything at all—I'll be right downstairs."

She smiled at him. "Thank you."

He nodded tightly and left the room. He stood outside the door until he heard the lock turn. Satisfied that she was safe for now, he went downstairs to check out the rest of the hotel. He would be vigilant this night. No harm would come to her. He would see to it.

* * *

Alyssa undressed and got ready for bed. It seemed she had not known a moment's peace in weeks. She longed for quietude. She doubted it would come any time soon, though, with the Kid vowing to come after her.

She lay down, wanting and hoping to rest, but sleep would not come. Memories of Slade kept returning—their dance, the way he'd kissed her that night in the moonlight and how he'd saved her on the trail. The image of the way he'd stood on the gallows was burned into her consciousness, and it preyed upon her unmercifully now.

Alyssa doubted she would ever forget that awful moment when the trap door had sprung beneath him. She'd believed he'd fallen to his death and was lost to her forever. The sight of him this very night standing resurrected before her had shaken her to the very depths of her soul. Even now, she found it difficult to believe that his execution had been an elaborate pretense. Slade was alive—alive!

Alyssa tossed and turned, and finally, in frustration, she got up and went to stand by the window. She stared out at the dark street, trying not to think about the man whose kiss haunted her days and nights.

Slade was pacing the jail like a caged lion. "I've got to get out of here for a while."

"See if you can find us a deck of cards. I'll play you a little poker," Ken offered, trying to distract him.

"I can't just sit here. The Kid could be out there watching Alyssa right now!"

"And that's why Rob is going to stay close by her all night."

"How close?" he growled, his expression as dark as his tone.

Ken would have been enjoying his torment if things hadn't been so complicated and so serious. "There's no way you can move around town freely. You're a dead man—in case you've forgotten."

"I haven't forgotten a damn thing!"

Slade raked a hand through his hair as he stopped pacing for a moment. He remembered far too much for his own peace of mind. He remembered Alyssa's kiss, her touch, her scent. . . . He remembered how she'd saved him in the river, and most of all, he remembered her tears when he had been about to be hanged. She had cried for him.

"So what's bothering you then?"

Ken leaned back in his chair and gave his friend a questioning look as he waited for him to answer. In all the years they'd worked together, he'd never before known Slade to let anything affect him personally. Slade had always been the perfect operative— aloof, distant, unemotional, a man in charge who was taking care of business. That was why Ken liked working with him. This was a complete change for Slade, and that troubled Ken.

When Slade didn't respond, Ken reminded him, "It doesn't pay to get involved with anyone while you're working on a case."

"It's too late for lectures."

Ken was surprised by his statement. "Did you

know Rob plans to marry Alyssa the first chance he gets?''

Slade slanted him an irritated look. He recalled the way Rob and Alyssa had embraced when they'd been reunited after the storm on the trip to Green River. And she had said earlier that she'd had dinner with Rob that very night.

''If you don't believe me, just ask him.''

''That's all right.''

''Just thought you'd want to know.''

''That doesn't change anything. I still need to get out of here and get some fresh air. I'll stay in the alleys and make sure no one recognizes me.'' He didn't wait for approval; he started out the back of the jail, pulling his hat low over his eyes.

''Be careful.'' Ken realized there was no point in trying to stop him.

Slade barely heard him. He was already out the door. Behind him in the jail, Ken and Jones exchanged looks.

''I hope he doesn't run into anyone with a weak heart,'' Jones remarked.

''I hope he doesn't run into anyone—period,'' Ken growled, less than pleased, but knowing he couldn't have stopped Slade even if he'd tried.

Slade was a man of his word. He moved soundlessly through the back streets and alleys of town. He passed only one person, an old drunk on his way home, and he was careful to keep his face averted from him.

The alley behind Alyssa's hotel was deserted, and Slade was glad, but he wondered where Rob was.

He'd said he was going to keep watch over her. Using his talent for picking locks, Slade let himself in the hotel's rear entrance and quietly made his way up the rear staircase, still with no sign of the lawman. Rob had said Alyssa's door was the last one down the hall, so he moved quietly, taking great care not to make any noise or disturb anyone else.

It was late, and the soft knock at the door startled Alyssa.

"Who is it?"

"Alyssa . . . It's Slade," he said in a low voice.

Her breath caught in her throat at the sound of his voice and her heartbeat quickened, but she held on to her control. "Go away. I'm tired."

"I want to talk to you for a moment."

"We've already talked," she replied sharply.

"In private," he added.

"There's really nothing more to say. I heard enough explanations tonight to last me a lifetime."

"Alyssa, I saw you today at the hanging—"

She heard the gruff emotion in his voice, and bit back a sob. She had to fight against the desire to open the door, and her arms, to him. She reminded herself that they'd all played her for a fool, and she hadn't liked it one bit.

But then the truth came to her.

Slade was an innocent man. He had not killed her father. He was everything she'd hoped he was that first night when they'd danced in the moonlight. And in spite of all the deception and lies that had kept them apart, she had fallen hopelessly in love with him.

"Alyssa, please. Open the door. I just want to ask

you one question. Then if you want me to leave, I'll go.''

He had expected no response, and his spirits soared as the door slowly opened to reveal Alyssa, standing before him clad only in her nightgown and wrapper. Her hair was down, brushed out around her shoulders in a tumble of pale curls, and she looked absolutely, positively beautiful.

''You'd better come inside before someone sees you,'' she said quietly, holding the door wide for him to enter.

Slade wanted to take her in his arms, to kiss her and hold her close. It took all of his considerable will-power to deny himself. He moved past her, taking his hat off, and waited, hat in hand, as she closed the door.

''Alyssa, I had to come and see you tonight. I had to thank you.''

''Thank me? For what?''

''For sending the wire to Denver. It couldn't have been an easy decision for you—not with Anderson's damning testimony against me. But you did it anyway. For some reason, you believed in me.''

She knew she should tell him to go. This wasn't proper at all. She was in her nightclothes and they were alone, unchaperoned. . . . But somehow, right now, none of that mattered. This was the moment she had waited for, hoped for, dreamed of for so long— she was with her mystery man again.

''I knew you weren't a cold-blooded killer,'' she said softly, gazing up at him.

''How did you know?''

"You saved my life that day on the trail when the others wanted to kill me, and you almost died yourself trying to rescue me from the river during the storm."

Slade was unable to help himself. He lifted one hand and gently caressed her cheek. "You're wonderful, Alyssa."

His one simple, gentle touch was almost her undoing.

"You said you only had to ask me one question—" Her voice was barely above a whisper as she stared up at his lean, darkly handsome features.

Slade's expression grew even more serious as he met her gaze. "I had to know, Alyssa. . . . I had to know . . . why were you crying?"

"I didn't want you to die—"

"Why?" His voice was hoarse with emotion.

"Because I love you, Slade Braxton. I think I've loved you since the first time I saw you that night of the dance."

Slade gave a growl of pure male satisfaction as he reached for her. He had hoped she cared, but he hadn't been sure until now. When she offered no resistance as he drew her into the circle of his arms, his heart soared.

"I love you, too."

He kissed her then, a sweet-soft exploration that revealed the true depth of his devotion. She sighed and melted against him. Alyssa's gentle surrender excited him, but there was still one thing troubling him. He remembered all too clearly Ken's words about Rob's intentions toward her.

"Alyssa—" He ended the kiss and held her slightly away from him.

"What?" She looked up at him, a little disoriented, wondering why he'd ended their kiss.

"There's just one other thing. . . . Rob . . . If you're promised to him, I'll go right now before we do something we might regret."

The look in her eyes grew warm as she stood on tiptoe to press another kiss to his mouth. "Rob and I are friends. I know he cares about me, but I've never returned his deeper feelings."

"You're not engaged to him?"

"No. He's not the man I want to spend my life with." Alyssa stared up at him, all the love she felt for him shining in her eyes. She had been given a gift. Slade was alive and well, and he had come to her tonight. "You are."

Slade smiled tenderly and held her close again. There was no longer any need for him to fight his desire for her. She was in his arms and she loved him.

Their first embrace the night of the dance had been forbidden and hurried; their second, when they'd been alone on the trail, had been startling and powerful. But tonight—now—he wanted more for them. He wanted the sweetness and the passion he knew could be theirs. He lowered his head and claimed her lips in a breathtaking kiss that set the world spinning wildly out of control around them.

Chapter Thirteen

Alyssa's senses reeled as Slade's lips plundered hers. She had never been held so intimately by a man before, and she found it most exciting to be crushed against the hard width of his chest. The feel of his hard-muscled body against her was arousing, and she found she wanted to get even closer to him.

When she'd kissed Rob earlier that evening, she'd experienced none of the wild emotions that were surging through her in Slade's arms. With Rob, she'd felt only safe and comfortable. But Slade's touch was ecstasy. His kiss and embrace awakened feelings in her that she'd never known existed—and they weren't feelings that made her feel safe and comfortable. They were feelings that made her want to forget everything—who she was and where she was—and just stay in his arms forever. Instinctively, Alyssa knew that this was where she belonged.

When Slade deepened their kiss, Alyssa met him in that passionate exchange and was caught up in a whirlwind of desire. She lifted her arms and linked them around his neck, drawing him even closer.

Slade . . . His name echoed through her mind as she met him in kiss after kiss. *He was there . . . He was alive . . . He had come to her. . . .* She moved against him, aching to be nearer.

Slade gave a low groan at her unspoken invitation. He held her even more tightly to him as his mouth slanted across hers in a devouring kiss. He could feel the soft fullness of her breasts crushed against him, and he marveled at how perfectly she fit in his arms. It was as if she'd been made especially for him.

Unable to resist the wondrous temptation, his hands began a restless foray over her slender curves. His knowing caress traced an arousing path and ignited fires wherever he touched her.

Alyssa whimpered as her passions ran wild. She clung to him, moving restlessly, wanting more from him. In her innocence, she didn't know what ''more'' was, and she didn't realize that her instinctive erotic movements were more enticing to him than the most learned caress by a practiced courtesan. She only knew that Slade was here holding her and kissing her, and she never wanted it to end.

Slade sought the soft weight of her breast in an intimate caress. She moaned against his mouth as a new and wildly wondrous sensation pulsed through her. His sensual exploration evoked an ache deep within the womanly heart of her that cried out for a fulfillment only he could give.

"Slade—"

Her whisper jarred him, forcing him to remember where he was and what he was doing. The woman in his arms was no saloon girl earning her keep. This was Alyssa. She was an innocent, untouched. He sighed and stilled his sensual assault.

He couldn't . . . no, he wouldn't take advantage of her. No matter how enthralling her kiss and her touch, he had to leave her and he had to leave her now. There was too much at stake.

"Alyssa—" His voice was hoarse with desire as he held her to his heart.

"What . . . ?"

She was caught up in the sensual web he'd been weaving around her. She looked up at him in confusion. It was blissful being in his arms, and she never wanted it to end.

Slade gazed down at her passion-flushed features and thought she'd never looked more lovely. Her color was high, her eyes bright with the knowledge of newly discovered desire. Her lips were red and swollen from the hunger of his kisses. He wanted her more than he'd ever wanted any other woman, but he would not hurt her.

"I have to go," he told her, pressing a gentle kiss to her slightly parted lips.

"But why?"

He silenced her with another kiss, tempted to lift her up into his arms and lay her upon the welcoming softness of her bed. His body was aching for oneness with her. He wanted to bury himself deep within her innocence and make her his for all time.

"I shouldn't stay—" he murmured against her lips.

"Why?"

She drew him down to her and kissed him fervently, arching up against him in an age-old invitation.

"Alyssa—" A muscle worked in his jaw as he fought to control his raging need for her. She was too tempting—too wonderful. "I should leave you now. I love you, and I won't be able to stop if I stay. I want you too badly."

"I want you, too." She smiled softly up at him, all the love she felt for him shining in her eyes.

"You don't know what you're saying."

"Yes, I do."

Her smile turned decidedly wicked, and Slade felt heat shaft through him.

"Are you sure?"

"Stay with me, Slade. Don't leave me tonight." She was innocent, but not so innocent that she didn't realize that she wanted to make love to him more than she'd ever wanted anything in her life.

Slade had meant to be a gentleman, to do the right thing, but at her invitation all was lost. Her request thrilled him, and he knew he would not leave her. Having her in his arms was his heaven, and he could no longer deny himself the joy of loving her.

His gaze never left hers as he lifted her up into his arms. He carried her to the bed and knelt upon it, laying her gently down on the soft expanse. He followed her down, stretching out beside her as his mouth claimed hers.

And heaven was theirs as they explored the wonder of their need.

With infinite care, Slade slipped her wrapper and gown from her, exposing the beauty of her slender body to his touch. At first, Alyssa was a bit shy being so unclad before him, but at the heated look in his eyes she grew more bold. She could see how much he desired her, and she lifted her arms to him.

Wanting to please her, to give her as much pleasure as he could, Slade went to her. He sought out her most intimate places with arousing caresses until she was writhing beneath him. His lips followed the sensuous trail his touch had forged, and Alyssa clung to him in breathless excitement. She had never known ecstasy so sweet.

When he moved away to shed his own clothes, she watched him, her gaze hungry upon him. She stared at his chest as he stripped off his shirt. She longed to run her hands over that muscle-sculpted bare flesh. Her gaze dropped lower as he shed the rest of his clothes, and her eyes widened in appreciation of her first look at an unclad male.

He was an Adonis, she decided immediately. His shoulders were broad, his chest and arms powerfully muscled. His waist was trim and his legs long and well-shaped. Alyssa thought Slade was male beauty personified.

Eager to touch him and kiss him, she rose up on her knees and smiled at him. "You're beautiful."

Slade was surprised by her words. "Men aren't beautiful," he denied.

"You are."

Alyssa took his hand and drew him back to the bed. He needed no encouragement to join her there. They kissed softly, then with more passion as their desire could no longer be denied.

Desperate to touch him, Alyssa reached out to caress him as he had touched her. His reaction to her boldness was immediate. He groaned and deepened their kiss.

Slade moved over her. She linked her arms around his neck as he came to her, seeking the sweet heat of her. Alyssa looked up at Slade as he moved to take her. There was the slightest feeling of pain and then pure rapture as he made her his.

She wrapped her arms around him, and they began to move together in love's age-old rhythm. They were one, giving and taking, until the perfection they'd sought crested within them, and they reached the peak of ecstasy together.

Alyssa cried out softly at the rapturous sensations that pulsed through her. Slade held her close, savoring her pleasure even as he achieved his own release.

She had never experienced such intimacy, such joy. She rested in his arms, holding fast to him, feeling more alive than she ever had in her life.

Slade had never known loving could be so beautiful, so giving. He cradled her to him, treasuring her nearness. He didn't know how he'd been lucky enough to find her, what quirk of fate had sent him to the dance that night, but he knew he would always be glad that he'd gone. The memory of the Kid's threat returned, and he vowed that he would protect her from all harm.

They drifted off to sleep, wrapped in each other's arms.

It was in the early morning hours that Slade awoke and forced himself to leave Alyssa's side. He wanted to stay there in bed with her, loving her for all eternity, but he had a job to do—keeping her safe and finding the Kid.

"I have to go," he told her quietly as he started to dress.

She smiled at him sleepily. "I wish you could stay."

"So do I."

Slade went to the bed and leaned down to kiss her. As he did, she ran a hand up his bare chest.

"Are you sure you have to go?"

"It will be dawn soon." He was staring down at her silken curves, wondering what the coming of the new day had to do with anything. He was here with Alyssa and—

She leaned forward just then and pressed a kiss to his bare chest. She smiled to herself as she felt him stiffen at her ploy, enjoying the newly discovered feminine power she had over him.

"It's still dark out."

"Yes, it is," he answered distractedly. He vaguely remembered that he was supposed to be getting dressed, but having Alyssa pressed against him, her lips upon him, was driving away all thoughts of anything but possessing her again.

"There's still time—" she whispered.

"Yes, there is."

They fell back together on the bed. Their coming together this time was fast and hungry. It was as if they couldn't get enough of each other. When at last their passion was spent, they collapsed together, panting from the fury of it.

It was long moments later that Slade realized he had to leave her. It would be light soon. He pressed one last, loving kiss on her lips and then quickly dressed without looking back at her where she lay looking so lovely on the bed. He feared she might tempt him into losing control again. For her own sake, he could not be weak where she was concerned. Her very life depended on his being strong.

"I have to go now."

"I know, but I don't want you to."

He loved hearing her say that. "Lock this door after me. I want to be sure you're safe before I leave."

"All right, but kiss me good-bye first." She rose and went to him, looping her arms around his neck.

Slade took full advantage and gave her a deep kiss.

"Now, lock the door when I'm gone. I don't want anything to happen to you," he told her as he opened the door and checked the hall before stepping outside. He didn't want to be seen leaving her room. He smiled tenderly at her as he closed the door behind him. "Good night."

Alyssa felt as if she'd dreamed the whole thing as she stood staring at the closed portal. With trembling fingers, she turned the lock and stood quietly, listening, wondering if Slade had really been there. The whole evening seemed almost a dream. And then she heard his footsteps move off down the hall, and she knew the truth.

She lifted a hand to her lips, tender now from the onslaught of his kisses. She could hardly believe that Slade had risked so much to come to her. His embrace had been wonderful—more wonderful than she could ever have imagined.

Turning away from the door, she put on her gown again and then lay down on her bed, reliving in her mind the events that had just happened. The memory of his touch and kiss enthralled her.

Tears of joy burned in her eyes, and she willingly gave in to them. As she'd watched Slade "executed," she had been torn by the knowledge that there had been nothing she could do to save him. But now all that had changed.

Slade was alive. . . .

Sleep came sweetly a short time later as Alyssa gave in to the exhaustion that threatened to overwhelm her. She slept contentedly, all the horror of the past few days forgotten for the moment. A sweet smile curved her lips as she dreamed of her strong, handsome mystery man loving her through the waning hours of the night.

Slade slipped away from the hotel unseen, and he was glad. He returned to the jail to find that Ken had gone back to his room and Jones was still there keeping an eye on things.

"You're back," Jones said by way of greeting as Slade came in the rear door.

"The streets were quiet. No one saw me."

"Good. Help yourself to a bunk down in one of the cells, but I doubt you'll get much sleep. Ken said he'd be back half an hour before sunrise so the two of you could ride out early."

"What about keeping a guard around Alyssa?"

"After you left, Ken and I talked. We decided it would be best if Alyssa and her family don't return to Black Springs on the regular stage. Rob and his deputies will be riding back, too, so we can hire Alyssa a private carriage, and everyone can make the trip together. It will be safer for her that way. She'll have a guard with her the whole time."

"Good idea."

It was fine with Slade that Alyssa would be surrounded by armed men on the trek back home. There were any number of places along the route where the Kid might try to ambush them. This way, they would have enough guns to fight him off if he tried anything.

"You could rendezvous with them outside of town later in the day."

"Good."

Slade almost hoped the Kid would try something right away. He wanted the upcoming confrontation with him over with as soon as possible. Until then, he would have to lie low and stay out of the public eye, for as Ken had reminded him earlier, he was a dead man.

But he was a dead man with a mission, and he was going to make sure the Dakota Kid faced justice before he could hurt Alyssa in any way. He wanted her out of danger as soon as possible.

No one was going to hurt Alyssa.

He would see to it.

"I'll be in the back. Call me when Ken shows up."

Slade disappeared into the jail cell he'd previously occupied with Johnson and Nash. He stretched out on the hard, narrow bunk and sought what ease he could find. As he lay there, staring at the ceiling, he thought of the comfort of Alyssa's wide, soft bed and regretted that he'd had to leave her. Even after all the loving they'd shared, his body was still on fire for her. He hadn't wanted to walk away from her tonight, and one day he was going to make sure he could stay.

But first, he had to bring in the Kid.

Once the Kid was under arrest and they'd learned the identity of the informant in the railroad express office, he would plan his future with Alyssa.

Chapter Fourteen

Alyssa felt like a different woman when she awoke in the morning. Though the night just past had had all the qualities of a dream, she knew it had truly been a dream come true. Slade had survived and he had come to her. Every now and then since she'd gotten up, she'd found herself stopping whatever small chore she was doing and staring off into the distance, smiling.

Memories of Slade left her weak-kneed and weak-willed. She wished he were there with her now. She wished he'd never had to leave her the night before. The time would come when he could stay, and she was eagerly looking forward to it.

As Alyssa was packing, a knock came at her hotel room door. For an instant, her heartbeat quickened, for she thought Slade might be returning, but then logic reasserted itself. It couldn't be Slade. It was broad daylight and the town was bustling with activity. He had to maintain his cover. Everyone thought he was dead.

"Yes?" she asked, refusing to open the door until she knew for certain just who was there. The Kid had gotten into her room the day before without any trouble. She wouldn't put it past him to try again today.

"It's Maisie from the front desk, Miss Mason," a woman answered. "I've got a letter here for you from Sheriff Jones."

Alyssa opened the door and took the missive from her. After going back inside, she sat down on the bed and read the short note. It informed her that the sheriff had taken the liberty of hiring a private coach for her and her family and that it would be ready to go whenever they were. She was pleased to learn that Rob and his deputies would be accompanying them on the trip back and that Slade and Ken would be meeting up with them on the way. The lawman wished them a safe trip home and thanked her for her help.

Alyssa quickly finished packing and then got ready to go speak with her mother and sister. It was going to be an interesting conversation—although "interesting" was far too casual a word for what she knew was about to come. Prepared for the worst, she left her room and crossed the hall to knock on her mother's door.

"It's me, Mother. I need to talk with you for a minute."

"Of course, dear." Loretta hurriedly opened the door to her daughter.

When Alyssa was inside their room, she sat down in a chair to watch them as they packed.

"Are you all ready to go?" Loretta asked.

"Yes, I'm all packed."

"Good, because the stage leaves soon. We really should hurry."

"That's one of the things I wanted to talk with you about," Alyssa began.

"What is, dear?"

"The trip home."

"Why?"

"Well, there's been a change in plans."

"A change?" Loretta looked troubled. "Has something gone wrong?"

"Well," Alyssa began, then paused.

At her hesitation, Emily's eyes narrowed suspiciously. "What's wrong, Alyssa? What happened?"

"All right," she began hesitantly. "I'll tell you everything, but you've got to promise not to be angry with me."

"Why would we be angry with you?" Loretta asked in surprise and then grew suspicious again.

"Because something happened last night that I didn't tell you about."

"What?" her mother demanded, instantly concerned.

"Well, when I got back to my room after visiting with Rob, I found a note on my nightstand. It was from the Dakota Kid."

"What!" Both Emily and Loretta almost shouted, they were so horrified.

"Somehow he managed to break into my room and

271

leave me a threatening letter. He said that he'd already killed my father and I was going to be next. He said it was my fault that his friends had been hanged because I'd ruined his chance to break them out, and he was coming after me.''

''Dear Lord . . .'' Loretta had gone ashen, and she was staring at Alyssa in horror. She sank down on the bed. ''This happened last night, and you're just now telling us?''

''There was no point in worrying you right then. That's why I went back to the sheriff's office to see Rob. I showed him the note, and he and Sheriff Jones both agree that we should travel home by private coach today. They think it might be too dangerous to make the trip on a regular stage.''

''Rob knows all about this?''

''Yes. We talked last night. He and his deputies will be riding with us to make sure everything goes all right.''

''Thank heaven for Rob. Somehow, he is always there when we need him.''

''Yes, he is,'' Alyssa agreed.

''But Alyssa, you should never have gone over to the jail alone!'' Emily scolded. ''Something terrible might have happened to you.''

''I had my gun with me, just in case.''

Loretta was terribly pale as she regarded her daughter. ''This terrifies me, you know. That man is a murderer, and he says he's after you now.''

''It's going to be all right, Mother,'' Alyssa tried to reassure her. ''We'll have Rob and the deputies with us. We'll be fine.''

"But he might not give up easily—"

"We'll just take things one day at a time. We'll be fine."

She desperately wanted to tell them the truth about Slade and Ken, but she knew better than to mention it now. According to Sheriff Jones's note, the two men would meet them somewhere on the trail, and that would be soon enough for her family to learn their real identities. The shock of hearing about the Kid's threat was enough excitement for her mother just now.

"Do you know when we're supposed to leave?" Emily asked.

"As soon as we're ready, they'll be ready. Shall I go tell them to plan on half an hour?"

"That'll be fine," they agreed.

"Why don't I come with you?" Emily suggested.

The two sisters went downstairs and found Rob waiting in the lobby for them.

"Good morning," he greeted them, his smile very real at the sight of Alyssa.

"Yes, it is," she responded. "We're going home."

They spoke of the arrangements for the carriage and about making sure Spartan was not left behind. They would tie him to the back of the carriage for the return trip.

"Rob, I was wondering," Emily began, looking around as if expecting someone. "Do you know where Ken Wiley is? I haven't seen or heard from him since yesterday afternoon."

Rob shot Alyssa a quick look and realized that she hadn't told her family everything yet.

"I heard he left town early this morning," he informed Emily.

Emily's expression faltered noticeably. "Oh . . . I'd hoped to speak with him again before he went back to Denver."

"I'm afraid he's gone, Emily. I'm sorry."

"Thanks, Rob." Her disappointment was very real, and she made no effort to hide it.

After agreeing to meet Rob downstairs at the appointed time, Alyssa and Emily went back upstairs to get their things.

"I didn't know you were that interested in the reporter," Alyssa remarked.

"I just thought he was intriguing, that's all." Emily tried to sound casual, but her earlier reaction had been the true one.

"Maybe you'll run into him again one day," Alyssa suggested.

"Why would a man like Ken come back to a small town like Black Springs? I'm sure he's gone forever."

Emily sighed to herself. Ken Wiley had intrigued her from the first. He'd been the one man she'd ever met who hadn't fallen all over himself trying to win her favor and court her. He had been a pleasant diversion from her usual over-eager cowboys, and she really had been attracted to him.

"We'll see," Alyssa said. "Right now, let's go home. We'll worry about everything else later."

"How can you be so at ease about everything when you know the Dakota Kid is still on the loose?"

"I'm not at ease. I just know that the safest place

for us is Black Springs. Rob and his deputies are going to protect us, and they're going to bring in the Kid and the gunman named Zeke Malone. Once they're locked up, we'll be able to live a halfway normal life again.''

"Listen to you. . . . You're so confident. The very thought that the Dakota Kid might still be around here terrifies me, and he says he's after you now!''

Alyssa stopped and took Emily's arm to bring her to a halt. She looked her straight in the eye. "Would you feel better if you had a gun with you? I'm sure I can get one for you if you want to carry one.''

"No, I'll be all right. Maybe once we get home, I'll take the one Papa gave me down to the store with us, but I'll worry about that when we get there.''

"It's going to be fine. Trust me,'' Alyssa told her as she gave her a hug.

"If you say so.'' Emily sounded less than convinced.

Within the hour, they had said their good-byes to Sheriff Jones and were on their way home. Spartan was securely tied to the back of the coach along with Deputy Hawkins's mount; the deputy was serving as their driver. Rob and Deputy Brown rode alongside, keeping an eye on their surroundings, watching for any sign of trouble.

They had been riding for about two hours when the coach began to slow down.

"Is something wrong?'' Loretta worried. "Why are we stopping?''

Alyssa glanced out the window and saw two men

riding toward them in the distance. She smiled, recognizing Slade and Ken.

"Nothing's wrong. In fact, I think now is the time I should tell you what's right."

"I don't understand—" Her mother looked puzzled.

"There's one more thing that I didn't tell you this morning, because we needed to be away from town before you could learn the truth."

"What truth?" Emily asked, not sure what in the world her sister was talking about.

"The truth about Slade Braxton . . . and Ken Wiley. Or should I say Ken Richards?"

Her mother and sister stared at her in open confusion.

"What about them?" Emily wondered.

"Slade Braxton wasn't a liar after all."

"I don't understand." Loretta could see a change coming over her daughter. As she was talking, Alyssa seemed suddenly almost lighthearted, and Loretta couldn't understand the change.

"When Slade and I were alone together during the trip here, he told me he was working undercover for the Pinkertons and asked me to wire Denver to verify his identity. I didn't believe him. I thought, as Rob did, that he was a cunning liar. But I learned last night that Braxton was telling the truth. He is a Pinkerton agent."

"You can't be serious!" Her mother and sister were both astounded.

"I'm very serious."

"But they hanged him!"

"Slade's execution was faked yesterday. He's alive and still on the trail of the Dakota Kid."

"He's a killer!" Loretta protested. "Les Anderson saw him shoot your father."

"For some reason, Mother, Les wasn't telling the truth. Slade did not shoot Papa. In fact, Slade was trying to keep Papa from being shot. Zeke Malone is the one who gunned him down."

"How do you know all this?"

"Slade told me."

"But he's—"

"Very much alive and joining us for the ride to Black Springs right now."

They could hear the horses drawing near then, and Emily and Loretta exchanged looks of complete astonishment.

Alyssa had known it would be difficult for them, so she hurriedly went on with the rest of the news. "And Emily, your Ken is not Ken Wiley from the *Denver Daily News*. He's Slade's supervisor, Ken Richards, out of the Pinkerton office there. They're working together to bring down the gang."

"I don't believe any of this," Emily said, staring at her in confusion.

"You'll be able to talk to Ken yourself in just a few minutes."

"But what about all the wanted posters on Braxton . . . all the bounties?"

"The agency created Slade's background to convince the Kid to let him ride with his gang. It was lies, all of it. Slade is no gunslinger. He never was. And he did not kill Papa."

Emily and Loretta could only sit there in silence. Everything they'd believed had just been turned upside down, and they were struggling to understand and come to grips with the truth.

"When did you learn all this?" Loretta demanded, outraged at having been lied to.

"Last night. When I rushed over to the sheriff's office to show Rob the note from the Kid, I walked in on Slade and Ken. Slade's faked death had to be kept secret. They want the Kid to believe he's dead, so Slade was hiding out at the jail until he could leave town."

Emily couldn't help laughing as she imagined the scene at the jail the night before. "I bet they were shocked to see you."

"Shocked wasn't the half of it," she told Emily with a grin. "You should have seen Rob trying to get me out of there before Slade came in the room, but it was too late."

"That must have been a terrible moment for you," Emily sympathized.

Alyssa was silent for a moment. "It was, and it wasn't. You know how I feel about Slade. I kept believing that I could find some way to save him, but I couldn't. Somehow, I knew in my heart that they were making a mistake by hanging him, but I couldn't prove it. It was horrible. . . . But then, on top of everything, to discover that he was not only still alive, but innocent of all the terrible charges against him, too—" She drew a ragged breath as she mentally relived the confrontation.

"I'm glad it turned out this way," her sister said,

truly understanding what Alyssa had gone through.

Loretta, however, was deeply troubled. "This is all so confusing. You're saying the man who was convicted of killing your father was innocent . . . but wasn't he there, robbing the bank? Didn't Les Anderson see him do the shooting?"

"Yes, he did ride with the gang on the robbery, and he did have his gun out during their ride from town, but Slade assures me that he did not shoot Papa. Zeke Malone was firing back in Papa's direction. He was the one who killed him."

"But Les—"

"Les probably just wanted to make sure that the Slade Braxton who is on all those wanted posters paid for his crimes. He probably saw Slade firing and took his testimony one step further than the truth to make sure he didn't get off."

Loretta looked suddenly very tired. "I know you cared for—I mean, care for this Braxton fellow, Alyssa, but it's hard for me to comprehend this right now."

Alyssa took her mother's hand. "It was hard for me, too. This is the best thing that could possibly have happened considering the circumstances, though. Now, not only do we have both the sheriffs from Black Springs and Green River after the Dakota Kid, we've got two Pinkertons working on the case. They're going to find the Kid and Zeke Malone, Mother. I promise you they will. The Pinkertons always get their man."

Loretta was a bit encouraged at the thought. "I just want to make sure they get the Kid and what's left

279

of his gang before he has the chance to hurt you."

"Don't worry, Mother. Nothing's going to happen to me. I'll be safe."

The coach had come to a complete stop, and the riders reined in beside it.

Alyssa didn't wait for anyone to come after her. She immediately opened the door and climbed down. She'd been aching to see Slade all morning and could hardly wait to feast her eyes upon him. When she turned and saw him dismounting from his horse, her pulse quickened. She had always thought him handsome before, but today, he looked absolutely magnificent to her. As he dropped his reins and walked toward her, it was all she could do not to throw herself into his arms. She had to remember who she was and what she was doing there.

"Good morning, Alyssa," Slade greeted her, giving her a half-smile.

His smile and the dark look of promise in his eyes took her breath away. She somehow managed to smile sweetly back at him.

"Hello, Slade," she said, nodding toward him. "It's good to see you up and about."

"It's good to be up and about," he countered. "The alternative isn't pretty."

"No sign of the Kid on your ride out?" Rob asked, as he insinuated himself into their conversation.

"Nothing," Slade told him. "It was quiet all morning. We stayed out of sight of the main road and kept a lookout for you."

"No news, I guess, is good news," Rob said. "You're comfortable in the coach, Alyssa?"

"It's fine, thank you, Rob."

"Good." He wanted to please her, especially after last night. He knew she wasn't happy with any of them, and he was determined to make it up to her.

"Slade, I think it's time you met my mother and my sister," Alyssa said, drawing him toward the coach door.

She quickly made the introductions.

"Mrs. Mason, my deepest sympathies on the loss of your husband," he said in earnest as he faced her. "If there had been some way for me to prevent it, I would have. I give you my word that I'll find the man who did it and bring him in."

Loretta had not been sure what to expect from Slade Braxton. She'd watched Slade at the trial and had been so full of hatred for him that it was difficult for her to see him in this new light and appreciate who he really was.

"Thank you, Mr. Braxton," she replied coolly, uncertain and still not fully trusting him.

"Miss Mason," Slade said as he looked to Emily, "it's nice to meet you, too."

"Mr. Braxton," Emily replied, looking past him to where she spied Ken sitting on his horse. Her chin lifted in irritation as she clearly recognized him now as the man she'd seen riding out of Black Springs the night she was putting up the sign. She hadn't been crazy! Ken Wiley really did have an alter ego! He truly was dangerous and deadly. He was a Pinkerton!

"I guess we'd better keep moving," Rob put in, wanting to get back home as quickly as they could.

"Slade, you ride in the coach with the ladies. Hawkins will tie your horse up in back."

Slade offered Alyssa his hand to help her climb back inside. As their hands touched, excitement surged through them both. Alyssa found it difficult to concentrate on anything but the feel of his hand on hers. She remembered clearly the gentleness of his touch and how he had caressed her and kissed her just hours before, and she fought down the blush that threatened.

Slade was not unaffected by the touch of her hand. He wanted to put his hands at her waist and lift her inside the vehicle, but he knew that would seem too forward an act for him. He had to satisfy himself with just being close to her, but it wasn't easy when all he could think about was the sweet taste of her kisses and how perfectly they had come together. It had been beautiful. She had been beautiful.

Slade started to climb inside, but Rob's call stopped him.

"Braxton! Here! Keep this with you!"

When Slade looked his way, Rob tossed him his rifle. He nodded toward the lawman and climbed into the now cramped carriage, shutting the door behind him. He'd hoped he'd get to sit next to Alyssa, and he was pleased to find the space next to her open. She smiled at him as he sat down, and he smiled back, enjoying having her pressed against him on the tight bench seat. He looked up and found himself facing her mother and sister. He knew then and there that it was going to be a long ride to Black River.

As Slade settled in, Ken decided he might as well

face Emily and get it over with. He rode up to the side of the coach where she was sitting by the window and smiled in at her.

"Morning, Emily," he greeted her.

"Hello, Mr. *Wiley*," she replied tightly, emphasizing his phony last name.

"I thought we'd agreed you'd call me Ken?"

"That was when I thought I knew who you were," she answered tartly. "Right now, I'm not quite sure."

"I *do* investigate stories," he told her.

"Just not for the *Denver Daily News!*" she retorted.

"Sometimes they do run stories about the investigations."

"But not because you've written them! They print them because they're big news and you happen to be involved with them!"

"Emily, I'm sorry I had to lie to you and your mother," he apologized. "It was important that I learn everything I could about the testimony against Slade before the trial so I could save him from hanging."

"I understand, I'm sure, sir," she said disdainfully.

"Good," he answered, though considering her tone, he really didn't believe her.

"Let's head out again," Rob ordered.

The coach lurched forward, and they continued on, anxious to return home. Once they were in Black Springs, they believed it would be easier to protect Alyssa, and that was Rob's main concern right now—keeping her safe from harm.

"It's difficult for me to accept all that's happened,'' Loretta told Slade as they faced each other across the narrow width of the conveyance.

"I understand,'' he sympathized, "and I'm sorry for all that you've been through. That's why we've been working so hard to bring down the gang.''

"Rob almost got all of them,'' Emily put in.

"He did a good job that day, better than any other lawman had before. Until Rob, there hadn't been a sheriff who'd even come close to catching up with the Kid.''

"Why didn't you bring them in?'' Loretta asked, voicing the question that was troubling her. Her gaze was piercing and almost condemning upon him as she went on. "You'd been riding with the gang for all that time, and you knew who they were. The Pinkertons are supposed to be the best. Why didn't you set up an ambush of your own and bring them in before they killed my husband?''

Slade had known this moment would come, and he'd dreaded it, because he knew the answer he had to give her wouldn't help explain anything. "There's more to our investigation than just arresting the gang. If that had been the case, I could have brought them down the first week I was with them.''

At Loretta's pained expression, he knew he had to explain further.

"I can't go into detail. Just realize that you already know more than most—you know I'm alive.''

Loretta felt a twinge of fear as she realized the dangers of his job. She looked over at him, studying him for a long moment, seeing the fierce determination and intelligence that made him the successful agent that he was.

"I wish our association had begun under better circumstances," she finally said. "Of course, Alyssa always believed that your heart was good."

Slade glanced over at Alyssa to find her gazing up at him, a gentle smile on her face. "She's a special woman."

"That she is," her mother agreed.

Emily was sitting quietly, feeling most put out. Ken had taken advantage of her. He had used her and discarded her when he'd gotten what he'd wanted from her, and that didn't sit well with Miss Emily Mason. She wasn't accustomed to being treated that way by men, and she was determined to do something about it. Mr. Ken Wiley—or Richards or whatever his last name really was—had just better watch out. He might be a master detective, but he hadn't seen anything like what she was planning for him.

The hours passed quickly, and they made good time. There was no sign of any trouble, and they neared the way station where they planned to spend the night just before dusk.

Hawkins drew the coach to a halt about two miles out, and Slade started to climb out of the coach.

"Where are you going?" Alyssa asked.

"The fewer people who see me, the better. I'll be close by tonight keeping watch, don't worry." His gaze met hers for an instant, telling her all she needed to know, before he was forced to leave her.

With that, he stopped to speak briefly with Rob,

then mounted his own horse and rode off across country. Hawkins got the coach moving again, and they rolled into the station just as darkness was claiming the land.

Chapter Fifteen

"Alyssa, I want you to stay inside tonight," Rob told her as he helped her down from the coach when they arrived at the station.

"Do you think the Kid might be close by?" she wondered, curious as to what was going on.

"We haven't seen or heard anything to lead us to believe that he is, but I don't want to take any chances."

"Whatever you say."

He kept an eye on Alyssa until she was safely indoors with her mother and sister. Once he was certain she was out of harm's way, he met with his deputies to discuss the plan for keeping watch that night.

"What can I do to help?" Ken asked as he joined them.

"We're going to be taking turns, starting now and

changing every two hours,'' Rob told him.

''Count me in. I'll take first watch if you want me to. That way you can all go get something hot to eat. It smells pretty good over by the house. The station manager's wife must be a fine cook.''

''Thanks.''

Confident that they'd done all they could to ensure Alyssa's protection, the three lawmen went off to get their dinner while Ken remained outside.

Ken checked his side arm and walked around the area to make sure everything was secure. He kept a careful watch, looking for any movement or flash of light that might give away an ambusher's hiding place. He saw nothing out of the ordinary, and he was grateful. He hoped they had a peaceful night.

''Ken?''

Emily's voice came softly to him. He looked back toward the house and was surprised to find her coming toward him, carrying a plate of food.

''Emily, you should stay inside where I know you'll be safe.''

''You're out here. If I'm with you, I know I'll be safe,'' she said simply, giving him her most coquettish smile. She hadn't used all her wiles on him before, and she was bound and determined to do so now. ''Here, I brought you something to eat. Rob told us how you volunteered to take first watch. It's nice of you to help them out.''

He wanted to tell her that his offer had nothing to do with being nice, that it was his job, but he didn't. He needed to concentrate on what he was doing, but the tantalizing smell of the food was distracting, not to mention Emily's presence.

"Well, it was nice of you to bring me out some food. Thanks."

"Someone has to take care of you," she said, "while you're so busy taking care of us."

They found a bale of hay near the stable and sat down there so he could eat.

Ken tried not to think about the lovely young woman sitting next to him as he ate the meal. He was working right now, and, as he'd told Slade, there was no time for emotional entanglements when one was investigating a case. Still, it was difficult for him to ignore the light, intoxicating scent of her perfume as it drifted to him on the cool night breeze.

"This is really delicious. The station manager's wife is a very good cook."

"Ken?"

"What?" He cast her a sidelong glance as he took another bite of his meal.

"Why are you ignoring me?" Here she was sitting right next to him, and he was far more interested in the dinner she'd brought him than he was in her. It was infuriating. She'd never played second fiddle to a plate of food before, and she was quite certain that she didn't like it.

"I'm not ignoring you," he answered, taking great pains not to look at her again. "I'm protecting you."

"What from? It's a beautiful night. The stars are out and the moon. . . . The Kid's nowhere around." Her voice grew softer as she spoke.

He cleared his throat as he set the empty plate

aside. "Emily, I am protecting you from me."

"What?"

Ken turned to her, and the rigid control he maintained over himself threatened to shatter as he stared down at her. She was the prettiest woman he'd ever seen, and she was there—with him.

"Damn it, woman—" he growled as his last fragment of control snapped. He took her in his arms and kissed her.

Emily met him fully in that embrace, delighting in the feel of his lips upon hers. She'd wanted to kiss him ever since she'd seen him that day in the sheriff's office, and she was thrilled.

Because the moment was forbidden and dangerous, it was even more exciting for them. His kiss was hungry and passionate, and Emily was swept away by the heat of his sudden, raging desire.

Only the sound of a horse stirring restlessly inside the stable nearby jolted Ken back to full awareness. He silently cursed his weakness for Emily as he abruptly put her from him. He stood up to put distance between them. A lapse like this in his iron-willed control could get him killed while he was on the job, and he had no intention of ending up dead any time soon.

"Emily—" He gazed down at her, seeing the hunger in her eyes and knowing his own need matched hers. Still, he denied himself that which he wanted most. "Go back inside and stay there." His tone was harsh.

"Didn't you enjoy kissing me?" she asked boldly, angered by his rejection. She stood up before him, as proud as any Valkyrie, fire flashing in her eyes.

"Good night, Emily," he said, deliberately sounding cold and indifferent. He wanted to discourage her, to make her mad enough to stay away from him. This was no game they were playing. They were dealing with the Dakota Kid. Lives were at stake. He couldn't afford any lapses in judgment—not even for her.

Emily was shocked by his dismissal. She all but stomped away from him. He was maddening! She'd never been treated so shabbily by a man before, and the worst part was, she was at a loss as to what to do about it. She wondered, too, why tears were burning in her eyes. She decided she just wanted to cry because she was angry. Not because she really cared about him.

When Slade left the coach, he sought out a secluded vantage point where he could safely bed down for the night. His thoughts were on Alyssa's safety, but Rob had assured him that he and his deputies were going to take turns standing guard all night at the station. He would have preferred to have protected her himself, but had resigned himself to hiding out. He would meet up with them on the road again the following morning.

He ate a sparse cold meal and, after taking a quick look around, tried to settle in. He'd had little rest the last two nights and needed sleep badly. He sought the comfort of his bedroll on the rough, rocky ground, but there was scant ease to be found. Stretching out as best he could, he kept his rifle close at hand and closed his eyes.

The images that teased him as he lay there helped him forget all about the hard ground. In his thoughts, he relived his night with Alyssa, holding her and kissing her—loving her until the threat of dawn had driven him from her arms. He thought of the long hours riding in the coach with her close by his side. He'd been hard-pressed not to take her in his arms any number of times when his imagination had conjured up fiery memories of the night just past. Only the presence of her mother and sister had held him at bay.

Slade wondered if Alyssa had felt the same way he had. He wondered, too, when he'd ever get to be alone with her again. The way things were going, he knew it wouldn't be any time soon.

Sleep finally eased over him, and his sweet dreams of his lovely lady offered him solace on the cold, lonely ground.

Alyssa awoke before daybreak and couldn't get back to sleep. She lay on the cot in the bedroom she was sharing with both her mother and her sister, thinking about Slade and wondering where he was and if he was all right. It had been difficult to watch him leave the day before, and she'd been worried about him ever since. He was alone in the wilderness, and if the Dakota Kid happened upon him, she knew it would be a terrible, deadly confrontation.

Rob had said that there had been no sign of trouble, though, so she believed that Slade was safe. She told herself that she would be reunited with him in just a few hours, but those few hours seemed an eternity to her.

The memory of Slade's lovemaking played in her mind as she tried to rest, and unbidden desire stirred within her. She ached to have him back in her arms. Only when she was with Slade did she feel secure; only then did she feel whole.

Rising quietly, Alyssa went to stand at the window. She parted the curtains to look out at the sky. She was pleased to see that it was brightening a bit. Daylight would soon be with them, and that meant Slade would be, too.

As she looked around, she could see Rob keeping watch, rifle in hand, near the stable where the men had bedded down for the night. She knew he cared for her, and it distressed her to think that at some point she was going to have to tell him that there could be no future for them. She couldn't tell him just yet, though, for it would be too awkward while they were making the trip. She would wait and explain things to him later, when they would have some privacy.

As she was looking out the window, she saw Ken emerge from the stable. Alyssa couldn't prevent a smile as she studied the other Pinkerton.

She wasn't quite sure what had happened between Ken and Emily the night before, but it had definitely upset her sister. Emily hadn't said much when she'd returned from taking him his dinner, but she'd almost seemed to be pouting when she went to bed. As accustomed as Emily was to having men panting after her, Alyssa supposed the trouble could be that Ken

293

wasn't chasing her—and her beautiful sister was not used to being ignored.

Under normal circumstances, Alyssa would have found the situation amusing and thought the challenge good for Emily, but not right now. There was too much danger to be considered. She would have to caution her sister about that.

Turning away from the window as Hawkins and Brown came out of the stable, she knew it was time to rouse her mother and Emily so they could be on their way. They wanted to be ready to ride as early as possible.

After feasting on a hearty breakfast and quickly loading up, they were on their way barely an hour after sunrise.

Slade met them about three miles on the other side of the station. He spoke briefly with Rob, checking to make sure everything had gone smoothly overnight, then tied his horse to the back of the conveyance and climbed inside.

"Good morning," he greeted Alyssa, Loretta and Emily as he sat down. "Rob says everything went fine last night."

"What about you? You didn't have any trouble?" Alyssa asked, concerned.

"No, it was quiet." The only trouble had been trying to keep his thoughts about her under control, and that kind of trouble he could stand.

Alyssa was so glad to see him that she wanted to kiss him. Instead, she played the sedate young woman, impressing even herself with her acting skills, for she certainly didn't feel the least bit sedate when Slade was around.

The traveling seemed endless that day. They were making good time, though, and would reach the next way station early in the afternoon, far ahead of schedule.

"What do you think?" Rob asked Ken and Slade when they stopped to rest the team at midday. "Shall we stop early at the station or keep going and camp out tonight?"

"Let's keep going," Slade said. "The sooner we reach Black Springs the better."

"Ken?" Rob looked to the other man.

"I agree with Slade. Let's keep moving. I'm sure there's a good, defensible campsite somewhere farther up ahead."

They were off again, moving at top speed, anxious to cover all the ground they could. They picked up what supplies they needed at the station and continued on. It was about an hour before dusk when they found a protected clearing just off the trail.

Though Loretta was concerned, Alyssa volunteered to sleep beside the campfire while her mother and Emily took the coach.

"It'll be all right, Mother. Don't forget I just made the trip up here unchaperoned," she told her with a smile.

"And I was concerned then, too!" Loretta responded with a wry smile.

"Well, Rob and the others are here to protect me, so I don't think you have to worry."

There was no delicious dinner this night. They

cooked their own meal over the campfire. It wasn't gourmet fare, but it was filling.

Slade was relieved that he didn't have to leave Alyssa tonight. Worrying about her the night before had been hellish. Tonight, he would keep her close at hand.

"I need to move around a bit," Alyssa said, standing and stretching after she'd finished her meal. The long hours cooped up in the coach had taken their toll on her and left her feeling cramped. It was still light out, so she figured she'd be all right.

"Don't wander too far," Rob cautioned.

"I'll go with her," Slade announced, taking advantage of the perfect opportunity to be alone with her for a while.

They walked off to a rock formation far enough away that no one could overhear their conversation. Alyssa leaned back against it and looked up at Slade. She was thrilled to have a moment with him during which they could talk openly.

Slade gave her a wicked grin. "I'm tempted to sneak off behind this rock with you and not come back until morning."

She returned his conspiratorial smile. "It sounds wonderful. If I'm going to be kidnapped by a gunslinger, I want it to be you."

"I'd be happy to oblige, but if I even think about trying it, Rob will be right over to check on us."

"He's a good man," she stated.

"A very good man." Slade took a step closer, aching to kiss her. It had been much too long since he'd last had the chance to hold her in his arms and taste of her sweetness.

"You don't suppose we could move just a few steps farther this way and watch the sunset from over here, do you?" she asked, noticing that there was a clear spot just beyond the rock where they could steal a few moments without an audience.

"I'd love to watch the sunset with you."

The moment they'd shifted out of sight of those sitting by the campfire, Slade caught Alyssa up in a warm embrace. His mouth claimed hers in a wild exchange, and she showed no shyness in returning his passion. It seemed she had been waiting for this moment for an eternity, and she gloried in having him near.

Kiss followed hungry kiss. Slade could not get enough of her. She was a fire in his blood. A thirst that could not be quenched. He had never felt this way about a woman before. No other female had ever enthralled him the way Alyssa did. She was beautiful and smart, and he never wanted to let her go.

Caught up in the rapture of their loving, they savored their temporary haven of intimacy. They forgot momentarily that others were keeping watch over them. There was only the sunset, and the heat of their need.

Rob had been eating when Slade and Alyssa went off on their own. As long as he'd had them in sight, he hadn't worried. When they first disappeared behind the rocks, he did not immediately become concerned because he knew they both were armed. But when they didn't reappear after a few moments, he grew troubled, and the silence that ensued only deepened his concern.

He had agreed to take the first watch tonight, so he didn't say anything to the others as he went to check on them. They were all busy getting ready to bed down. Loretta and Emily had already climbed into the coach to seek what comfort they could find there, and Hawkins and Brown were spreading out their bedrolls in hopes of getting at least some sleep.

Rob carried his rifle with him, fearful of what he might find, for as he drew nearer to the rocks, he could hear no conversation. He frowned, listening carefully, wanting and hoping to hear them talking, but there was only silence. His hold on his weapon tightened. He feared the Dakota Kid had somehow overpowered Slade and hurt Alyssa.

Tense, his nerves stretched taut, Rob quietly moved past the rocks. He wasn't sure what he expected to find. He had prepared himself for danger or a confrontation with the Kid. And so he was completely taken aback by the sight that greeted him—the sight of the woman he loved in the arms of another man.

Rob took a step backward as if struck a physical blow by the vision of Alyssa blissfully returning Slade's kiss. They were completely unaware of his presence and so he silently backed away, trying to deal with the heartbreak of learning the truth of her feelings.

He had thought he and Alyssa might have a future together. He had thought that she would be open to his courting after a respectful amount of time for her mourning, but obviously he'd been wrong—very wrong. Alyssa didn't love him, and from the looks of things, she never would. He wasn't the man for her.

The pain of acknowledging the truth of her feelings for Braxton stabbed at him as sharply as any blade. He moved away, giving them privacy, not wanting them to know that he'd seen them together.

Right now, he had a job to do and that was to get her back to town without incident. No matter how she felt about him, he still loved her, and he would do everything he could to ensure her safety. He could do no less.

It was only a short time later when Slade and Alyssa returned to the campsite. No one else had been concerned about their absence.

Later, when Hawkins relieved him and it was his turn to rest, Rob didn't sleep. He lay staring up at the stars, thinking of what might have been and wishing that somehow things could have been different.

Slade's kisses had only served to make Alyssa all the more miserable. She wanted to be with him, always, and they'd practically had to tear themselves apart when it was time to return to the campsite. They'd realized that their need for each other was so powerful that if they hadn't stopped then, they wouldn't have stopped at all.

"I told Ken to make sure your bedroll was between his and mine," Slade told her as they walked slowly back, each taking great care not to have any physical contact with the other.

"I guess I can't get any better protection than that—spending the night in between two Pinkertons."

"That's the way we're looking at it," he said with a grin.

They reached the fire and spread out their bedrolls. The temptation of knowing they were so close and yet couldn't reach out to each other kept them from sleeping soundly that night.

The following afternoon when they stopped to rest the horses for a while, Rob managed to get a moment alone with Slade. He'd had a lot of time to think about what he was going to say to him, and he'd purposely waited until now to say it. He'd wanted to make sure he wasn't speaking to him in anger or out of jealousy.

Not that he wasn't jealous of Slade's relationship with Alyssa. He was, and he was angry, too. He'd wanted to be the man in Alyssa's life, the man she cared for, but things hadn't worked out that way. He was going to have to accept that reality, for he knew he couldn't change it. But when he spoke of the situation to Slade, he wanted the other man to know that his interest in their relationship was out of concern for Alyssa, and not for any other reason.

"Braxton, I need to talk with you," he said tersely.

Slade followed him as he walked away from where the others were gathered. "What is it?"

Rob turned on Slade and looked him straight in the eye. "I've got something to say to you, and it needs to be said in private."

"What?"

"It's about Alyssa—"

"What about her?" Slade was cautious, wondering where the conversation was going.

"Let me put it this way—I care about Alyssa. She means a lot to me, but it's obvious to me now that she doesn't feel the same way about me."

"I don't understand."

"I saw the two of you together last night."

Slade was surprised. He hadn't realized that Rob had come upon them when they'd stolen their few minutes alone. He didn't say anything, but waited for him to go on.

"I just want you to know, Braxton, that if you ever hurt her in any way, I will personally see to it that you are very sorry."

Slade realized how deeply Rob cared for Alyssa. She had a champion in her sheriff, and he respected the other man all the more for it.

"You don't have to worry, Rob. I would never do anything to cause Alyssa any pain."

Rob glared at him, studying him, trying to read him to see if he was hiding anything. But Slade was facing him forthrightly. There was no hidden meaning behind his words.

"She's a very special woman," Rob said.

"Yes, she is. I love her."

"You'll do the right thing by her." It was a statement of fact, not a question.

"As soon as all this is over with the Kid, I intend to propose to her."

Rob nodded slowly, approvingly. If he couldn't marry her, at least he was glad it would be Slade. "She could do worse."

Slade smiled at him, sensing that the tension was easing between them. He respected Rob and hoped the lawman respected him. "She could probably do better, but I'm hoping she won't want to try."

They stood there, sizing each other up for a moment, before moving apart.

Rob felt better for having championed Alyssa, yet he still wished there had been some way she could have loved him as he loved her.

Slade walked away from Rob, glad to know that there was no hostility between them over Alyssa. They still had too much danger to face ahead of them. He wanted Rob by his side as a friend, not an enemy.

Chapter Sixteen

Zeke smiled at the Kid as they broke in the back door of the Mason home in Black Springs. "That was easy, wasn't it?"

"Keep quiet. We don't want anybody to know we're here," the Kid said as they crept inside.

"There ain't nobody around."

"And we want it to stay that way."

They lit one candle and made sure to stay away from the windows as they checked out the deserted home and memorized the floor plan. When the time came to pay the lady judge back, they wanted to be prepared. Until then, they didn't want anyone to know what they were up to.

"I'm thinkin' we should just make ourselves at home here and enjoy their hospitality 'til they show up."

"That would be entertaining," the Kid agreed, speaking in a low voice. "Can you imagine the look on her face if she found us relaxing all comfortable-like in her house?"

"I'd enjoy that, but not nearly as much as I'd enjoy havin' some of her. I've had a hankering for her ever since that first night we were in town and I saw her dance with Braxton."

"He's damned lucky nobody recognized him and tried to take him in right then."

Zeke shrugged his indifference, glad that the other man was dead now. "Either way, his luck finally ran out."

The Kid nodded in the darkness. "I miss all three of them. They deserved better than what they got, and I intend to see that Judge Alyssa Mason suffers for all the trouble she caused."

"I'll be glad to help you with it."

"I knew you would be."

They finished going through the house. Zeke found Alyssa's bedroom and lingered a little too long in there for the Kid's peace of mind.

"Let's get out of here," he ordered, eager to be gone.

"Damn, but I'd like to sleep in her bed tonight," Zeke said, going through her bureau drawers and handling her more intimate things.

"Go ahead and take something of hers if you want it. It'll just let her know that we've been here and could have done anything we wanted to."

Zeke took a silken garment from her lingerie drawer, and then they left the house.

They would keep watch, and wait. When the time was right, they'd meet up with Alyssa Mason and have some fun with her—fun that only they would enjoy. And Zeke intended to enjoy himself with her the most.

When they finished with the lady judge, the Kid was going to make sure that the word got out around the territory that it didn't pay to mess with him. He wanted the lawmen and other judges to see what was done to Alyssa Mason, so they would know that he would stop at nothing in seeking revenge. He wanted to put fear of the Dakota Kid in them.

The coach rolled into Black Springs early on their fourth day of traveling. They were all relieved to have made it home without incident.

Once more, fearful of being seen, Slade had left them on the outskirts of town. He planned to stay to the back roads and meet them at Alyssa's house as soon as possible. They had to decide the best way to keep watch over her, now that they were back.

Alyssa was smiling as she climbed down from the coach in front of her house. They were home. The three women started inside, but Rob stopped them.

"Let me go in first."

"You think they may have been here?" Loretta asked, worried.

"It's hard telling where the Kid might be, but we're just going to be careful."

"Rob!" Ken's call came from around back.

They rushed to the rear of the house to see the back door standing slightly ajar, the lock forced.

"I found it this way," Ken told them, his gaze seeking out Emily. He noticed how she'd gone pale at the discovered intrusion.

"Oh, God!" Loretta cried, terrified. She clutched at Emily, her belief that they could get back to leading a normal life destroyed.

"Easy, Mrs. Mason," Rob said, trying to soothe her as he drew his gun. "You ladies stay out here with Hawkins and Brown, while Ken and I take a look around."

He gave his deputies a look that told them to stand close guard and was about to go inside when Slade appeared, coming out from behind their small barn. Slade had made good time once he'd separated from them, and he'd been waiting and watching for their arrival from his hiding place. He'd wondered why there seemed to be a commotion around back, and then he saw the frightened looks on the women's faces.

"What is it?" He rested his hand on his gun, ready for trouble should it come.

"Somebody broke into the house," Alyssa explained quickly.

She wanted to go straight to him, to be held in the shelter of his embrace, and the thought amazed her. She was used to being independent and taking care of herself, but now she liked having Slade's protection. Even so, she knew she had to be strong and not show any weakness before her mother and sister. If they thought she was afraid, it would only make things worse.

"You think they might still be inside somewhere?"

Emily asked, looking at Ken, her eyes wide with fear.

Ken wanted to tell her that there was nothing to worry about, that everything was fine, but it would have been a lie.

"It doesn't look like it, but we'll make sure," Ken told her.

It was the first time she'd spoken directly to him since he'd kissed her at the way station. She'd taken great pains to ignore him since then, and he had to admit that at first he'd been glad. It had allowed him to concentrate on business, but when she'd begun flirting with Hawkins, he'd found himself annoyed. He'd forced himself to focus on his job, but it had been tough. The only good thing was that now when she really was afraid, she'd look to him for comfort and not to Hawkins.

"You wait here. We'll be right back," Rob said.

Drawing their guns, Slade, Rob and Ken disappeared inside. They began a careful search room by room. It was Slade who discovered that the outlaws had gone through Alyssa's personal things in her bedroom.

"Rob," he called. "Look at this."

Rob saw the open drawers and Alyssa's underthings strewn haphazardly about. He swore under his breath.

"Zeke Malone did this." Slade was certain of it.

"How do you know?"

"The Kid only cares about his revenge. But Zeke—" Slade explained about the night before the robbery. "We've got to make sure he never gets the chance to lay a hand on her." His tone was fierce.

"Don't worry." Rob was angry, too. "We'll put a guard on the house around-the-clock."

"You won't have to. I'm going to stay here," Slade stated. "I can't very well move around town with her, but I can damn well guard the house."

The sheriff knew his proposal made sense. Having Slade secretly under the same roof with the women would certainly add an element of surprise to their defense of them. Anything they could use to their advantage against the Kid and Zeke was important.

"Let's tell the ladies what we're going to do. I'll make sure Alyssa has an escort to and from her office every day," Rob decided.

The men were grimly determined as they went back outside.

"Is everything all right?" Loretta asked. She was upset and angry.

"Nothing's missing as far as we could tell," Rob assured her. "And there was no vandalism to speak of. We'll get the locksmith over here right away and get your door repaired."

"Thanks. Then it's all right for us to go in now?"

"First, let me tell you how Slade, Ken and I want to handle this," Rob said. He quickly related their plan.

"Having Slade in the house can only help," Loretta agreed. They had a spare bedroom, and she knew she would rest easier having him close at hand. "We want to do everything we can to help you catch the Kid. If there's anything you need from us, just say so."

Rob smiled at the older woman. "We will. Mostly,

308

I just want you to be constantly aware of your surroundings and to make sure you don't give the Kid a chance to hurt you.''

"Don't worry. We won't.''

Ken looked at Emily, who appeared a bit more relaxed. "Are you feeling better?''

Now that her initial terror was over, she wasn't about to let him know that she'd needed him.

"Of course. Deputy Hawkins here reassured me that everything is just fine,'' she said, looking up at the deputy adoringly.

Ken turned and walked back around to the front of the house, his jaw clenched in irritation. *Women!*

Loretta and Emily went on inside as Rob and the deputies began to unload the coach. Slade looked over at Alyssa.

"Before you go in . . . I have to tell you, one of them tore your bedroom apart. It doesn't look like they took anything, but you'd better check and make sure.''

This time she couldn't suppress the shudder that racked her. "It's an awful feeling to know that they could get into the house so easily.''

"The good news is, you weren't here when they broke in.''

"But next time—'' She looked up at him, fear evident in her expression.

"If there is a next time, I'll be waiting for them.''

She managed a smile then, and they went inside together. As horrible as the discovery of the break-in was, it thrilled her to know that Slade would be close.

* * *

The rest of the day passed quietly. They learned that Deputy Clemans had gone by their house two days before and nothing had been amiss. Ken went with Rob and the deputies to ask around town to see if anyone had seen any strangers or noticed anything unusual recently, but their quest turned up nothing. Discovering that the Kid had been there so recently was unsettling, but it also encouraged them that they were doing the right thing by waiting in town for him and not getting up a posse to go on a wild-goose chase around the territory.

The Kid had said he was after Alyssa, and Slade knew they could believe him. The outlaw leader was out for revenge.

Even after the lock on the back door had been replaced, Loretta did not feel entirely secure anymore. Only Slade's manly presence helped to calm her. When it was finally time to retire, Loretta and Emily said good night and went upstairs to bed, leaving Slade and Alyssa alone in the parlor.

"I'm glad you're staying here with us," Alyssa said. "I doubt I could have gotten through today without you."

He smiled gently at her. "Sure you would have. Look at what you've been through in the last few weeks."

"Sometimes I get tired of being strong," she admitted out loud. "Just thinking about the Kid and Zeke being here in the house makes me want to scream! I hate them!"

"You're not alone in this, sweetheart," he told her softly as he went to sit beside her on the sofa.

"Slade, I was wondering . . . I found a small, one-shot derringer in Papa's desk drawer, and I thought maybe I should start carrying it with me. What do you think?"

"I think that would be smart. It would be difficult for you to carry your six-gun all the time, but the derringer can fit in your pocket."

She nodded. "I'll do it, then. I'll feel better if I have it with me, since you and Rob can't be here all the time."

Slade realized it was time to tell her what had happened between him and Rob. "There's something I need to tell you—"

"What?" She looked at him questioningly.

"That second night of the trip when we were enjoying our view of the sunset—" he said, with a half-smile.

"Yes?"

"Well, Rob was standing guard, and he got worried about us because we'd moved out of sight. He went to check on us to make sure we were safe, and he saw us together."

"Oh." She was saddened by the news. "How did you find out?"

"He took me aside and spoke with me about it. I would have told you sooner, but this is the first time we've been alone since it happened."

"How is he?"

"It wasn't easy for him, but he knows how we feel about each other now, and he's handling it."

"I'm so sorry. . . . I wanted to tell him myself when we got back here and things quieted down."

"I would have picked a better way, too, but it's too late to worry about that now."

She looked at Slade and could only imagine what the two men had said to each other. "I hope he finds happiness some day."

"I do, too. He deserves it."

Slade caressed her cheek as their gazes met, and then he kissed her as he'd been longing to do all day. He wished the terror was over, so he could concentrate on her and their future, but reality had too firm a grip on him. He had to make sure they got the Kid and Zeke first. As long as the gunmen were on the loose, he couldn't afford the luxury of dreaming about living happily ever after with Alyssa.

She melted against him, savoring his kiss and his nearness. She had been so wrapped up in her studies with her father that she'd never really thought she'd fall in love. None of the men around town had intrigued her or delighted her the way Slade did. He was everything she'd ever wanted in a man, and she couldn't believe the circumstances that had brought them together.

"I'm glad you asked me to dance that night," she said when they finally moved apart.

They were very aware of her mother's and sister's presence in the house, and so had to control their desire. Not that it wouldn't have been sweet to give in to their need, but Slade respected Alyssa too much to cheapen their love that way.

"I am, too, although I must have been crazy to do it . . . or maybe just in love."

"You believe in love at first sight?"

He smiled at her. "Why not?"

"What about Emily? Weren't you attracted to her? Every single man at the dance seemed to be vying for her attention."

"Your sister's beautiful, there's no doubt about that, but when I looked at you—" He leaned closer, giving her a soft kiss. "I knew you were the woman I wanted."

"I like the sound of that." She lifted her arms around his neck and drew him to her for another fiery kiss.

They were both breathing heavily when they broke apart. They sat quietly, just enjoying being together.

"You're lucky to have such a wonderful family," Slade told her.

"You would have liked my father," she said, sadness coming into her eyes. "And he would have liked you."

"He must have been a good man to have so many friends."

She smiled at Slade as she thought of her father. "Papa was. He was honest and fair, and he never knew a stranger. I don't think we'll ever really be convinced that he's gone forever."

"Death is like that." He was solemn.

"Tell me about your family," Alyssa said. "Where do you call home?"

"I was raised in St. Louis, but my parents both died of the fever when I was seventeen. I've been on my own ever since."

"You didn't have any other relatives to take you in? No brothers or sisters?"

"No."

"What did you do? You were so young to be by yourself—"

He shrugged slightly, preferring not to think about those hard times. "I headed west to Kansas and began working on the cattle drives. From that I got work as a range detective for a while, and then I met Ken on a trip to Denver. He recruited me to be a Pinkerton, and I've been working as an operative ever since. It's been just over five years now."

"Do you enjoy the work?"

"Some days I do. . . . Like the days when I see the outlaws I've been chasing finally locked up. That makes it all worthwhile, but sometimes, like in the situation with your father, it's hard being undercover . . . real hard."

She reached over and touched his hand. "I love you, Slade Braxton, and I know that you had nothing to do with my father's murder. There was no way you could have stopped it."

His gaze met hers, and he saw reflected in her eyes all the peace, acceptance and understanding that his soul so desperately needed.

"I love you, too, Alyssa."

He crushed her to his heart, loving the feel of her soft curves pressed against him. His mouth slanted across hers in a hot, possessive kiss that could easily have led to more . . . much more.

With a groan, Slade realized he had to set her from him right then, or in another moment, he might not be able to release her at all. In a herculean effort of self-mastery, he ended the embrace and stood up.

"You'd better go on up to bed now," he ordered. "I'll stay down here and keep watch."

Alyssa ached to kiss him and touch him and love him, but she also knew he was telling her to leave him because he wanted to protect her, not hurt her.

"Good night, Slade." Her voice was soft as she rose and left him standing there alone.

He raked a hand through his hair as he stared off in the direction she'd gone. If he had known at that moment exactly where the Kid and Zeke were hiding, he would have gone after them that very night, just to put an end to the fear and terror that was threatening their lives.

He resented being forced to play the Kid's game, and that was what they were being forced to do—whether they liked it or not. But with Alyssa's life at stake, he had little choice in the matter.

Slade turned off the lamps and sat down in the darkness alone, watching and waiting for trouble he hoped would never come.

Rob came to escort Alyssa to her office bright and early the next morning. Her mother and Emily were ready to reopen the store, too, so they all left together. When they had gone, Slade retired after having been up all night. It was near noon when the sound of Ken's knock roused him from a deep sleep. He quickly got up to let him in.

"What brings you here?" Slade asked wearily. "Did you find something out?"

"No, things are very quiet. I sent a wire to Denver, letting them know where we were and what we were doing. If they have anything to tell us, they'll contact me here.''

"Good. This waiting isn't sitting well with me."

"I know. I feel the same way. I want this to be over. I want Alyssa out of danger."

Slade nodded. "I just wish we'd get some kind of break. The Kid's managed to elude us at every turn. Even after all my weeks of riding with him, I never did learn anything that would help us identify the informant in the express office. I'm beginning to wonder if there's any way we can still find out."

"I don't know. The good news is that they're working on it from the other end, too. The last I heard, we had a man undercover in the office itself."

Slade nodded. "Good, because I just don't see the Kid robbing another train any time soon—or ever again, once we bring him in."

"Amen."

"How's Emily?"

Ken shot him a quick glance that was less than kind. "How should I know?"

Slade tried not to grin at him, but he couldn't help himself. "I thought you liked her."

Ken muttered an expletive. "I'm working on a case. I don't have any time for women."

"That must be why I heard her talking about how Deputy Hawkins wanted to come courting her as soon as her mourning period was over. And here I thought you were the man she wanted."

Ken gave a snort of derision. "She's just a baby. She's barely out of the cradle."

"I heard Alyssa say that she was almost nineteen."

Ken scowled at him. "This is no time to be concerned about females."

"Not even females you love?"

"Who said anything about love?"

"In all the years we've worked together, I've never seen you pay attention to any good woman—until Emily."

Ken looked uncomfortable. "Damn it, Slade, we're investigating a case."

"All the more reason why you can't escape her. She's involved in this, whether you like it or not. You're going to be seeing her daily, whether you like it or not. You may as well face it. You're going to have to deal with the problem."

Ken scowled. "It's a problem, all right."

"I feel the same way about Alyssa. I'd give anything for her not to be involved in this. I want her out of danger. I know my original assignment was to learn the informant's name and bring down the Kid and his gang, but that's all changed. Alyssa, inadvertently, has become a big part of this operation, and now my first and foremost priority is to make sure she comes out of it unscathed. If that's becoming personally involved, then so be it. I love her, and I won't stand by and let anything happen to her—not when I'm partially to blame for what happened to begin with."

"How do you figure any of this is your fault?" Ken asked, puzzled by his statement.

"If I'd only been ordered to bring in the gang, we could have brought them down long before the Kid decided to rob the Black Springs bank. If I'd done that, her father would never have been shot, and none of this would have happened.''

"There are a lot of times in life when things happen that you can't control.''

"I know. Alyssa even said that no one blames me, but I still wish I could have done something.''

"You are doing something. You're helping to bring in his killer. As soon as we bring in the Kid and Zeke, the one responsible for John Mason's murder will pay with his life.''

"I was riding with them when it happened.''

"It was your job to maintain your cover.''

"And watch innocents die?'' He voiced the dilemma that had been troubling him for some time.

"If necessary in the line of duty—yes.''

They were both grimly silent. As painful as it was, Slade knew that Ken was right.

"So, what are you going to do about Emily?'' he asked.

"Nothing.''

"You aren't going to let her know how you feel about her?''

"She already knows I care.''

"Then why are you avoiding her?''

"Because I don't want to be distracted while I'm working on this investigation with you.''

"But aren't you being even more distracted by trying not to be distracted? Go talk to her.'' Slade waited for him to say something, but he didn't. "Go on. Straighten things out with her. You'll feel better if you do.''

"There's nothing to straighten out.''

Slade gave him a disbelieving look. "All right. But just remember that Hawkins has been coming by to talk with her, and she's even mentioned how nice Deputy Clemans is, too."

"I'm glad she likes them," Ken ground out, standing up to leave. "I'll talk with you later."

Slade watched him go and would have smiled, if his friend hadn't looked so perturbed. Emily was a light-hearted flirt, but he also knew that she was interested in Ken. He'd watched her as she'd tried to ignore Ken during the last few days. She hadn't been entirely successful in her attempts. He'd seen the flicker of emotion in her expression that had proven to him that her interests lay not with the deputies she was charming, but with Ken.

Ken left the house, determined not to do anything about Emily. As he made his way through town, though, he found himself walking toward the general store. He stopped himself, then deliberately went to the stable to saddle his horse. He rode out of town with no particular destination in mind. As he passed the store, he saw Deputy Clemans coming out, looking rather pleased with himself and smiling quite broadly.

Though he rode for over an hour, Ken's mood did not change. He kept thinking of Emily and wondering what Clemans had been smiling about. Despite his best effort to stay away, he returned to town and reined in before the store.

"Afternoon, Ken," Loretta greeted him as he entered.

"Mrs. Mason," he replied, glancing around but seeing no sign of Emily anywhere.

"What can I do for you?"

"I was just stopping by to make sure you were all right."

"It's been pretty quiet today, but quiet is good right now."

"Have you seen Rob since this morning?"

"No, but Deputies Clemans and Hawkins were both by and said they'd heard nothing new."

Ken nodded. He knew exactly what the Dakota Kid was up to—he was going to stall and make them wait and make them sweat. The Kid was a cautious man. He was a man who liked to be in control. When he finally did make his move, it would be lethal.

"Emily just stepped out a few minutes ago to run an errand for me, but she should be back soon if you want to wait and visit with her for a while."

"No, just tell her I said hello," he said, starting for the door. He didn't need to be there. It was ridiculous that he'd come.

"Oh, Ken?" Loretta called out to him.

"Yes?" He looked back but did not stop his retreat.

As he was glancing toward Loretta, Emily came through the door and almost collided with him.

"Why, Ken, what a pleasant surprise. I didn't know you were going to stop by," she said sweetly, trying to ignore the way her heart skipped a beat at the sight of him. He was so handsome—and so irritating.

"I just dropped in to see how things were going."

320

"Ken, why don't you come by the house for dinner tonight," Loretta asked.

"I'd be delighted, thank you for the invitation. What time?"

"Six-thirty will be fine."

"I'll see you then," he said and then left the store, nodding to Emily as he went.

Emily was annoyed as she watched him go. Wasn't that just his way? Instead of visiting with her for a while, he couldn't wait to escape. She was surprised that he'd actually agreed to come to dinner. He probably had only said yes so he could see Slade for a while. She was sure he wasn't coming to see her.

"Do you think he'll really come?" she asked her mother.

"Why wouldn't he?"

"I don't know. . . . Sometimes I don't think he likes me very much."

"Oh, that's nonsense, Emily. Of course Ken likes you."

"Well, would you mind if I invited Deputy Clemans to dinner, too?" she asked, already planning what she was going to do that night.

"I don't suppose there would be anything wrong with that."

"Good."

Emily watched out the store door for the lawman. As soon as she saw him, she was going to issue her invitation. She'd show Ken that she wasn't a woman to be so easily ignored. She'd show Ken that other men found her quite attractive and irresistible, no matter what he thought.

Dinner that night was delicious, though not fancy, and those gathered spoke of everything but the Kid. They deliberately took care to avoid the topic, wanting to share a relaxed meal and, for just a little while, pretend that everything was fine.

When dinner was over, they moved into the parlor. Ken sought out Slade, while Emily made a point of sitting beside the deputy on the love seat. Ken was trying to concentrate on what Slade was saying, but he kept glancing over at Emily, who seemed enraptured by the lawman's every word.

"What do you think?" Slade asked, then waited to see what his friend's response would be.

"About what?" Ken countered.

"That's what I thought. You haven't heard a word I've said."

"Yes, I have. You were talking about, uh . . ."

"Exactly." Slade was disgusted with him.

"Mother," Emily said as she stood up with the deputy. "Vernon has to leave, so I'm going to show him out."

Emily had barely made it out the front door with the lawman when Ken stood up.

"I'd better go, too," he announced. "I'll talk to you tomorrow, Slade. Mrs. Mason, thank you for a delicious dinner. Alyssa, good night."

Slade knew why he wanted to go so quickly—he didn't want Emily alone outside with Clemans. "I'll see you then."

"Good night, Ken," Loretta said.

He walked out of the house to find Emily standing alone on the porch watching Clemans walk away up the street.

"He's gone already?" Ken was surprised. He'd thought for sure the other man would be trying to kiss her out here in the dark.

Emily turned to look at Ken. "Yes. He had to go."

"Well, er . . . I'm leaving, too. Good night, Emily."

"Good night, Ken."

She gazed at him invitingly. She ran the tip of her tongue over her bottom lip in unspoken invitation. She all but tackled him as he started to move past her, but Ken did not respond.

Emily had never been at her wit's end before, but this man was pushing her to it. She wondered what her father's advice would have been if he'd still been alive and she'd confided in him. As she thought about it, she knew her father would have told her to go after what she wanted. And that was just what she decided to do.

Ken reached the edge of the porch and started down the steps just as her hand snaked out and grabbed him by the arm.

"Are you really going to leave me without a good-night kiss, Ken?" she said daringly.

Without waiting for his answer, she pulled him toward her and brazenly, wildly kissed him. When she ended the kiss and let him go, she did not say a word. She turned her back on him and, with her head held high, went inside and closed the door firmly behind her.

Ken stood staring at the closed door, a silly half-smile on his face.

Emily had kissed him.

Chapter Seventeen

Alyssa was tense as she left her office early and started toward the jail to seek out Rob. It had been over a week since they'd returned from Green River, and so far nothing had happened. The Kid had made no move. It had been quiet. Too quiet.

At the direction of her thoughts, Alyssa realized how ridiculous she was being. She should have been thrilled that nothing had happened. She should have been thanking God that the week had been uneventful, but the constant, unrelenting threat of danger was draining.

"Alyssa, is something wrong?" Rob asked, looking up in surprise as she entered the sheriff's office. He was scheduled to pick her up at her office in two hours.

"No, everything's fine. I just finished work early

today and wanted to let you know. I think I'll stop by the store and visit with Mother and Emily for a while, before I go on home.''

''Well, let me walk you down,'' he offered, standing and grabbing his hat.

''Thanks.''

She had been tempted to go about her business normally, but she knew Rob would have been angry if she had. He'd made it plain that he wanted to be at her side whenever she moved around town.

Rob held the door for her as they left the office. He was slowly coming to terms with their relationship—or rather their lack of a relationship. It had been painful for him to accept, but at least he had her friendship. He still loved her. He knew he would never stop. It wasn't possible to turn off such a strong emotion, and his love for her was enduring. He glanced down at her as they made their way to the store, and he smiled to himself because he had, at least, this much time with her.

''There's been nothing new today. Everything's peaceful,'' he said.

''I guess that's the good news. Ken hasn't heard anything from Denver?''

''No. I spoke with him this morning. Everything has been quiet there, too.''

''You don't suppose the Kid and Zeke have gone somewhere else, do you?''

''I wish I could tell you that they had, but there have been no sightings of them anywhere. There's been no word of any robberies or shootings . . . nothing. Judging from what Slade says about the Kid,

326

though, he doesn't give up. When he makes up his mind to go after something or someone, he doesn't stop. The Kid is cold, methodical and thorough. As hard as it is for us to remain vigilant, I think we have to continue to act as though he's somewhere close around.''

''I'm sorry this is so much trouble for you.''

''Alyssa,'' he said seriously, as he stopped walking to look down at her. There was no one around, so he knew he could speak from the heart. ''There is nowhere else I'd rather be than with you.''

She lifted her gaze to his and smiled tenderly up at him. ''Thank you, Rob.''

He stared at her for a moment, wishing things could be different, then forced himself back to reality. He started on, not speaking, letting his sharp-eyed gaze sweep the streets and alleys as they walked. He would take no chances with her life. She was too precious.

''Hello, you two,'' Loretta said as they entered the store. ''What are you doing here this time of day?''

''I got done early, so I decided to leave the office. Rob's doing the honors again.''

''Afternoon, Loretta,'' Rob returned, smiling at her. ''Anything interesting going on around here?''

''No, just business as usual.''

''Nothing wrong with that.'' He walked through the store, checking things out, then returned to Alyssa's side. ''Did you want to stay here or go on home?''

''Do you need any help?'' Alyssa asked.

''We're pretty much caught up.''

"Then I'll have Rob walk me home, and I'll start dinner for you tonight."

"We'll see you at six," her mother said as she watched them go.

Loretta remembered how much John had wanted Alyssa to marry Rob, and she was sorry that it would never be. Not that she didn't like Slade. In the days that he'd been staying at the house guarding them, she'd come to like and respect him. He was a smart man—he had to be to be a Pinkerton—and he was handsome, too.

She understood why Alyssa had fallen in love with Slade. She'd felt the same way about John all those years ago. Loretta sighed, missing the gentle life of loving she'd led with her husband. A tear traced a path down her cheek at the thought of him. She missed him so much, and she wondered if the ache in her heart and the emptiness in her soul would ever go away.

Rob escorted Alyssa to the house. There was no sign of Slade, so he went inside with her to make sure everything was all right. Rob found the door to Slade's room ajar and looked in. He was sleeping. He quietly closed the door and went back downstairs to tell Alyssa.

"Do you want me to wake Slade up for you?" Rob asked, concerned.

"No. He stays up all night, so he needs all the rest he can get. Just let him sleep."

She could tell Rob was worried about leaving her because he was frowning.

"Rob, don't worry. There are times at the office when I'm alone during the day, and nothing's happened. I'll lock the door when you leave, and I'll be fine. Besides, if anything should happen, I've got my derringer in my pocket and I'd only have to yell and Slade would come."

"All right. I'll be back first thing in the morning."

"I'll see you then."

Alyssa closed and locked the door as Rob left, then sighed as the tension drained from her. She was home. Another day was over. She started upstairs to her own room, and, as she did, she passed Slade's room.

The temptation to enter was great. She paused before his door, wondering if she dared. They'd had little time alone during the last week, and she thought perhaps she should wake him. With great care, she opened the door and looked in.

Slade appeared to be sleeping soundly. He lay on his stomach, his face turned toward her. A dark shadow of beard covered his jaw. In sleep, his defenses were down, and there was a look almost of innocence about him as he slumbered. He was irresistibly handsome and virile, and her heartbeat quickened.

Alyssa took a step into the room, drawn to him, wanting to be close to him. Slade did not stir. She moved nearer, amazing herself with her brazenness, yet unable to stop herself. She didn't want to leave. She wanted Slade.

Going to stand beside his bed, she could no longer resist the temptation of him. She bent to him and pressed a soft kiss to the corner of his mouth.

"Slade . . ." she whispered.

His eyes opened, and at the sight of her, a slow, sexy smile curved his lips. He had just been dreaming of having her in his arms, of kissing her and making her his own. For a moment, he thought he might have conjured her up, that he might still be caught up in the pleasure of his fantasy. He reached out to touch her, wanting to see if she was actually there. His hand closed on her wrist, and he knew she was real.

The Alyssa in his dream had been wonderful, but she was only a figment of his imagination. He wanted this woman—the flesh and blood Alyssa, the Alyssa who dominated his thoughts every minute of the day and night.

Slowly, he drew her to him, and she did not resist. He shifted on the bed, and she accepted his unspoken invitation, moving to lie beside him.

"We're alone," she told him in a quiet voice, wanting him to know that at last they had some time together.

At the very welcome news, Slade pulled her into his arms and brought her full length against him.

"For how long?" he asked, knowing he didn't want to start anything they couldn't finish.

"Long enough," she said in a voice just above a whisper. She'd wanted this for so long, had ached for him so long, that she didn't want to think about leaving his embrace.

"You're sure?" He rose up on one elbow to look down at her.

She stared up at him, at the wide, bare expanse of

his hair-roughened chest, and she nodded, drawing him down to her. "I love you, Slade."

He decided to show her how much he loved her this time, rather than tell her. With infinite care, he kissed her, and his kiss spoke volumes. His touch was restrained as he unfastened the buttons on her dress and helped her slip the garment from her. Then he stripped away the rest of her clothing, leaving her perfect beauty bared to his hungry gaze.

Slade's eyes were dark with passion as he visually caressed her. Her breasts were tempting, her hips full and inviting, her legs long and slender. He was on fire for her, and he could wait no longer. It had been too long already.

Alyssa lifted her arms to him, and he went into them, fitting himself to her. She opened to him like a flower to the sun, and she gasped at the intimacy as he claimed her for his own.

They began to move together, seeking the joy they knew would be theirs. She met his eager thrusts, matching him, urging him on. Holding him close, she caressed him, glorying in the domination of his powerful body. They were perfect together. One in body. All that mattered was that they were together. All thoughts of danger were burned away in the heat of their joining. There was only the two of them, each seeking to please the other, each wanting only the other's happiness.

They sought the heights of desire together. With kisses and heated caresses, they explored the wonder of their love. The flames of their need burned higher and hotter until there could be no turning back, no denying the prize that they sought—the gift they wanted to give to each other—the ultimate pleasure of ecstasy's promise.

Their excitement crested and waves of rapture swept them away to bliss and beyond. Clasped in each other's arms, their bodies joined in love's embrace, they surrendered to the perfection of their union.

"I love you, Alyssa," Slade said as he shifted away from her and brought her into the circle of his arms.

She sighed and nestled against him. "I wish I never had to leave you again."

He smiled at the thought. "Well, we could stay like this forever as far as I'm concerned, but I think your mother might not approve."

"I know . . . I have to go. They could be back at any time," she said in a soft voice, but she made no effort to leave him. Being here with him was her heaven.

Slade sought her lips in a gentle kiss. "You don't suppose that if we closed the door, she would never know we were here, do you?"

"Somehow, I think she and Emily would figure it out."

He pretended to scowl. "Too bad."

"I know. I like your idea."

"The day's going to come, my love, when you will never have to leave my bed."

"I'm looking forward to it." She linked an arm around his neck and pulled him to her for a kiss.

His need stirred again, surprising him. He'd never wanted any woman the way he wanted Alyssa. He started to move to make her his again, but she eluded him, slipping from the bed to stand before him in all her feminine glory.

She began to dress, and he resented the garments that hid her from him.

"I'll be glad to help you," he offered.

She gave a small laugh; she saw through his offer to his real plan. "I think I'd better do this on my own."

"Pity."

"I know. There's nothing I'd rather do than spend the rest of the day and night in your arms. You promised me an all-night ride not too long ago, and, trust me, one day I'm going to make you deliver on your promise."

"You'd torture me that way?" he asked, grinning.

"Yes, and I'd enjoy every minute."

"I hope so," he growled, his imagination running away with him. He rose from the bed and went to help her fasten the buttons on her dress.

"I liked unfastening them better."

"So did I."

They embraced, his mouth seeking hers in sweet emphasis.

"So this is it? Tonight we're finally going to get her?" Zeke asked the Kid eagerly. He was hot, and he was ready. He'd been wanting to go after the lady judge for days now, but the Kid had refused—until now.

"We'll wait until after ten. I want it nice and quiet around there when we make our move."

"Hell, I'm ready now!" Zeke declared.

He was finally going to get a taste of her, and his body hardened in response to thoughts of the night to come. If he enjoyed thinking about it this much, he could just imagine how much he was going to enjoy actually doing her.

"Slow down," the Kid said sharply, knowing how Zeke sometimes let the wrong parts of his body do his thinking for him.

Zeke shot him an angry look. "I'll slow down for now, but tonight, she's mine."

"You can do whatever you want to once we've got her out of town, but until then you'll listen to me and do what I say."

The other outlaw was resentful of those orders, but shut up. He knew the Kid was right. That was why he rode with him.

Zeke settled in to wait out the afternoon. They were camped about an hour out of town, so they wouldn't leave for the Mason house until close to sunset. It would be a long couple of hours, but it would be worth it. He smiled.

It was near dark when they finally rode out for Black Springs. They were both more than ready for the action to come. They reached the outskirts of town after nine o'clock and skirted around the area until they reached Alyssa's house. After leaving their horses in the secluded spot they'd discovered when they'd first searched the house, they approached on foot. The Kid's leg had healed, and he had no problem covering the terrain. He was ready. Tonight was the night.

Zeke was beside him all the way. He was eager, hot and hungry for a taste of that lady judge.

The knock on the door shortly after dark surprised everyone. At Slade's direction, Alyssa called out and asked who it was before she opened the door.

"It's Ken. I need to talk to Slade. It's important."

Slade stepped forward and opened the door as he holstered his gun.

"What's wrong?"

"I just got a telegram from the Denver office that sounds promising," he said as he came inside. "I thought you'd want to know right away."

They went to sit at the dining room table so he could read the missive to them. Loretta and Emily gathered around, too, to see what the big news was.

"According to the operatives working undercover out of Cheyenne," Ken began, "they've narrowed down the number of suspects in the express office to two men. An arrest is imminent. We should be hearing something in the next day or two."

Slade was relieved. He wanted the entire gang out of operation. "Good. That's one less thing we've got to worry about. Now all we have to do is finish what I started—bring in what's left of the Kid and his gang."

"We'll do it. Pinkertons never rest until they get their man," Ken said, his determination evident in his voice.

They shared looks of satisfaction across the table, unaware that just outside the window, the Kid and Zeke were watching everything in silent fury.

335

Slade Braxton was still alive! Slade Braxton was an undercover Pinkerton agent!

"The bastard!" the Kid swore under his breath as he took aim at Slade.

The power of his rage was so great that he was physically shaking. His knuckles were white as he gripped his gun. He'd been betrayed! He'd been set up! And Nash and Johnson had paid with their lives for Braxton's deception and lies!

As the Kid thought of his two dead friends, his anger grew even more. The hanging had been faked! Everyone believed that Braxton had been hanged, too, but there he was—alive and well.

But not for long!

The Kid took careful aim, ready to put an end to Slade's miserable life. No one betrayed the Dakota Kid and got away with it! No one!

"Don't!" Zeke said in a hushed voice as he grabbed the Kid's arm to stop him. "We're going to end up dead if you fire that gun right now. There's only two of us, and there are five of them. There's no way we can pull it off and get out of town in time. Not now. Not tonight."

"Bullshit!" the Kid cursed, jerking free of Zeke's hold. "I want that bastard dead now!"

"So do I, but if you fire that gun, we ain't gonna be alive to see his funeral, and believe me, I'm looking forward to seeing him six feet under."

The Kid was past logic and past using any well-thought-out plan. He had never been so furious or so close to being out of control. He wanted nothing more than to pump bullets into Braxton. He started to squeeze the trigger.

"No!" Zeke snarled. He'd never had to face down the Kid before, but he wasn't ready to die—especially not over Slade Braxton. "Think about what you're doing! We need a new plan. You want to kill Braxton, fine, but we need to let him know who's pulling the trigger and why. Right now he thinks he's pretty smart, riding with us like he did and coming out of it looking like a damned hero. We need to think this through. We still got time. There ain't no hurry. We got the upper hand."

The Kid was filled with bloodlust. He was ready to kill. There would be no stopping him until he'd gotten what he wanted. And he wanted Braxton dead. But there was a grain of truth in Zeke's words. Somehow, the Kid managed to get a temporary grip on his fury.

"All right," he relented, "but I'm not gonna wait long. We gotta get word to Patterson that the Pinkertons are on to him. He's gotta get out of there while he still can."

They fell silent as they continued to watch what was happening inside from their hiding place by the window.

"I'll let you know the minute I hear anything more. Otherwise, I'll be close by in case you need me," Ken was saying as he stood up to leave.

He glanced over at Emily, but she was talking to her mother and paying no attention to him. He'd been hoping that she would walk him out tonight, but she didn't even look his way. The woman was maddening.

"I appreciate your letting me know about this," Slade told him as he showed him out.

When they were standing at the front door, Ken's expression grew serious.

"I've got an uneasy feeling about all of this tonight," he said, troubled.

"I'm not sure if that's good news or bad news."

"Neither am I, and that's why I mentioned it. Be careful the next day or two. It's not going to stay this quiet forever, and we have to be ready." He looked back toward the dining room, wondering if Emily was going to come out and say good-bye, but there was no sign that she'd followed them. "I'll be going."

"You keep an eye out, too."

"I will."

With that, he left them.

Emily and Loretta came out into the front hall, passing Slade on his way back into the dining room to speak with Alyssa again. They bade him good night before they went up to bed.

"You didn't have much to say to Ken tonight, Emily," Loretta remarked thoughtfully.

"He doesn't seem to be interested in me, so I thought I'd just ignore him for a while."

Her mother looked thoughtful. "Sometimes, men need a wake-up call, but Ken is different from the other men in town, being a Pinkerton and all."

"I know," Emily said simply.

When they reached the door to her room, she gave her mother a kiss on the cheek and went in to bed. A short while later, though, as she lay trying to fall asleep, thoughts of Ken plagued her—Ken in the

338

moonlight at the way station telling her he was protecting her from himself . . . Ken rushing outside to protect her honor from Vernon and then almost walking off without kissing her . . . And Ken tonight, glancing her way several times, but never seeking her out . . .

Emily wondered dismally what it was going to take to break down his iron self-control. She hoped her new plan of playing hard to get worked.

With a sigh, she rolled over and closed her eyes.

The Kid and Zeke looked on in silence as Slade spoke with the lady judge for a moment. They were completely surprised when she went into his arms and kissed him.

"That's what we'll do!" the Kid said, his vicious plan already formed in his mind.

"What?"

"We're gonna use her to get to him."

"I like the way you think."

"I knew you would," the Kid said with a leer, looking at Zeke. "I'm gonna enjoy this. Braxton's caused us a lot of grief, and I'm gonna return the favor."

"We know her routine. That sheriff comes for her first thing in the morning. We'll grab her then and have time to get out of town before Braxton even finds out what happened. We'll be the trap, and she'll be the bait."

"That's right. And I want the bait alive until we lure him up there. After I get my hands on Braxton, I don't care what you do with her."

Zeke had never heard sweeter words. He could hardly wait for daybreak.

"Let's go send the telegram to Patterson. Think the operator will open the office for us this late at night?"

"I think we can get him to help us if we use the right kind of persuasion." Zeke pulled out his knife and smiled. The savage-looking blade gleamed lethally in the moonlight.

They moved off into the night, unseen and unnoticed. When they reached the telegraph office it was closed, but Ralph White, the man who ran it, lived in a room in back. The Kid stayed in the shadows as Zeke pounded on the door. The beleaguered man finally answered the summons, a small lamp in hand.

"It's after hours. What do you want?" Ralph growled, eyeing Zeke coldly.

"It's an emergency. I've got to send a wire to my brother in Cheyenne."

"Come back in the morning. I'll send it for you then." He started to shut the door in Zeke's face, thinking he looked disreputable.

Zeke wasn't about to be dismissed that way. In one swift, deadly move, he drew his knife, grabbed the man and held the blade at his throat.

"I don't think you understand just how important it is to me to get this message to my brother, friend," he snarled, as he held him in an iron grip. "Do you suppose you could help me out?"

Ralph was too terrified even to speak. He just nodded.

"Good. I like people who are easy to get along

with. Let's go inside," Zeke said, shoving the man toward the counter. "It's clear, Kid."

The telegraph operator wondered whom he was talking to, and he went even more ashen when he saw the Dakota Kid slip into the office behind them.

"It's you!" he croaked, horrified, recognizing him from his wanted poster.

"You make any noise and you won't live long enough to send the damned wire!" the Kid told him, the threat evident in his tone.

Ralph hurried to sit at the table before the telegraph, and he picked up a pencil, ready to write out their message. "What do you want me to send?"

"Don't write anything down! Just send this," the Kid ordered and he started to dictate to him. "To Harlan Patterson, in care of the Railroad Express Office in Cheyenne, Wyoming."

The operator started keying in the message.

"Get out of town as fast as you can. The Pinkertons are on to you."

Ralph blinked and swallowed nervously. "Anything else? Do you want your name on it or anything?"

"No. That's it."

The Kid and Zeke exchanged looks.

"How much do we owe you?" Zeke asked, moving to stand behind the man.

"Uh . . . er, nothing. This one's on me. I'm glad I could help you," he lied, only wanting them to leave.

"You can help us even more by keeping your mouth shut."

"I won't tell nobody," he promised, fearing for his

very life, wondering if there was any way to save himself.

But there wasn't.

Zeke struck from behind, stabbing him savagely in the back. He slumped forward, face down on the table. The Kid went to him and kicked the chair, knocking the man to the floor. He watched him for a moment, and when the man did not stir, but lay still in a growing pool of blood, he was satisfied.

"Let's get out of here."

They put out the lamp and quit the building, making sure everything looked normal from the outside.

Inside the darkened room, Ralph moved. He could feel his life ebbing from him as his blood pulsed from his body. He didn't have long, and he had to leave something for the sheriff to let him know who'd done this to him and why.

It took all his fading strength, but Ralph dragged himself to a sitting position. He groped on top of the table and found the pad of paper and pencil he needed. His fingers were numb as he tried to write. Blood was staining everything, but he somehow managed to record the truth. He had just scrawled 'The Kid' and 'Patterson'—'Express'—'Cheyenne', when the pencil slipped from his hand for the last time.

Chapter Eighteen

"Did you get the chance to speak with Ken last night?" Alyssa asked Rob as they left her house on the way to her office the following morning.

"No, I didn't. Why?"

"He came by to see Slade and to let him know that he'd gotten a wire from Denver. It seems they've had some luck identifying the informant at the express office, and they should be making an arrest any day now."

Rob was pleased by the news, but it had little effect on the situation in Black Springs. "They hadn't heard anything about the Kid?"

"No, not a word."

He nodded in silence, knowing their ordeal was still far from over. They continued on, greeting the other townspeople as they passed them on the street.

It was a typical, uneventful morning in Black Springs.

Alyssa's office was on the second floor of the building that housed the local doctor's office. The only entrance was through the side alley by way of outside stairs.

"Unless I hear from you, I'll be back for you around four o'clock," Rob was saying as they climbed the steps.

He always unlocked the door and checked things out inside for her. He wouldn't have felt right just leaving her there without taking a look around first.

And the Kid and Zeke knew it. They'd managed to watch them in their routine for a few days without being detected. They had picked the lock on the office door and were waiting inside for them this morning. It was time.

Zeke was so excited that he hadn't slept at all the night before. He'd lain awake thinking about the night to come and how much he was going to enjoy having the lady judge all to himself. Even now, as he waited with knife in hand for Rob to enter, he was smiling.

The Kid was excited, too, but for different reasons. He couldn't wait to be face-to-face with Braxton again. He'd already written the note and left it on her desk where someone would be sure to find it later on, once they were long gone.

They heard the key turn in the lock, and the door swung open. Rob drew his gun as he walked in, alert and looking for anything out of the ordinary that might mean trouble, but Zeke was crouched and hidden behind the door, ready. He launched himself at the lawman, aiming with deadly accuracy with his knife. Rob started to turn, to call out a warning to Alyssa, but he was silenced immediately, the blade striking him in the throat and ending his life.

Alyssa was right behind him. At the sight of Rob falling forward, she let out a small scream and turned to flee.

The Kid had planned well, though. He was there before she could take a step. He grabbed her around the waist and clamped a hand over her mouth as he hauled her inside and slammed the door behind them.

Alyssa struggled and kicked in an effort to free herself from his brutal hold. She tried to work one hand loose so she could get to her derringer, but it was useless. There would be no escape.

"I got her!" the Kid said with pride as he forced her further back into the office, away from the windows. "Is the lawman dead?"

"Yeah," Zeke announced as he stood up and wiped the blade off on his pants leg. He turned toward the Kid, knife still in hand. "You need help with her?"

"Get her hands tied behind her while I keep hold of her. She's a feisty one."

Zeke grinned as he closed in on Alyssa. He could see the terror and anger in her eyes, and it only excited him more. "I know I'm gonna enjoy this one a helluva lot."

He made quick work of binding her hands. When that was done, the Kid released her long enough to gag her.

"You're not going to get away with this!" she cried before he tied the cloth around her mouth.

"Little lady, we already have," the Kid told her with a menacing chuckle as he tied the gag extra tightly. "Take a look at your sworn protector there. He should have been more careful coming in here this morning."

Alyssa stared at Rob, her heart breaking at the sight of him slain by these savage killers. Tears ran down her cheeks. He had been her friend . . . and now he was dead. All because of her.

"Ah, look, Zeke. She's crying for him. Maybe she liked him as much as she likes Braxton . . . and we know how much you like Braxton," the Kid said.

Alyssa's eyes widened at his mention of Slade.

"Oh, yeah, lady judge, we know all about Braxton being a Pinkerton, and we're going to thank him in a real personal way for all he's done to us. This isn't just about you ruining the jailbreak anymore. Now, it's *real* personal."

She tried to run for the door. It didn't matter that it was closed and her hands were bound behind her. She had to get away! She had to warn Slade that they knew everything! The outlaws' mocking laughter followed her as the Kid easily caught up with her and slammed her back against his chest.

"That wasn't too smart, bitch," the Kid snarled at her. He looked at Zeke. "Pull his body over here, so no one can see him by just looking in the window. We need all the time we can get for a headstart."

Zeke did as he was told, dumping Rob in a corner out of sight.

"Now, check outside and see if it's clear."

Zeke took a quick look around and came back inside. "Nobody's out there. If we leave right now, we should be able to make it to the horses without being seen."

"Good. Let's get the hell out of here."

The Kid drew his gun. Dragging Alyssa with him, he led the way from her office. Zeke left last, and he took care to lock the door behind them. They wanted to slow down any possible pursuit.

Alyssa was praying frantically that someone would see them as they descended the steps. She hoped that someone might walk by and notice the men leading her away, but the street and alley were deserted. It was too early in the morning for many people to be about.

The Kid and Zeke had planned well. They reached the horses and mounted up, throwing Alyssa across the back of the third horse they'd brought along. They made quick work of tying her down and then covered her with a canvas tarp. Once they were far enough away from town, they would let her ride astride, but for now all they cared about was getting her away undetected.

They rode out at a slow pace, keeping to the alleys and the quietest streets. They didn't want to draw any attention to themselves.

The pounding pace of the horse jarred Alyssa painfully, yet bound as she was, she was helpless to do anything about it. Her mind was racing, seeking ways to escape from the killers, but for now, there was nothing she could do. She could only stay alive and wait for a chance—a chance to avenge Rob and her father.

The image of Rob lying dead before her was seared into her consciousness. She doubted she would ever be able to erase the horror of the attack from her mind. It had happened so quickly. Alyssa knew Rob hadn't been negligent. He'd had his gun drawn as he entered the office, but the attack had been too fast and too deadly. Zeke was every bit the amoral murderer Slade had said he was, and Rob had had little chance against his surprise assault.

The fact that she hadn't been able to help him in some way weighed heavily on Alyssa. She'd had her derringer in her pocket, but she'd had no time to use it. Guilt haunted her. Alyssa agonized, wondering if she could have done anything differently, but she could find no answer to her torment. The terror of the Kid's triumph was burned into her soul.

As they'd feared all along, the Kid had played his game and won.

"Where's Sheriff Emerson?" demanded Brett Lee, a local businessman, as he ran into the sheriff's office shortly after nine o'clock that morning.

Deputy Hawkins saw the man's panic and jumped to his feet. "He's off taking care of business. Why? What happened?"

"It's Ralph! Somebody killed him!"

"Ralph?" Hawkins was shocked. He grabbed a rifle and ran from the jail, following Brett toward the telegraph office.

A crowd was beginning to gather as Hawkins rushed inside. He took one look around and knew who'd done it. Zeke Malone had murdered Ralph, for he'd been stabbed just like the two deputies during the attempted jailbreak in Green River.

"Damn..." He knelt beside the body, but he could tell just from looking at Ralph that he'd been dead for a while. "Brett, run over to Judge Mason's office and see if you can find Rob. He escorted her to work this morning, and he might still be over there."

"Right away!" The other man hurried away in search of help.

Ken was just coming out of the restaurant after having breakfast when he saw the crowd gathering at the telegraph office. Instantly concerned, he went to see what the trouble was.

"Something wrong here?" he asked a woman at the edge of the crowd.

"It's so terrible!" she said, looking up at him, her expression horrified.

"What is?"

"Someone's killed Ralph."

"Did anyone send for Sheriff Emerson?"

"Deputy Hawkins is already in there, and he just sent Brett to find the sheriff."

Ken shouldered his way up to the front of the crowd and went in to see if he could help.

"What happened to him?"

"He was stabbed, sometime late last night," Hawkins explained.

Ken went to examine the body. As he checked the floor around the man, he found the note pad in a pool of drying blood. Ken lifted it up carefully. Though the paper was stained with Ralph's blood, he could make out the few words written on it. He was grim as he looked over at Hawkins.

"It must have been Malone."

"Why would he kill poor Ralph?" Hawkins was at a loss.

"Zeke was here, and it looks like the Kid was, too. I think they had him send a telegram last night." He held out the note pad for the deputy to see. "It looks like the operator wanted us to know who'd killed him and why."

The deputy studied the scrawled words. *"The Kid . . . Patterson . . . Express . . . Cheyenne . . .* What does it mean?"

Ken frowned, remembering the news he'd discussed with Slade the night before and wondering if there was any way the Kid and Zeke could have overhead them. "I'm going to have to send a wire to Denver myself as soon as things settle down. There's an ongoing investigation in Cheyenne that's connected to the Kid's gang, and this may be related to it."

Hawkins nodded. "So the Kid was actually here, in town, last night."

"That's right." Ken tensed as he realized the danger. "Has anyone seen Alyssa this morning?"

"I haven't, but then I was taking care of the office for Rob while he went to walk her to work. He left at his regular time. It was right around eight o'clock."

"Where is he now?"

"I don't know—" Hawkins suddenly looked concerned, and he wasn't a man who worried easily. "He didn't come back by the office. I just figured he was out checking around town.''

Ken swore violently as he ran from the room, shouting over his shoulder, ''Get the other deputies!''

Hawkins was nervous as he emerged from the telegraph office. He sent one of the townspeople to find Clemans and Brown, and another to get the doctor.

Ken rushed toward Alyssa's office.

Emily had been hard at work at the store. They had only been open an hour, and there was a lot to do in the morning. She had just placed some merchandise outside on display when she noticed the people standing around in front of the telegraph office. She was wondering what was going on when she saw Ken come running out of the office, headed down the street toward her. She was instantly afraid.

''Ken! What is it?'' she called out to him as he drew near.

He stopped for only a moment to explain. ''The telegraph operator was murdered last night. I'm going to find Rob right now. Have you seen him?''

''No, not since he came for Alyssa earlier this morning.''

''Well, stay close to the store, and if Rob does come by, send him down there. Hawkins is in charge right now.''

''I will.''

''Emily?'' Loretta came out to see what was going on.

Emily went back to her mother and told her what Ken had said.

Ken ran on toward Alyssa's office. When he got

there, he saw Brett at the top of the stairs knocking on the door.

"She's not there?" he called up to him.

"No. It looks deserted inside," Brett answered.

Ken mounted the steps, gripped by fear. Alyssa should have been there, and they should have seen some sign of Rob somewhere.

"Let me take a look," Ken said, moving past the other man and peering in the window of the door.

There was no sign of Alyssa. The room was empty. Yet Ken sensed something was wrong—very wrong. Instinctively, he tried the door, only to find that it was locked. Undeterred, he put his shoulder against it and broke in.

"What are you doing?" Brett yelled. He'd seen the other man around town, but had no idea who he was or what his interest was in Alyssa Mason. "Who are you? I'm going to get Deputy Hawkins." He made it sound like a threat.

"The name's Richards, Ken Richards. I'm a Pinkerton detective working to bring in the Kid's gang."

At the news that Ken was a Pinkerton, Brett looked at him with open respect. "Oh."

Ken didn't have time to explain further. He had to find out where Rob and Alyssa were.

As he forced the door completely open and went inside, he knew he'd found his answer.

"Go for Hawkins! Now!" Ken ordered as he saw Rob lying off to the side of Alyssa's desk.

Brett went inside to see what Ken wanted the deputy for, and he caught a glimpse of the sheriff's body. "Is he dead?"

"It looks like it. Hurry!"

He rushed from the office as Ken went to tend to Rob. One close look at the fallen sheriff told him all he needed to know. Rob was dead, and it looked as if Zeke was responsible again. Somehow, they'd taken Rob down before he could get off a shot, for if he'd had time to use his gun, half the town would have heard and come running.

Sorrow and rage filled Ken at the lawman's senseless death. He searched the rest of the office. There was no trace of Alyssa, and he was certain the Kid had taken her. He wished one of the deputies would show up so he could get Slade. They needed to go after the Kid as soon as possible. The longer they delayed, the bigger headstart the Kid would have, and from the looks of things, he'd already been gone for a couple of hours.

Ken stalked to the door and glanced out toward the street. He was glad to see Hawkins running his way, but it troubled him when he spotted Emily trailing after him. He didn't want her to see any of this. He wanted to protect her.

He took one last look around the office, meaning to go downstairs to speak with Hawkins and to keep Emily from witnessing the tragedy. It was then, though, that he spied the boldly scrawled note on top of Alyssa's desk.

Ken recognized the handwriting right away. It matched that of the threatening missive the Kid had left for Alyssa back in her hotel room in Green River. He picked it up and read through it quickly.

Braxton—

I know you're alive and I know you're a Pinkerton. I've got your woman. Zeke's wanting her for his own, so if you want to see her alive again, be at Lattimer Canyon by sunup tomorrow. Come in alone and unarmed. If you do, she'll live. Try anything, and she's a dead woman.

We'll be waiting for you.

The Kid

Just as Ken finished reading, Hawkins came charging into the room.

"What's going on?" he demanded.

Emily was right behind the deputy, dogging his steps, trying to get a look around him. "Where's Alyssa?"

"Emily! Alyssa!" Loretta's call came to them as she hurried up the steps, intent on ascertaining her daughter's safety.

"They got Rob," Ken said.

The deputy moved past Ken to see his friend lying dead on the floor. "Oh, God, no!"

It had been terrible enough dealing with Ralph's murder this morning, but this . . . this was different. Rob had been Hawkins's friend. He'd respected and admired him. And now he was dead. Murdered by the Dakota Kid's gang. Hawkins was inconsolable.

"What is it?" Emily insisted as she moved forward into the office, too, only to see Rob lying there.

She would have swooned, but Ken was instantly beside her, slipping a supportive arm around her waist. She leaned into him, glad for his strength, glad for his calm presence. She needed him so.

"Emily?" Loretta had almost reached the top of the steps.

"Mother . . . Don't come in, please," she managed.

Ken walked Emily to the door, so she could take care of her mother.

"Will you be all right for a minute?" he asked her. He saw how pale she was and he could feel her trembling.

"Yes . . . but where's Alyssa?"

"They've taken her."

Emily gazed up at him, fear and anger shining in her eyes. Her voice was filled with hatred as she spoke. "You get Slade, and you two go find those bastards! Don't let them hurt my sister! Don't let them get away with this! Bring Alyssa home!"

Ken met her regard, and when he answered her, he meant it. "We will."

"Emily!"

She hurried out the door to turn her mother away from the carnage within. Ken could hear the older woman demanding to know where Alyssa was and then, after Emily spoke to her, starting to cry. He was glad that they knew she was still alive—for now. He turned back to Hawkins.

"Here, read this." He handed him the note.

Hawkins's expression turned to one of pure hatred as he finished reading and gave the note back to Ken. "We'll be riding with you."

Ken nodded. "I'm going to take this to Slade. Once we've talked, we'll let you know what we've decided. There's not much time. Whatever we're going to do, we have to do fast."

"Whatever you need, just let me know. Rob wanted those bastards locked up. I'm telling you right now, if I do nothing else for the rest of my life, I'm going to track them down and see them hang."

Ken understood the deputy's anger completely. He said no more, but went to get Slade.

Half an hour later, Slade walked into the sheriff's office followed by Ken. He'd walked down the streets of Black Springs, unmindful of the stares he'd received from those who'd seen him and the hushed, horrified whispers that had followed.

Hawkins had been sitting at the desk, and he looked up as Slade came into the room. He wasn't a man easily intimidated, but the sight that met his eyes sent a chill down his spine. He realized that in all his years of being a lawman, he'd never seen a more dangerous-looking man than Slade Braxton at that moment.

Dressed all in black, Slade had pulled his hat low over his eyes. He was wearing his side arm and carrying his rifle. His expression was emotionless, his jaw tight. There was tension etched in every line of his lean body, and Hawkins knew the man would just as soon shoot as ask questions right then.

"You're ready to ride?" Hawkins asked.

"The horses are tied up out front."

"I'll be riding with you and so will Brown. Clemans is going to stay here and run the office while we're gone. Ursino's feeling good enough now to help him out a little."

Ken spoke up. "How soon can you be saddled up?"

"Ten minutes."

"Fine. We'll wait for you outside."

Slade and Ken went to check their mounts one last time.

"If we ride hard enough, we should be able to get there before dusk."

"What if they see us?"

Slade slanted him a deadly look. "They won't. I've been to this canyon before with the gang. I took a look around when we were there. They'll be expecting me at dawn, but I'm not going to wait that long. I'm not leaving Alyssa in Zeke's hands overnight. There's no telling what the man might do to her—no matter what the Kid said in the letter."

Ken understood his determination. He would feel the same way if Emily was the one in danger. At the thought of her, he looked up to see her standing before the store watching them.

"I'm going to go speak to Emily and Loretta."

"I'll go with you."

The two men approached the store, and as they did, Emily called to her mother to come outside.

"Oh, Slade . . . Thank God!" Loretta threw herself in his arms, sobbing. "Save Alyssa, please! With Rob dead now, you and Ken are my only hope!"

Slade held her as she cried. "I'll bring her back to you, Loretta. You have my word on it."

She looked up at him, her face tear-stained. She saw the hardness in him, but she also saw the goodness. She reached up to touch his lean cheek. "Thank you."

Ken went to Emily as Slade spoke with Loretta. "You'll be all right while we're gone?"

"I'll be fine," she answered.

She wanted to cry, but was struggling to control herself. So much had happened . . . the telegraph operator being murdered, then Rob being killed and now Alyssa kidnapped. She was terrified of what might happen to her sister, but she also found herself worrying about Ken. They all knew how vicious the Kid and his men were. She knew what they would do to Ken and Slade if they got their hands on them.

"You'll be careful?" she asked him.

"Don't worry about me. I'll be fine. Let's just pray we can get your sister back."

"Oh, Ken . . ."

"Wish me luck?"

Emily couldn't help herself. She was so afraid that she might never see Ken again, that he might be killed just like Rob, that she went to him. She boldly put her hand on his chest as she looked up at him. She didn't say another word, but kissed him full on the lips. Ken was shocked and thrilled by her open display of affection.

"For luck," she said, her eyes shining with tears as she started to move away from him. "Be careful."

But he wasn't quite done with her yet. Unable to bear the thought that she was worrying and desperate, he caught her arm and brought her back to him. Without a word, he kissed her again, deeply, softly. It was a kiss that promised many wonders to come.

"We'll be back—and don't worry. When we come, we'll be bringing your sister with us."

Emily managed a wavering smile, trying to lighten their mood. "I'll expect a full report from you when you get back, Mr. *Wiley*."

"I can't think of anyone else I'd rather report to than you."

"I'll be waiting."

"Slade! Ken!" Hawkins's call drew them away.

"Be careful," Loretta and Emily called out as the two men went to mount up.

Emily could not stop the tears that began to fall as she watched them ride out of town.

Darlene Hays came hurrying over to where Emily and Loretta were standing. She looked fit to be tied as she asked, "Loretta, wasn't that man you were just talking to Slade Braxton?"

Emily and Loretta could just imagine the buzz of gossip that would be going around town soon, now that Slade had emerged from hiding and some of the folks had seen him.

"Yes, Darlene, that was Slade."

"But—but—" She was so excited, she couldn't form a sentence.

"He wasn't an outlaw at all," Loretta explained. "He was working undercover for the Pinkertons."

"Slade Braxton is a Pinkerton detective?"

"Yes. They faked his hanging so he could continue to work to bring in the Dakota Kid."

"Dear Lord!" Darlene gasped, staring at them in amazement. "When did you find out about all this?"

"We learned the truth about his identity when we were in Green River," Emily informed her. "Ken Richards is an operative, too. They swore us to secrecy about Slade's situation. They didn't want the word to get out, just in case it might get back to the Kid somehow.''

''Well, you both are as good as your word! Imagine keeping that secret for so long,'' she said, impressed. ''Now, if they can only bring back Alyssa—''

''They will,'' Loretta said with conviction. ''They're Pinkertons. They'll get the Kid and bring Alyssa home safe.''

''We'll be praying for them.''

''So will we.''

''Loretta!'' It was Al Carson from the newspaper and he had an anxious look on his face as he came hurrying toward them.

''What is it, Al?'' she asked, worried that something else terrible had happened.

''Is it true what I just heard? Is it true someone just saw Slade Braxton alive and well riding off with Deputy Hawkins? Did Braxton kill Rob? I thought he'd been hanged! Do you know the truth?''

''Come on in the store, Al. I'll tell you everything you want to know,'' Loretta said, knowing there was much to tell him.

Emily lingered outside just a moment longer. She looked off in the direction Ken and Slade had ridden with the two deputies, and she offered up a silent prayer for her sister's safety and for theirs.

Frustrated and saddened by the knowledge that there was nothing more she could do to help, she followed her mother and the newspaperman inside. The next few days were going to be the longest of her life.

Chapter Nineteen

Alyssa's misery was so great that she almost cried from relief when they finally stopped their headlong flight from town.

"You about ready to ride normal, sweetmeat?" Zeke asked as he pulled the tarp off her.

Had she not been gagged, Alyssa would have told him what she thought of him, but she had no chance. She realized that it was probably just as well. She doubted the outlaws would have been too pleased with her opinion of them.

Zeke's hands were far too familiar on her as he untied the ropes that held her and pulled her off the horse's back. He tried to fondle her, but she jerked away from his vile touch, glaring at him in disgust.

"My, my . . . You are a little spitfire." He chuckled. "Kid? You think she's gonna be this wild tonight?"

The Kid looked over at them. "She'll probably be worse once she figures out what we got planned for her boyfriend."

Sudden panic showed in Alyssa's eyes, and Zeke saw it.

"*Oohee*, she sure does care about Braxton." He grabbed her and pulled her close so he could look her in the eye. He ground his hips against her in an imitation of what he planned to do to her that night. "Honey, I'm gonna make you forget all about him. After I get done with you, you ain't gonna want anybody else."

Had she not been gagged, Alyssa would have retched. This was the man who had killed her father. Never in her life had she despised anyone the way she despised Zeke Malone. He was mean, vicious and without conscience, and what made him even worse was that he seemed proud of being that way.

"Let's get going again, Zeke," the Kid ordered. "We can't be sure how much of a headstart we've got on them, and I want to be ready when Braxton shows up in the morning."

"What if he doesn't come?" Zeke asked, deliberately wanting to taunt Alyssa. "What if he doesn't care enough about her to show up and save her?"

"He'll come, whether he cares about her or not," he answered. "He's a Pinkerton. This won't be over until one of us is dead."

"Don't worry. By this time tomorrow, Braxton will be."

Zeke gave Alyssa a little shove away from him as he drew out his knife. She watched in terror, fearing what he might do to her next.

"Scared of me, are you?" He'd seen the way her eyes had widened at the sight of his weapon. "Good."

He reached out and turned her around. He startled her when he sliced the ropes that bound her hands.

Alyssa wanted to go for her gun. She wanted to shoot him right then and there, but she fought down the need. This was not the time or the place. She only had one bullet. No matter how fast she might be, there was no way she'd have time enough to shoot Zeke, grab his gun and shoot the Kid, too. As desperate as she was, she was going to have to wait.

"Now, let me just tie your hands in front of you so you can ride."

When she didn't immediately hold out her arms to him, he grabbed her and gave her a hard shake.

"When I tell you to do something, woman, you damned well better do it!" he snarled, his face close to hers.

She looked up at him, this time refusing to show any fear. Her defiance earned a leering look from him.

"You don't look so scared anymore," he said with a grin. "Maybe I should give you a little preview of what I got in store for you tonight—"

She still didn't blink or try to squirm away as he retied her hands. He made the rope even tighter than it had been before, and she twisted her wrists, trying to loosen it a bit.

"I think I should take you real slow, so we can both appreciate it more," he said thoughtfully. He looked her up and down, and then his lustful gaze settled on the top button of her dress. "I think I should use everything I got to make it exciting for you. What do you think, Kid?"

The Kid laughed. "I thought you always made it exciting for your women."

Zeke turned back to Alyssa and brought his knife up for her to see. Alyssa gasped in terror as he came at her with the weapon. She was expecting him to stab her. She braced herself for his attack, and she was shocked when, in one quick, slicing move, he simply cut off the top button from her dress. Her dressed gaped open slightly with the button gone, and Alyssa knew she was lucky that he hadn't slit her throat. Of course, this was a game he was playing. He was flaunting power over her.

"There," he said in satisfaction as he stared at her bared flesh. He reached up and ran one finger down the line of her throat to where the dress was still fastened. "Now I got a little more of you to look at on the rest of the ride."

"Let's go, Zeke."

Zeke heard the impatience in the Kid's voice and put his knife away. It was time to ride.

"Get on the horse," Zeke ordered.

Alyssa turned to mount and cringed when she felt Zeke's hands at her waist helping her. She jerked free of his hold as soon as she'd gotten her foot in the stirrup and could pull herself up.

"Don't think you're going to be smart and try anything," the Kid said as he edged his horse closer to hers. "Zeke may want to keep you alive, but you're just as valuable to me dead."

Alyssa didn't flinch at his words, but she knew he meant them.

The Kid sidled even closer until she could almost feel his breath on her face. "Remember this. Nobody—I mean nobody—plays me for a fool. Braxton's gonna get what's coming to him, and so are you. Johnson and Nash are dead because of you."

She had never seen such cold, deadly hatred in her life as she saw mirrored in the Kid's eyes. She thought Zeke was horrible, but the Kid was even more savage. Suddenly, she was afraid not only for herself, but for Slade, too. This man would stop at nothing to seek his revenge.

The Kid turned his horse away from her. "Let's ride."

He led the way, and they kept Alyssa between them on the trail. Zeke was enjoying the view, watching her hips as she rode her horse. He knew that tonight, he'd be the one she was riding. His imagination kept him busy for the duration of the ride to the canyon.

Alyssa felt battered and bruised. The one hope she could cling to was the knowledge that she still had her derringer in her pocket. It was her last line of defense, and she knew she would use it without hesitation when the time came.

She thought of Slade and Ken and prayed that they

were following her by now. If anyone could save her, it would be Slade.

They rode on for hours, stopping only briefly to rest the horses as they needed it. It was late in the afternoon when they finally reached the entrance to the box canyon.

Alyssa took one look around and understood immediately why the Kid had picked this place to confront Slade. It was easily defensible, for the outlaws could see anyone approaching for at least a mile. She cast a quick glance back, hoping to see some sign that they were being followed, but there was no indication that anyone was closing on them. The Kid had planned well. They had gotten completely away from town without anyone being the wiser.

She wondered how long it would be before Slade showed up. She wondered, too, if she could face the possibility that he might not get there in time to save her from Zeke.

Firm resolve filled her. She would not submit to him easily. She would not give him the satisfaction of seeing her cower and beg before him. He might be able to overpower her with brute strength and force her to his will, but she would never give in to him. No matter how much she suffered at his hands, she would not submit willingly to his domination, and she knew that was what he wanted. He wanted to break her spirit.

"We'll camp here," the Kid said as they reached a clearing near a small creek. "It'll be the best place for us to watch for Slade."

The rocky walls of the canyon offered good protection from any attack. It looked impregnable, and Alyssa feared that it was.

Zeke came to her and started to reach up and grab her by the waist to help her down. But Alyssa wasn't about to suffer his touch without a fight. She lifted her foot and kicked him squarely in the chest, shoving him away.

He was taken by surprise at her action and staggered backward a step. The Kid laughed out loud at her daring. Her action infuriated Zeke.

"So you want to play rough, do you?" he growled, standing back and waiting until she'd climbed down by herself.

When she'd dismounted and turned to walk away, he deliberately tripped her, sending her to her knees.

"That's where I want you, bitch—on your knees. Remember that."

She looked up at him from where she knelt in the dirt, her hatred for him showing plainly in her expression. But he just walked past her, leaving her there.

The two men set up camp quickly. They planned to be there only one night, so there wasn't a lot to do.

"Take first watch," the Kid told Zeke. "If you see anything suspicious at all, let me know. We aren't taking any chances tonight. This is too important."

"What are you going to do with her?" Zeke looked over to where Alyssa now stood.

"I know she's not going anywhere, but I think I'll tie her up in plain sight just in case Braxton gets any ideas about trying to sneak in here and free her. If there's any trouble, any trouble at all, my first bullet goes into her.''

Zeke nodded. ''Where do you want her?''

The Kid looked around and saw a medium-sized tree that would be perfect for what he had in mind. ''There. Tie her standing up to that one limb, her arms above her head.''

Zeke went to get Alyssa and do as the Kid had told him. He liked the idea that she'd be tied up right where he could keep an eye on her while he was standing guard. She would be far better scenery than the surrounding countryside.

''Let's go, sugar. It's almost time for some fun,'' he said, leering at her as he grabbed her by the arm and led her off toward the tree.

In short order, he had her tied up just the way the Kid wanted her. She was standing, her arms above her head, completely helpless to do anything to free herself.

''You look real good that way,'' he said. ''Course, you've always looked real good to me. Should I take her gag off?''

''Sure, there ain't nobody gonna hear her out here,'' the Kid answered.

Zeke reached behind her head and loosened the rag that had silenced her during the trip. He expected her to scream and curse him when he did, but she only stared at him and did not speak.

''What's the matter, honey? Ain't you got nothing to say?'' He leaned toward her.

Alyssa's rage was so great, she didn't even think; she just spat in his face.

Zeke swore loudly and pulled out his knife. He wiped his cheek off with the back of his arm as he glared at her. He wanted to teach her a lesson right then, but he stopped himself.

"Don't worry. I'll pay you back for that later." He smiled coldly. "But maybe I'll give you something to think about until then, what do you say?"

He dropped his gaze to her bosom and lifted the knife to sever another button on the front of her gown. She gasped as the button fell away. Intrigued by her reaction, he sliced off another one. When he finally stopped, her dress was open to the waist. Alyssa was thankful that her chemise still covered her, but her breasts swelled above it, giving him a hint of the fullness shielded from his view.

"We are going to have some good times when I get done with my turn at watch," he said hungrily.

Alyssa didn't respond. She found herself holding her breath as he pressed the cold blade of his knife against her bared skin.

"Some real good times," he repeated, lifting his gaze to hers.

The look he gave her was unnerving, yet Alyssa didn't show her terror. She looked him straight in the eye. Only when he finally gave a maniacal laugh and turned and walked away, did she allow herself to exhale in relief.

Alyssa glanced up at the sky, trying to judge how much time there was until sundown. The sun was low in the western sky, and she knew it wouldn't be too long before she'd have to face the coming night—and Zeke.

"It's not much farther," Slade told Ken and the others as they neared the canyon. "We'll have to be careful from here on out, though. It'll probably be best if we stop after another mile and wait for dark."

"His site's that good?"

"If he's camped where I think he is, he'll be able to see almost a mile out. Going in after dark is the only way."

"You're sure about this?" Ken repeated, wanting to confirm their plan.

"There's nothing else we can do. I have to get to Alyssa now. Zeke's wanted her ever since the night we went into Black Springs to check out the bank. He isn't going to stop tonight, and the Kid won't care what he does to her. All the Kid cares about is getting even with me."

They were silent and grim as they urged their mounts forward. The next few hours would be critical and dangerous. They would have to shoot straight and move swiftly when the time came. Alyssa's very life depended upon it.

The Kid started a small campfire near the tree where Alyssa was restrained, so he could keep a close watch over her. He was certain that Braxton was on his way by now. He wondered if the Pinkerton would be stupid enough to try to rescue her tonight. If he did, she was a dead woman.

One way or the other, once any shooting started,

the Kid's first shot would be at her. Killing her would be the thing that would affect Braxton the most, and that was what he wanted to do. Braxton was going to suffer for his part in seeing Johnson and Nash hanged.

Getting up from where he'd been sitting by the fire, the Kid walked over to Alyssa. He took the canteen with him.

"Do you need a drink?" he asked.

She looked at him, taking care to keep her expression blank. "Yes." She hadn't had anything to drink for most of the day.

Alyssa grew worried as he came toward her. With her clothes torn away as they were, she was afraid that he might decide to start what Zeke wanted to finish later that night. She tensed, but said nothing more. Relief flooded through her when the Kid merely held the canteen to her lips and waited.

The Kid paid little attention to her. Women were the last thing on his mind tonight. He was too concerned with trying to figure out what trickery Braxton might try to pull off. He wouldn't put anything past the Pinkerton.

When Alyssa had finally finished drinking, the Kid glanced up the canyon as if he expected trouble to come riding in on them at any moment. He saw no sign of anyone trying to sneak up on them, so he relaxed again for a while.

He was going to have to relieve Zeke as lookout soon, and he wasn't looking forward to it. Zeke had no intention of being distracted from the lady judge tonight, and the Kid had no intention of trying to distract him. He just didn't want to lose sight of what was really important—watching for Braxton.

It was an hour past sundown when the Kid finally decided to take over for Zeke. He made his way up to his vantage point.

"All right, go on."

Zeke looked up at the Kid, his eyes shining with an eagerness born of waiting. "I'm gonna be busy for a while."

He was all but drooling in his rabid excitement. At last! The lady judge was going to be his!

"I figured that. Just keep it quiet. Gag her again if you have to, but I don't want no screaming. Braxton could be out there listening and waiting."

"Yeah, yeah."

The last thing Zeke wanted to hear about from the Kid right then was Braxton. His body was hungry for the woman, and he intended to sate that hunger. He was going to take her as many times as he could.

Zeke started down to the campsite. He was ready. He'd already waited longer for her than he'd ever waited for any woman. He thought back to the first time he'd seen her and thought about how different things would have been if he had knifed Slade and gone after her then, when he'd wanted to. The Kid would have been angry with him if he had, though, for an attack that night could have ruined the robbery they'd pulled off successfully the next morning. Still, if he'd gotten rid of Braxton that night, none of this would have happened, and Johnson and Nash might still be alive.

"Evening, darling," he said as he put his rifle aside

and walked toward Alyssa. "I can tell you've been missing me while I was gone."

"You're wrong, Malone," she said. "I didn't miss you at all."

"Too bad. I sure was thinking about you." He grabbed himself explicitly to show her where his thoughts had been.

Alyssa was disgusted by his action and looked away from him. He was a low, vile man, and she hoped she could get to her gun before he had the chance to lay a hand on her.

"Would you like me to cut you down? I could be real good to you if you'd let me." He thought he'd try being nice to her at first to see if she'd cooperate a little. Either way he was going to get some of her right now, so it didn't really matter.

"Go to hell."

"Oh, no, sweetheart, getting between your thighs is going to be heaven, not hell." He chuckled lasciviously as he came to stand before her. "Let's have us some fun tonight."

Alyssa felt almost physically ill. Though he hadn't touched her yet, she still felt violated. She kept hoping and praying to be rescued from the horrible fate that awaited her at Zeke's hands, but there was no sign that Slade was riding in to her rescue. She was trapped.

Held captive as she was by two killers, her one-shot derringer out of reach, Alyssa realized she was on her own. She was going to have to save herself. It wasn't going to be easy, but she would choose her moment carefully and pray her attempt worked.

"Here . . . Let me free you so you can enjoy this as much as I'm going to," Zeke said as he used his knife to cut her down.

Alyssa's arms felt leaden, and she could barely move. She rubbed at her wrists, trying to get the feeling back in her hands as quickly as she could. She couldn't afford to fumble when she went for the derringer. She was going to have one chance and one chance only. She would have to move fast and shoot straight if she was to survive the night. She stood staring at Zeke, waiting, trying to anticipate his next move.

"Come on, sugar," he said in a low voice, not quite believing that the moment he'd waited so long for was actually upon him. He took a step toward her.

"No!" Alyssa said, backing up.

Her move broke his mood and he grabbed her, not about to put up with any protests. She was his to do with as he pleased.

"You're mine. Get used to it," he said in a low, threatening voice as he pulled her along with him to the campfire, where he'd spread out his bedroll earlier.

He shoved her roughly to the ground and stared down at her as he unbuckled his gunbelt and set it aside. His gaze grew hot, and he could wait no longer. He dropped to his knees beside her and reached for her.

"Get away from me, Malone, or I swear I'll kill you."

"That ain't no way to talk. All I want to do is show you a good time. Lift up your skirts and spread your legs. I don't want to waste no more time—''

He moved over her, lying down upon her, forcing her legs apart with his knees when she refused to accommodate him willingly. He pressed hot, wet kisses to her throat and then lower, to the tops of her breasts. He moved against her, showing her exactly what he wanted to do to her.

Alyssa was in a panic. Bile rose in her throat at his touch, and she wanted to scream in frustration. She looked over to where the Kid was keeping watch, only to find him staring at them with open interest. She started to go for her gun, but Zeke caught her hands and pulled them up above her head. She was pinned there, the weight of his body holding her fast. Bucking wildly, Alyssa hoped to throw him from her, but he was too heavy.

"That's it, honey. Give me a good hard ride."

He slipped one hand down to pull up her skirt. His fingers groped at her legs as she squirmed desperately, trying to avoid his touch.

"You know, I owe you an apology," he said, talking low to her as he continued to paw at her. "I really am sorry about your father."

Alyssa had been fighting and twisting and turning, trying to escape his degrading possession, but at his mention of her father, she went completely still.

"What?" she demanded.

"Your daddy . . . I'm real sorry I killed him."

"You bastard! What do you care about my father? You are a killer! A murderer! You shoot people down in cold blood!"

"Well, that's just it, honey," he said, stopping his

groping at her while he spoke. "You see, I wasn't aiming at your daddy when I was shooting that day. He just sorta got in the way. I was trying to kill Braxton, but the shot went wide and hit the old man instead."

"How dare you—!"

"I'd dare anything for you, sugar. You see, you're the reason why I was shooting at Braxton in the first place. That night at the dance, I was wanting you." He moved against her to emphasize his words. "I told old Slade to dance you over to me, and then I'd get some of you right there in the back alley. I was real hard for you that night, just like I am now." He gave a fierce thrust of his hips against her, wanting her to know the strength of his desire.

"You're horrible!"

"You won't be saying that once I give you what I got," he said, grinning down at her. "But that night, Slade told me you weren't for the likes of me. He even hit me to make his point. Now I don't know what that boy could have been talking about, 'cause look at us now. You're here with me, and you're just loving every minute of it. Ain't you, sweetheart?"

"I hate you, Malone!" Her fury was beyond control. She began to fight and kick, trying to break free any way she could.

"Hate me all you want, honey, but let's face it. It's your fault your father got himself killed. If Slade had let me have at you that night instead of protecting you like he did, your daddy would still be alive."

Alyssa had never experienced mindless rage before, but she did now. There was no thought of saving herself, there was only the driving, primitive need to see this man dead. Giving a violent twist to one side, she managed to dislodge him so that he let go of one hand. In that instant, she tried to dig in her pocket for her gun, but he grabbed her and stilled her movements.

"What are you trying to do?" he asked, growing irritated by her continued struggles. "Lie still, bitch. It's time now. I want what's mine!"

He ripped at her chemise, baring her breasts to his view. She fought him even harder. He grew angrier and slapped her, splitting her lip.

At his blow, Alyssa screamed in pain and frustration.

Chapter Twenty

When Slade had started in toward the campsite, he'd sent Ken to the south rim of the canyon and Hawkins to the north. Brown had stayed back out of sight near the entrance with the horses, just in case Alyssa somehow managed to escape on her own. If she did, he could stop her there and protect her until they returned.

Slade had been slowly making his way on foot through the rocky terrain, staying off the main trail and avoiding places where the Kid might be able to catch sight of him. But when the sound of Alyssa's scream came echoing through the night to him, the unrelenting terror of it pierced him to the depths of his soul.

No longer able to restrain himself, Slade charged forward. He had meant to be cautious in his assault.

He had meant to outsmart the Kid, to outmaneuver him and entrap him before he and Zeke could hurt anyone else, but Alyssa's cry erased any intention he'd had of moving slowly. There was no time. She was in danger now. He had to go to her. He had to save her.

Zeke's physical abuse only enraged Alyssa even more. She was not subdued by his brutality, but empowered by it. She did not stop struggling with him, but fought harder against his cruel attack.

"Shut her up!" the Kid commanded angrily. "Gag her if you have to!"

"All right!"

Zeke had wanted to cow Alyssa by hitting her, to have her begging him not to strike her again. He hadn't thought she'd fight back. She was a nasty little bitch, but he was sure going to enjoy the final act when they got to it. And it wouldn't be long now. He clamped a hand over her mouth to silence her, never knowing that his move gave her just the freedom she needed to go for her gun.

"You need help?" the Kid called out to Zeke, witnessing his continuing struggles with the woman. "I'll be glad to come hold her down for you, if you ain't man enough to take care of it yourself. Or maybe you need help some other way?"

"Hell, no, I don't need your help! We're just enjoying each other, that's all," Zeke ground out.

He was angry that the lady judge wasn't surrendering to him easily, angry that he had to keep fighting her, and angry at the Kid for his insulting remarks.

As hard as it was proving to be to take her, though, he knew it would be all the more sweet once he'd put it to her. A little rough stuff always made sex better for him.

Alyssa got her hand in her pocket just as Zeke pushed her skirt up to her waist and shifted his weight to free himself from his pants.

"You grabbing for me, honey?" he asked, feeling her hand between their bodies and believing that she was finally coming around to his way of thinking. "You're gonna like what I'm going to give you. . . . Let me help you a little. Move your hand this way," he encouraged her, smiling. He liked her feisty and struggling, though, so he deliberately taunted her again. "You know your daddy wouldn't mind you doing me this way tonight. He'd probably want to watch us, seeing as how pretty you are and all—"

Those words were the final ones Zeke Malone would ever say. At his filthy suggestion, Alyssa was pushed beyond all reason. She only knew hatred and the driving need to avenge both her father's death and Rob's. She didn't even bother to pull the gun out of her pocket. As her hand closed on it, she twisted it around and pointed it up at Zeke's most vital organs.

Then she pulled the trigger.

The sound of the shot echoed through the night.

Zeke's body jerked violently.

"You—you bitch—" he gasped in shocked horror, and then he collapsed on top of her.

Alyssa heard the Kid shouting as he came running down from his vantage point, and she reacted quickly. She pushed Zeke's dead weight off her and grabbed his six-gun from the holster where he'd laid it on the ground near them. A shot hit the dirt near her; she stayed low and ran for cover out of the light of the campfire. As soon as she was safely behind some rocks, Alyssa took aim and fired off a round at the Kid as he came running into the clearing.

"Zeke! What the hell—?" the Kid yelled as he charged back the way he'd come.

Alyssa didn't make a sound. She didn't want him to know where she was hiding. She only had five bullets left and couldn't afford to waste any of them without a clear shot. A silent prayer was on her lips that somewhere out there in the moonless darkness of the night, Slade had heard the shooting and was on his way.

The sound of the gunfire sent Slade running toward the campsite at full speed. He was terrified that Alyssa had been wounded or killed. He had to get to her! He had to help her!

Casting all concern about his own safety to the wind, he drew his gun and rushed headlong toward the flickering light of the campfire ahead. When he reached the edge of the clearing, he stopped. He saw Zeke's body on the far side of the fire, but there was no sign of Alyssa or the Kid.

"Alyssa!"

Slade had barely called her name when a shot hit the tree near his head. He instantly dove for cover.

"You're early, Braxton!" the Kid shouted at him from somewhere across the way. "The note I left for you said to show up at dawn tomorrow!"

"I couldn't wait to see you again, so I came tonight!" he yelled back.

"I'm glad you did. We'll just get this over with all the sooner."

"Get what over with?"

"Killing you, Braxton."

"Slade! Be careful!" Alyssa called out to him, wanting to let him know that the Kid did not have her and that she was unhurt.

"Stay down!" he ordered.

"Why, Mr. Pinkerton? You worried she might get hurt?"

"This is between the two of us, Kid. Leave her out of it."

"You're wrong. She's in this. She's the one who ruined the jailbreak in Green River. If it hadn't been for her, Johnson and Nash would still be alive!"

"Maybe, maybe not. I was one of the men you were trying to break out, too, Kid. I would have brought you down myself, with or without her help. It's over now. You may as well just throw down your guns and come on in. You're finished in the territory."

"Like hell, I am!"

"Hell's where you're going," Slade shouted back.

The Kid tightened his grip on his weapon as he looked around for some clue to Braxton's hiding place. He shifted his own position, hoping to get a clean shot at either him or the woman. He wanted them both dead, and if he managed to put a bullet in her, he was sure it would lure Braxton out into the open.

Slade moved slowly around the edge of the campsite, taking care to stay low, making his way in Alyssa's direction. He thanked God that she was still alive, and he planned to make sure that she stayed that way.

"Kid! Listen up! I've got men moving in on both sides of the canyon. There's no getting out of here for you. You'd be smart to surrender now."

Silence was the Kid's answer. Slade paused to listen, hoping to hear him moving around, but he heard nothing. It was quiet. He reached an opening and darted across it. The Kid fired at him immediately and only narrowly missed.

Alyssa had remained crouched behind some rocks, with Zeke's gun ready. When the Kid took his shot at Slade, she returned his fire. Her aim was good, but she did not hit him. He quickly disappeared again behind the rocks and foliage.

Slade heard her shot and knew he was getting close. In a frantic effort, he kept moving forward until he finally reached her side. He had never been so glad to see anyone alive and well in his entire life. Alyssa turned to him, and he clasped her in his arms, his embrace almost painful.

"Are you all right?" he whispered, his gaze sweeping over her, seeing her ruined clothing and the faint bruise already swelling her lip and cheek.

"Now that you're here, I'm fine," she whispered back, holding him tightly, never wanting to let him go.

Slade took Alyssa by the shoulders and held her

back away from him for a moment, so he could feast his eyes upon her. "Thank God."

"I killed Zeke. I shot him with my derringer," she said softly, looking up at him with troubled eyes.

"I'm proud of you. If ever a man deserved killing, it was Zeke."

"I never thought I was capable of killing anyone, but—" She paused, trying to voice her deepest thoughts, thoughts that shocked her with their fierceness. "But I think I actually enjoyed pulling the trigger."

Slade touched her cheek gently, understanding exactly what she was feeling. "It's all right. You had to save yourself. If you hadn't shot him—" He let the sentence drop, not even wanting to consider what might have happened to her had he not been able to reach her in time.

"But I'm a justice of the peace. I'm supposed to uphold the law," she agonized. "I wanted to shoot him, though. . . . I had to shoot him . . . He had already killed my father and Rob, and God knows how many other people."

"And he would have killed you if he'd had half a chance. You did the right thing. It was self-defense," he said simply. "I'm just thankful you still had the derringer with you. I was so worried about you when Ken told me that Rob had been killed and you'd been kidnapped . . ."

He gave her a quick, tender kiss, taking care not to hurt her already injured lip.

"Oh, Slade," she sighed, agonizing over all that had passed and worrying about what was to come.

"We're going to end this with the Kid—right here, right now," Slade declared, looking back out across the clearing to see if he could spot the outlaw. "Do you have any idea where he's hiding?"

"The last shot he fired at you came from that big rock on the far end near the bushes," Alyssa said, pointing out the exact location to him.

"You stay here and cover me. Ken and Hawkins are working their way in, too. I'm going to try to circle around and see if I can get the drop on him."

"Watch out for him, Slade. Be careful. He wants you dead."

"I know."

He was grim as he tore himself away from her. He was going out to finish the job he'd started so many months ago. It was time to put an end to the Dakota Kid once and for all.

The Kid was usually very cool under pressure, but not tonight. He was beyond reason. He was furious. Zeke was dead, and he was left alone to face Braxton. He knew he could sneak away into the night and take him on another day, but it was too late for that. He was going to kill Braxton right here, right now.

"Kid! Give it up!" Slade called out again.

"Never, Braxton!" He wasn't about to turn himself in just so they could hang him. He'd rather be cut down in a shoot-out like a man than face a hangman's noose.

"You can't win. There's a posse waiting for you at the canyon entrance."

"Yeah, they may get me eventually, but even if they do, you and the lady judge will already be

385

dead!'' the Kid answered with a crazed laugh.

The Kid fired off two rounds in the direction of Slade's voice. As he did, a shot came from high above him, and he realized that Slade's men were almost in position. He wasn't about to sit there and let the men in the posse pick him off. If he was going to die, then he was taking the Pinkerton down with him!

Johnson, Nash and Zeke were all dead because of Braxton. Now it was his turn to die. The Kid's burning need for revenge was ruling his every thought, his every action. He fired off more shots in Braxton's direction. When he caught sight of the Pinkerton moving past some rocks, he fired again and ran out from his place of hiding to follow. He was going to chase his enemy down and shoot him like the dog he was.

Alyssa saw the Kid going after Slade, and she fired at him. Her shot came close, but missed. He returned her fire as he charged toward the spot where he'd last seen Slade. She shot again and again, but he was moving too fast for her. Her shots went wide. She knew she was down to her last bullet, so she waited, hoping for a better chance.

''You're a dead man, Braxton!'' the Kid was yelling as he closed on him.

But Slade was ready. Though the Kid's shots were coming close to him, he did not run for better cover. He waited patiently, and when at last he had his best opportunity, he took it. He stood up, and as his gaze met the Kid's straight on, he fired at him. The bullet hit the gunman squarely in the chest.

''No, you're the dead man,'' Slade said tersely as

he watched the outlaw's expression change from fury to complete shock.

"You bastard—I'll see you in hell!" the Kid swore as he collapsed to the ground.

Slade remained where he was, watching and waiting. The Kid lay unmoving. It was over. The Dakota Kid and his gang had been brought down.

"Oh, Slade!" Alyssa ran from her hiding place straight into his arms.

He held her close as relief surged through him. She was safe. It was over.

"Slade! Are you and Alyssa all right?" Ken shouted from his place above them on the canyon wall.

"Yeah. We're fine."

"And the Kid?"

"He's dead," Slade called back.

"We'll be right there!"

"I'm going to check on the Kid. Stay here," Slade told Alyssa as he gave her a soft kiss.

He released her as he looked over to where the Kid was sprawled in the dirt. They had won this night, but there was no real joy in the victory, for in winning much had been lost. The Kid and his Gang had left a trail of bloody death and destruction all across the territory. Slade was glad that it was over.

Slade walked toward the Kid, holstering his side arm as he went. There would be no more killing tonight. He stopped at the Kid's side and was reaching down to take the gun from his hand when the Kid's eyes opened.

The Kid stared up at Slade, his eyes aglow with

the fever of his hatred. With the last of his strength he lifted his six-gun and shot at close range. The Kid gave a triumphant laugh and fell back.

Slade staggered a few steps. He turned toward Alyssa, and his gaze met hers for a fleeting moment before he collapsed in the dirt.

"Slade!" Alyssa screamed in horror.

She ran toward them, lifting the gun she held and firing her last bullet into the Kid point-blank.

Epilogue

One Year Later

At the soft sound of the baby's cry, Alyssa instinctively stirred and awoke. She was about to rise to go check on her son when the crying suddenly stopped. Alyssa frowned wondering at the silence, and then she heard Emily talking softly.

"Shhh, J. R. Don't cry," she was telling her nephew in a whisper. "Aunt Emily's going to take care of you this morning, so your mama and papa can sleep a little longer."

Alyssa smiled and lay back. It was sweet of her sister to take him like that, and she would be sure to thank her later—after she'd gotten a little more rest.

"Maybe we should invite Emily and Ken to come and visit us more often," Slade suggested in a sleep-husky voice as he turned to take his wife in his arms.

"That's fine with me. Since they got married and moved to Denver so Ken could take that office job for the agency, we haven't had the chance to visit very often. Maybe you should offer Ken a job as one of your deputies," she said with a smile. She doubted Ken would take it, though, for he'd been promoted at the agency. Slade had quit the Pinkertons just before they'd married to become sheriff of Black Springs.

"It's about time I got to enjoy time alone with you in bed," Slade said with a smile.

"Oh?" Alyssa played the innocent, but she smiled back at him invitingly. "I have to admit, it does feel decidedly decadent to just lie here like this while Emily takes care of J.R."

"Decadent? I like the sound of that."

Slade pulled her into his arms, his mouth taking hers in a hungry exchange. In all the months they'd been married, he'd never tired of loving her. She was everything he'd ever wanted in a woman.

Alyssa returned his kiss with fervor, wrapping her arms around him. She loved him with all her heart, and she wanted him to know it.

There had been many times over the months since they'd married when the memory of the terrifying showdown with the Kid and Zeke crept into her thoughts. To this day, that memory still had the power to leave her almost paralyzed with fear. Slade meant so much to her that if he had been killed that day, she was certain she would have died, too—from a broken heart.

She still remembered the horror that had gripped

her when she'd watched the Kid shoot Slade in that final, deadly confrontation. His treacherous attack had taken her by surprise, and she'd been helpless to prevent it. She thanked God every day that he'd survived his devastating wound.

When the kiss ended, Alyssa trailed her lips down his throat in a sensuous caress and then moved lower to press them to the terrible scar on his chest from the near-deadly gunshot. Slade gave a low groan at the intimacy of her touch and drew her back up to him for another passionate kiss.

"I almost lost you that day," she said, gazing down at him, all the love she felt for him shining in her eyes.

"It would take more than just a gunshot wound to get rid of me. I think you're stuck with me for eternity, lovely lady."

She smiled. "I can't think of anyone else I'd rather spend eternity with."

"I love you, Alyssa."

They came together then to celebrate the joy of their union. They had their son, John Robert, and they had each other. Their happiness was complete.

They would live happily ever after.

BOBBI SMITH

THE LADY & THE TEXAN

"A fine storyteller!"—*Romantic Times*

A firebrand since the day she was born, Amanda Taylor always stands up for what she believes in. She won't let any man control her—especially a man like gunslinger Jack Logan. Even though Jack knows Amanda is trouble, her defiant spirit only spurs his hunger for her. He discovers that keeping the dark-haired tigress at bay is a lot harder than outsmarting the outlaws after his hide—and surrendering to her sweet fury is a heck of a lot riskier.

___4319-X $5.99 US/$6.99 CAN

THE LADY'S HAND
BOBBI SMITH
Author of *Lady Deception*

Cool-headed and ravishingly beautiful, Brandy O'Neal knows how to hold her own with the riverboat gamblers on *The Pride of New Orleans*. But she meets her match in Rafe Morgan when she bets everything she has on three queens and discovers that the wealthy plantation owner has a far from gentlemanly notion of how she shall make good on her wager.

Disillusioned with romance, Rafe wants a child of his own to care for, without the complications of a woman to break his heart. Now a full house has given him just the opportunity he is looking for—he will force the lovely cardsharp to marry him and give him a child before he sets her free. But a firecracker-hot wedding night and a glimpse into Brandy's tender heart soon make Rafe realize he's luckier than he ever imagined when he wins the lady's hand.

_4116-2 $5.99 US/$6.99 CAN

MIDNIGHT FIRE

MADELINE BAKER

"Lovers of Indian Romance have a special place on their bookshelves for Madeline Baker!"
—*Romantic Times*

A half-breed who has no use for a frightened girl fleeing an unwanted wedding, Morgan thinks he wants only the money Carolyn Chandler offers him to guide her across the plains, but halfway between Galveston and Ogallala, where the burning prairie meets the endless night sky, he makes her his woman. There in the vast wilderness, Morgan swears to change his life path, to fulfill the challenge of his vision quest—anything to keep Carolyn's love.

_4056-5 $5.99 US/$6.99 CAN

LOVE FOREVERMORE

MADELINE BAKER

The West—it has been Loralee's dream for as long as she could remember, and Indians are the most fascinating part of the wildly beautiful frontier she imagines. But when Loralee arrives at Fort Apache as the new schoolmarm, she has some hard realities to learn...and a harsh taskmaster to teach her. Shad Zuniga is fiercely proud, aloof, a renegade Apache who wants no part of the white man's world, not even its women. Yet Loralee is driven to seek him out, compelled to join him in a forbidden union, forced to become an outcast for one slim chance at love forevermore.

___4267-3 $5.99 US/$6.99 CAN

A WANTED MAN.
  AN INNOCENT WOMAN.
   A WANTON LOVE!

Renegade Heart
Madeline Baker

When beautiful Rachel Halloran took Logan Tyree into her home, he was unconscious. A renegade Indian with a bullet wound in his side and a price on his head, he needed her help. But to Rachel he was nothing but trouble, a man whose dark sensuality made her long for forbidden pleasures; to her father he was the answer to a prayer, a gunslinger whose legendary skill could rid the ranch of a powerful enemy.

But Logan Tyree would answer to no man—and to no woman. If John Halloran wanted his services, he would have to pay dearly for them. And if Rachel wanted his loving, she would have to give up her innocence, her reputation, her very heart and soul.

_4085-9 $5.99 US/$6.99 CAN

Dorchester Publishing Co., Inc.
P.O. Box 6640
Wayne, PA 19087-8640

Please add $1.75 for shipping and handling for the first book and $.50 for each book thereafter. NY, NYC, and PA residents, please add appropriate sales tax. No cash, stamps, or C.O.D.s. All orders shipped within 6 weeks via postal service book rate. Canadian orders require $2.00 extra postage and must be paid in U.S. dollars through a U.S. banking facility.

Name_____
Address_____
City_____ State_____ Zip_____
I have enclosed $_____ in payment for the checked book(s).
Payment <u>must</u> accompany all orders. ❑ Please send a free catalog.

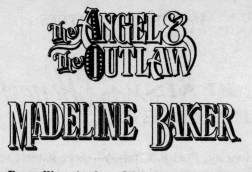

THE ANGEL & THE OUTLAW

MADELINE BAKER

Bestselling Author Of *Lakota Renegade*

An outlaw, a horse thief, a man killer, J.T. Cutter isn't surprised when he is strung up for his crimes. What amazes him is the heavenly being who grants him one year to change his wicked ways. Yet when he returns to his old life, he hopes to cram a whole lot of hell-raising into those twelve months no matter what the future holds.

But even as J.T. heads back down the trail to damnation, a sharp-tongued beauty is making other plans for him. With the body of a temptress and the heart of a saint, Brandy is the only woman who can save J.T. And no matter what it takes, she'll prove to him that the road to redemption can lead to rapturous bliss.

_3931-1 $5.99 US/$7.99 CAN

Dorchester Publishing Co., Inc.
P.O. Box 6640
Wayne, PA 19087-8640

DANGEROUS VIRTUES:

ELAINE BARBIERI *Honesty*

Honesty, Purity, Chastity—three sisters, very different women, all three possessed of an alluring beauty that made them...DANGEROUS VIRTUES

When the covered wagon that is taking her family west capsizes in a flood-swollen river, Honesty Buchanan's life is forever changed. Raised in a bawdy Abilene saloon by its flamboyant mistress, Honesty learns to earn her keep as a card sharp, and a crooked one at that. Continually searching for her missing sisters, the raven-haired temptress finds instead the last person in the world she needs: a devastatingly handsome Texas ranger, Sinclair Archer, who is sworn to put cheats and thieves like herself behind bars. Nestled in his protective embrace, Honesty finds the love she's been desperately seeking ever since she lost her family—a love that will finally make an honest woman out of her.

_4080-8 $5.99 US/$6.99 CAN

Purity, Honesty, Chastity—They were all admirable traits, but when they came in the form of three headstrong, spirited, sinfully lovely sisters, they were...

Dangerous Virtues

From the moment Purity sees the stranger's magnificent body, she feels anything but what her name implies. Who is the mysterious half-breed who has bushwhacked the trail drive she is leading? And why does she find it impossible to forget his blazing, green-eyed gaze?

Though Pale Wolf attacks her, though he is as driven to discover his brother's killer as she is to find her long-lost sisters, Purity longs to make him a part of her life, just as her waiting softness longs to welcome his perfect masculine form. There may be nothing virtuous about her intentions toward Pale Wolf, but she knows that their ultimate joining will be pure paradise.

___4272-X $5.99 US/$6.99 CAN